The Homecoming of Samuel Lake

RANDOM HOUSE TRADE PAPERBACKS NEW YORK

The Homecoming
of Samuel Lake

A NOVEL

Jenny Wingfield

2012 Random House Trade Paperback Edition

Published in the United States by Random House Trade Paperbacks,
an imprint of The Random House Publishing Group,
a division of Random House, Inc., New York.

RANDOM HOUSE TRADE PAPERBACK and colophon are
trademarks of Random House, Inc.
RANDOM HOUSE READER'S CIRCLE & Design is a registered
trademark of Random House, Inc.

Originally published in hardcover in the United States by Random House,
an imprint of The Random House Publishing Group,
a division of Random House, Inc., in 2011.

LIBRARY OF CONGRESS CATALOGING-IN-PUBLICATION DATA
Wingfield, Jenny
The homecoming of Samuel Lake: a novel / Jenny Wingfield
p. cm.
ISBN 978-0-385-34409-8
eBook ISBN 978-0-679-60360-3
1. Teenage boys—Fiction. 2. Brothers and sisters—Fiction.
3. Arkansas—History—20th century—Fiction 4. Domestic fiction. I. Title.
PS3623.I66255H66 2011
813'.6-dc22   2010035309

Printed in the United States of America

www.randomhousereaderscircle.com

9 8 7 6 5 4 3 2 1

Book design by Dana Leigh Blanchette
Title-page image: © iStockphoto

*For Taylor, Amy, and Lori—who never once said
they wished I was normal.*

*For Jim, Ruth, Clif, and Hal—who probably said it,
but not where I could hear.*

And for Charlie and Leon—because.

The Homecoming of Samuel Lake

Chapter 1

Columbia County, Arkansas, 1956

John Moses couldn't have chosen a worse day, or a worse way to die, if he'd planned it for a lifetime. Which was possible. He was contrary as a mule. It was the weekend of the Moses family reunion, and everything was perfect—or at least perfectly normal—until John went and ruined it.

The reunion was always held the first Sunday in June. It had been that way forever. It was tradition. And John Moses had a thing about tradition. Every year or so, his daughter, Willadee (who lived way off down in Louisiana), would ask him to change the reunion date to the second Sunday in June, or the first Sunday in July, but John had a stock answer.

"I'd rather burn in Hell."

Willadee would remind her father that he didn't believe in Hell, and John would remind *her* that it was *God* he didn't believe in, the vote was still out about Hell. Then he would throw in that the worst thing about it was, if there did happen to be a hell, Willadee's husband, Samuel Lake, would land there right beside him, since he was a preacher, and everybody knew that preachers (especially Methodists, like Samuel) were the vilest bunch of bandits alive.

Willadee never argued with her daddy, but the thing was, annual conference started the first Sunday in June. That was when all the Methodist ministers in Louisiana found out from their district superintendents how satisfied or dissatisfied their congregations had been that past year, and whether they were going to get to stay in one place or have to move.

Usually, Samuel would have to move. He was the kind who ruffled a lot of feathers. Not on purpose, mind you. He just went along doing what he thought was right—which included driving out into the boonies on Sunday mornings, and loading up his old rattletrap car with poor people (sometimes ragged, barefoot poor people), and hauling them into town for services. It wouldn't have been so bad if he'd had separate services, one for the folks from the boonies and one for fine, upright citizens whose clothes and shoes were presentable enough to get them into Heaven, no questions asked. But Samuel Lake was of the bothersome conviction that God loved everybody the same. Add this to the fact that he preached with what some considered undue fervor, frequently thumping the pulpit for emphasis and saying things like "If you believe that, say 'AMEN'!" when he knew full well that Methodists were trying to give up that sort of thing, and you can see what his churches were up against.

John Moses didn't give a hoot about Samuel's obligations. He wasn't about to mess with Moses tradition just because Willadee had been fool enough to marry a preacher.

Of course, Samuel wasn't a preacher when Willadee married him. He was a big, strapping country boy, strong as an ox, and dangerously good-looking. Black-haired and blue-eyed—Welsh and Irish or some such mix. Several girls in Columbia County had taken to their beds for a week when Samuel married that plain, quiet Willadee Moses.

Samuel Lake was magic. He was wonderful and terrible, with an awful temper and fearsome tenderness, and when he loved, he loved with his whole heart. He had a clear tenor voice, and he could play the guitar or the fiddle or the mandolin or just about any other in-strument you could think of. Folks all over the county used to talk about Samuel and his music.

"Sam Lake can play anything he can pick up."

"He can make strings talk."

"He can make them speak in tongues."

Every year, the day after school let out for the summer, Samuel and Willadee would load up their kids and take off for south Arkansas. Willadee already had freckles everywhere the sun had ever touched, but she would always roll the window down and hang her arm out, and God would give her more. Her boisterous, sand-colored hair would fly in the breeze, tossing and tangling, and eventually she would laugh out loud, just because going home made her feel so free.

Willadee loved this ritual. This once-a-year road trip, when she was snugged into the car with her good, healthy family—all of them fairly vibrating with anticipation. This was her time for thinking about where they'd been and where they might be going and how well the kids were growing in to their names—the names she'd given them as blessings when they were born. The first boy, she'd called Noble. Her clear call to the universe to infuse him with courage and honor. The younger son was Bienville. A good city, or as Willadee thought of it, a peaceful place. The girl, she had named Swan. Not be-cause a swan is beautiful but because it is powerful. A girl needs power that she doesn't have to borrow from anyone else, Willadee had thought. So far, her blessings seemed to be working. Noble was honest to a fault, Bienville was unfailingly amicable, and Swan radi-ated so much strength that she wore everybody else to a frazzle.

Columbia County was located down on the tail end of Arkansas, which looked just the same as north Louisiana. When God made that part of the country, He made it all in one big piece, and He must have had a good time doing it. There were rolling hills and tall trees and clear creeks with sandy bottoms and wildflowers and blue skies and great puffy clouds that hung down so low you'd almost believe you could reach up and grab a handful. That was the upside. The downside was brambles and cockleburs and a variety of other things nobody paid much attention to, since the upside outweighed the downside by a mile.

Because of the annual conference, Samuel never got to stay for the reunion. Just long enough to unload Willadee and the kids, and talk awhile with Willadee's parents. At least, he talked with her mother, Calla. John would invariably gag and go outside the minute his son-in-law set foot in the house, but Calla thought Samuel hung the moon. Within an hour or so, Samuel would be kissing Willadee goodbye and patting her on the backside, right there in front of God and everybody. Then he'd hug the kids and tell them to mind their mama, and he'd head back to Louisiana. He always said goodbye to John as he left, but the old man never answered back. He couldn't forgive Samuel for moving Willadee so far away, and he couldn't forgive Willadee for going. Especially since she could have married Calvin Furlough, who now had a successful paint and body shop, and lived right down the road, and had the best coon dogs you ever laid eyes on. If Willadee had cooperated with her father by falling in love with Calvin, everything would have been different. She could have lived nearby, and been a comfort to John in his old age. And he (John) would not be stuck with a granddaughter named Swan Lake.

The Moses family lived all over Columbia County. *All over.* John and Calla had loved each other lustily, and had produced five children. Four sons and a daughter. All of these except Willadee and their youngest (Walter, who had died in a sawmill accident the year he turned twenty) still lived around Magnolia, all within forty miles of the old homeplace.

The "old homeplace" had been a sprawling hundred-acre farm, which provided milk and eggs and meat and vegetables and fruit and berries and nuts and honey. It took some coaxing. The land gave little up for free. The farm was dotted with outbuildings that John and his sons had erected over the years. Barns and sheds and smokehouses and outhouses, most of which were leaning wearily by 1956. When you don't use a building anymore, it knows it's lost its purpose.

The Moses house was a big two-story affair. Solidly built, but it leaned a little, too, these days, as if there weren't enough souls inside anymore to hold it up. John and Calla had stopped farming several years back. Calla still had a garden and a few chickens, but they let the fields grow up, and walled in the front porch of the house, and turned it into a grocery store/service station. Calla had John paint her a sign, but she couldn't decide whether she wanted the thing to say "Moses' Grocery and Service Station" or "Moses' Gas and Groceries." While she was making up her mind, John ran out of patience and nailed the sign above the front door. It said, simply, MOSES.

Calla would get out of bed every morning, go down to the store, and start a pot of coffee perking, and farmers would drop by on their way to the cattle auction or the feed store, and warm their behinds at the woodstove, and drink Calla's coffee.

Calla had a way with the customers. She was an ample, comfortable woman, with capable hands, and people liked dealing with her. She didn't really need John, not in the store. As a matter of fact, he got underfoot.

Now, John liked to drink. For thirty years, he'd laced his coffee with whiskey every morning before he headed out to the milk barn. That was to keep off the chill, in the winter. In the summertime, it was to brace him for the day. He no longer went to milk at dawn, but he still laced his coffee. He'd sit there in Calla's store and visit with the regulars, and by the time they were on their way to take care of the day's business, John was usually on his way to being ripped. None of this sat well with Calla. She was used to her husband staying busy, and she told him, finally, that he needed an *interest*.

"I've got an interest, woman," he told her. Calla was bent over, stoking the fire in the woodstove at the moment, so she presented a mighty tempting target. John aimed himself in her direction, and wobbled over behind her, and slipped his arms around her middle. Calla was caught so off guard that she burned her hand on the poker. She shrugged her husband off and sucked on her hand.

"I mean, one that'll keep you out of my hair," she snapped.

"You never wanted me out of your hair before."

He was wounded. She hadn't intended to wound him, but after all, wounds heal over. Most of them.

"I never had time to notice before if you was in my hair or not. Isn't there anything you like to do anymore, besides roll around in bed?" Not that she minded rolling around in bed with her husband. She liked it now, maybe even more than she had in all the years they'd been together. But you couldn't do that all day long just because a man had nothing else to occupy his time. Not when you had customers dropping by every few minutes.

John went to the counter where he'd been drinking his coffee. He poured himself another cup, and laced it good.

"There is," he announced stiffly. "There most damn certainly is something else I like to do. And I'm about to do it."

The thing he was talking about was getting drunk. Not just ripped. Blind drunk. Beyond thinking and reasoning drunk. He took his coffee and his bottle, and a couple more bottles he had stashed behind the counter, plus a package of doughnuts and two tins of Prince Albert. Then he went out to the barn, and he stayed for three days. When he'd been drunk enough long enough, and there was no further purpose to be served by staying drunk any longer, he came back to the house and took a hot bath and had a shave. That was the day he walled in the *back* porch of the house and started painting another sign.

"Just what do you think you're doing?" Calla demanded, hands on hips, the way a woman stands when She Expects an Answer.

"I'm cultivating an interest," John Moses said. "From now on, you've got a business, and I've got a business, and we don't either one stick our noses in the *other* one's business. You open at dawn and close at dusk, I'll open at dusk and close at dawn. You won't have to roll around with me anymore, because we won't be keeping the same hours."

"I never said I didn't want to roll around with you."

"The hell you never," said John.

He took his sign, with the paint still wet, and he climbed up on his stepladder and nailed that sign above the back door. The paint was smudged, but the message was readable enough. It said, NEVER CLOSES.

Never Closes sold beer and wine and hard liquor seven nights a week, all night long. Since Columbia County was dry, it was illegal to sell alcohol to the public, so John didn't call it selling. He was just serving drinks to his friends, that's all. Sort of like gifts he gave them. Then, when they were ready to call it a night, his "friends" would each give John a gift of some sort. Five dollars, or ten dollars, or whatever his little ragged notebook indicated the gift should be.

The county sheriff and several deputies got into the habit of dropping by after their shifts, and John really *didn't* sell to them, just poured them anything they wanted, on the house. Those fellows never saw so much free liquor, so it just stood to reason that there would be a lot of other things they didn't see. But they were used to not seeing, under certain circumstances, so it all felt pretty right.

Before long, John got his own share of regulars who would drop by to play dominoes or shoot pool. They'd talk religion and politics, and tell filthy stories, and spit tobacco juice in the coffee cans John had set around, and they'd smoke until the air was thick enough to cut into cubes.

John took bitter pride in his new venture. He'd have dropped the whole thing in a heartbeat, would have torn down his walls and burned his sign and told his regulars to go to hell, if Calla would have apologized, but she had her own pride. There was a wedge between them, and she couldn't see that she'd been the one to drive it.

After a while, Calla took to staying open seven days a week, too. Sometimes her last customers of the day would walk right out the front door and go around the house to the back door and drink up whatever money they had left over from buying groceries. Sometimes, it was the other way around. John's customers would stagger out the back door at dawn and come around to the front (there was a well-worn path). They'd sober up on Calla's coffee, then spend the rest of their money on food for their families.

You could go to the Moses place, any time of the day or night, and buy what you needed, provided your needs were simple. And you never had to leave until you were ready, because neither Calla nor John had the heart to run anybody off, even when they ran out of money. Nate Ramsey had stayed once for almost a week when his wife, Shirley, took to throwing things at home.

And that's the way things went along, right up until the day John Moses died. Moses Never Closes was something folks counted on. It was a certain place in an uncertain world. Folks wanted it to stay the way it was, because once you change one part of a thing, all the other parts begin to shift, and pretty soon, you just don't know what's what anymore.

Chapter 2

This is the way it happened.

Samuel dropped Willadee and the kids off on Saturday, and Willadee spent the rest of the day helping her mother with the cooking and cleaning. The kids weren't going to be any help, so they were banished from the house and had to endure such punishments as romping in the hayloft, fishing for crawdads in the creek, and playing War Spies all over the hundred acres.

Noble was twelve years old, all arms and legs and freckles. He had his daddy's eyes, but you didn't really notice them because of his glasses, which were so thick and heavy they continually slid down his nose. He wanted, more than anything, to be *formidable,* so he walked with a swagger and talked in low, menacing tones. Problem was, his voice was changing and would take the high road when he least expected it. Just when he might say something sinister like "You make a move, and I'll cut your heart out," his voice would jump to falsetto and spoil the effect completely.

Swan was eleven. A gray-eyed, compact bit of a girl who could pass for a boy, dressed in her younger brother, Bienville's, clothes, as she was now. Samuel would have had a fit if he'd known that Willadee allowed such things. The Bible clearly said that women were not to dress as men, and Samuel Lake always tried to follow the Bible to the letter. But then, Willadee had a habit of letting the kids do whatever they wanted to when Samuel wasn't around, as long as they didn't violate the Moses Family Rules—which meant no lying, no stealing, no tormenting animals or smaller children.

The most delicious thing in Swan's life was this one week every summer of wearing boy clothes and forgetting about modesty. She could scoot under barbed-wire fences and race across pastures without those confounded skirts getting in her way. She was little. She was quick. And she was just what Noble dreamed of being. Formidable. You couldn't get the best of her, no matter how you tried.

"That child is a terror," Grandma Calla would say to Willadee when she thought Swan wasn't listening. (Swan was always listening.)

"She's her father's daughter," Willadee would answer, usually with a small sigh, which indicated that there was nothing to be done about the situation, Swan was Swan. Both Willadee and Calla rather admired Swan, although they never would have said so. They just indicated it with a slight lift of their eyebrows, and the least hint of a smile, whenever her name came up. Which was often. Swan got into more trouble than any other child in the Moses tribe.

Bienville was nine years old, and he was another story altogether. He had a peaceable nature, a passion for books, and a total fascination with the universe in general. You just couldn't count on him for things like surveillance, or assassinations. You could be playing the best game of Spies, and have the Enemy cornered, and be just about to move in for the kill, and there Bienville would be, studying the pattern of rocks in the creek bed or examining the veins in a sassafras leaf. He couldn't be *depended on* to do his part in a war effort.

Noble and Swan had learned how to deal with Bienville, though. Since he never seemed to commit to either side, they made him a double agent. Bienville didn't care, even though being a double agent generally meant he was the first one to get killed.

Bienville had just gotten killed for the fourth time that Saturday afternoon when Things Started Happening. He was lying on his back in the pasture, dead as a stone, staring up at the sky.

He said, "Swan, did you ever wonder why you can see stars at night but not in the daytime? Stars don't evaporate when the sun comes up."

"You're supposed to be dead," Swan reminded him.

She had just shot him with an invisible submachine gun, and she was busy digging an invisible trench with an invisible shovel. Bienville didn't know it, but he was about to be rolled over into the trench, dead or not. Noble was still lurking somewhere out there in Enemy Territory, so Swan had to keep a watchful eye.

Bienville said, "I'm tired of being dead," and he sat up.

Swan pushed him back down with her foot. "You are a corpse," she told him. "You can't be tired, you can't sit up, and you can*not* talk."

She had forgotten to be watchful. Sudden footsteps behind her told her so. She whirled, brandishing the invisible shovel. Noble was running directly toward her, arms pumping. The area he was crossing had been designated as a Minefield, but Noble wasn't looking for mines. Swan let out a ferocious *roar* and brought her "shovel" down across Noble's head. That should have done him in, but he didn't fling himself on the ground and commence his death agonies, like he was supposed to. He grabbed Swan and clamped one hand over her mouth, and hissed at her to get quiet. Swan struggled indignantly but couldn't get free. Even if Noble wasn't formidable, he was strong.

"I just—killed you—with a shovel!" she hollered. Noble's hand muffled the sound into mushy, garbled noises. About every other word, Swan tried to bite his fingers. "No way—could you—have survived. That—was a fatal blow—and you know it!"

Bienville was looking on like a wise old sage, and he made out enough of what Swan was saying to have to agree with her.

"It was a fatal blow, all right," he confirmed.

Noble rolled his eyes and clamped his hand tighter across Swan's mouth. She was kicking up a storm and growling, deep in her throat.

"I said *shhh*!" Noble dragged his sister toward a line of brush and brambles that ran between the pasture and a patch of woods. Bienville flipped over on his belly and crawled across the Minefield after them. When they got close to the brush line, Noble realized he had a problem. He needed to let Swan go, which promised to be something like releasing a wildcat.

He said, very calmly, "Swan, I'm going to turn you loose."

"*Irpulmbfrmlmb, ustnknbzzrd!*" she answered, and she bit his hand so hard that he jerked it away from her mouth to inspect it for blood. That split second was all Swan needed. She drove an elbow into Noble's gut, and he doubled over, gasping for breath.

"Dammit, Swan," he groaned. She was all over him. Noble drew himself into a wad, enduring the onslaught. He knew a few Indian tricks, such as Becoming a Tree. A person could hit and kick a tree all day long without hurting it, because it was Unmovable. He'd learned this from Bienville, who had either read about it or made it up. Noble didn't care whether Bienville's stories were true, just so the methods worked.

Swan hated it when Noble Became a Tree. It was something she had never mastered (*she* was not about to stand still for anybody to hit *her*), and it wore her out fighting someone who wouldn't fight back. It made her feel like a loser, no matter how much damage she inflicted. Still, she had to save face, so she landed one last blow to Noble's wooden shoulder and licked her sore knuckles.

"I win," she announced.

"Fine." Noble let his muscles relax. "You win. Now, shut up and follow me."

John Moses was sitting under a tree, cleaning his shotgun and talking to God.

"And another thing," he was saying. "I don't believe the part about the Red Sea opening up and people walking through on dry land."

For a man who didn't believe in God, John talked to Him a lot.

Whether God ever listened was anybody's guess. John was generally drunk during these monologues, and the things he said were not very complimentary. He'd been mad at God for a long time, starting when Walter had fallen across that saw blade, over at the Ferguson mill.

John was pulling a string out of the end of his shotgun barrel. There was an oily strip of cotton cloth tied onto the end of the string, and the cloth came out gray-black. He sighted down the barrel, squinting and angry-looking.

"You expect us to believe the damnedest things." He was talking in a normal tone of voice, just as if God were sitting two feet away from him.

"For instance, all this stuff about You being love," he went on, and here his voice grew thick. "If You was love, You wouldn't have let my Walter get split wide open like a slaughtered hog—"

John began polishing the butt of his gun with a separate rag that he'd had tucked away in the bib of his overalls. Tears welled in his eyes, then spilled over and trailed down his weathered face. He didn't bother to wipe them away.

"If You are love," he roared, "then love ain't much to crow about."

The kids were all crouched behind a thick wall of razor wire (blackberry vines), peering at the Enemy through the tiniest of openings between the thorny canes. They had a good, clear view of the old man, but he couldn't see them.

Swan had a feeling that they shouldn't be here. It was one thing for her and her brothers to spy on each other, since they only said things they meant each other to hear. But this was Papa John. They had never seen him cry, or believed it was possible for him to cry. Usually during their visits, he just slept the days away and ran his bar at night. If they saw him at all, it was only as he walked through a room without speaking or sat at the supper table, picking at his food. Their mother said he hadn't always been this way, that he had really been something beautiful when she was growing up, but he had let life get the best of him. From the looks of him now, she was right about that last part.

Swan tugged on Noble's sleeve, intending to tell him she wanted to leave, but he drew one finger across his gullet, indicating that he would slit her throat for sure if she said a word.

Just then, Papa John gave up on talking to God and set in singing. "Coming home," he quavered. He had to be tone-deaf. "Cominnng—hommmme—"

Swan shot a look at Bienville, and he shot one back. This was getting harder to swallow by the minute.

"Never more to roammmm—" Papa John caterwauled, but he couldn't remember any more of the words, so he switched over to a Hank Williams song, which he also couldn't remember.

He hummed the first few bars tunelessly, while he dug a shell out of his pocket and loaded his shotgun.

"I'm so lonesome, I could—" he sang, suddenly loud and clear. Then his voice broke and quavered. "I'm so lonesome, I could—"

Swan thought he sounded like a stuck record.

"I could—" he sang again, but he couldn't make himself say that last word. He shook his head and blew out a long, discouraged breath. Then he stuck the shotgun barrel in his mouth.

Swan screamed. Noble and Bienville sprang up in the air like flushed quail.

Papa John hadn't had time to get his finger situated on the trigger, so instead of blowing his brains out in full view of his grandchildren, he jerked to attention and banged the back of his head on the tree. The shotgun barrel slipped out of his mouth, bringing his upper plate with it. The false teeth went sailing and disappeared in the blackberry vines, directly in front of where the three kids were now standing, shaking like maple leaves. Papa John jumped to his feet, shocked and humiliated. His mouth was working, open and shut. Slack-looking without that upper plate.

The kids hung their heads and stared at the ground for the longest time. When they looked up again, Papa John was cutting through the woods, going back toward the house. Shade and sun rays fell across him, dappling and camouflaging, making him indistinguishable from his surroundings. He never really disappeared from view. He just blended in with the trees and the underbrush, like he was part of the woods and they were part of him.

Papa John didn't show up for supper, just went into Never Closes and opened for business. Calla and Willadee and the kids could hear the hubbub through the wall that separated the kitchen from the bar. John had bought himself a used jukebox during the past year, and his customers were giving it a workout. Swan and Noble and Bienville kept sneaking anxious glances at each other while they ate.

Finally, Calla couldn't take it anymore. "All right," she said. "I want to know what's up, and I want to know now."

Bienville gulped. Noble pushed his glasses up his nose. Swan reached into the pocket of her jeans and pulled out Papa John's false teeth.

"Papa John lost these this afternoon, and we found them."

"That's all you're looking guilty about?" Calla asked sharply.

Which made Swan mad. Grown-ups had a way of interpreting every single, solitary expression that ever lit on a kid's face as guilt. "We're not *guilty*," she said, a little louder than was necessary. "We're *worried*. Papa John came within an inch of killing himself this afternoon, and if it hadn't been for us, he would've made it."

Willadee sucked in a sharp breath.

Calla just shook her head. "He wouldn't have made it. He never does."

Willadee looked at her mother accusingly.

Calla poured some tomato gravy onto her biscuit. "Sorry, Willadee. I can't panic anymore. I've been through it too many times. You kids eat your okra."

Willadee didn't say anything, but you could tell she was thinking. As soon as supper was over, she offered to clean the kitchen and asked her mother to put the hellions to bed. Grandma Calla said, "Oh, sure, give me the dirty work," and both women laughed. The kids all turned up their noses while they allowed themselves to be herded upstairs. They knew better than to complain, but they had their own ways of getting back at people who insulted them. Next time they played War Spies, they would probably take a couple of female prisoners and get information out of them the hard way.

Willadee washed all the dishes, left them to dry in the drain rack, and went out the back door into Never Closes. This was the only bar she'd ever been inside in her life, and the first time during business hours. At least once every summer, she'd insisted on cleaning and airing out the place for her daddy, marveling every time that his customers could stand the bitter, stale burned-tobacco odor that no amount of scrubbing could drive away. She was surprised tonight to find that the smell was entirely different when the place was full of life. The smoke was overpowering but fresh, and it was mingled with men's aftershave and the heady perfume worn by the few women customers. A lone couple danced in one corner, the woman toying with the man's hair while his hands traveled all up and down her back. There was a card game going on, and a couple of games of dominoes, and you couldn't even see the pool table for all the rear ends and elbows. The way people were laughing and joking with each other, they must've checked their troubles at the door. John Moses was standing behind the bar, uncapping a couple of beers. He passed them over to a middle-aged bleached blonde and smiled, lips closed, self-conscious about the missing upper plate. He pretended not to see Willadee until she came over and leaned against the bar.

Willadee passed his teeth across to him. Discreetly. John's eyes narrowed, but he took the teeth, turned away for a second, and put them inside his mouth. Then he turned back to face his daughter.

"What are you doing in here?"

"Just thought I'd see how the other half lives," Willadee said. "How're you doing, Daddy? I never get to see you much anymore when I come home."

John Moses coughed disdainfully. "You didn't live so far away, you'd see me plenty."

Willadee gave her daddy the gentlest look imaginable, and she said, "Daddy, are you all right?"

"What do you care?"

"I care."

"My eye."

"You're just set on being miserable. Come on. Give me a grin."

But it looked as if he didn't have a grin left in him.

She said, "It's not healthy to manufacture trouble and wallow around in it."

"Willadee," he grumbled, "you don't know trouble."

"Yes, I do, you old fart. I know you."

That sounded a lot more like the kind of thing a Moses would say than the kind of thing a preacher's wife would say. So, as it turned out, John did have a grin or two left in him, and he gave her one, as proof.

"You want a beer, Willadee?" He sounded hopeful.

"You know I don't drink."

"Yeah, but it would tickle the pure-dee hell outta me to see you do something that'd make Sam Lake have a stroke if he knew about it."

Willadee laughed, and reached across the bar, and goosed her daddy in the ribs, and said, "Well, give me that beer. Because I surely would like to see you get tickled."

It was after 2:00 A.M. by the time Willadee left Never Closes and sneaked back through the house. Her mother was just coming out of the bathroom, and the two bumped into each other in the hall.

"Willadee, have you got beer on your breath?"

"Yes, ma'am, I have."

"Well, forevermore," Calla said as she headed up the stairs. She was going to have to mark this day on the calendar.

Later on, when Willadee was in her old room, she lay in bed thinking about how the first beer had tasted like rotten tomatoes, but the second one had simply tasted wet and welcome, and how the noise and laughter in the bar had been as intoxicating as the beer. She and her daddy had left the customers to wait on themselves and had found an empty table and talked about everything on earth, the way they used to, before Willadee got married. She had been the old man's shadow, back then. Now, he had become the shadow. Almost invisible these days. But not tonight. Tonight, he'd had a shine about him.

He didn't want to die anymore. He certainly did not seem to want to die anymore. He'd just been feeling unnecessary for so long, and she'd shown him how necessary he was, by sitting with him those hours. Joking with him, and listening with her heart, while he poured out his.

"You've always been my favorite," he had told her, just before she left Never Closes. "I love the others. All of them. I'm their daddy, and I love them. But you. You and Walter—" He shook his head. All his feelings stuck in his throat. Then he kissed her cheek, there at the back door of the bar. John Moses, ushering his beloved daughter back into the solid safety of the house he had built when he was a stalwart, younger man. John Moses, feeling necessary.

Willadee was groggy, but it was a pleasant sort of grogginess. Like she was floating. Nothing to tie her down and hold her to earth. She could just float higher and higher, and look down at life while it turned all fuzzy and indistinct around the edges. She promised herself that, one of these days, she was going to have another couple of beers. One of these days. She was a Moses, after all.

Her father's favorite child.

Chapter 3

Kinfolk started pouring in early the next morning. Pulling up in the front yard, and piling out of their cars, and opening the trunks of those cars with a flourish. Huge bowls of potato salad and dishpans full of fried chicken were produced like rabbits out of hats. And corn on the cob, and squash casseroles, and dilled green beans, and fifty kinds of pickles, and gallon jugs of iced tea, and enough pies and cakes to founder a multitude. Which was what was on hand.

John and Calla's sons, Toy and Sid and Alvis, had been the first to arrive, along with their wives and offspring. Toy didn't have any children, but Sid had two and Alvis had six, so what with Willadee's three, nobody was worried that the family line might fade out any time soon.

"It's unbelievable how many grandkids I've got," Grandma Calla said, not to anybody in particular.

Willadee sang out, "But not inconceivable!"

All her brothers howled with laughter.

Calla said, "I can see I've raised a whole passel of heathens." She was trying to look as if she disapproved, but it wasn't any use. She approved of a good time, and everybody was having one.

The womenfolk laid the food out on the tables, and the kids started helping themselves before they were supposed to, so somebody had to say the blessing quick. Nicey (who was married to Sid, Willadee's oldest brother) was selected, since it would have hurt her feelings if she hadn't been. She was a serious churchgoer and had been teaching the Sunbeams practically ever since she'd gotten too old to be one. She prayed a fancy prayer, full of *Thine*s and *Thou*s, ending up with "Ah-men." Sid and Alvis followed that with "Dive in!" which just about gave Nicey the vapors, it sounding so irreverent and all.

"You married into an irreverent family," Alvis's wife, Eudora, told her. "You got to take the bad with the worse."

John had closed the bar just before sunup that morning and had gone straight to bed, figuring that would give him five or six hours of sleep, enough sleep for a well man, and he was certainly feeling like a well man. Calla's store was operating on the honor system, the way it always did on reunion day. Folks who needed to buy something just went in and got what they wanted, and left the money or a note in a jar on the counter. There weren't many customers until after church, when folks started drifting in, picking up last-minute items like brown 'n' serve rolls and whipping cream for their Sunday dinners. It was the most natural thing in the world that quite a few of the customers would drift from the store into the yard, and would visit for a while, protesting that they really had to be getting on home until somebody put a plate into their hands and they were forced to stay and eat.

Swan, Noble, and Bienville had a hard time figuring out who was kin and who wasn't. The closest relatives they remembered from year to year, but there was this sea of nonrelatives, not to mention second cousins, and third cousins, and great-aunts twice removed. This cracked the kids up. "If that old bird's been twice removed, how come she keeps coming back?" they would whisper to each other, and then they'd snicker until they got the hiccups or a swat on the pants from their grandmother, whichever happened first.

John Moses woke up just before noon and wandered down to join the celebration. His sons and Willadee all came up out of the yard onto the side porch to greet him. The side porch had been added onto the house way back, shortly after John had walled in the back porch. John said a house wasn't a home if it didn't have a porch, a man had to have something to pee off of. Indoor plumbing was fine, as far as it went, but it never would offer a man the same sense of freedom that a porch would. The daughters all hugged John's neck (Willadee rubbed his stubbled chin lovingly), and the sons all shook his hand. John smiled from ear to ear.

"Somebody said there was a party," he boomed.

"They was right," Toy Moses said.

Toy looked nothing like his name implied. He stood six foot four, with muscles that rippled powerfully beneath his cotton shirt. He walked real straight and stiff-starched. Straighter than anyone Swan and her brothers had ever seen. There was a scar on his forehead and a tattoo of a belly dancer on his arm, and all told, he had the look of a man you wouldn't want to mess with. He was soft-spoken, though, especially when he was talking to his daddy. He said, "You better come on out here and get some grub, before it's all gone."

John said, "You won't have to twist *my* arm," just as cheerful as you please, and he led his brood back down the steps.

When everybody had eaten until they were stuffed, the grown-ups flopped down into lawn chairs and onto the grass, and commenced talking about the good old days. The littlest kids all got put down for naps, and the teenagers meandered out to the cars to listen to the radio and talk about things they ought not to know about. Noble tried to join this worldly crowd, but he was coolly rejected, so he slunk off to the creek to think his own thoughts. Swan and Bienville crawled under the house (which was pier and beam, a good four feet off the ground) with a couple of cousins their own age and built toad houses. This was accomplished by mounding dirt over their bare feet and patting it down good, then carefully pulling their feet out, leaving perfect toad dwellings, suitable to accommodate the pickiest of toads.

It was about three o'clock when John Moses started feeling a serious need for a drink. He'd been fighting the feeling ever since he woke up, and he'd thought he was winning the battle, but all of a sudden his fighting spirit waned, and he decided what could it hurt, he wasn't going to drink himself into a stupor after all he was too happy for that. So he got to his feet and announced, ceremoniously, that he had to go to the bathroom.

All his kids looked at all his other kids, and the looks they were giving each other were looks of dread. John Moses couldn't help noticing.

"Anybody find anything wrong with that?" he demanded. After all, he had just as much right to go to the bathroom as anyone else.

Nobody made a sound.

John said, "Well, if nobody has any objections . . . ," and he took off for the house.

No one said anything for a minute or so. They just sat there looking as if they'd been waked up from a good dream. Then Alvis said, "Well, sonofabitch. I thought for a while there we had it made."

Willadee was chewing a hole in her lip, trying to decide whether or not to follow her daddy and head him off before he could get drunk and ruin the reunion. But then she remembered the beers she'd had the night before, and the pleasant grogginess that had followed, and she thought, Maybe he won't ruin anything, maybe he'll just relax a little, and go to sleep, and that will be the end of that. She stayed put in her lawn chair.

Calla stood up and got herself a clean paper plate. "I don't believe I've tasted Eudora's friendship cake," she said. "Anybody else want a piece of Eudora's friendship cake while I'm up?"

. . .

John went through the house and into the bar, and he sat down on the first barstool he came to. Giving in and having a drink wasn't something he wanted to do today. He *wanted* to make them all proud of him. They had *seemed* proud of him all afternoon.

By the time he poured the first two fingers of Johnnie Walker into a glass and drank it down, he had come to realize that every one of them (except for Willadee, who was above reproach) had been stringing him along, in order to manipulate him into staying sober. He poured three fingers the next time, instead of two. Willadee's face seemed to be swimming before him, so he squenched his eyes closed, trying to shut her out.

"Willadee, you just get on out of here," he commanded, but she refused to leave.

"I said get out of here, Willadee. You and I can have a beer and talk about this, after everybody else is gone."

When he opened his eyes, the image of Willadee had disappeared.

"Where's Walter?" John Moses asked. He had just come from the bar back through the house, and from the house out onto the side porch. The porch was full of people, and the yard was running over with people, and altogether, it was more people than John could deal with comfortably, since he was looking for just one face, and it was nowhere to be seen.

It got so quiet even the wind quit blowing.

"I said, where's Walter?" John bellowed.

Toy was sitting in the porch swing with his arm around his wife, Bernice, who was outlandishly pretty, even though she was thirty-five years old and ought to be starting to fade.

Toy left Bernice and came over beside the old man. "Walter's not here today, Daddy."

"The devil you say." John's words were slurring into one another. "Walter wouldn't miss a Moses reunion."

Then John remembered why Walter wasn't there. "You shouldn't have let him go to work, Toy. You shouldn't have ever let him go when he wasn't feeling good, and you knew it."

Toy got a sick look on his face. "You're right, Daddy. I know that."

John said, "Split open, like a slaughtered—"

But he didn't get to finish. Calla had come up the steps and stood facing him.

"Why don't you and me just go inside and take us a rest?" she asked. Which changed the world John Moses was living in. All of a sudden, he wasn't thinking about Walter anymore. He was thinking about the fact that he'd been sleeping alone for more than a decade.

"What?" he ripped out, raucous-sounding. "You're saying you wanta go roll around in the old marriage bed?"

Calla just stood there. Wordless. Her lips going white. Out in the yard, relatives and nonrelatives began skittering around, loading up kids and leftover food. There was a storm brewing, and they wanted to be gone before it hit.

John hollered, "Where the hell you folks going? Don't you know it's not nice to eat and run?" But they kept leaving, like salt dribbling out of an overturned shaker. It was getting sparse out there.

Calla said, "John, quit making a fool of yourself."

"I'll make of myself what I damn well please," John informed her. "I am a self-made man." He did a lurching sort of dance step and nearly fell off the porch.

"You are a self-made jackass," she muttered under her breath.

That's when John Moses slapped her. The sound rang out, and Willadee came running across the yard. Pushing people aside. She stepped in between her mother and father and looked John Moses dead in the eye.

"I—am so—ashamed of you," she said to him. Her voice was shaking.

That sobered John up. He looked back at Willadee for what seemed like eternity extended. Then he turned on his heel and walked inside the house.

Nobody felt much like visiting anymore. They all just hung there for a little bit, wishing none of this was happening. Willadee was patting her mother's arm, but she was staring at the door John Moses had walked through. All at once, she knew what was about to happen, just as surely as if a voice had come out of the sky and told her. She took a quick step toward the door.

"Daddy!" she cried out, sharp and clear, but not one soul heard her say it, because the gunshot was as loud as a big clap of thunder.

Chapter 4

The first hour was the worst. Willadee's brothers kept the women out of the house, but Willadee saw it all just as vividly in her mind as if she'd been the one to find the body. For the rest of her life, she would be pushing that picture back, fighting it, hating it. Trying to reduce the dimensions. Dull down the colors. She would never succeed.

She allowed herself to be led over to a chair in the yard, but she could not sit still. She leapt to her feet and crammed her fingers in her mouth to keep from wailing. Then someone took her arm and walked her in circles, from the porch to the well to the garden to the porch. Circles. Talking. Gentle words, pouring, one on top of another, running together. More circles. Later on, Willadee would be unable to remember who this person was who saved her from hysteria.

"My fault," Willadee said to whoever it was.

"Hush, shhh, hush that talk, it wasn't anybody's fault."

But Willadee knew better. She knew.

She managed to get Samuel on the phone, and he said what she knew he'd say. That he was going to get in the car and come back. He should be there, with her and the kids and Calla. Willadee wouldn't hear of it. He needed to be right where he was. There were enough menfolk around to handle things, and if he came up, he'd just have to turn around and go back, and it was all too much driving, too dangerous, and she couldn't stand it if anything happened to him, too.

"How could he do this to all of you, Willadee?" Samuel asked angrily, but she pretended not to hear.

After she hung up the phone, Willadee didn't know what to do. The body had been taken into Magnolia, to the funeral home. Friends and neighbors had pitched in to clean up the mess John had made. People were milling around in the yard. There wasn't a private place anywhere to sit down and think. Willadee wondered briefly whether she should find her children and comfort them, but there weren't any kids in sight. Someone must have gotten them out of there, taken them home with them, and would bring them back later, tomorrow morning probably.

Alvis came over, and put his arms around her, and said, bitterly, "That old man."

Willadee rubbed her forehead against his shoulder, then turned away. It bothered her for everybody to be so upset with her daddy for what he'd done. His life was broken, and he couldn't figure out how to fix it, so he'd just killed the man who was responsible. She picked her way through the crowd. Every way she turned, there was another sympathetic face. Someone telling her to just let go and cry it out— when she was dry and crumbling inside. Someone inquiring about the arrangements. What a word. *Arrangements.* What was left of John Moses to arrange? He was dead. He would rot. He had been beautiful once, and now he would rot, but not before arrangements were made, and a profit taken. Arrangements were expensive, even in 1956.

Finally, she found her way into the bar and locked the door behind her. It was dark in there. Murky and stifling hot. But she didn't want any lights. Didn't want to open doors and windows to let in air, because then that sea of people outside would begin to seep in, and she would drown for sure. She felt her way along the bar, thinking about her father and the night before, and the talk they'd had, and how she'd gone to bed thinking it was all right now, everything would be all right. She stood there, holding on to the bar with both hands, not even aware that she had started crying. Great, gusty sobs. After a while, she stopped, and just laid her head against the scarred wood. That was when she realized that she was not alone.

"I never once set foot in here, until today." It was Calla talking. She was sitting way back in a corner, at one of the tables, all by herself. "I was so mad at him, all these years. I keep trying to remember what I was so mad about."

Calla Moses spent the night at the funeral home. Ernest Simmons, the funeral director, said the body wouldn't be ready for viewing until the next day, and that she should go on home and get some rest, but she informed him that she didn't come to view the body, she came to be close to it, and she wasn't going anywhere.

Willadee and her brothers all offered to stay with Calla, to keep her company. She said she didn't want any company.

"You don't need to be alone right now," Willadee insisted.

"I'd feel more alone at home," Calla answered stoutly. "And don't any of you get the idea that you can start telling me what to do now that your daddy's gone. You never had the nerve to try it before, so you'd best not start now."

Everybody backed off except Toy, who refused to leave. He was just as stubborn as his mother.

"Bernice can sleep at your house, so she won't be by herself," he told her. "You won't hardly know I'm here."

And she didn't. Toy saw all the others off, then spent most of the night standing outside smoking one cigarette after the other and staring at the sky. Calla took a seat in an empty viewing room and closed the door, and thought about the life she'd had with John Moses.

"It was a good life, John," she whispered into the stillness. "We had our rough spots to go through, but it was a good life, mainly."

Then she demanded, fiercely, "Why the hell did you give up on it?"

They didn't close the store for the funeral. Calla said "Moses Never Closes" had been such a tradition for so long, and you know how Papa John was about tradition. Swan couldn't help thinking that Papa John had pretty well played the wild with tradition by shooting himself, right in the middle of a family reunion, but you didn't go around saying things like that. Besides, they didn't make any *money* that day, didn't charge for anything, so it wasn't as if they were staying open out of greed. What if somebody in the community needed a jug of milk, they said. Or a jug of whiskey. Anybody had a touch of flu, there was nothing like lemon juice and sugar and whiskey to put them out of their misery while it ran its course. It wasn't exactly flu season, but you never knew.

Toy kept the store. He didn't like funerals anyway. Said they were just more examples of people trying to fit other people's expectations. When Walter had died, Toy had slunk off into the woods with his .22 and taken potshots at squirrels while the rest of the family was doing what was expected of them. He figured his brother's spirit was still close—maybe with a few things heavy on his mind that he'd been meaning to say but never got around to. So Toy went to the woods, and he listened. He and Walter had hunted those woods together since they were towheaded kids. They were close, the two of them. More than blood close.

Toy knew all the stumps and fallen logs where Walter liked to sit down and have a smoke, and just enjoy the peace. So that's what Toy had done. For an hour or so at a time. Then, when the peace was too much for him, and he couldn't take it anymore, and his chest would feel like it was about to bust from the tears he'd been holding in, Toy Ephraim Moses would shatter the peace with a shot or two from his rifle. If he hit something, fine. Toy hoped Bernice would outlive him.

If she should happen to die before he did, that was one funeral he'd have to go to, and he was afraid he'd turn out taking potshots at the mourners.

Swan found out early the morning of the service that Uncle Toy wasn't going.

"Uncle Toy has no respect what-so-ever for the dead," Lovey had said at breakfast. Lovey was Uncle Sid and Aunt Nicey's youngest child. Ten years old, and spoiled rotten. She had insisted on sleeping over the night before, mostly so she could rub it in to Swan and her brothers how much better she'd known Papa John than they had, and also, so she could shame them for not crying as much as she thought they ought to. They had squeezed out a few tears, but nothing like the gallons Lovey produced. They hadn't needed to grieve, because Papa John had lived and died a stranger.

"You hush your mouth, young lady," Grandma Calla had said to Lovey. "Your uncle Toy has his own ways, is all."

Swan had been hearing about Uncle Toy and his "ways" ever since she could remember. For one thing, he was a bootlegger—not that Swan had a clear idea of what that meant. She knew it was against the law, though, and that it could be dangerous. If Uncle Toy wanted to break the law, why not just work in Never Closes with Papa John? That sure seemed like a safe proposition. But it was like Grandma Calla said. Toy had his own ways.

He'd been in the war, and was decorated for valor. Something about going through enemy fire to save a comrade. A colored man, no less. He got shot doing it, too. Got one leg blown clean off. That was why he walked so stiff-starched. His artificial leg didn't have any give to it. But bootlegging when he could have been working in the bar and getting his leg blown off to save a Negro weren't the only things that got Uncle Toy talked about. He'd killed a man once, right here in Columbia County. A neighbor named Yam Ferguson, whose family had "connections." Yam hadn't had to go off to war. He got to stay home and help run the Ferguson Sawmill, and chase after the wives and girlfriends of the boys whose families weren't so well connected.

Yam lived through the war, but not through the night Uncle Toy got home from the V.A. hospital.

By the time the rest of the family was dressed for the funeral, Swan had made up her mind not to go. She got ready, along with everybody else, but she told her mama she was going to ride with Aunt Nicey, and she told Aunt Nicey she was going to ride with Aunt Eudora. Then, while everybody else was piling into the line of cars parked out in front of the store, Swan sneaked upstairs into Papa John's bedroom. She would not look at the bed Papa John had sat down on to finish what he had started out in the pasture, under that tree. She would not look at the wall that the neighbor women had washed clean. She especially would not look at the Bible on the bedside table. It made her shudder to think that Papa John was in touching distance of the Holy Word when he did what he did, as if he just had to insult God one last time. There was no doubt in Swan's mind that Papa John was already burning in Hell by now, unless by some chance, God took insanity into consideration. But, she figured, why have a hell if you're going to let folks get off on technicalities?

So she didn't look at *anything* in the room. She had the feeling that, if she looked, she would see Papa John, still there, just the way his sons had found him, and she wasn't about to chance a thing like that. Papa John was scary enough when he was alive.

Swan walked over to the window and watched through the curtains while the caravan drove away. When the red dust had settled in the wake of the last car, Swan crept down the stairs. She could see the open door that led from the living room into the grocery store.

Uncle Toy was standing in the store, leaning against the counter, using his pocketknife to peel the bark off a stick that he must have picked up on one of his treks into the woods. A lit Camel drooped from between his lips, and he smoked no hands. Swan stood in the doorway, watching him. She knew that he knew she was there, but he didn't look up or say a word.

Swan eased into the store, climbed up on top of the ice cream box, and started worrying the heel of one shoe with the toe of the other. Toy lifted his eyes, peering at her through a blue-white fog of smoke.

"Guess you don't like funerals, either."

"Never been to one." Swan was lying, of course. Preachers' kids attended more funerals than any other kids in the world. Toy had to know that.

"Well—" Toy left the word hanging in the air for a while, like that said it all. He shaved down a little knob that jutted out on one side of the stick. Finally, he said, "You ain't missed much."

Swan had been afraid he might say something adult like "Does your mama know you're here?" Since he didn't, she considered the two of them immediately bonded. Swan yearned to get close to somebody. Really close. Soul deep. She wanted the kind of friendship where two people know each other inside out and stick up for each other, no matter what. So far, she'd never had that, and she was convinced the reason was because her father was a minister.

From Swan's observations, there seemed to be a conspiracy among church members to keep the preacher and his family from knowing them too well. Playing cards were hidden when they came to visit. Liquor was stuck back in the pantry behind the mason jars of home-canned green beans and crowder peas. And you didn't even *talk* about dancing. They just didn't know Sam Lake's background—but Swan did. She'd heard it said that her daddy had been a rounder back before God got hold of him. Samuel Lake had danced the soles off his shoes many's the time, and he'd drunk his share of whiskey.

"His share, and everybody else's," Willadee would say, grinning. Willadee was not a woman for protecting her husband's image. She was a Moses, and the Moses family didn't believe in lying. There were a lot of things the Moseses would do without a qualm, but they plain would not lie. This didn't necessarily hold true for their children. Swan lied daily. Took pleasure in it. She fabricated the most wondrous, the most atrocious tales, and told them for the truth. The good thing about lies was that the possibilities were limitless. You could make up a world that was just like you wanted it, and if you pretended hard enough, it would start to feel real.

The point is, church members might try to impress the preacher with how righteous they were—they might tell him what a blessing he was, and they might talk about brotherly love as if they'd invented it, but they never showed him their real faces, and they sometimes said ugly things behind his back. One thing Swan had overheard frequently was the meanest utterance since "Off with his head."

"Preachers' kids are the worst kind."

Nobody ever said the worst kind of what, but the implication was that all preachers' kids had illicit adventures, and Swan could never feel close to anyone who looked down on her for things she hadn't had a chance to *do* yet.

Swan didn't have a ghost of an idea how to go about getting close with Uncle Toy. It stood to reason, though, that if you wanted to get in tight with somebody named Moses, honesty would be the best policy. Since they believed in it so strongly.

"Lovey said you have no respect for the dead what-so-ever." Swan hoped that was enough honesty to get his attention. She also hoped that he would take offense at Lovey for saying such a thing, and that the two of them could dislike the brat together.

Uncle Toy just smiled a lazy smile. "Lovey said that?"

"She damn sure did."

Swan figured that any man who wouldn't go to his own brother's or his own daddy's funeral ought to be a safe bet to practice cussing around. She had him pegged right. He never even flinched.

"Well . . ." Toy said that word like a sentence again. "I reckon I respect a person after they're dead to about the same degree as I respected them while they was alive."

"Did you love your daddy a-tall?"

"I did."

Which seemed to pretty well take care of the funeral issue.

"Are you really a bootlegger?"

"Who said I'm a bootlegger?"

"Near 'bout everybody."

Toy turned the stick in his hand, examining it for flaws. It wasn't shaped like anything, but he had gotten it perfectly smooth.

Swan made her voice real low and ominous and warned him, "I just might be a revenuer. You better be careful I don't find your still and run you in."

"You got me mixed up with a moonshiner. Moonshiners, they're the ones have stills and fight revenuers. A bootlegger is just a middleman. Meets the deacons in the thickets, or out behind the barn, and sells them what they wouldn' be seen buyin' in public. How come so many questions?"

"I'm just curious."

"Curiosity killed the cat."

"I'm not a cat."

He squinted at her. "You sure? I think I see whiskers."

She laughed. Out loud. Loving this. They were friends. They were going to get to know each other. She was going to find out everything about him, and tell him everything about herself, and she bet sometimes he'd ride her on his shoulders, and no telling what they would do together.

"You really kill a man once?" she asked suddenly. This time, he flinched. Swan was practically sure she saw him flinch.

"I killed a lot of men," Toy said. Flat. "I was in the war."

"I don't mean in the war. I mean did you kill Yam Ferguson deader'n a doornail, for messing with Aunt Bernice."

Toy had started whittling again, and now he raised his eyes to hers. Swan thought suddenly that she had never seen eyes so piercingly green. Toy's shaggy, rust-colored brows were rearing up a little. She had touched a raw nerve, and wished she had not. But she knew the answer to her question all right.

"You watch how you talk about your aunt Bernice," Toy said. His voice sounded tight, like his throat was parched. "Now, get your fuzzy butt out of here."

"I didn't mean anything," Swan said.

Toy didn't answer. He got a dingy old rag from behind the cash register and started polishing the countertop. The countertop did not need polishing.

"I was just making conversation."

Toy didn't even look up. Just kept rubbing at some imaginary stain. Swan didn't exist for him anymore.

Swan turned her attention to the window. She was not about to leave the store just because Uncle Toy had ordered her to. Leaving in disgrace was not her style. Outside, a shiny red Chevrolet Apache pickup truck was stopping beside the gas pump. The driver—a sharp-featured, raven-haired man—was bearing down on the horn. There was a woman in the front seat beside him. A plump, blondish woman, holding a baby. Another, bigger baby stood in the seat between the woman and her husband. And in the back of the truck, there were two little boys, about four and eight years old. The sharp-featured man laid on the horn again. Louder.

Swan cast an uneasy glance at Uncle Toy, who was putting the cleaning rag back behind the cash register. Taking his time about it.

"Well, *damn!*" the man outside hollered, and he swung out of the truck. He was little bitty. Maybe five-two or five-three. He looked strong, though. Wiry and tough-muscled. He was walking toward the store. Walking fast, hunched forward, like he intended to drag everybody inside outside and stomp them good. He reached the door and started in at the precise same moment that Toy was starting out, so they ran smack into each other, the little man's head slamming into Toy's diaphragm. It should have knocked him down, but all it did was stop him in his tracks. He backed up a step, and tipped his head back, and glared up at Toy.

Swan had slid down off the ice cream box by now and sidled over near the door. For a second, she thought the little man was going to spit in Uncle Toy's face. He must not have heard the story about Yam Ferguson.

"Anything I can do for you, Mr. Ballenger?" Toy asked, easy-sounding.

"You can pump me some damn gas, if it's not too damn much trouble," Mr. Ballenger snapped. His eyes—which were so black you couldn't tell where the pupils left off and the irises started—those were snapping, too.

"No trouble," Toy said easily. He stepped past Ballenger, out into the sunlight. Swan followed, hanging back a little, staying out of her uncle's line of vision. While Toy was pumping the gas, the two little boys in the back of the truck watched him silently. Their hair and eyes were as black as their father's. Their features had the softness of childhood, but the man's stamp was on them, no doubt about that.

"How you fellers doin'?" Toy asked them. They sat as stiff as tin soldiers, staring back at him. The woman holding the baby turned a little in the seat, and smiled, just slightly. Toy must not have noticed, which was a good thing, because her husband *did*. Swan could tell by the way the keen black eyes flicked back and forth, from his wife's face to Toy's. The woman turned back around in the seat. Toy finished pumping the gas and hung up the hose.

"How much I owe you?" Ballenger asked. He had his chest pooched out and was fooling with his belt. Running his fingers over the buckle. Sort of half smiling, as if he might be anticipating something nobody else knew about.

"No charge today," Toy said.

Ballenger eyeballed Toy narrowly, then glanced into the truck, at his wife. She was busy wiping the baby's nose on the hem of her dress. Wiping it raw, she was being so diligent. Swan could see now that this "woman" was barely more than a girl. Must have started having babies about the same time she found out where they came from.

"You got a reason for doing me favors, Mr. Moses?"

Toy's jaw tightened.

"They're burying my daddy today, Mr. Ballenger. Mama wanted the store kept open, just in case anybody needed anything, but she drawed the line at charging money."

Ballenger's expression became carefully, properly sorrowful.

"You give my condolences to Miz Calla," he said, and swung up into the cab. In the back of the truck, the older boy had gotten more trusting and was inching toward the side. Toward Toy. Ballenger caught the movement in the rearview mirror. Reached one hand out and back, and slapped at the boy, carelessly. He could have been swatting a fly. His palm caught the kid across the face, hard.

"How many times do I have to tell you not to move around back there?" Ballenger yelled over his shoulder. And to Toy, he said, "Sometimes you gotta help 'em remember."

Toy glared at Ballenger the way you look at something you'd just like to step on. The kid's lips were quivering, and he had a dazed look on his face, but he refused to cry. That little, and already he knew that, if you don't cry, you're not licked.

Swan had gasped loudly and was standing there now with her hand over her mouth, wishing she could take back the sound. She had a feeling that drawing Ballenger's attention to your existence was like prodding a cottonmouth moccasin with your bare foot. A cottonmouth is deadly poisonous, and it will come after you. It will strike from behind.

Ballenger cut his glance in her direction. His black eyes widened, and he grinned. Swan wanted to shrink up inside herself and disappear, but it was too late.

"Where'd you come from, little pretty?" he asked.

Toy looked at her. Hard. "I thought I told you to git."

She got. Turned and hustled into the store. There was another car pulling up, but she didn't look to see who it was. She wouldn't know them anyway. She leaned against the ice cream box and peeked through the bug-specked window. The new customer was a middle-aged woman in a flowery cotton dress. Some farmer's wife. She was chattering to Toy as she started toward the store, and Toy was answering her. His voice was a deep, low rumble. Swan wasn't paying any attention to them, though.

She was watching the red pickup truck as it peeled out onto the road. The two little boys were sitting like soldiers again. Straight as arrows. *Two* little boys. But Swan was focused on just one. The one who'd gotten struck by the cottonmouth. That kid. The way he was sitting there, with his head cocked to one side—looking like he didn't care, like it was nothing. That kid's face was burning a hole in Swan's mind.

She watched until the truck made the bend in the road and was blotted out by a bank of sweet gums and pin oaks. Until the whine of the tires and the chug of the motor faded down to a whisper that hung in the air for the longest time, unwilling to die.

Chapter 5

Sometimes, when Geraldine Ballenger wasn't trying to think, but was letting her thoughts just drift, some quick, shining idea or insight would start to churn faster than the rest and would rocket to the surface, glimmering. She could never quite catch hold of these. They were like shooting stars. Fast gone.

She was letting her thoughts drift now, enjoying the pleasant flow. There was a small, bright stab of light that had surfaced, a little earlier, back at the store, and it was still bobbing along in her consciousness. She gazed at it, mentally, fascinated by it. She knew better than to attempt to examine it for brilliance or for flaws. If she tried too hard to capture it, it would dissolve, or sink, or shoot out of reach. And, anyway she was content, for now, just to look at it.

Her husband was smiling to himself while he drove. This she saw out of the corner of her eye, and her stomach did an uneasy flip-flop. When most folks smiled, it meant something good. With Ras, it could mean anything. Still, she wouldn't let him and his smile take her mind off the lovely, shimmering Idea. She wanted to keep it in view as long as possible.

"How long you had your eye on that ugly bastid?" Ras asked. He prided himself on his craftiness, as well as on his ability to throw her thinking off. He sure knew how to throw her thinking off.

She just looked at him, without saying anything. When Ras was getting wound up, it was bad to talk, because he could find something incriminating in any words that came out of your mouth—and it was bad not to talk, because silence indicated guilt. It meant you couldn't think of anything to say that would hide whatever dirty secret he was in the process of discovering.

"I seen you droolin' back there," he accused. "Don't you think I didn'."

Geraldine was irritated. The Idea was starting to dim a little. If only Ras would shut up so she could concentrate. She said, "Oh, you think you see so much." She had already forgotten about it not being good to talk.

He laughed. An obscene, snorting sound. "You'd best believe I do."

Geraldine shifted the baby from her lap to her shoulder and patted its back, rhythmically. She was so disgusted. The stab of light was gone. There was nothing to do now but go ahead and fuss with Ras. If you didn't give him back a little of his own, he just got worse. Nothing made Ras worse quite so fast as knowing he had the upper hand.

"Well, there wasn't nothin' to see," she snapped.

Ras spat a rusty stream of tobacco juice out the window and wiped his mouth on his shirtsleeve. "I reckon I know when I see a woman askin' for it."

"You better quit accusin' me of things, Ras Ballenger." She made her voice go high and haughty. "You sure are somebody to go accusin' people of things. Why, I don't even know that man."

"Not as well as you'd like, is that it?"

In fact, Geraldine did not know Toy Moses, had never even seen him except for times like today when he had happened to be keeping the store and she had stopped by with her husband and kids. Always with her husband and kids. She was not allowed to go anywhere alone. She knew the stories, though. About how Toy had lost his leg to save a life, and had taken a life to save his wife's honor. These things she had heard and taken note of. Toy Moses looked out for those who couldn't protect themselves. It was this realization that had been dancing through her mind like a will-o'-the-wisp a few minutes ago.

She'd met and married Ras when she was only fourteen. Fourteen! Just a little split-tailed girl, and there he'd come along, a soldier back from the war, and he wasn't bad-looking, even if he wasn't any bigger than a mess of minutes.

He had come strutting into her life, all quick moves and jaunty airs, and he had fair turned her head. After all, not many girls her age got courted by men who'd been everywhere and seen everything and sent more of the enemy than they could count to meet their Maker. Back then, the killing Ras had done hadn't bothered her. Wasn't that what soldiers are supposed to do? The only reason it bothered her now was that now she knew how much he'd enjoyed it. For Ras Ballenger, war had been a once in a lifetime opportunity.

Oh, she had learned things about him, all right.

Their courtship had lasted barely long enough for him to ascertain her virginity. This he had done by testing it, rather roughly. As soon as he had convinced himself on that one point he had brushed away her tears and told her there wasn't anything to cry about. It was her fault, really, for making him so crazy, plus, he had had to *know*. He could never have loved a woman who had been used by another man.

That word *used* should have tipped her off. Should have. But then he started talking about getting married, and she more or less forgot about everything else. She hadn't known what she was getting into. She'd been finding out ever since.

This upset her more at some times than at others. The first time that it had upset her badly—which was the first time Ras took a strap to her—she had begged her folks to let her come home, but they said she'd made her bed, she could wallow in it. After that, leaving never seemed to be an option.

Actually (and Geraldine didn't understand this herself), she didn't always *want* to leave. Sure, Ras was rough with her, but he made up for it, afterward. After a while, it got to where the roughness just made everything more intense. There was a part of her that had come to believe nothing else could match that intensity. Even when she did want to get away, it was hard to imagine life without—that.

Ras reached over now, across the bigger baby, another boy, who was staring off, exploring his nose and mouth with his fingers. Ras ran his hand under his wife's skirt, and up the inside of her thigh, and gave the tender flesh a vicious squeeze. Geraldine was still patting the baby (her only girl) on the back, and she stopped, just for a second, gritting her teeth.

"You wimmen are all alike," Ras said. "Always wantin' whatever you ain't had. We'll be to the house in a minute, and *I'll* give you something you ain't never had."

That laugh again. Edging higher, threatening to go out of control. His laugh could ricochet, change tone and direction all at once, and then hit you like a bullet in the heart. Or the head.

Geraldine shut him out. Sometimes you had to do that, with Ras. You just had to think about other things, that was the only way. She turned her mind back to the river of her thoughts, but they had gotten sluggish and dark. With all her might, she tried to find that lovely stab of light again, that shimmering Idea that had been Toy Moses, Protector of the Helpless. But the Idea had lost its shining fire. Even if she found it now, it wouldn't amount to anything. Once a shooting star goes out, wishing on it doesn't do a lick of good.

"What did Uncle Toy use to kill Yam Ferguson?"

"What?"

"What did he use? A gun? A knife? What?"

Swan was sitting in the bathtub, shoulder-deep in bubbles. Her mother had been bending over the sink, washing her hair, but her head had snapped almost straight up when Swan asked her first question, and now she was swabbing shampoo out of her eyes.

"Who told you Uncle Toy killed anybody?"

"Lovey."

"Lovey talks entirely too much."

"She's not the only one who's said it. I heard you and Grandma Calla talking about it once, a long time ago."

Willadee bent back over the sink and twisted around until her head was under the flowing tap. Shampoo foamed and cascaded and ran in rivulets.

"What did you hear your grandma and me saying?"

"I don't remember exactly."

"Good."

"Well, I just think when a relative of mine has committed a *murder,* I deserve to know the details," Swan complained.

"You deserve a licking about nine tenths of the time."

Willadee pulled a strand of hair between her thumb and forefinger to see whether it squeaked. It did. She flipped her head back, wrapped a towel around it, and started out of the bathroom.

"Well, *did he kill him or not*?" Swan hollered after her.

"Yes!" her mother yelled back. It might take Willadee a while to get around to telling the truth, but if you pinned her down, she wouldn't lie. She was Moses, through and through.

"So what did he *use*?"

"His hands!"

His hands. Uncle Toy had killed a man with his bare hands. Swan sat there for a minute, thinking about that, Uncle Toy growing bigger and more powerful in her mind by the second. He had captured her imagination, and she couldn't stop thinking about him. Strangely enough, Aunt Bernice didn't appear to be all that impressed with him. Often as not, she acted as if her husband wasn't there, even when she was sitting right beside him. And they were so *perfect* together—him being so strong, and sure of himself, and her with that heartbreaking body, and skin like silk. If Aunt Bernice were just a little entranced with Uncle Toy, it would be the most incredible love story, the kind that lives on after the people are gone.

Swan stood up in the tub. Bubbles glistened everywhere. She reached down, scooped up a double handful of suds, and plastered them on either side of her chest, teasing them into pointy breast shapes, just like Aunt Bernice had. Willadee came back into the room in search of a comb and caught her in the act.

"Will you stop doing that."

It was not a question. Swan slithered back down into the water. Her fabulous foamy breasts lost all their pointiness.

"Did he beat him to death? Did he strangle him?"

Willadee had found her comb and was leaving the room again.

"He broke his neck."

Chapter 6

Uncle Toy had not spoken to Swan once since the funeral. He'd been around enough. His brothers had "real jobs," so it was up to him to run Never Closes. His own customers would just have to buy their liquor in public or do without for now.

Every afternoon, an hour or so before Grandma Calla closed the store, Toy would come rolling into the yard in either his blue outrun-the-law Oldsmobile or his black hit-the-woods Ford pickup. Bernice always came with him, never failing to explain that she was afraid to stay home alone. While Willadee was making supper, Toy would busy himself around the place, finding things that needed a man's hand—a door hanging out of plumb (all the doors were out of plumb), a hole to be patched in the chicken yard fence, a dead tree that needed to come down before some storm blew it over on the house.

The first day, Swan had followed Toy around, hoping he'd notice her, and forgive her, and they could become close, the way it had looked like they might. But Toy never looked her way. He just worked until it was time for supper, then ate like a horse and disappeared into the bar. Swan sat at the kitchen table after he left that first night, listening to her mother and Aunt Bernice talk while they cleaned the kitchen.

"I still can't hardly stand to think about your daddy doing what he did," Bernice said. She shuddered, indicating that she was thinking about it all right. In color. She was the only one in the family who seemed bent on bringing that subject up. Everybody else pretty much left it alone. It hung in the air, though. Always there.

Willadee said, "Let's just let Daddy rest."

Bernice looked over at her like maybe she felt a little insulted that her conversation starter hadn't gone anywhere.

"I don't know how all of you are holding up so well. If I were in your shoes, I don't think I'd be able to even get out of bed in the morning."

"If you had kids, you would."

Having kids was something Bernice didn't like to talk about, so the kitchen got quiet for a minute. Nothing but the clink and clatter of dishes. Then, as if it just occurred to her, she asked, "When's Sam coming back?"

"Friday evening," Willadee answered. "Like always."

"Wonder where you'll be next year."

"God knows."

"Well, maybe you won't have to move."

"Moving's not that bad."

"I couldn't handle it myself, I don't think."

"Good thing you didn't marry Sam."

End of conversation. There was empty silence, until Willadee started humming "In the Gloaming," and then Bernice just up and left the room. Like that. No warning. Willadee wiped her hands on her apron and watched her go. Then she noticed Swan, sitting there all eyes and ears.

"Swan Lake, what are you doing?"

"Nothing."

"Well, do it somewhere else."

"Yes, ma'am."

Naturally, Swan didn't move. If you didn't actually refuse to mind Willadee, you could frequently get by with not minding, at least for a little while.

"What's Aunt Bernice's problem?" Swan asked when her mother had started back washing dishes.

"Somewhere *else*, Swan."

That had been Wednesday night, and now it was Friday, and time was running out. Swan's father would be back this evening, and he would tell them where they were going to live next year, and in the morning, Willadee would have all their clothes packed up before they even got out of bed. As soon as breakfast was over, they'd be off. Going home to Louisiana. Either getting back into the swing of things in Eros, the tiny town they'd been living in for all of a year now, or else getting ready to move.

Swan hoped they moved. People felt sorry for her and her brothers because they moved so much, but she could never resist the excitement of it. When you went to a new place, everybody welcomed you, and church members had you over for dinner and made over you, and things were peachy. For a little while.

As far as Swan was concerned, once the new wore off, it was time to move again. After that, life got to be a dance, careful, careful how you step, mustn't get on anybody's toes, but her father did, all the time. He specialized in it. Just couldn't resist telling sinners that God loved 'em, and he loved 'em, and why didn't they put in an appearance at the Lord's house, come Sunday. And we're talking the *rankest* sinners, here. Men who were too lazy to work, and couples who were living in sin, and even one frowsy old woman who used to be a stripper, down on Bourbon Street, until her looks played out. Samuel didn't stop at trying to get ordinary sinners saved. He wanted everybody on God's green earth saved, and acted like the whole thing was up to just him. Like the Lord didn't have any other helpers.

Sometimes Swan wished her father did almost anything else besides preaching. Probably, if he were the postmaster, or owned a hardware store, or something, and everybody in town wasn't always watching her, hoping she'd mess up so they could gossip about it, *probably,* she could just be a regular kid. It must be lovely to be like everybody else.

But there were bigger things to think about right now. She had less than a day to get in solid with Uncle Toy. Once she and her family drove away in the morning, she wouldn't see him again for a year, and the whole world could come to an end by then.

Swan started scouting around for Uncle Toy as soon as she woke up. Noble and Bienville were nowhere in sight, thank heaven. They had gotten disgusted with her the past couple of days, what with her trailing around after Uncle Toy all the time, and they'd started playing by themselves. Which suited Swan just fine. Everything that had seemed exciting less than a week ago had paled in comparison to Uncle Toy, who was bigger than life, bigger than anything *she* had ever seen in life, or could imagine ever seeing.

She found him out beside the house. He was on the ground, under Papa John's old truck, just his feet sticking out, and he was tinkering with something. Swan squatted down and looked under the truck, and cleared her throat loudly. Uncle Toy didn't have to glance over to know who it was.

"Can I help?" Swan asked.

"Nope."

"Well, I wouldn't mind."

"Well, I would."

His voice was blunt as a sledgehammer. Swan narrowed her eyes into slits and got this faraway, *thoughtful* look on her face.

"Do you know what?" she asked, after a while.

"What."

"I have purely been wasting my time on you."

"Is that so."

"It damn sure is."

She stood up and tapped her foot a couple of times. Disdainfully. She had her arms crossed in front of her chest, and she was staring down at his feet. If she'd known for sure which foot was the real one, she'd have given it a good hard kick. But she didn't know, so she just used words to try to hurt him.

"Here I've been, dogging your tracks like you were some kind of hero, when all you really are is an old, one-legged bootlegger. I bet you never saved anybody's life. You prob'ly lost your leg running away from a fight. And as for Yam Ferguson, he must have been one puny sombuck if he let himself get done in by the likes of you. I wouldn't be scared of you in a graveyard on a dark night."

It was awfully quiet. Uncle Toy wasn't tinkering anymore. He could come sliding out from under that truck any minute. But Swan didn't care. She really wasn't scared of him. She had decided not to care one way or the other about him. He had become completely insignificant to her, the way she had to him.

She said, "And I don't want to be your friend anymore, either." That part was hard, because she didn't mean it, even more than she hadn't meant all the other things she'd been saying. She had a heavy feeling in her stomach, the way you do when you close a door that you don't want closed, not ever. But she had had it with him. Begging wasn't in her. So she turned, and stalked off, too proud to look back.

Toy slid out from under the truck and sat up. He could see her, heading into the house. Shoulders straight, head erect. "Well, I'm so glad," he said softly.

Not that it was entirely true.

By the time Samuel's old car pulled into the yard, it was almost dark. Swan was sitting on the porch steps waiting for him. The instant his feet hit the ground, she hurled herself across the yard and tackled him, hugging him and dancing up and down.

"Hey, hey, wait a minute," Samuel protested, but he liked the reception.

"Are we moving?"

"We are."

"Good. Where to?"

"We'll talk about that later. Where's your mama?"

Just as he asked, Willadee appeared on the porch and waved, and the two of them started walking toward each other. Bernice was sitting in the swing, sort of off to one side, almost hidden by the morning glories that meandered across the porch rail. She watched while Samuel and Willadee moved into each other's arms. Noble and Bienville, who had been off in the pasture, were charging into the yard, bearing down on their parents—hugging them both at once, because those two were still standing welded together. One thing about Samuel and Willadee. They sure said hello like they meant it.

Eventually, Samuel turned loose of his wife and picked Bienville up and shook him like a rag, and made noises like an animal roaring, and set him down again. He greeted Noble by boxing him on the shoulder. Noble boxed back. Samuel grabbed his shoulder, as if that had hurt more than he expected, and while Noble was wondering whether he'd hit his old man too hard, Samuel cuffed him another good one.

All this, Bernice observed from her perch in the swing. Samuel and Willadee and the kids were starting up the steps, all jabbering at once. When they got even with Bernice, she stood up, sleek and graceful as a cat. She was wearing a soft little cream-colored dress that clung to her curves when she moved. And when she didn't. Everybody stopped stock-still. Bernice had that effect on people.

"How you doing, Bernice?" Samuel asked.

Bernice said, "Fine as wine." Smooth and warm, like butter melting.

Willadee rolled her eyes up in her head and drawled, real slow, "I've got something on the stove, Sam. You just come on in whenever you're ready." And she went inside the house. Talk about trust.

"Where's that husband of yours?" Samuel asked Bernice. She motioned toward the backyard. A vague gesture. Samuel glanced in the direction she had pointed and nodded, as though indicating approval of Toy's presence out there, somewhere. "I hear he's been keeping things going around here the last few days."

"Some things, yes."

Samuel's eyes played over Bernice's face. No fondness, no malice.

Just a look that said he knew where she was heading, and he wasn't going along with her. He looked at her like that until she looked away. Then he opened the screen door and waved his children inside.

"C'mon, c'mon, your mama's waitin'."

"Sure am, preacher boy," Willadee called out. Drawling again.

All during supper, Swan and Noble and Bienville kept after Samuel to tell them where they were moving, but he kept putting them off. This wasn't like their father. Usually, he couldn't wait to give them the news, and to embellish it with every single positive comment he'd been able to drag out of anybody who'd ever seen the place. As a rule, the new town was so small that it wasn't easy finding people who'd been there, even just passing through—except for the pastor who was leaving, and he was apt to be more full of warnings than full of compliments. But Samuel always managed to find something good to tell about it. The people were the salt of the earth, or the countryside was a sight for sore eyes, or the church building was a relic and there were rumors that it had secret passageways, or the parsonage yard had a good spot for a playhouse, or *something*.

Tonight, though, was different, and everybody noticed. Even Calla and Toy and Bernice had questioning looks on their faces.

"Anything wrong, Sam?" Willadee asked.

"I was planning to tell you about it first, and then break it to everybody else."

Willadee passed the speckled limas across to Toy. "They must be sending us to bayou country. We've been everywhere else."

Samuel said, "They're not sending us to bayou country." He set down his tea glass and rested both arms on the table. Everybody's eyes were on him. Waiting.

"They're not sending us anywhere."

Swan broke all records getting out of the house after supper. She had to find a place to think this thing through. She would have settled into the swing, but Aunt Bernice would be out there again before you could even spit. She always hogged the swing as soon as she'd finished helping to clean the kitchen. Swan herself never had to assist with such chores, although she knew unfortunate kids her age who did. Willadee was of the opinion that you're only a kid once. Grandma Calla thought that once was a dandy time to learn some responsibility, but Swan could wear you to a frazzle, so she never pushed her point. If Aunt Bernice had an opinion, she kept it to herself. She just did her share of the work as quickly as possible and disappeared into the porch shadows until bedtime. You wouldn't have known she was there, except for the gentle squeaks the swing made.

Swan wondered sometimes what Aunt Bernice found to think about, sitting out there all alone. She had asked her once. Aunt Bernice had lifted her hair up off the back of her neck and murmured, "Hmm? Oh. Things."

Anyway, the swing was out, so Swan passed it by and went on through the yard, past the haphazard jumble of vehicles parked between the house and the road. The regulars had been gathering in to Never Closes for over an hour now.

Any other time, Swan would have crept around to the back of Never Closes and hid out, trying to get a peek inside. She and her brothers were strictly forbidden to do that, but they did it anyway, every chance they got. So far, they hadn't seen anything worth looking at, and they'd have given the project up if it hadn't been forbidden. But the fact that it was had to mean something, so they'd kept after it.

Tonight, though, Swan didn't feel much like spying. All she wanted was privacy. She reached the road and walked along the grassy shoulder. She could see perfectly well, even once she'd gotten away from the lights of the house and bar. The moon was almost, almost full. She'd never realized before that the moon could shed enough light to give the world any real brightness. She'd also never strayed far from her family in the dark. But it *wasn't* dark. The night was luminous.

Out there, walking along beside that easy-curving road, Swan decided she didn't need to find a *place* to think. Who needed a *place*, when you could just keep moving, putting one foot in front of the other, enjoying going nowhere.

By now, her father's situation had pretty well sorted itself out inside her head. At first, when it had struck her that she and her folks didn't have an income, or a house to live in, she'd felt guilty for wishing that her life was different. Maybe this was what happened when you wished for something you didn't know enough about.

The real gravity of the situation had escaped her, though. The Lake family changed homes every year or two anyway, so it wasn't as though they were being jerked up by the roots. They didn't have any roots. Besides, grown-ups worked out problems every day. That's what grown-ups *did*. Plus, she figured, this had to be the Lord's will. Hadn't her daddy preached, time and again, about how God had a Plan, and how everything works together for those who love God? Her parents certainly loved God. Swan did, too, she was sure, even though she bent His rules with some degree of regularity, and prayed only When It Was Important. She'd never been one to wear God out with small talk.

Anyway, if you looked at it right, there was a Bible guarantee of a favorable outcome to all this, so her conscience was off the hook.

She sucked in a deep, glad gulp of honeysuckled air. The tall grass bent beneath her feet and straightened as she passed. She wasn't ready to turn back just yet. This moment was too delicious. Ahead, and to the left, a narrow lane forked off the main road. She knew she shouldn't take the lane, shouldn't even be out here, but it couldn't do any harm. Bad things happened on Dark and Stormy Nights, not on nights like tonight, when all of creation wore a soft satin sheen.

Chapter 7

The little lane wound and twisted and tapered down to almost nothing, and kept on going. Every bend promised some new discovery. And delivered. A slim young tree, silvered by moonlight. Dancing stars, mirrored in the rocky stream that tumbled alongside the rutted lane. Nothing was ordinary tonight. Even cow pastures and falling-down fences had an otherworldly look.

And the silence! It was like the immense quiet of snowfall, right here in summer. This had to mean something. Something good. Only good could come from so much light where there would ordinarily be darkness.

These were her thoughts as she rounded a final bend, and saw the house. It was smallish, built of faded wood and topped off by a tin roof. There were lights on inside, so the windows glowed golden against the silver of the night. An extremely neat yard wrapped around the house, and in that yard, there was a gleaming something. A vehicle. A pickup truck. As clear and brilliant as the night was, the light was no good for telling color. But Swan knew in her bones. It was red.

She heard a dull, grunting noise, like a person makes when they've been socked in the stomach. It took a second for her to realize that she'd made the sound herself. She couldn't seem to move. Surely, her heart had stopped.

Only her mind was not immobilized. *It* was racing wildly, imagining the unimaginable. What if that little viper of a man was out here, somewhere, slithering around in the dark? What if he was watching her right now?

She whirled and fled. Running, scrambling, away and away, back along the rutted lane. She could *feel* Ballenger, back there, behind her—and could *sense* him, up there, ahead of her. No direction was safe. The June breeze was his hot breath. The rustle of leaves was a sinister whisper. *The snakeman, hissing her name.*

Swan thought of herself as a person who was prepared for anything. But she wasn't prepared for this. And she wasn't prepared for what happened next.

The moon slid behind a thick bank of clouds, and the world went dark. Suddenly, Swan couldn't see where she was going—so she stumbled. There was nothing to catch hold of, to break her fall. She threw her arms out, flailing every which way like twin windmills, but that didn't stop her from falling, either.

It seemed as though she fell for the longest time. Head over heels, and heels over head. When she stopped falling, she lay still, afraid to move. The reason she was afraid to move was that her hand was touching something soft and warm. Another hand.

Her eyes were closed, and she kept them that way, afraid of what she might see if she opened them.

"Well, are you dead?" a voice asked.

It wasn't Ballenger's voice. Swan could have died then, from relief. She opened her eyes, just enough so that she could peer through the darkness. Then she sat bolt upright.

The person talking to her . . . was the kid. Ballenger's little boy. The one who had gotten slapped that day outside the store. He was sitting in the ditch, dressed in a ragged T-shirt and underdrawers. A skinny little fellow, his hair standing on end, his eyes studying her soberly. Swan made herself stop trembling and studied him back.

"What are you doing out here?" she asked him, finally.

"Waiting."

"Waiting for what?"

"Till it's okay to go back."

"Back where?"

The kid pointed toward the house.

Swan said, "Why isn't it okay to go back right now?"

"*Because.*"

"You're too little to be outside by yourself at night," Swan said. "*Why* can't you go back?"

The kid just shrugged.

Swan sighed. She figured she could guess the answer. Still, this kid really *didn't* need to be out here alone, and she couldn't stay here with him.

She said, "Well, maybe you ought to go back now, because I've got to get on home."

He shook his head again, vigorously.

Swan said, "Well, I can't babysit you."

"Nobody ast you to."

She stood up. "Well, don't let a bobcat see you. A bobcat could eat you in two bites."

He said, "I can kill bobcats."

"Yeah? With what?"

He just stared at her. Swan was beginning to feel cross, because she knew she'd get into trouble if she didn't turn up at Grandma Calla's pretty soon. They'd have people out looking for her, and nothing makes grown-ups quite so mad as finding a child safe when they'd been scared silly that they might find that child dead.

She said, "Well, look. I know you're probably afraid of your daddy. I'm afraid of him, myself, and I only saw him once. So why don't I have my daddy talk to your daddy? My daddy's a preacher. He talks people into changing their ways all the time."

He said, "My daddy would kill your daddy."

Swan dropped back down on her knees, facing him. The moon had come out of hiding, and she could see the kid's face real plain. It was a beautiful face, with fine, high cheekbones and lush black lashes and a mouth that was fuller than it looked right now—because right now it was pulled tight, into a hard, brave line. Those black eyes of his were cutting right to her soul. Those fierce black eyes. He was, she thought, the damnedest thing she'd ever seen.

"You," she said, "talk an awful lot about killing, for somebody who's not hardly big enough to pee standing up."

But you couldn't even insult him. He just cocked his head to one side to show that nothing bothered him.

She got up again. "Go home," she said.

He didn't budge.

"Go home," she *pleaded*. And this was Swan Lake, who never begged.

He still didn't budge.

"Well, I'm going," she warned. And she did. One step at a time. Hating every minute of it. Worrying all the way about that kid, and what was going to happen to him, whether he'd get snake-bit, or spider-bit, or be some animal's supper. And where was he going to sleep? Would he dig a hole and curl up in it? Were his instincts that good? Or would his hateful daddy come raging out in search of him, and if he found him, what would happen then? What?

Maybe she should go back and get the kid, and take him up to his house, and give him over to his mother—but she had a feeling that mother wasn't much protection. So maybe she should go back and get him, and take him home with *her*. But you can't do that sort of thing. It's kidnapping, even if it's a kid who does the 'napping. Swan didn't really think she'd go to jail for it, not as long as the law was still drinking for free at Never Closes, but she knew the story wouldn't have a happy ending.

She made up her mind that, as soon as she got back to Grandma Calla's, she was going to get her daddy to go find that kid and take him home and talk to his parents. Nobody would *really* dream of killing Samuel Lake, and even if they did *think* about it, they couldn't succeed. Samuel Lake enjoyed the Protection of the Lord.

The hard part about this plan was going to be coming up with a good enough lie to explain why she'd been where she'd been, but Swan had tremendous confidence in her lying ability. And if worst came to worst, she could always tell the truth.

As it happened, she didn't have to tell anybody the truth, or a lie, or anything else. She was almost back to Grandma Calla's when she sensed something or someone behind her. She glanced over her shoulder, and there he was. That tough little guy. Walking ten or twelve paces behind her, as silent as an Indian.

"Do we have a plan?" Willadee was asking Samuel. They were lying in bed, curled together, the same way they had been for the past hour. They'd gone to bed before anyone else, which was something they almost never did. As wild about each other as they were after all these years, they still didn't like to be too obvious about things like hustling off to their bedroom before it was really bedtime. This once, though, it had seemed to be the only way to get some privacy.

Willadee had told Samuel about John Moses, and the things that happened the day he died. (She didn't mention the things that had happened the night before. She reasoned that Samuel had enough of a load to bear right now, she could tell him about the beer some other time. Maybe.) She'd also told him about how Calla had taken to going down to the living room in the middle of the night, wearing one of John's old shirts over her nightgown, and just sitting there by herself, for hours at a time. Willadee had found her there one night, and asked her if she needed to talk about anything.

"It's too late for talking," Calla had told her sadly. "I had a million chances to tell John how I missed having him in bed beside me. How I wanted to smell his hair, and feel his skin, and touch him in the night. I should have swallowed my pride, but I wouldn't, and now I'm choking on it."

Samuel had listened while Willadee poured out her story, and when she asked him please not to ever let walls grow up between them, he'd promised that he wouldn't. Then he'd told her about the annual conference, and how the superintendent had explained to him that, nowadays, churches had different needs than they'd had in the past, but that it wasn't *over* for him, he still was *licensed* and all, there just didn't seem to be a suitable place for him this year, so maybe he should contemplate, really contemplate, positive changes he could make, improvements he could make, in his ministry.

"They don't want preachers anymore," Samuel had told Willadee, his voice heavy. "They want social directors."

"Well, you have to stand for what you think is right."

"I think feeding my family is right, but I don't know how I'm going to manage."

"We'll manage."

"Will we?"

"Why, yes, you know we will."

Several times, they had almost started making love, but the bed was so old and the springs so creaky that they'd decided to wait either until everyone else in the house was bedded down, asleep, or until inspiration struck and they figured out a way to have each other without risking getting funny looks at breakfast the next morning.

"Do we?" she asked again now. "Do we have a plan?"

"I could go looking for some oil," Samuel said. "I could oil the springs."

"I didn't mean that kind of plan."

"I know you didn't."

"We have to figure someplace to live."

"I know we do."

He was quiet for a moment. Just his breathing, the only sound. Strong and deep and steady. Then he said, "Willadee? What about the floor? Would you be really insulted, if we just did it on the floor?"

"Not insulted. But they'd still hear us."

"We could be quiet."

"Maybe *you* could."

He laughed. Couldn't help it. She hushed him with a kiss. After a little bit, he said, "I think I'm supposed to be scared or something, Willadee. I mean here I am with a wife and kids, and no job, and no house, and you know what, Willadee?"

"What, Samuel?"

"I'm scared, all right."

She didn't like this. Him being afraid. Him hurting. It was the worst part of this thing, that he should be hurt. Samuel, of all people.

She said, "Damn these springs."

"What was that?"

"I said, 'Damn these springs,' Samuel."

Willadee kicked off the covers and sat up in bed. She drew her knees up underneath her and knelt beside her husband, leaning over him, kissing his neck, his chest, his stomach. Her hands touching, giving. He shifted his weight, pushing up against her hands. The bedsprings creaked rudely.

He let out a low moan that wasn't quite as low as he'd meant it to be and said, "Love of God, Willadee," and then, "Willadee, I need you so."

Her mouth moved against his skin. Taking. Talking.

"Good thing, preacher boy. 'Cause if you didn't, you wouldn't be able to live *through* all I'm about to do to you."

Downstairs in the swing, Bernice Moses was having a glass of iced tea with lots of lemon. Her ear was trained to the upstairs bedroom that happened to be right above the spot where she was sitting. She was listening intently. Listening, and not smiling. For the most part, Bernice had gotten everything she'd ever wanted out of life, and none of it had made her happy. There was only one thing she'd really wanted that she hadn't gotten, and she was positive that if she could get it (no, when she got it), she would be deliriously happy. At last.

What she wanted was Samuel. And what was in her way was Willadee. What had *been* in her way, until tonight, had been miles. But the miles weren't going to be a factor anymore, so that left only

Willadee. And how much competition could she be, when you thought about it?

Bernice had been one of those Columbia County girls who had taken to their beds for a week after Sam got married. She was the *only* one who had the distinction of having been engaged to him—and having jilted him—and she was convinced that he had married Willadee on the rebound. Why else would he have married her, she wasn't even pretty. Not according to Bernice's definition of prettiness. She had all those freckles that she didn't even try to bleach out or cover up, and she was plain as a board fence except for her eyes, and everybody had eyes.

Anyway, it wasn't supposed to have turned out like it did. Bernice had meant only to jilt him for a little while, to teach him a lesson about not being too friendly with other girls. Samuel was friendly with everybody, male and female, young and old, he made no distinctions. It was enough to gnaw a hole in a woman's insides. So she had simply done what any woman with any technique at all would have done. She had Given Him Something to Think About. You couldn't blame her for that. Besides, she was planning to give in and marry him, as soon as he came around to her way of thinking.

Only Samuel never came around. While he was thinking about the lesson Bernice was teaching him, he met Willadee, and you never saw a man get so carried away over a woman. You'd have thought he'd struck gold. Of course, Bernice knew, always knew, that Samuel didn't really love Willadee as much as he made out, but she never could get him to talk about it. Never could get him to talk to her again at all, except in the politest, most conversational sort of way, and that was worse than being totally ignored.

Bernice had gotten herself engaged to Toy, trying to teach Samuel another lesson, which he also refused to learn. He'd just gone ahead and married Willadee, and Bernice had had no choice but to go through with marrying Toy; it had just been awful.

Poor Toy. He was the kindest thing, and he was so crazy about her he couldn't see straight. But when a person loves you so much that he asks for nothing in return, it's only to be expected that that's about what he gets. It's like a Law of Nature.

So here Bernice was, sitting in the swing, thinking about how things had gotten to the sorry state they were in, when all of a sudden—springs started creaking upstairs. Not actually all of a *sudden*. It came on kind of gradually, and just increased in tempo.

That first little sound sliced Bernice's heart almost in half, and the rest of them—coming louder and faster like they did—finished the job. It was absolutely enough to make a woman do Things She Wouldn't Ordinarily Do.

What Bernice did was, she leapt out of the swing so fast that the contents of her glass flew upward like steam out of a geyser, and she had to cram her fist in her mouth to keep from screaming. There was tea and ice showering down around her, not to mention soggy lemon wedges, some of which lodged in her hair. Bernice groped for the lemon wedges, and flung them at the ceiling, and commenced to stamping her feet like a child having a hissy fit.

What's important here, though, is that, all in all, Bernice Moses was too caught up in the moment to even notice when Swan crept up the steps and into the house, followed by a wide-eyed eight-year-old boy, who was dressed in just his underwear.

That kid was marching along behind Swan like she was the path to salvation.

Chapter 8

The bed Swan slept in was so high she always used a stool to climb up onto it. The little boy was sitting on the bed, backed up against the headboard. His legs stuck straight out in front of him like sticks. Swan had stretched out on the other end of the bed and was lying there propped up on one elbow, wondering how this deal was going to come out.

She said, "Okay. I've got you here, now what am I going to do with you?"

The black eyes gazed steadily back at her.

She said, "Well, what's your name?"

"Blade."

"That's not a name."

He nodded. It was so.

Swan turned the name over and over on her tongue, getting the feel of it. "Blade Ballenger. Blade Bal-len-ger. Your name is bad as mine."

With a perfect lead-in like that, most folks would have asked her name, but Blade didn't, so she volunteered it.

"Swan Lake. You laugh, I'll cream you."

He didn't laugh. He didn't even change expressions. Swan sat up, and bounced on the bed a little, and tried to think of something else to talk about. Finally, she said, "This is where I live. This week. That lady you saw a while ago—out on the porch? Don't worry, she's not crazy or anything. I think she's mad 'cause her husband works nights."

Still nothing.

"How come you followed me home?"

He lifted his shoulders, and let them fall.

"You know you're going to have to go back."

He slid under the covers and pulled the sheet up to his chin, as if he were putting on armor.

She said, "I didn't mean right now. I meant sometime."

He settled back into the pillow and closed his eyes. He must have been awfully tired. His little hands loosened their grip on the covers, and his body seemed to relax one section at a time. Blade Ballenger, at eight years of age, was too cautious to let go of consciousness all at once.

A lump formed in Swan's throat. No way could she have explained just why. Slowly, carefully, she stood up on the bed, never taking her eyes off the kid's face. There was a knotted string dangling from a bare lightbulb overhead. Swan tugged at the string, and the room went dark. For a minute, she just stood there. Later on, years down the road, she would look back on this moment as a time when the world had changed. All the moves she would make from now on would be in a different direction than she'd ever been headed before. But she wasn't thinking about that now. She wasn't even thinking that Blade Ballenger had changed anything, although he had. And he would. She was thinking about the fact that her daddy didn't have a church, so she wasn't technically a preacher's kid anymore, and now she could be normal.

Through her open window, she could hear the music from Never Closes. Some country song. "Gonna live fast, love hard, die young—and leave a beautiful memory." Why in the world would anybody write a song about a thing like that when nobody, but nobody wanted to die young?

Swan eased herself down onto the bed, and felt her way along, and crawled under the covers. Blade stirred slightly, then got still again. Sometime later on, when Swan was drifting into sleep, she heard him murmur drowsily, "Swan Lake. That's a goofy name."

In the wee hours before daylight, Willadee and Samuel did come up with a plan, which Samuel announced the next morning at breakfast.

"We'd like to stay here for a while. Until we can make other arrangements. If it's all right."

Noble and Bienville sure thought it was all right. They both let out war whoops. Swan thought it was all right, too, although she didn't holler. You don't holler when you're sneaking food off the table to take upstairs to a Fugitive, and hoping nobody will notice.

Calla said it was all right with *her,* she wouldn't have it any other way. She just hoped Samuel could cope with living in a house that had a bar attached. Samuel assured her that the bar wouldn't bother him, he didn't see how a bar could bother him if he didn't go in it, and anyway, he was going to find a job of some sort, somewhere. It wasn't as if he'd be lolling around the house making judgments about things.

What about preaching, Calla inquired. She knew Samuel well enough to know that, if he wasn't preaching, he wouldn't be happy. And she knew Life well enough to know that if one person in a house gets really miserable for any length of time, the misery spreads like smallpox.

"We've got that figured out," Samuel informed her. "On weekends, I intend to do some relief preaching."

"What on earth is relief preaching?" Bernice purred. It was a good southern purr, designed to tweak heartstrings. She was sitting there at the breakfast table, in this sleek white satin robe that must've been designed for the same purpose. Her hair was all brushed out over her shoulders—gleaming—quite possibly from the lemon juice. She looked for all the world like a picture out of the Sears and Roebuck.

Willadee gave Bernice a patient look and explained that sometimes a pastor needs some time off, like for a family vacation, or an emergency, or whatever. She went on to say that someone like Samuel, who was licensed to preach but didn't have a congregation, could hold services in another pastor's absence, and it could be very helpful and beneficial to all concerned.

"Lots of churches need relief preachers," Willadee finished brightly.

Calla thought about that, and sipped at her coffee, and shook her head mournfully. "They won't get any relief if they get Samuel," she said.

Swan was in a terrible hurry to get back upstairs after breakfast. She was worried that Blade Ballenger might wake up alone in a strange place and be afraid. Or that he might come tumbling down the stairs any minute, and then everyone would discover that she had been hiding him. But her anxiety was nothing compared to something else she was feeling. Blade Ballenger had chosen her as a refuge. Hadn't she been wishing fervently for someone to bond with? All of a sudden, her wishes were coming true right and left.

Just as she was about to bolt out of the kitchen, Samuel nabbed her. He and Willadee led her and her brothers into the living room, and closed the door, and gathered them into a circle, just like a scene from *Ideals* magazine.

"Our lives are about to change in a lot of ways," he told them. "We'll have to work at keeping our equilibrium. But I don't want you to worry or feel afraid. Whatever is about to happen to us, it's going to be good, because all God's purposes are good."

"Will one of the changes be that I can wear blue jeans?" Swan wanted to know. "Because I think that would be good. Us being here on a farm and all." (She had gone back to wearing dresses the day before. Naturally. When Samuel came back from conference, the kids always immediately stopped breaking all the rules they'd been breaking while he was gone.)

"You know better than that, Swan," Willadee said. Swan blinked indignantly at her. Willadee gave her back a placid look. She could look mighty innocent when she wanted to.

"Well, it's not like there'll be a whole church full of people watching every move we make anymore."

"We don't decide how we'll live according to what other people think," Samuel said. "We just try to live by the Bible."

Swan argued, reasonably, that the Bible never said one solitary word about how a kid should dress to play in a cow pasture, but Samuel was already moving on to other things. They wouldn't have much money—not that they had ever had much money—but their income would be uncertain now, so they'd all have to make sacrifices. And he hoped they would understand, and pitch in, and do their part without complaining.

Swan wasn't sure what the word *sacrifice* signified, in present-day terms. In Bible times, it had meant offering something precious on the altar in order to gain God's favor. In Abraham's case, that something had been Isaac, but God had sent a scapegoat, so Abraham didn't actually have to slay his son. Swan had always secretly thought that sounded just a little too convenient. She didn't say this out loud, of course. You don't go around questioning the Bible, not if you want to go to Heaven one of these days. Besides, once you start picking holes in things, it's hard to figure out which parts to throw away and which parts to keep.

Still, if Samuel was asking them not to complain, that meant there might be something to complain about. This not being a preacher's kid was sounding less and less appealing. What worried her most was the niggling thought that maybe her father had fallen out of God's favor. She couldn't imagine how that could have happened. Nobody tried harder to do the right thing than Sam Lake. Surely God was aware of that.

Naturally, Blade didn't hang around waiting until Swan got back to her room. By then, he'd already slipped out of the house and trotted home. He told his mama he'd been playing down by the creek, and she said he must've followed it north to Alaska, he sure didn't answer when she called him half an hour ago, and since when did he go out to play before the rest of the family got their eyes open.

Geraldine had the ironing board set up in the living room (she took in ironing for pay), and she was smoking a Pall Mall. Her face was about five different colors, mostly shades of blue, with cuts and scrapes crisscrossing each other along her jaw. What had happened the night before was, Blade's daddy had been teaching his mama how to behave right, and Blade had just wanted to get away. It was scary when his daddy taught anybody about anything. Sometimes, when it happened, Blade pretended to be asleep, but last night, there'd been no pretending. Ras had been pulling Geraldine around the kitchen by the hair of her head and whacking her with a metal spatula. Geraldine had gone from crying and begging him to stop to trying to fight back, which was never a good idea. Blade had tried not to hear, and tried not to hear, and finally, he had just climbed out the window.

At first, he had sat huddled against the well shed, drawing pictures in the dirt with his fingers, which was something he did a lot at times like this. He didn't have to see what his hands were doing when he was drawing, and he didn't have to be looking at something to draw it. He'd always drawn in the dark, usually without even thinking about it. Anyway, he could still hear everything, so he had walked out farther in the yard, and then down the lane, until he was far enough away that it all got pretty quiet. And then that girl had come along.

Blade didn't know why he had decided to follow her. Maybe it was because he had the feeling that, wherever she was headed, nothing scary was going to happen. She sure didn't seem afraid of anything— except for when she first fell down. She was awful scared then, for a minute, like she thought the devil was about to get her. But once she got over that, she was solid as a rock.

Anyway, he was glad that he had trailed along behind her. In his own mind, he had already laid claim on Swan Lake. She was a safe place—and something more that he was too young to understand or put into words. All he knew was that he wanted to hold on to the feeling he'd had the night before, and to let it wrap around him like a warm blanket on a cold night.

Chapter 9

Bernice could hardly stand the way she felt the next few days. For one thing, she kept imagining the whole family knew about her throwing that fit the other night. Everybody except Toy. Generally, Toy was careful not to know things he'd be happier and more comfortable not knowing. He'd been that way ever since that ugly business with Yam Ferguson, back after the war. But as for the rest of them—with everybody living in a heap like this, nobody would be able to poot without somebody smelling it.

Not that Bernice ever pooted.

The other thing that was making Bernice miserable was that, lately, she'd been having this time's-a-wasting-and-so-am-I sort of feeling. You don't go along for years being the prettiest thing around, and then realize that you're in full flower, without getting a little anxious, since the next stage after full flower is when the petals start to droop and fall. So here she was, ripe and lush, with all her petals still pointing in the right direction, and Sam Lake didn't even notice.

Well, she'd have to do something about *that*.

Bernice tried to think of ways to make Sam notice. She thought about it in the daytime, after she and Toy got back to their own house. He always hit the sack as soon as they got home from Calla's, and usually didn't wake up until midafternoon. While he was asleep, Bernice would roam from room to room, as silent and graceful as a butterfly. Briefly lighting here and there. On a chair. On the couch. Sometimes, outside, on the porch rail. There were gardenias blooming beside the steps, and the smell was so sweet, it would catch in her throat and make her want to cry.

She thought about it at night, when she sat alone in Calla's swing, with the music from Never Closes rollicking in the background. She thought about it when Samuel and Willadee and the kids headed back to Louisiana to have their farewell service at the little church they were leaving. She thought about it all the time. Somehow there had to be a way to make Samuel see the truth—that he was miserable without her.

With every hour that passed, Bernice felt an increasing sense of urgency. She wasn't getting enough sleep, she wasn't getting what she wanted, and she wasn't getting any younger.

It was late Friday night when Samuel's car chugged into the yard, pulling a trailer that was piled so high with furniture and boxes it was a wonder it had made it under the railroad trestles along the way. Grandma Calla was waiting up for them. She came down off the porch, picked her way through the muddle of customers' vehicles, and leaned in the car window, talking loud above the juke joint racket.

"Just unload the kids, and go park the trailer in the barn," she told Samuel. "It's too late to move your stuff inside, and you wouldn't want anybody pilfering through it."

Samuel did as she said.

On Saturday, Calla's toilet backed up, so Samuel had to spend the day digging up the septic tank field line. He had no trouble finding it, since the grass on top of those things always grows so much greener and brighter than the grass around it, but he had plenty of trouble chopping out the sweet gum roots that had grown through it and tangled around it. The job took all day. The car and the trailer stayed shut up in the barn, and nothing got unloaded, so there was none of the usual commotion that occurs when a family moves into a house. Which is why folks around the community were pretty much in the dark about the fact that Sam Lake and his family had moved back home to Arkansas.

Bernice didn't go down to breakfast on Sunday morning. She just stayed in bed thinking about how wrong this situation was. And that's how it happened that she first got the Inspiration.

Actually, it was Samuel who inspired her, although he didn't know it. He and Willadee were in their room getting dressed for church, and their voices drifted through to her, clearer than clear. Bernice didn't even have to press her ear to the wall to hear. It was as though This Moment Was Meant to Be.

Willadee was asking Samuel if he was all right about this—about going to church this morning, knowing that people were going to be asking him why he wasn't back home in Louisiana, preaching to his own congregation. (For sure it was going to be humiliating for him to admit that he didn't have a congregation.) And Samuel was saying that he wasn't about to let the Lord down by not showing up at His House on His Day.

"I have to believe that there's a reason for all this," he said. "Maybe there's something I'm supposed to do right here that I couldn't do if I were anywhere else. Maybe there's someone that I'm supposed to reach out to, or some problem I'm supposed to help with."

Bernice sat straight up in bed.

In the next room, Willadee was agreeing with Samuel. It must be that God had something for him to do here, and the only way to bring it about was to uproot him from Louisiana loam and replant him in

Arkansas clay, and probably the fields were right now ripe unto harvest.

Bernice flung back her covers and leapt out of bed. The fields were ripe, all right. She being the fields. And she was so ready for harvest she couldn't see straight.

Before Bernice could hardly turn around, Samuel and Willadee were loading the kids into the car. Calla had long since opened the store, and Toy had headed down to the pond to do a little fishing as soon as he'd closed the bar—so neither one of them was around to gum up the works. Even so, Bernice barely had time to wash her face, and brush out her hair, and slip on the dress she'd worn to Papa John's funeral. It was a pale gray number, with a slightly scooped neckline, just perfect for this occasion. Proper and tantalizing, all at the same time. She didn't bother with makeup, because her skin didn't need makeup, and besides, when you cry, makeup runs, which makes a woman look absolutely scary, and she intended to cry this morning.

She came running out of the house at the very last moment, letting the screen door slam behind her. Samuel jerked his head around and looked back in her direction, and then he did a double take. It wasn't every day you saw Bernice Moses run.

"Something wrong, Bernice?"

She waited until she was right up close to him before she answered, so that he'd be able to smell her perfume while he listened.

"I was wondering if I could ride to church with y'all," she said softly.

If Sam was surprised, he didn't show it. He smiled that big, wide, handsome smile of his and said, "Well, come on, then. There's always room for one more in God's house."

As if God had one little thing to do with this.

Samuel took her arm, led her around the car to the passenger side, opened the door, leaned in ahead of her, and said, "Willadee, Bernice wants to ride to church with us."

Willadee gave her husband a knowing smile and slid over to make room. Bernice got into the car the way she'd seen movie stars do, gracefully lowering herself onto the seat, and managing to show just enough flesh to be tempting as she swung her legs in. She glanced demurely up at Samuel, to see whether he'd been tempted, but he was busy making sure none of the kids had their fingers in the way as he shut the car door.

Bernice hadn't counted on what the ride to church would actually be like. She'd imagined herself and Samuel in the front seat, with Willadee in between them feeling ugly and awkward. Samuel would sneak longing glances at her over Willadee's head, and she would favor him with an occasional enigmatic smile. If Willadee caught on, she'd probably pout, which fit right into Bernice's plan, since nothing makes a man want another woman as much as being reminded that the one he has is determined to hang on to him.

As for the kids, they were more or less background color, part of the scenery that surrounded Samuel. She'd never thought much one way or the other about Samuel's kids. She'd also never been shut up in a car with all three of them at once.

Before long, she realized that there would be no longing looks from Samuel. He and Willadee were holding hands in Willadee's lap, and Samuel pretty much had the air of a man whose longings had been recently satisfied.

The kids were unobtrusive enough for about the first half mile, but then Noble took to leaning forward and sucking in deep breaths through his nose.

"What are you doing back there, Noble?" Samuel finally asked.

"Sitting here." Which was true.

"He's drinking in her perfume," Bienville said. You read enough books, you learn to spot these things.

Noble turned as red as a beet and gave his brother a look that said he'd tend to him later. Bienville wasn't worried. He'd been tended to before, and always lived over it.

"Why do women wear perfume, Aunt Bernice?" Bienville asked.

"To attract males," Willadee drawled.

"We just like to smell nice," Bernice corrected.

"Well, you sure do smell nice, Aunt Bernice."

"Thank you, Bienville."

"Do you attract many males?"

Willadee felt the laughter coming and tried to stifle it, but it wouldn't be stifled. Pretty soon it started gurgling in her throat. Bernice was sitting there with her mouth open and her brain working overtime, trying to come up with a good, workable answer. She couldn't say "More than my share," because there are times when the truth just gets in the way of a woman's purposes. And she couldn't say "Only my husband," because that would make her sound dull, which was totally unacceptable. And she for sure couldn't say "I'm *trying* to attract one right now."

Finally, she said, "Oh, I never pay any attention to things like that."

Samuel managed to keep a straight face, but only because preachers learn early on not to laugh when they shouldn't. Another thing preachers learn early on is that the best way to pull a congregation together is to get everybody singing. So he asked Swan if she knew any new songs.

"Does it have to be a hymn?"

"No, just something everybody can sing along to."

Swan told him that Lovey had taught her "My Gal's a Corker," and *that* sure was a good sing-along song. Ordinarily, Samuel would have nixed that one, but not today. Today he said, "Well, let's hear it."

Nobody ever had to ask Swan twice to sing. She had a great big voice for such a small girl, and she wasn't afraid to turn it loose. She set in to singing, verse after verse, and the other kids joined in. Noble made sound effects. They were clapping their hands, and stomping their feet, and getting louder and louder, and Willadee and Samuel never even told them to pipe down. They didn't let up until they pulled into the yard of the Bethel Baptist Church. (The Moses family had always been Baptists, those who went to church. When Willadee had married Samuel, she became the first Methodist Moses ever.) As the car rolled to a stop, Noble bellowed the last note of the song in the most rutting-buck tone he could muster.

Bernice made up her mind then and there, whenever the sweet day came that she finally got Samuel, Willadee would get the kids.

She flung open the car door and stumbled out, and wouldn't you know, the first thing she did was step into a hole. The dainty little heel of her dainty little shoe broke clean off with a snap you could have heard all the way to El Dorado.

"Are you all right?" Willadee asked, when she could see clear as day that Bernice was in pain. Breaking a heel on a pair of shoes that make your feet look simply precious is a painful experience for any woman.

Bernice pulled herself up straight and hobbled toward the front door of the church. With every step, she kept reminding herself that, when you're on a mission, you don't let little things distract you. She had come here this morning to get saved, and she'd be damned if she was going to let anything or anybody ruin it for her.

When they got inside the church, the congregation was singing the first hymn. Lifting their hearts in song, Samuel thought—and that thought was followed by a rush of emotion. A yearning for a congregation of his own. Most men in Samuel's shoes might have asked themselves whether they had done something to displease the Lord, but Samuel didn't think like that. The God he knew was giving and kind, so he was convinced that this experience was going to turn out to be a blessing, maybe the greatest blessing of his life. That didn't keep him from hurting, though.

Bernice hobbled down the aisle, slipped into the first vacant pew, and stepped on over to make room for the rest of them. The kids filed in after her, then Willadee, then Samuel. Swan started singing lustily before she came to a full stop. People turned their heads to look at her, the way they always did when she opened her mouth and that big voice came out. Swan didn't notice. Anytime she was singing, she was in a world of her own. She would pour herself into the music, and it would pour out of her, tumbling like a waterfall, and there was nothing else she'd ever known that compared to the feelings that took her over.

Samuel and Willadee nudged each other and smiled. The boys were wincing at their sister's volume. Bernice stood erect, gazing straight ahead. Involuntarily, Samuel cut his eyes to see what she was looking at. It couldn't be the scrawny, red-faced song director, because he was a constant blur of motion—strutting around, waving his arms in time to the music. Whatever Bernice was looking at was stationary. But knowing Bernice, she might not consciously be focusing on anything at all. She had a curious way of living inside her own head. You never knew what was going on in there.

One thing was for sure. She was up to something this morning—and Samuel figured it had to do with her trying to get him back. You'd think, after all these years, she'd have given up, but if she gave up, what would she have? A marriage she never wanted, to a good man who loved her so much that she despised him.

It wasn't that Bernice ever actually chased after Samuel. She just managed every time he was around to drape herself someplace where he couldn't help seeing her, and she talked to him in that silky, honeydrip voice, and she acted, well—amused. As if there was some powerful electric current between them and she found it comical to watch him trying to resist it.

Samuel responded by treating her the same way he treated everybody else. He was gracious and polite, and respectful as you please. He never avoided looking her in the eye. He never looked away first. He never let her get under his skin.

Truth was, Samuel felt sorry for Bernice. She was the most alone person he had ever met—so intent on staying forever breathtaking that she could never let any of life's glories take her own breath away. He hadn't felt a tingle for her since the day he met Willadee. (Talk about one of life's glories. Talk about something taking your breath away.) But that didn't mean he wasn't going to be extra cautious around his sister-in-law. An electrical cord doesn't have to carry a charge in order to be dangerous. It can still be used to tie people up. And strangle them.

Chapter 10

The way you trained a horse was, you taught it that life was uncertain and punishment was sure. At least, that was the way Ras Ballenger trained horses. If the people who entrusted their animals to him had known his methods, most of them would have found another trainer.

A few people would have used Ras anyway. Those who only cared about results. Ras definitely got results. He could get a horse to do damn near anything. You wanted it to be a high stepper? He could turn it into a high stepper, all right. You wanted it to prance around with its head at an elegant but unnatural angle? He could get it to where it would prance all day long and never bob its head once. You wanted it to be a good kid horse? He could turn it into a horse a three-year-old could ride.

The thing was, the reason the horses Ras trained were so obedient and eager to please was that they were terrified of humans, and broken in spirit. They came away from his place groomed and gleaming, but with a vacant stare and a tendency to shudder when they were petted. Sometimes owners questioned Ras about that, and he had all sorts of explanations. The weather was changing, and you know how squirrelly horses can get when the weather is changing. Or they weren't used to the owners anymore, after all they hadn't seen them in a couple of months, but they'd get back to normal soon enough. Or they knew they were about to be moved, and horses hate being hauled. That sort of thing.

Ras never let the conversation linger long on such trivia. The thing that kept people coming back to him was performance, so he never wasted any time getting down to showing them what their horses could do now that he had worked with them so diligently.

He'd get up on the horse and ride it around, and start it and stop it and back it and make it step sideways. He'd lope it and canter it and trot it and run it at a gallop. If it happened to be a cutting horse, he'd turn some calves into the lot, and he'd do a little cutting demonstration, which never failed to please the owners. Few things in the world are as pretty and flashy as the intricate dance a fine horse does when it's separating a calf from a herd.

At some point, Ras would go no-hands. He'd loop the reins around the pommel, and rest his hands on his thighs, and let the horse do the work on its own. He always wound up the performance by putting a kid in the saddle. He'd use one of his own if the folks hadn't brought one along. Then he'd tell the kid what to do, and they'd go through a little replay of Ras's original demonstration, and by that time, nobody was worrying anymore about whether the horse had a vacant stare. They'd be clapping Ras on the shoulder, and asking him how he did it, and pressing money into his ready hand.

"A horse is smart," Ras would tell them. Smiling. "All you have to do is show it what you want, and it'll do it, or die trying."

So far, none of the horses that had been brought to Ras had died trying, although a few had come close.

If you wanted Ras Ballenger to work with your horse, you had to take it to his place and leave it. After all, he could put in more time with it that way, and besides, he was already set up for it.

The owners didn't know it, but Ras's setup included a twitch, a whip, and a place in his barn where the beasts could be cross-tied so that they couldn't move an inch in any direction. A horse could be left for hours or days without food and water, so that it would be grateful and docile when it was finally released and given a drink. It could be tormented in any number of ways, and Ras Ballenger knew them all.

At about the same time that Samuel Lake was sitting in church wondering what was going to become of his life, a big white gelding named Snowman was standing in Ras Ballenger's holding pen, probably wondering the same thing. Ras was standing outside the pen, leaning against the wood rails, watching the horse watch him.

They'd been like that—the two of them, watching each other—for a couple of hours now. Ever since the owner, a fellow named Odell Pritchett, from over around Camden, had dropped the horse off. Odell had explained that Snowman was green broke, but he needed some finishing work. He was a little high-headed. A little unpredictable.

Ras had assured Odell that he would do what he could. Generally, all a horse like that needed was a little experience. (He didn't say what kind.) A lot of special attention. (He didn't explain that, either.) What he would do was, he'd work with Snowman every day. He'd be consistent, and show him what was expected of him, and before you could pour piss out of a boot, he'd have him whipped into shape. (He for sure didn't elaborate on that one.)

Right now, Ras was doing what he always did first with a new horse, which was to let the animal's anxiety take over. He could stand here all day, if it took all day, just giving the horse a chance to realize that whatever happened next would be something it would have no control over whatsoever. An uncertain horse was a horse that made mistakes. And a horse that made mistakes was a horse that could be corrected. And that was the point where Ras Ballenger would start to truly enjoy his work.

"You're thinkin' 'bout it now, ain't you?" he asked. Talking soft. Laughing low.

Snowman moved to the far side of the pen and turned his head away.

"You're thinkin' 'bout how you're bigger than me, and faster than me, and how you got four feet to my two," Ras went on, and his voice sounded deceptively kind. "You're wonderin' whether this is all gonna be hard or easy, ain't you, Snowman?"

He stepped inside the pen, and walked over to the horse, and took hold of its halter, and snapped on a lead rope, which was already attached to a sturdy post that was cemented into the ground.

"Well, I'm here to tell you, Snowman—it won't be easy. 'Cause easy just ain't no fun."

When Brother Homer Nations got up to make the announcements, the first words out of his mouth were the ones Samuel dreaded.

"We've got a very special visitor this morning, folks," Brother Homer proclaimed. "One of the best and most devout men I've ever been privileged to know. Samuel Lake. Stand up, Samuel. Let us get a look at you."

Samuel stood up. He hated to, but he did it. He looked around at all the people, and smiled at them, and nodded to them, and they all smiled and nodded back. Brother Homer beamed and cleared his throat, to indicate that he had more to say. The congregation dutifully turned their eyes back to him.

"Ordinarily, we don't get the honor of having Samuel with us for services. But tragic circumstances have brought him our way this morning. Samuel, I know you're here to be with your wife's family in their time of grief. I just want to say that you all have our deepest sympathies, and our heartfelt prayers."

"Thank you, Brother Homer," Samuel said. "We appreciate that." And then he added, "I just hope you folks don't get tired of looking at me, because Willadee and the kids and I are moving home."

Brother Homer said, "Well, praise the Lord! Where will you be preaching?"

Samuel looked around at the people, these people he had grown up with, who respected him and looked up to him, and he said, in that calm, resonant voice of his, "I don't have a church this year. I'll be preaching wherever God provides me with a pulpit."

You could have knocked those folks over with a feather. If Sam Lake didn't have a church, that meant that the Methodist conference hadn't seen fit to appoint him to one. And if that were the case, there had to be a reason. Methodists might be dead wrong about not believing in closed communion and once-saved-always, but they seemed to do right by their preachers. Surely they didn't lay them off for nothing, like mill hands during a slow season. Something bad must have happened, and Samuel must have been unfairly blamed for it.

At this point, nobody was even thinking, at least not seriously, that maybe Samuel himself had done anything wrong. Those thoughts would come later. For the moment, the people were all for Samuel.

Brother Homer's sermon was all full of hellfire and brimstone, which wasn't really the side of religion that Samuel liked to emphasize, but concentrating on the message kept his mind off of what would come next, which was visiting with people after the service and having to explain over and over that he and the Methodist church weren't seeing eye to eye these days. Willadee had been right. It was humiliating, and the more people he had to talk to about it, the more humiliating it would become.

What he didn't know was that, by the time the service was over, everybody there would be thinking about something else entirely.

When Calla heard about Bernice getting religion, it just made her so mad she could spit. Not that she had anything against salvation. She'd taken the plunge herself, back when she was just a slip of a girl, and she still prayed and tried to do the right thing, even though she had decided by now that God was all over the place, and you didn't have to go to church to find Him. The thing was, she'd had a bellyful of Bernice a long time ago, and she was way past the point of giving that woman the benefit of the doubt. She never said as much to anybody, but Calla had always been of the opinion that when Toy came home from the war, and killed Yam Ferguson, the biggest mistake he made was that he wrung the wrong neck.

It was the kids who just had to tell Calla the big news. They were piling out of the car before their father even cut off the engine, and they went racing and scrambling straight into the store.

"Aunt Bernice got saved!" Noble was yelling, not paying the slightest attention to the fact that Calla had a couple of customers who really didn't need to know Everything About Everything.

Calla very nearly dropped the dozen eggs and the can of Calumet baking powder she was ringing up. The customers—a sweet-faced old lady and a weather-beaten old man—looked pleased as could be, the way you ought to look when you find out that somebody has come to the Lord.

"You don't say," the old lady chirruped.

"Oh, yes, ma'am," Swan warbled back. The three kids had all skidded to a stop right across the counter from Calla, and Swan was trying to shove Noble out of the way so that she could be the spokesperson for the delegation. "She went down the aisle as soon as they started singing 'Just As I Am,' and she flung herself down on her knees—"

Swan flung her own self down next to a stack of fifty-pound sacks of chopped corn, the kind of corn Grandma Calla fed her chickens. The sacks were made of printed cotton fabric, most of them colorful florals, so they made a nice backdrop for the reenactment.

"And she was holding her head up?" Swan said. "Like this? Like she was looking up to the Lord? And she was just crying her heart out, only her face didn't crumple up like most people's faces do when they cry, you know how ugly most people look when they cry? But she didn't look ugly *at all*, she looked just like an angel."

"And just about everybody there went down and knelt around her and helped her pray through," Noble added.

Bienville nodded soberly. "She got saved as all get-out."

Calla got this kind of squinty-eyed stare, and handed the old couple their purchase, and told them to have a good day. The old couple cast confused glances at each other, knowing they'd just been dismissed and wondering what in the world had gotten into Calla Moses, who was usually so nice and pleasant, and always had a kind word for everybody.

Calla's garden was a beauteous jumble of flowers and vegetables that seemed to spring up of their own accord wherever they pleased. Sunflowers towered ten feet in the air, with runner beans and cucumbers climbing their stalks and blooming all along the way. Tomatoes were surrounded by peppers, which were set off by marigolds of orange and bronze and gold. Graceful okra cast a fan-leafed canopy over a frilly patchwork of lettuces. Scarlet zinnias and pastel cosmos danced among hip-high summer squash, and purple hull peas hugged the sturdy legs of strappy sweet corn. It was a sight to behold.

Toy was scaling crappie at a rickety old table between the garden and the toolshed. He glanced up at the sound of all the car doors slamming, and then he focused his attention back on what he was doing. He knew Bernice had gone to church with the others—not because he had seen her leave, and not because he had gone to their room and discovered that she wasn't there. He just knew because he knew, the same way he often just knew things, especially where his wife was concerned.

Toy wished with his whole heart that he didn't care so much about what Bernice did, or whether *she* cared about *him*. He wished he could numb it all out and not hurt over her or yearn after her, or give a damn one way or the other. He wished that she were not still in love with Sam Lake, or that at least he didn't have to be so acutely aware of it. The hardest thing he did every day was to pretend not to be aware, and the only way he managed it was to just keep on doing whatever work was at hand to do, from the time he got up until the time he lay down, day after day, after day.

Right now, the work at hand was cleaning fish. So he gutted and scaled, and gutted and scaled. He had a kind of rhythm to his movements that would have caused anybody watching him to think, Now, there's a man who's at peace with his world.

He could hear the cooking sounds starting up in the kitchen. The clatter of pots and pans. The low murmur of female voices. That would be Bernice and Willadee. He didn't strain to hear what they were saying, partly because that was not his way and partly because they wouldn't be saying much worth listening to anyway.

Pretty soon, Samuel came out and joined him. He had changed into khakis and an everyday shirt, and he was holding a paring knife.

"How about some help?" Samuel asked.

"No sense in both of us smelling like fish," Toy said. "Anyway, I'm almost done."

Samuel hadn't figured Toy would want or accept help. He had just brought the knife along to show that he was willing to do his part. Since he felt useless, and didn't know what else to do with himself, he leaned against a tree and tossed the knife from one hand to the other.

"How was church?" Toy asked. Just making conversation.

"Uplifting," Samuel said.

And Toy said, "That's good."

He kept on cleaning fish, and Samuel kept tossing the knife back and forth. After a while, Samuel said, "Bernice surrendered her life to the Lord this morning."

There was a slight break in Toy's rhythm. Ever so slight. He finished the fish he was working on, chunked it into a dishpan with the rest of the already cleaned ones, and scooped another one out of the washtub where the last few live ones were thrashing around.

He said, "I guess that means she'll be going to church a good bit from now on."

"Maybe you'll want to start going with her," Samuel suggested. He was really hoping, although he didn't believe it for a minute, that Toy might do just that. Besides the obvious consideration of Toy's eternal soul, there was the fact that, if Toy started going to church, his wife would be riding with him, instead of with Samuel and his family. Willadee was an awfully good-natured woman, but she had her limits, and Samuel knew in his bones that those limits were about to be tested.

Toy shook his head. "Wouldn't want the roof to cave in."

Samuel grinned. Tossed the knife up higher into the air, and caught it with the same hand this time.

"I don't imagine the roof would cave in," he said.

"Be a shame for folks to find out the hard way," Toy answered.

By the time the women got lunch ready, Toy had packed the fish into empty milk cartons, and filled the cartons with water, and asked Samuel to put them in the deep freeze. Then he had wrapped all the innards and scraps in newspaper and buried the mess in a bare patch in Calla's garden. Come spring, whatever got planted there would flourish, and somebody would say, "Looks like Toy had a good catch sometime last summer."

He drove a stake in the spot and hammered it down good, so it wouldn't get knocked over by accident. Calla always wanted to know where he'd planted fish scraps, so she could be sure not to plant peas or beans anywhere near it. Peas and beans make lush, showy vines when they get a big dose of fertilizer, but that's all they make. Calla was mighty particular about her garden. She had a system that worked, and she didn't take kindly to anybody upsetting the balance.

Toy hosed down the table where he'd been cleaning the fish, and stripped off his shirt, and hosed himself down, too. He still smelled to high heaven, so he went into Never Closes and washed up with soap and water at the sink behind the bar.

He didn't know why he'd been so surprised at what Samuel had told him. Trust Bernice to come up with the one thing nobody could fault her for. The one way she could be thrown together the most frequently, and under the most favorable circumstances, with the man she considered to be the love of her life.

Toy had nothing but respect for his good-looking preacher-boy brother-in-law, and he couldn't imagine Sam Lake ever letting himself get sucked into a situation where his honor might be compromised.

Even so, Toy Moses couldn't help feeling mighty sick inside.

Chapter 11

Swan and her brothers had given up playing War Spies because now, every time they found themselves running across the Minefield, dodging enemy bullets and trying not to get blown to Kingdom Come from blundering onto a land mine, they couldn't help thinking about what it must really be like to get shot, or to have some body part suddenly explode. They kept picturing in their minds what Papa John must have looked like two seconds after he pulled the trigger.

All of a sudden, they had found that they couldn't think about dying the same way as before. Used to be, they could shoot each other and watch each other fall and roll around moaning and twitching, and they never thought about death as something you couldn't get up and walk away from. Now all that had changed.

They had switched from being War Spies to being Cowboys and Indians, and that had worked out all right. Cowboys and Indians killed each other all the time, but it didn't seem so real. Besides, Swan and Noble and Bienville never shot each other anymore. Sometimes, just to keep things interesting, they'd let themselves get bushwhacked by a gunslinger, but they mainly suffered flesh wounds from those encounters. None of them ever wound up on Boot Hill.

Swan wanted to be the sheriff, but Noble wasn't having that. Whoever heard of a lady sheriff? And besides, she'd probably get them all killed, the way she was always going off half-cocked. He was going to be the sheriff. She could be his deputy if she wanted to be a law woman.

Swan wasn't about to settle for being anybody's deputy, so she became a United States marshal. Bienville was a deaf and dumb Indian scout, and he worked up a variety of hand signals to communicate with them. At first, it was confusing, since he couldn't speak a word or hear one either (he had to explain the hand signals with more hand signals), but after a while they got the hang of it.

The kids had a big shoot-out planned for the afternoon. They'd been chasing a band of Outlaws and had finally hemmed up the sorry, lily-livered snakes in the Box Canyon (their new name for the old calf lot). There were about fifty or so Outlaws, judging from the number of hoofprints where they'd all crossed the Big River (their new name for the creek), so the Good Guys were hopelessly outnumbered. As usual.

The way they had it figured, the deaf and dumb Indian scout would circle around behind the Box Canyon and throw in a lit torch, and the sagebrush would all catch fire, and the Bad Guys would have to hightail it to keep from being barbecued. The mouth to the canyon (the gate to the calf lot) was a tight fit, just room enough for one man to ride through at a time, so the sheriff and the United States marshal would have no trouble picking off the low-down, no-account sidewinders as they tried to escape.

Bienville wasn't the one to come up with the plan, and he didn't like it much. The way he saw it, even an Outlaw ought to be given a fair chance. Swan just hooted over that one. Fifty or so Outlaws against one local sheriff and one United States marshal didn't sound exactly fair to *her*. Anyway, if the crooks wanted a fair chance, they shouldn't have robbed the bank, shot up the town, and peed in the watering trough out in front of the saloon.

. . .

Of course, by the time lunch was over and the posse was ready to ride out, plans had changed. Swan was so inspired by what had happened at church that morning that she decided they should swipe a tarp from the shed, put up a tent back by the creek, and hold a Revival Meeting. That way, if they had any converts, they could baptize them before they had a chance to backslide.

She aimed to have converts. One in particular. Grandma Calla had mentioned at lunch that she thought Sid and Nicey and Lovey would be dropping by later, and wouldn't Swan enjoy getting to play with a girl for a change.

Grandma Calla just didn't know.

Swan reckoned that, by the time the company got there, she (the evangelist) and her deacons could have the tent all set up, and they'd be ready to lead their first sinner to salvation. They'd drag her if they had to. Swan told Grandma Calla that she would love to have a girl to play with, and wouldn't she please tell Lovey, as soon as she got there, to just come on back to the creek.

Grandma Calla gave Swan one of those I-can-see-right-through-you looks and said, "You'd better not be up to anything, Swan Lake."

"All I'm *up* to is trying to be nice to Lovey," Swan explained archly.

And Grandma Calla said, "Um-hmm."

The Revival Meeting was harder to coordinate than Swan had anticipated. Noble had been in charge of doing all the necessary stealing, and the only thing he could find to support the corners of the tent were some old cane fishing poles, which kept bending under the weight of the tarp. Finally, Bienville came up with the idea of draping the tarp over a low-hanging tree limb. Then they could tie the corners to some young saplings.

Only—they didn't have any rope.

So Noble had to go back and burgle the shed again. While he was gone, Bienville scouted around for trees with low-hanging limbs, and

Swan meandered down to the creek to pick out a good spot for the upcoming baptism.

For the most part, the little stream was less than a foot deep, which would be okay for a Methodist baptism, since Methodists let people choose between sprinkling and pouring. But Swan had no plans for performing a Methodist baptism. She also did not plan to give her baptismal candidate a choice. This was going to be a Baptist baptism. A baptism by immersion. All she had to do was find a spot that was deep enough.

She knew there was at least one spot in the creek that was deep enough, because she and her brothers had been warned never to go there without an adult. The Old Swimming Hole. That's what her mother and her uncles always called it when they talked about how much fun they'd had, back when they were kids, swinging on grapevines and cannonballing the water.

It didn't dawn on Swan that, if the water was deep enough to cannonball into, it was too deep for wading into with a new convert who was probably the biggest sissy in Arkansas. Especially since Swan herself didn't know how to swim. How *could* she, when her daddy was always too busy to teach her? She had begged him to, and he had promised to, and he had surely intended to, but there had always been something more pressing. For instance, somebody out in the boonies had a kid with a fever of 103. And the kid had to get to the doctor, but they didn't have a car. So somebody would call the preacher, and he would drop everything and go do what had to be done.

Swan wasn't thinking about any of this, though. All she was thinking about was that Lovey was stuck on herself and needed to be taken down a few notches.

The swimming hole hadn't been used in years, and there were no paths leading down to it anymore, so finding it wasn't easy. Swan followed the creek bank, looking and hoping, and looking and hoping, but the swimming hole just did not seem to exist. The bank sloped and slanted, sometimes level with the water, sometimes rising high above it.

When she finally found what she was looking for, it came as a huge surprise, because she almost charged off the bank and landed in the middle of it. She had just reached one of the high points and was picking her way through some underbrush that seemed to go on forever when, all at once—it didn't. There was a clear space right ahead, and she was heading for it, and it turned out that the clear space was where the bank dropped off, straight down and down and down. If it hadn't been for the fabled grapevines, and for the fact that Swan happened to get an arm tangled up in one as she was pushing toward the light, she'd have been doing a cannonball off the side whether she wanted to or not.

But then, the grapevines *were* there, and she *did* get her arm (not to mention her skirt tail) tangled up in one, and so she turned out not falling in but dangling above the water with her panties showing. She was screaming bloody murder.

Noble had gotten back with the rope, and Bienville had found a tree with an appropriately low-hanging limb. The two of them were busy setting up the Revival Tent when they heard all the commotion. The thing was, their sister had gotten far enough off from the Revival Grounds that her terrified voice didn't exactly come through loud and clear. It was muted. Distant. And not altogether believable, since Swan had a history of making make-believe seem like the real thing.

The two boys kept working on the tent.

Blade Ballenger had been trailing Swan ever since she had left Bienville behind and struck out on her own. He'd stayed out of sight, and had made no sound at all.

When Swan went crashing through the underbrush, Blade started to holler out, to warn her that there was a drop-off. He'd been here before. He knew this place. He knew a lot of the places in these parts, because he'd explored most of them, at one time or another, when he was trying to stay away from whatever was going on at home. But she was moving faster than his thoughts. One second she was on land, and the next second, she was in the air, and the only thing between her and the water was a gnarled old grapevine.

Blade went racing to the side of the bank, terrified that Swan Lake was about to go plunging out of his life once and for all. He had to do something.

He was afraid to say anything to her. Afraid that anything he did would be wrong. But he had to do something.

So he cannonballed. Just took a flying leap off the side, passed her on the way down, and ploinked into the water. Little as he was, he didn't even make much of a splash. He went under and kept heading down for a bit, then bobbed to the surface.

Swan had seen him whizzing past and was gaping down at him. Hanging on to the vine that was hanging on to her, and just gaping.

"Well, let go!" he yelled.

She shook her head and held on harder.

"I can't swim!"

He said, "You go down, you come up!"

"And then I'd go down again."

"No, you won't. The way I learned to swim was somebody threw me in."

Which was true. His daddy had thrown him out of a boat into a pond when he was three years old. He couldn't remember exactly how it all happened, but he had swum like a fish.

Swan wasn't buying his story.

"Well, I'm not letting go! You go down three times, you're done for."

"I'll save you!"

"Who's gonna save *you*?"

"*I* don't need saving."

He was dog-paddling in circles, and it certainly did not look as though he needed saving, but Swan wasn't taking any chances.

"I'm going to swing back to the bank," she said.

She gathered her feet up beneath her, and pushed the air with them, and went nowhere in particular. She tried again. Same result.

"Go get somebody!" she hollered. She was hanging on with both hands now and didn't dare let go, so she jerked her head in the general direction of the Revival Grounds. "Go get my brothers! They're right back over yonder."

Not that her brothers could swim, either.

But Blade wasn't about to leave her. It would take too long. What if she lost her grip while he was gone? That was a chance he couldn't take. He didn't know for sure what he would do if she let go now, but if she fell, he was going to be there.

Swan had gone with her daddy plenty of times over the years to visit elderly parishioners who reveled in reciting the details of their latest brushes with death, heart attacks being the most frequently mentioned and dramatically described. She knew the symptoms of a heart attack and was pretty sure she was having one. Her chest felt tight, her pulse was pounding in her ears, and her left arm was going numb.

Swan was an optimistic sort, but she couldn't help thinking that one of two things was about to happen. Either she was going to die in the air or she was going to die in the water. When the snakeman appeared out of nowhere on the creek bank a few seconds later saying not to worry, that he'd have her back on solid footing in a jiffy, Swan just had one more thing to worry about.

Maybe she was going to die on dry land.

Chapter 12

Ras Ballenger had better things to do with his day than chase around through the woods after a kid who kept wandering off. Lately, every time he'd needed Blade to go fetch him his Bull Durham, or to bring him a jug of ice water from the house, the boy was nowhere to be seen. Used to be, Blade disappeared only to put off getting a strapping when he'd done something he shouldn't, or to keep from having to hear his mama blubbering when she'd gotten out of line. But nowadays, he was like swamp fire. Here, there, and gone. It looked like he'd have figured out by now that running off only made things worse, but that young'un had to learn everything the hard way.

Ras had made up his mind that, when he caught up to him this time, he'd get his point across good and proper. A horse wasn't the only thing that could be cross-tied.

But here he was, standing high on the rise over the creek, and there Blade was down in the water, and there that little bit of a girl was hanging out over the swimming hole, with her skirts hiked up. All of a sudden, Ras wasn't so mad anymore.

He had his whip all rolled up in one hand. He didn't have to tell the little girl to get still, because she did that as soon as she laid eyes on him.

"Now, don't be scared," he said, real nice and soft. "I'm just gonna snag that vine with this whip and pull you over here and get you untangled."

Swan's eyes were big as saucers. She was trying hard to swallow, but her throat didn't want to cooperate. She sure did wish she could fly.

Still, maybe Ballenger didn't intend to hurt her. Maybe he was only mean to his own kids. A lot of people were like that—nicer to everybody else than they were to their own flesh and blood.

And anyway, the snakeman was rearing back with his whip, about to let it fly. If she moved a muscle, he might take her arm off.

The tail of the whip whistled through the air and popped as it wound around the grapevine, about two feet above Swan's head. Ras jerked back on the whip and dragged Swan through empty space like she was on a trapeze. As soon as she swung into reach, he grabbed hold of the grapevine with his free hand and steadied it.

"That wasn't so bad, was it?" he asked. Swan was trying to get free from the vine, but her hands were shaking, and her legs were like water. It was all she could do to stand up. She shook her head timidly.

Ras laughed and started easing her arm free from the vine. Her stomach lurched when he touched her.

"You ain't got nothing to be afraid of, little pretty," he said, just as cheerful as sunrise. He made sure not to put his hands anywhere except on her arm and shoulder while he worked. He made sure not to look as she tugged her skirt tail back down where it was supposed to be. He even patted her on the head.

The tough old vine had scraped and bruised the top of Swan's arm, and now that she was safe, she could feel the pain. She gritted her teeth, trying not to cry.

Ras made a sympathetic clucking sound. "You need to git home and let your mama put something on that."

She nodded and backed away from him.

Ras Ballenger bowed grandly. "Any time you need savin', you just holler."

She sure could holler. That's what he was thinking later on, when he and Blade were headed back to the house. Ras was covering ground fast. The boy was trotting alongside, looking up at him and talking a mile a minute.

"That was something, what you did with the whip," he was saying. "You just let 'er fly, and popped that ole grapevine a hummer. That was sure something, what you did with the whip."

Ras reached down and patted his son on the head, just the way he had patted the girl on the head a few minutes earlier.

"Bet you're hopin' I don't pop you a hummer, too," he said.

The little boy gulped. He had been thinking maybe his father had forgotten that the reason he'd had to come off down to the creek and the reason he was carrying the whip had anything to do with each other.

Ras looked down at him and smiled. It wasn't a bad smile, like sometimes. He sifted through the boy's hair with his hand.

"Well, you're wrong," he said. "I ain't goin' to take the whip to you."

Blade gulped again, this time from blessed relief. "You're not?"

"Nawwwww," Ras said.

Then, snake-quick, he knotted his fingers in the boy's hair, yanked him up off the ground, gave him a toss off to one side, and kept on walking.

When Swan got back to the Revival Grounds, the deacons had the tent up and were constructing a pulpit out of rocks and deadwood. It wasn't going to be a very high pulpit, Noble explained. If they tried to build it too high, it would fall down. But he had seen this one evangelist once who was so tall that he had to kind of hunker over the pulpit to see his sermon notes. Swan could, maybe, play like she was tall.

Swan told him he was crazy as hell if he thought she was going to hunker over anything. Then she slunk off toward the house. Which meant that Noble got to be the evangelist, and Bienville had to be the whole congregation.

Sid and Nicey and Lovey weren't the only relatives who had shown up while Swan was off where she had no business being. Alvis was there, too, with Eudora. Their kids were all in town at the movies— something Swan and her brothers never got to do, going to the movies being a sin in Samuel's eyes. The grown-ups were lolling around on the porch and in the yard, finger snapping and foot tapping while Samuel played "Foggy Mountain Breakdown" on his five-string banjo.

When Samuel saw Swan scurrying past, he stopped playing and called out to her. "Hey, little girl. You want to sing a song with your daddy?"

She shook her head and kept walking.

He sweetened the offer. "We'll do 'Faded Love.' "

But not even the thought of those sweet harmonies could tempt her to join the fun.

Alvis, the worst cutup in the bunch, was leaning against the biggest old oak tree in the yard. He grabbed Swan, out of the blue, and started dancing her around. She jerked away from him like he was poison and kept on going.

Alvis looked perplexed, and sniffed his armpits, and said, "I can't smell that bad."

As a matter of fact, he smelled like Dial soap and Old Spice. Alvis Moses was an auto mechanic, who spent half his life covered with grease and sweat and the other half so clean he gleamed.

"She's just going through a stage," Grandma Calla said.

"Then y'all better look out," Alvis offered. "Them stages can drain you."

. . .

Swan stomped up onto the porch and stepped around Lovey, who was playing with a couple of walking dolls near the screen door. Lovey was allowed to wear shorts and had on a navy blue pair, with the cutest little white sailor top. For a second, Swan thought about hauling her back down to the swimming hole and baptizing her good. But no way was she going back to that swimming hole. There were dangers down there that even her parents didn't know about.

Lovey didn't ask her to come play dolls, which was just as well. Swan hated dolls. She slammed into the house and on to the bathroom, to doctor her scrapes with Mercurochrome—otherwise known as Monkey Blood.

She wished she could tell the men of the family that she was scared to death of Ras Ballenger, and ask them to be on the lookout for him and protect her from him. But she couldn't. If she asked for help, she'd have to explain about breaking the rules, and that would take more courage than she had in her. You have to figure the percentages in these things. If she stuck close to home from now on, there was probably at least a fifty-fifty chance that she could avoid Ras Ballenger. But if her folks ever found out what she had done, the odds were double to nothing that she'd have no place to hide.

The Moses family was used to the ebb and flow of music from Never Closes. Used to car doors slamming and muffled voices, and voices that needed to be muffled. They never locked their doors at night, and never worried about anyone slipping into the house. After all, no one ever had. But several times that week, doors were eased open, and hallways explored, and stairs were climbed silently, and no one asleep in the bedrooms was any the wiser.

Sometimes the visits took place in broad daylight—although, in the daytime, the prowler stayed away from the house, peering through a chink hole in the shed, or hiding in the hayloft, or crouching at the edge of the woods. Patient, and observant, and silent as a stone.

On one sultry afternoon, Samuel was standing beside his and

Willadee's bedroom window, picking out a song on his guitar. It was a lonesome kind of song, and he knew he ought to switch over to something more upbeat, since it's not good to stay in a melancholy mood too long, but the lonesome song kept winning out. He closed his eyes and rode the notes, and it was almost like a prayer, just feeling that sweet, sad music. When he opened his eyes, he looked out over the Moses farm. It was a comforting sight, even in its present state of neglect. Sam Lake had been a farm boy before he got to be a preacher. He loved good earth—the smell of it, and the feel of it in his hands. Loved what could be done with it when a person cared enough to sweat over it, and give to it.

Somebody ought to do something with this place. Somebody ought to lay into it and love it and woo it back to what it used to be. That's what he was thinking. Then his thoughts were interrupted, because something caught his eye. Down there, in what used to be the hay meadow, half-hidden by the fuzzy, gray-green sea of goatweed. A small, dark-haired boy, gazing at the house.

Samuel went downstairs and out into the meadow, but there was no sign that anyone had been there. Nothing except a bare spot of ground where someone had been drawing in the dirt.

Other than that, Blade Ballenger had left without a trace.

Chapter 13

Bernice was wise enough not go on too much about the difference the Lord was making in her life. She knew full well that the more you talk about a thing, the less likely folks are to believe it, so her plan was to let her actions speak louder than words.

First off, she was determined to start being at church every time the doors opened. Willadee had never made a secret of the fact that she thought worshiping God and going to church were two different things altogether, and she had been known to miss a service now and then. Bernice was positive she could show Willadee up in that department.

Second, she was going to start singing solos, as soon as somebody noticed how pretty she could sing and asked her to.

Bernice hadn't sung in a while, not so much as a note, because who wants to sing when they're sad, and she had been sad so much for so long. But she used to sing, back before she lost Samuel to Willadee. That was one of the things that had gotten her and Samuel together to start with. Samuel used to come over and sit on the front porch with Bernice's brother, Van, both of them picking on their old guitars. Bernice would sit out there with them and sing up a storm, and Samuel would just get lost in the music. And in her.

Third, she supposed she was going to have to start living differently, although the only thing she really wanted to change about her life was the man in it. Still, church people were forever talking about how God had made them over, so she guessed she could make herself over and let God take the credit.

She could handle that. A woman can handle almost anything when she's got a good enough reason. And Bernice looked across the supper table at that reason every night. Sometimes it was all she could do to keep from reaching over and touching him.

But she was not that stupid. She could pass him the mashed potatoes, and let her fingertips brush his for an instant. Stand behind him, and lean across to set the corn bread on the table, and let her body press against his shoulder for one electric second. So easy. But not smart.

Good works were smart.

So she offered to help out more around Calla's house, and wouldn't you know, Calla put a mop in her hand. Far be it from Calla Moses to just let Bernice do the things that came to mind, such as— Well, nothing really came to mind, but she had offered to help, and it seemed to her that Calla could have thanked her for being so thoughtful and let it go at that.

She contemplated other good works she could do, such as visiting the sick and the elderly, but that wouldn't help her to be around Samuel, unless she asked him to drive her, which she couldn't get by with, since she knew how to drive. Besides, being around the sick and the elderly made her skin crawl.

Toy was surprised when Bernice started making over him again the way she had back when they were courting. Surprised—but so glad he could have cried. He knew that Bernice might be doing all this for show, just to impress Samuel with how virtuous she was becoming, and he told himself that no man should be as big a fool over a woman as he was over his wife. But his "self" didn't listen. His "self" was just eating this up, like a kid sucking on candy.

Toy Moses couldn't believe the *taste* life had these days. Bernice would be smiling when he woke up late in the afternoon. She would bring him coffee and talk to him while he drank it. When they were driving to Calla's, she would sit right beside him instead of way over on the other side of the car—and when he'd slip his arm around her, she'd snuggle like a bird into a nest.

One night, at the supper table, about a week after her conversion, he caught her looking at him with this kind of glow, the way a woman does when she's falling in love, or falling back into love. Toy wasn't the only one who noticed. Samuel and Willadee both blinked, and Calla nearly choked on her collards.

Toy didn't care. Let them all think that Bernice was building him up for another fall. Let them think any damn thing they wanted. Toy wanted more than anything to trust Bernice, and he was the kind of man who would risk everything for something he believed in.

"Shameless" was what Calla had to say about it. It was Thursday morning, and she and Willadee were hanging laundry on the line out in the backyard. Bernice had gone to prayer meeting the night before with Samuel and Willadee and the kids, and she had looked simply luscious, wearing this virginal smile and a modest little princess-style dress that showed off how much tinier her waist was than the parts above and below it. It had been all Calla could do not to drag her out of the car and tell her she could do her praying at home.

"We can't say she's not sincere," Willadee said. Although she knew better.

"She's sincere, all right," Calla muttered. "And we know what she's sincere *about*."

Willadee hung a sheet, making sure to smooth it out and keep the corners straight. You hang a sheet right, it comes off the line looking like it's been ironed.

"Mama," she said, "it doesn't matter what Bernice does. It's what Samuel does that counts. And he's too good a man to let go of his principles."

Calla grunted under her breath. She believed in Samuel's goodness, too. The trouble was, she believed just as strongly in Bernice's ability to take anything good and flat-out ruin it.

Willadee felt guilty for talking about giving Bernice the benefit of the doubt when she wasn't doing that herself. To tell the truth, though, she didn't think her sister-in-law's case of religion would last very long. Bernice would keep up her act for a little while, but when she saw it wasn't going to get her what she wanted, she'd give it up.

The worst thing about it was that Toy was bound to get hurt again, and he'd been hurt enough. Willadee said as much to Samuel early one morning, right after Toy and Bernice had left for the day. Bernice had been especially attentive to Toy at breakfast, calling him honey, and buttering his toast, and laying her hand on his arm when she probably hadn't touched him on purpose in years. Butter wasn't the only thing she could spread on thick.

"I wouldn't be too worried about him," Samuel told Willadee. The two of them were in the bathroom with the door closed. She was perched on the side of the bathtub shaving her legs while he stood at the sink shaving his face. It had been three weeks since he'd come back from the Methodist conference, and he was about to go job hunting. He kept one side of his face taut while he drew the razor down across it. "He's been looking pretty happy lately."

"That's what worries me. She's got him fooled again."

"Now, we don't know that."

Samuel's voice was patient and kind—and just the slightest bit reproving. Willadee jerked around so fast she nicked her ankle.

"Don't tell me she's got you fooled, too," she said. Her leg was stinging like crazy, but that sting wasn't the one that was smarting the most.

"I'm not taking up for her," he protested. "I'm just saying that we can't possibly know what's in somebody else's heart."

"I know what's in hers." Willadee hated herself for saying that. As a rule, she and Samuel were on the same wavelength about things. She waited for Samuel to say something else, but he was shaving again, paying close attention to what he was doing. Willadee turned back around and started shaving again, too. For the first time since she was fifteen years old, she cut herself in three different places.

Outside, the sky was dull gray, and the air felt heavy, like the elements were about to turn loose and do something terrible. Willadee tried to talk Samuel into staying home, but he wasn't about to let his kids see him sitting around idle. He figured the weather was like a lot of people. Most of their threats never got carried out. Besides, the Bible said that a man who didn't provide for his family was worse than an infidel. And even if the Bible hadn't said a word about it, Samuel couldn't stand the idea of living off of Calla.

Already, he had been making phone calls, and sending out letters, offering his services to other pastors he had known for years.

If they were wanting to go on vacation and needed a relief preacher . . .

If they felt the Lord leading them to hold a revival anytime soon and hadn't yet selected an evangelist . . .

Try as he would, Samuel could not think of himself as an evangelist. To his way of thinking, an evangelist was kind of a lone wolf who roamed from flock to flock, driving strays into the fold. Maybe *wolf* wasn't the right term, precisely, since the sheep were in no danger of being eaten alive. And they *were* being driven into the fold for their own good. But a shepherd didn't drive his flock, he led it. And Samuel was a shepherd, pure and simple. All he wanted was to have a flock of his own, and lead it beside the still waters, and protect it from harm, and seek out the lost, and gently bring them home to peace and safety. Traveling from town to town, spending a week here and two weeks there, and leaving folks behind without really getting to know them—none of that appealed to him at all.

He needn't have worried. All the ministers he contacted already had their vacations and revivals planned, and their pulpits filled. They seemed to feel bad about turning him down, though, and they all promised to keep him in mind, in case anything came up.

Sam Lake knew how to do a lot of things. He could sing, and make music, and help people to see the best in themselves and each other. He could get a couple who were on the verge of divorce to start talking, and he could guide the conversation along until they remembered why they had fallen in love in the first place, and forgot about whatever had convinced them that the love was gone. He could persuade a thief to give back what he had taken, and to be a man and come clean about it. He could talk a judge or a constable into going easy on someone who deserved a second chance. He could visit a teenage girl who had just given birth out of wedlock, and by the time he left, she would be feeling proud of her child instead of ashamed of herself.

But none of the things Sam Lake knew how to do were mentioned in the Magnolia *Banner-News* help wanted ads.

The first place he stopped was at the Eternal Rock Monument Company, in Magnolia, where they needed a salesman in the worst way. The man who ran the office, Mr. Lindale Stroud, took one look at Samuel and decided what everybody always decided when they looked at Samuel: that he was the kind of man nobody could say no to. He hired him on the spot.

The way Samuel's new job worked was, he drove around calling on people who had recently lost a loved one, and he told them how he sympathized with them in this their time of grief—which was no exaggeration. He really did have compassion for people who were suffering. He would visit with them, just getting a feel for their circumstances, and then he'd ask them whether they had thought about picking out a monument to commemorate their beloved. If they hadn't, he'd talk with them a bit more, helping them to see the importance of doing it now instead of putting it off, since time slips away when we're not looking. Finally, he would open the three-ring binder that Mr. Lindale Stroud had provided and show the folks the glossy photos of all the various styles of monuments available.

To make it all easier for the families who couldn't afford to pay in full (and most couldn't), the monument company had an E-Z payment plan. The plan had a not so E-Z interest rate, which bothered Samuel. He would work it all out for the folks, showing them how they'd be paying the full price several times over if they took the E-Z plan, but nobody wanted to hear those explanations. It was just too tempting to sign on the dotted line and pay the small down payment. All those future weekly payments seemed worlds away.

By the time the storm hit, at 3:08 P.M., Samuel had already made his first sale.

Willadee had kept the kids inside most of the day, because she had a bad feeling about the weather and didn't want to have to track them down if it turned ugly. Swan and her brothers had never lived in tornado country, and had never witnessed a twister during their visits to Arkansas, so they didn't understand what all the fuss was about. The ominous cloud banks hanging above the horizon didn't seem nearly as threatening as the thunderheads they were used to back home in Louisiana. The long, lead-colored banks looked as if they had been sheared off, flat across the bottom, and regular sky showed underneath. Rain drizzled, and lightning feathered through the clouds, and thunder rumbled, and the treetops churned in the wind. None of this seemed especially scary to the kids, even when little tails dipped down out of the flat bottoms of the clouds and felt around, like they were looking for something to lock on to.

All day long, Willadee had kept going to the window and looking out, or stepping onto the porch and frowning at the sky, and saying she wished Samuel would hurry up and get back. About midafternoon, Calla came through the house from the store, and stood on the porch with Willadee, and frowned at the sky, too.

"I never saw a man had a lick of sense," Calla said. Which wasn't true at all. Her sons had plenty of sense, and so did Samuel. Even John had had a good head on his own shoulders, back before the liquor scorched his brain. But griping about men not having any sense was easier for Calla than admitting that she was worried about Samuel.

"Well, I know he's all right," Willadee said, trying to convince herself.

The kids had been hanging half in and half out the front door, and now they ventured out on the porch, to help with the weather watch.

"Why is the sky turning green?" Bienville wanted to know.

"Why is your bee-hind about to turn red?" Grandma Calla asked. Then she saved him the trouble of answering. "Because I'm about to swat it, that's why."

Swan said, "Well, the weather's not doing anything. The wind's not even blowing anymore."

She was right. Willadee had been so busy watching the sky that she hadn't noticed the sudden, eerie stillness. Now she looked at her mother, who was looking at her, and they both went grim around the mouth.

"Get inside, and get your pillows off your beds," Willadee told them. "And go climb in the bathtub with the pillows over your heads, until I tell you."

"But nothing's happening!" Swan persisted.

Grandma Calla hollered, "Swan Lake, if this storm rips your head off your shoulders and slings it out there in the cow pasture, I guess you'll learn to listen."

Swan thought that was hilarious. A head, in a cow pasture, listening. She didn't dare laugh, though, because Grandma Calla was stomping her foot and waving her apron, like she was shooing her hens into the chicken yard. Swan, Noble, and Bienville stampeded through the door, and up the stairs, then grabbed their pillows and clattered back down. They charged into the bathroom and dove into the tub. So far, Swan thought, this was kind of fun.

Grandma Calla and their mother had run back inside and were throwing windows open, because they had heard somewhere that

that could help keep a house from exploding if a twister hit it. Then they rushed into the bathroom and sat down on the floor beside the tub. Willadee told the kids that she bet their daddy was praying right then for God to keep them safe, so there wasn't one thing to be afraid of.

Swan pulled the pillow down off her head and said that if there wasn't anything to be afraid of, she personally didn't see the point of hiding in the bathtub. Before Willadee could open her mouth to ask Swan to please shut hers, they heard what sounded like a freight train, screaming out of nowhere. All the kids could think about at the time was that that was odd, since there wasn't a railroad track around for miles.

Chapter 14

Samuel was out on the Macedonia highway, heading for the home of Birdie Birdwell, daughter of T. H. Birdwell, recently deceased. According to Mr. Lindale Stroud, who had gotten it from Avery Overbeck, whose third cousin was Birdie's next-door neighbor's uncle Frank, T.H. had been out in the privy looking at the lingerie section of the Montgomery Ward catalog when he suffered a massive heart attack.

Samuel didn't dwell on the details. His job was to provide comfort—which he felt good about—and to try to sell Birdie a monument—which he did *not* feel completely good about. Already, he was beginning to view himself as a vulture, swooping down after death had struck, hoping to feed off the unfortunate. The biggest difference he saw between himself and the buzzards was that they fed off the dead, and—as long as he was in this line of work—he would be feeding off the living.

Still, there was no moral reason not to sell monuments. He'd just make sure to give the people on his prospect list his best by being careful never to take advantage of them.

Now, if he could make this sale, that would give him two checks to hand over to the Eternal Rock Monument Company. And it would give him two commissions. Samuel could go home with money in his pocket. Not only that, but next week, he could drop back around and collect the installment payments from the sales he had made this week. Theoretically, the whole thing should keep on growing to the point where, eventually, he would have substantial income whether he made any new sales or not.

Samuel wasn't a gullible sort, so he already knew that things wouldn't actually turn out quite that rosy. Once the people got their headstones set up, the payments were likely to be perceived first as an inconvenience, then as a burden, and finally as something the customers didn't actually owe anyway, considering the interest rate was so ungodly. But Samuel would cross those bridges when he came to them. Right now, he was looking for the Birdwell mailbox. The weather had been getting nastier by the minute.

He was trying to decide whether to turn in to the drive or turn around and head home when the bottom fell out of the sky. The rain was sudden and savage and impossible to see through. The wind came back to life with a vengeance, slamming into Samuel's car, rocking it back and forth. Unless that car picked up and flew, which seemed a possibility at the moment, Sam Lake wasn't going anywhere. Whatever was going on at home, it was too late for him to show up and help out. So he did something even better.

He cut the engine, and took his Bible from the passenger seat, and held it to his heart, and calmly began to pray. From the tone of his voice, he could have been asking his best friend for a glass of water.

"Lord," he said, "I'm asking you for one thing, and one thing only. If the storm is headed toward Calla's house, please make it go around."

...

Two hours later, when the weather had finished having its say, and the western sky was just turning mauve and gold, Samuel's car rolled over the crest of a hill about a half a mile away from Calla's front door. From the top of that rise, Samuel could see the Moses place, all spread out below. He hadn't been worried about whether his family was safe. It never occurred to him to doubt that his prayer had been answered. But he wasn't prepared for the sight that lay before him. His first impression was that parts of the place must now be scattered all over south Arkansas. Samuel had to stop the car and get out and stand there for a few minutes, just staring. It looked like a bulldozer had headed through the woods, mowing down trees like so much tall grass, and then had continued straight toward the house. An old feed silo was in its way. It shredded the silo. An abandoned outhouse was in its way. It flattened the outhouse. Calla's chicken coop was in the way, but it was spared, because the twister had veered off abruptly, cutting a semicircle around the yard and the closest outbuildings and the Moses home before straightening back out and resuming its path of destruction.

Samuel got down on his knees, right there in the middle of the mud-puddled road, and looked up at the heavens. He could feel his eyes filling with tears.

"Anything You ask of me, Lord," he said, simply. "Anything You want."

Samuel spent the rest of the afternoon helping Toy pick up broken limbs and shattered boards and mangled pieces of tin.

"I reckon it'll take a while to rebuild everything," Samuel said, when the two stopped for a breather.

"I reckon it won't," Toy returned. He waved one arm, indicating the casualties. "We don't need an outhouse, since we have indoor plumbing. Don't need a silo, since we got no cattle to feed. I was gonna take down that fence over yonder, because it was falling apart anyway. And all those sheds were just places for rats and snakes to breed. Nothing we had any use for was even touched. Damnedest thing I ever saw."

Later on, in bed, Samuel told Willadee that he had a feeling God was about to teach him a thing or two about trust.

"But you always trust," she said.

"I know. But it's always been easy, Willadee. Everything has always come easy for me."

"Because you trust," she insisted.

"I used to think that, too," Samuel said. "I thought things came easy for me because I had such strong faith. But anybody can trust as long as everything's going their way. You think about it. I've never lost anybody except my parents, and they had lived long lives, and everybody expects to lose their parents someday. I've never had a broken heart, except when Bernice jilted me, and that was the best thing that ever happened to me. Other than being without a church right now, I've never asked for anything I didn't get, my whole life."

"Samuel," Willadee said. "You're the best person I've ever known. God blesses you because you're good."

"God blesses me because *He* is good," Samuel corrected her.

Willadee wanted to remind Samuel that, even though God is good, an awful lot of people seem to suffer from the cradle to the grave. But Samuel was trying to tell her something important, and she didn't want to get him off the track.

"You've got to wonder about it," he went on. "I asked God to make the storm go around this house, and He did precisely that. The twister didn't pick up on one side of the house and set down on the other. It didn't head out in a whole new direction. It went *around* this house. It was real close. Real tight. Real obvious."

He traced the twister's path on her bare stomach.

"Like this," he said. "It was coming straight at the house, and then it circled around like this, and then it headed out straight again. Like that. I'll have to take you up there to the rise and let you see for yourself, because you can't get the full picture down here."

Willadee sat upright in the bed and looked at him through the darkness. "What are you getting at, Sam Lake?"

"What I'm getting at is—I think God gave me this thing today as a sign."

"What kind of sign?"

"One I can look back on, and hold on to." He was silent again for another moment, and then he said, earnestly, "He just made it so *vivid*, Willadee. Like He wanted to make sure I could never forget."

Chapter 15

On the first Friday in July, Odell Pritchett called from Camden to ask Ras Ballenger how Snowman's training was coming along, and Ras told him he'd never seen an animal so eager to please. Odell was tickled pea green to hear that, since his teenage daughter, Sandy, was pure-dee in love with that horse. She had watched him come into the world, and had claimed him immediately, and right now she was missing him something terrible. What Odell was thinking was, he'd like to bring Sandy over and let her watch Ras work with Snowman, and maybe Ras could give her some pointers for later on.

Ras had a dozen reasons why he wasn't about to let Odell bring his daughter over to watch him work with Snowman, not the least of which was that right now Snowman had angry, oozing welts all over his flanks from being worked over with Ras's whip. Another few weeks, and the wounds would be healed up enough so that they could be explained away, but right now they looked like hell. Naturally, that wasn't the reason Ras gave Odell.

"Now, Mr. Pritchett," he said, "you know I don't allow owners on the place while I'm workin' with their horses. It undoes their trainin'. Gets 'em all excited, and they forget what they're supposed to be doing. Then we lose half the ground we've already made, and you turn out wastin' money you could have spent buyin' that little girl of yours a fancy saddle or somethin'."

Odell suggested that maybe he and Sandy could watch from a distance. Snowman would never have to know they were even on the place.

"You just don't know how smart that horse is," Ras told him. He was always telling owners how smart their horses were, since that was the thing owners most wanted to hear. "You come within a mile of this place, and that boy is gonna know it. I swear, he can read my mind. He knows what I want before I even tell him."

That was music to Odell Pritchett's ears. "You really think he's that good a horse?"

Ras said, "Well, I don't like to exaggerate, but I've worked with a lot of horses in my time, and this one keeps on surprisin' me."

That last part was true. Snowman had surprised him a couple of times by throwing him (which very few horses had ever managed to do), and he had surprised him several times by not cowing at the whip (which almost all horses did do). He had even surprised him once by rearing up and trying to stomp his ass (which was why Snowman now had the oozing welts all over his flanks).

Odell argued and cajoled, but Ras stuck to his guns. He knew full well that controlling the owner was every bit as important as controlling the horse, sometimes more important, since unruly owners could ruin your whole operation by blabbing to other owners things you didn't want or need to have blabbed. They could take the bread right out of your mouth, which was just plain wrong.

Finally, Ras said, "Mr. Pritchett, if you don't trust me to know what's best for your horse, maybe you'd better find yourself another trainer."

He was taking a gamble, but it was one he had taken before. So far, nobody had ever called his bluff. This time wasn't any different.

"Aw, now," Odell protested. "I didn't say I don't trust your judgment."

Ras said, "I reckon I was hearin' things."

Odell hem-hawed around, saying how he knew Ras was the finest trainer in the country, everybody knew that, it was just that he hated to disappoint his little girl, her being so attached to Snowman and all. Ras told him he'd hate it a sight more if that horse forgot his manners and pitched the kid off and broke her neck, all because he'd had his training interrupted at the worst possible time.

"It's your call, though," he said. "He's your horse, and she's your daughter, and I can't tell you your business. As a matter of fact, the more I think about it, why don't you just get on over here and pick him up. I wash my hands of the whole thing."

Well, Odell wasn't about to come and get his horse after being told a thing like that. He backtracked, and stammered around, and finally asked, with the proper degree of humility, how long Ras would estimate it might take to get Snowman finished right. No shortcuts. He wasn't asking for shortcuts, and he wasn't pushing or trying to hurry Ras, he was just wondering.

"End of August," Ras snapped. "Just like I told you in the beginning."

Geraldine was ironing again. Lost in her own thoughts. When you get up before sunrise, and spend the day doing some other family's ironing for money that you'll never get to hold in your hand because you're not the one in *charge* of the money, you have to find some way to occupy your mind. A lot of times, like today, Geraldine occupied her mind planning her husband's funeral. She never really planned the way he would arrive at the point of being dead and she would arrive at the point of being a widow, although she frequently hoped that the last thing Ras saw in this world would be some horse's hooves, flashing down like swords of justice. That would be fitting.

She sometimes thought, for brief moments, when she allowed herself, that it would be even more fitting if she herself did him in with a number 10 Griswold cast-iron skillet. Just smack him upside his little bullet-shaped head. She'd never have the nerve to try it, though. Ras was too quick. Any attempt to do him in would backfire, and it would be her brains that wound up on the kitchen floor.

Besides, how he came to be dead wasn't important for the purposes of her daydream, and she told herself that she wasn't even really *wishing* him dead. She was just thinking about what it would be like if it happened. There was nothing at all wrong with contemplating what life would be like if some certain thing happened.

In her fantasy, she could see him all laid out, looking natural, and she could see herself wearing a nice black dress, crying silent tears, while the members of the little Church of the Nazarene they sometimes attended felt sorry for her, and held her up in case her strength failed, and sang shouting songs. She didn't actually have a black dress, and didn't know how she might get one, but the best thing about daydreaming was that every little detail didn't have to be filled in. Maybe some kindly neighbor would lend her a black dress or, better yet, buy her one. Maybe she would find where Ras stashed his cash, and the kindly neighbor would drive her into town, and she'd buy her own black dress. She didn't know where she'd get the silent tears, either, but she figured those would come on their own. Sometimes she got misty-eyed just thinking about it.

"I suppose it would just be too damn much trouble to get me a cup of coffee," Ras snarled, out of nowhere. Geraldine had been so deep into her reverie that she hadn't noticed when he slammed down the phone and sauntered into the kitchen. Right now, he was plopped down at the table, mad as a hornet.

Geraldine thudded back into the world of reality, laid the iron over on its side, and hustled to the stove to get his coffee. It wasn't going to be right, because nothing was ever right, but she measured sugar and milk into it, and handed it to him, and waited to hear what was wrong with it this time. Ras took an experimental sip.

"How come you're standin' there lookin' like a walleyed heifer?" he demanded. "Don't you have anything else to do besides stand around lookin' like a walleyed heifer?"

So at least the coffee must be all right. Geraldine went back over to the ironing board and took up her work where she had left off. Ras kept sipping his coffee and glaring around the room—not at anything in particular.

"Bastid thinks he's gonna come on my place without bein' invited," he said.

"Which bastard?" Geraldine asked. After all, you never knew. In Ras's book, everybody was a bastard.

"Odell Asshole Pritchett."

Geraldine mouthed a silent *oh* and put the shirt she'd just been ironing on a hanger, which she hooked over the top facing of the wide-open back door with several other freshly ironed garments.

"Bastid might just get a phone call one night before long," Ras said.

What he meant, Geraldine knew, was that Odell Pritchett might get a phone call saying that his horse had foundered and had to be put down. Or that it had stepped in a hole and broken its leg and had to be put down. Or that any number of other things had happened to it, with the end result being that it had to be put down. Ras could always find an excuse to kill.

He was bad about shooting hunting dogs that wouldn't hunt to suit him, and he was bad about catching stray cats and throwing them to the hunting dogs. He poisoned rats, although you couldn't blame a man for poisoning rats. He hunted squirrels and deer and rabbits for food, and raccoons and foxes and beavers for their hides, and wolves and coyotes and bobcats for the noble reason that, if he didn't kill them, they'd kill somebody's livestock. He had no qualms about killing armadillos and possums and skunks, because they didn't have any reason for living anyway. He had never killed a customer's horse. Yet. But then, he'd never hated a horse as much as he hated this one.

Ras slapped his hand down on the table, signifying that he had just decided something. Then he got up and strutted out the door, slowing down enough to give Geraldine a vulgar, bruising goose as he went by.

She didn't react. She didn't have to. Her fantasy was waiting. All she had to do was slide back into it. By the time Ras was off the porch, Geraldine could already see it all again. There he was, laid out and looking natural. And there she was, in her nice black dress, crying silent tears. All around her, the people from the Church of the Nazarene were feeling sorry for her, and holding her up in case her strength failed her, and singing shouting songs.

Blade's little brother Blue, at four and a half, was curly-headed and round as a teddy bear, and thought his daddy hung the moon. Probably, he wouldn't have thought that if he got whacked and whipped as often as Blade, but he didn't. Blade didn't hold that against him. You can't hold it against somebody that they're not getting switched till the blood runs down their legs or that they're not getting thumped on the head till they've got punk knots sprouting everywhere.

Instead of resenting his little brother, Blade tried to figure out what Blue was doing right that he himself was doing wrong. He figured it must have something to do with the fact that Blue was smart, and he (Blade) was dumb. That was what their daddy had told them, time after time.

"Blue, you're smart as a whip and sharp as a tack."

"Blade, you are too dumb to know it."

Blade would have loved to be smart as a whip and sharp as a tack, like Blue, except that he couldn't really see any way that Blue *was* all that smart. He still wet the bed, he still talked baby talk, he still sucked his thumb. One way he was smart, though, was that he tried at every opportunity to be just like his daddy. He walked like him. He talked like him. If Ras picked up a piece of straw and stuck it in his mouth and chewed on it, Blue would pick up a piece of straw and stick it in his mouth and chew on it. If Ras hitched up his britches and hooked his thumbs in his belt loops, Blue would hitch up his britches and hook his thumbs in his belt loops. If Ras kicked one of the Catahoula curs out of his way as he was coming down off the porch, Blue would kick one of the Catahoula curs out of his way as he was coming down off the porch.

Ras thought it was the funniest, cutest thing he had ever seen, that little chubby shaver trying to act like his old man. Every time he would see Blue aping him, he would shake his head and grin and tell anybody who might be listening that that boy was a caution.

Blade didn't want to be like his daddy, but he wanted his daddy to *like* him, so he tried once in a while to imitate him, just the way Blue did. It never worked out. Whenever Blade aped Ras's gestures, Ras would ask him what he was being so cocky about, who did he think *he* was? Blade never had an answer for those questions, which just proved to Ras that he'd been right about his oldest son all along.

"You ain't right bright, are you, boy?"

"Boy, you are Dumb, with a capital *D*."

"Blade, you are too dumb to know it."

When Ras came across the yard, Blade and Blue were out by the holding pen, watching Snowman through the spaces between the wooden rails. Blade felt awfully sorry for the horse—something he could never admit, because nothing infuriated Ras Ballenger quite so much as somebody who was Dumb with a capital *D* feeling sorry for an animal that he had been abusing. Blade had seen what happened the few times his mama dared to express her pity.

Blue never felt sorry for the animals. In fact, he seemed to get a kick out of observing Ras's methods, and he participated whenever his daddy let him. Ras never allowed him to mess with the horses, unless they were cross-tied, because he was little and the damn sonsabitches might hurt him. Cats were another situation entirely. They couldn't very well hurt anyone, even a little kid, if they were tied up in a gunnysack, which they generally were when they were thrown to the dogs. Anytime a stray cat came around, Blue was always the first to tell Ras. It was a dog-eat-cat world at the Ballengers', and Blue, at four and a half, sure knew how to score points.

Ras came swaggering out to the holding pen, and leaned up against the rails, and eyeballed Snowman—who stood very still, trying not to attract attention. He was a proud horse, or had been a few weeks earlier. The pride was what had gotten him into so much trouble. A man like Ras Ballenger, who had killed filthy Germans (many of whom had not been in uniform) with a bayonet, couldn't be expected to tolerate insolence from a horse. The German civilians had begged to be spared. Not that it had done them a speck of good. Ras had found that immensely pleasurable—having two-legged animals beg for mercy.

Four-legged animals (horses, at least) do not beg. If you inflict pain on a horse, it will do one of three things. It will try to get away. Or it will take the abuse, and stand there quivering, willing to do anything that's asked of it. Or it will try to fight back.

Most of the horses Ras had worked with had started out with the try-to-get-away response and graduated rather quickly to the quivering,-willing-to-do-anything-that's-asked response. Snowman had started out plumb ass-backwards, somewhat willing to do what Ras asked, but (when nothing he did was good enough, and everything he did brought on punishment of one sort or another) he had opted to fight back. It hadn't done him any more good than begging had done the filthy Germans, but there was one difference. Snowman was still alive.

Ras Ballenger didn't have a license to kill another man's horse, the way he had believed he had a license to kill another country's people in the war. He couldn't just bayonet this horse. To do in somebody else's horse, and get away with it, you had to have a reason. You had to be saving the animal from some unspeakable agony that couldn't be fixed. Or you had to find a way to let the horse die on its own.

Everybody who knows anything much about horses knows that

the surest way to get one to die on its own is also the simplest. You just leave the door to the feed room open, and you go off to town (if it happens to be daytime) or you go off to bed (if it happens to be night). A horse doesn't know when to stop eating and doesn't have the ability to throw up. That's all right on the open range, or out in a pasture. Out there, the horse will just get a big grass belly, or it might get the squirts, but if it stands in one place and eats fifty pounds of grain, it will die a hard death.

When horses are afraid of a person, they won't look that person in the eye. It's as if they think that, if they don't see the danger, it has disappeared. Or maybe they just can't stand the stress. Snowman was standing with his eyes turned away from the wiry little man who was leaning against the fence and grinning at him.

Ras laughed out loud. "You best look away, you sonofabitch," he cackled.

"Best look 'way, sum'bitch," Blue parroted.

Ras laughed again, and informed Blue that he was a caution. Blue may or may not have known what a caution was, but he looked up at his daddy and told him that *he* was a caution. Ras laughed out loud again, and picked Blue up and set him on the top fence rail, and pointed to Snowman.

"Do you know what you're lookin' at there?" he asked.

"Horsee," said Blue.

"That's right. Horsee. Dead horsee."

Blue's eyes got wide with surprise, and Blade's eyes got wide with horror.

"Dead horsee," Blue chortled.

Ras sang out, "You hear that, Snowman? You're a dead horsee."

Blade didn't say a word. He just stood there holding on to the fence with both hands. Blue might be the one perched on the top rail, but Blade was the one who felt like he might fall if he let go.

"Just as soon as those welts go down," Ras said.

"Soon's whells go down," echoed Blue.

"Because Mr. Odell Pritchett is gonna wanta examine his horse," Ras said. "And I don't intend to deprive him of the privilege."

Blue had gotten a little lost in all that, but he said it back the best he could.

"Mister Oh hell Pritchett wanta 'zamin he horse, and I don't ten-prive-prittilege!"

Chapter 16

Blade had no idea how long it would take for Snowman's welts to go down, but he knew that, once it happened, that horse was done for. Sickness welled up inside him, followed by fury.

Nothing else his daddy had ever done had had quite this effect on Blade. Everything else he had accepted as just being the way things were. He didn't know and didn't ask himself why this was different. But it was.

All day long, he stewed over it. Ras buzzed around the place mending tack, mucking stalls, cutting the grass in the yard with a sling blade. Blue dogged his tracks, as usual, and (as usual) got patted on the head and told how smart he was. Blade crawled under the porch and sat there in the shadowy semidarkness, drawing pictures with his fingers while his mind tried to figure out what to do.

It wouldn't do any good to plead with his daddy not to kill the horse. That would just get it killed sooner, and maybe ensure that it suffered more in the process. Blade would have liked to call Mr. Odell Pritchett, and tell him what was going on, and ask him to please come get Snowman. But to do that, he'd have to get the man's phone number out of his daddy's billfold, and figure out how to make a long-distance call, and somehow manage to make the call without getting caught. Three mountains he didn't feel nearly big enough to climb.

He wished his daddy would disappear. He didn't exactly wish, the way his mother did, that Ras would die. That kind of wish would have been hard for a boy Blade's age to live with. He just wished that Ras would walk off into the woods, or take off in the truck, and never come back. Now you see him, now you don't. He's gone.

But Ras wasn't gone. He wasn't gone today, and he wouldn't be gone tomorrow. He was here, and he was going to kill the horse, and there was nothing Blade could do to stop him. Unless . . .

(And here, Blade's mind balked a little. Shied away like bare feet from broken glass.)

Unless . . . *he could make the* horse *disappear.*

Blade Ballenger had never been more afraid of his daddy than he was in the moment when he unlatched the chain on the gate to the holding pen and stepped inside with Snowman. Up until that precise instant, if he'd gotten caught, he could have made up some story about why he was outside in the middle of the night, or he could have just clammed up, like anybody would expect from a kid who was too dumb to know it. Either way, there would have been consequences, but Blade was used to consequences. His life was pretty much one consequence after another.

If he got caught now, that would bring consequences of a kind that he'd never known but had had nightmares about. As a precaution, he had kept on his sleepers (his mama's term for whatever shirt and underwear he'd had on that day), instead of putting on britches, because what if his daddy heard him rustling around getting dressed and came in there to see what he was up to?

There was no use thinking about it. Thinking about it wouldn't do any good, and besides, nothing was going to change his mind. He was going to let Snowman out of that lot, and watch him run away to freedom, and then he was going to slip back into the house and get back in bed, and hope that that horse would get all the way to Odell Pritchett's house before Ras Ballenger woke up and the devil came to breakfast.

Of course Blade couldn't begin to guess how far it was to Camden, or how long it would take to get there, or whether a horse had enough gumption to find its way back to where it came from. He was just hoping.

When he had crawled out through his bedroom window, a few minutes ago, the curs had all lifted their heads and trained their eyes on him. He had worried they might set in howling, and wake everybody up, but they'd been seeing him crawl through that window two or three times a week for a while now, so it must have just seemed like business as usual. They didn't even follow him across the yard.

Snowman was standing facing away from the gate, and he didn't move a muscle when Blade came into the lot with him. Blade walked over beside him and stood looking up at him, wondering what to do next. He knew better than to try to drive Snowman out of the lot, because then the horse might take to rearing and whinnying and crashing around, which would get the dogs to barking, and then all hell would break loose. Blade thought about leading Snowman, but Ras had left the horse unhaltered, so there was nothing to reach up and grab hold of. While the boy was examining his options, Snowman wandered over and walked out of the lot on his own.

"Good boy," Blade whispered, almost silently. "Go on. Go!"

But the horse stopped outside the gate and stood beside the fence, like it was waiting for something.

Blade couldn't imagine what the horse could be waiting for. There for sure wasn't one good thing going to happen to it if it stayed around here. But maybe animals don't know those things. A dog, for instance, won't generally run away from home, no matter how it's treated. It might go off to a convention once in a while, but it'll come back when the party's over. If it's able.

Anyway, Snowman should have been lighting a shuck out of there, but he kept standing beside that fence, still as a statue. On impulse,

Blade climbed the fence, and swung one leg over, and maneuvered himself astride the horse, hoping against hope that his luck wouldn't play out now. He tangled both hands in Snowman's mane, and squeezed with his knees to keep from falling off, and dug his bare heels ever so gently into the big horse's sides to get him moving.

"That way," he was saying, silently, inside his mind. "Over there, Snowman. To the creek. All we have to do is follow the creek."

A couple of hours before daylight, Toy Moses did something his daddy never would have done. He cut off a paying customer.

The customer was Bootsie Phillips, a logger, who was one of Never Closes's most faithful regulars. You could always count on Bootsie to come in early, stay until everybody else had gone home, and spend every last dime he had. Never mind that he had a house full of hungry mouths at home, and the money could be better spent on groceries. He'd been there since the bar opened, and he was so drunk he had to hold on to the jukebox to feed it change, but he wasn't showing any signs of being ready to call it a night.

After a while, Toy asked him if he was determined to stay there until his money was all gone, and Bootsie said he damn sure was.

Toy said, "Just a minute," and walked out the back door of the bar, through the house, and into the grocery store. He gathered milk and eggs and bread and bacon and canned goods and flour, and a double handful of penny candy, and he sacked it all up. Then he marched back through the house and into the bar. Right over to where Bootsie was trying not to fall off his stool.

"Your money's all gone," Toy said.

Bootsie tried to look at Toy, but his eyes wouldn't focus.

"Th'hell y'say," he mumbled.

Toy held out his hands and waggled his fingers. Bootsie obediently dug in his pockets, and brought out all his money, and handed it over. Toy jerked his head toward the door.

"Come on. I'll drive you home. You can get somebody to bring you back to get your truck tomorrow."

Bootsie slid down off the stool and informed Toy darkly that he could drive his own damn self home. Either that or he said he was running for president. The way he was slurring his words, you couldn't be sure.

Didn't matter what he said, Toy was propelling him out the door. When they got outside, and Bootsie was stumbling ahead of Toy, making for the parking lot, Toy Moses slipped the money Bootsie had given him into the grocery sack. One logger's wife was about to get a triple surprise. Her husband, home before daylight, with food for the family, and enough money to buy more.

Toy got back to Calla's just at the beginning of what he thought of as the pearly grays—the soft perfection that envelops the world right before dawn. Toy's favorite time of day. Or it used to be, when he was just getting out of bed at that hour, instead of just getting a chance to fall into it. The lights were on in Calla's store, so he knew she was already in there starting coffee and getting ready to take care of her regulars as they began straggling in.

He swung down out of the truck and started toward the store, but then he saw something off to one side that made him do a double take. Out there beside the chicken pen, in Calla's pretty garden—or what was left of Calla's garden—was a horse. A big, white horse covered with filthy smudges. The animal had already gone through the corn, which had been coming on strong, thanks to the fish guts that Toy had been planting out there all spring, and now it was working on the purple hull peas.

Toy didn't wave his arms or holler at the horse, because if it spooked and trampled the squash and tomatoes, that wasn't going to fix the corn and peas. Instead, he just walked on out to the garden, moving easy, keeping his arms to his sides. There was nothing to do but catch the horse, and pen it up, and ask around until he found out who the owner was. That shouldn't take long. You didn't see many horses as pretty as that one would be if somebody gave it a bath and took a brush to it.

When he got closer, he felt like a fool for thinking the horse was just dirty. For not realizing straight off that those dark smudges were dried blood. At first he figured the animal had gotten tangled up in a barbed-wire fence, but that theory didn't hold up. Barbed wire leaves jagged wounds, and the barbs can gouge out chunks of flesh. These marks were straight, crisscrossing each other. They'd been laid on with a whip. It had been a long time since Toy Moses had felt the kind of anger that boiled up in him now.

When he was about ten feet away from the horse, Toy stopped walking and stood still. The horse stopped eating and eyeballed him warily.

"It's all right, boy. You can run away, if you want to. But you'd be better off here than wherever you come from." His voice was soft as well water.

The horse backed away several steps. Toy backed away just as many.

"I sure wish you could talk," Toy said. Then he backed off another couple of feet and broke eye contact with the beast. So, of course, the horse moved toward him. Just a little. Just a fraction. Toy still didn't look at the horse, but he kept on talking, low and peaceful.

"If you could tell me who did this, I'd give him a taste of his own. See how he likes being on the receiving end."

The horse must have had kind treatment at some time, Toy thought, because now he came closer. Toy stood still and waited. When the horse was near enough to touch, Toy resisted the urge to reach out to him. Just breathed in and out, deep and slow. And waited.

The horse offered his face. Toy told it hello the way horses say hello to each other, by breathing into his nose. The horse bobbed his head up and down as if to say that Toy Moses was all right, and he didn't mind visiting with him. In slow, slow motion, Toy took off his belt, and looped it around the horse's neck, and led the mighty Snowman out of Calla Moses's garden.

. . .

The kids didn't know what to think when they came down for breakfast and there wasn't any. Well, there was a pan of cold biscuits on the back of the stove, and a bowl full of eggs on the cook table that Willadee must have been planning to scramble but hadn't gotten around to. Swan's first thought was that somebody else must have died, because she'd never in her life known her mother to forget to feed her children.

When she looked out the kitchen window and saw the sheriff's car parked under a shade tree, she knew for sure that she'd been right. Not that the sight was all that unusual. That car was in that same spot for an hour or so most nights, while the sheriff and his deputy were in Never Closes, but the sheriff had never come around in the daytime except when Papa John shot himself. So this was bad.

The only person left in the family who was old enough to die was Grandma Calla, but it couldn't be her, because there she was standing beside the sheriff, both of them watching something that Swan couldn't see because Uncle Toy's truck was in the way.

"Oh, no," Swan breathed. Tragic. Her mind was going ninety to nothing, conjuring up images of all the terrible things that could have happened, and who they could have happened to.

"Oh, no, what?" Noble asked. He and Bienville had gotten themselves cold biscuits, and were poking holes in them with their fingers. Pouring Blackburn-Made syrup into the wells they'd made.

Swan didn't answer. She was already out the door.

Chapter 17

Sheriff Early Meeks was born prematurely, back at the turn of the century, and he'd been Early ever since. Early was the name his daddy gave him, thinking it was cute, and everybody agreed that it was, even Early, once he got big enough to have an opinion. Early was more than a name. It was who he *was*. Sunday School started at 10:00 A.M., so he was there at 9:45. He was supposed to show up for work at 8:30, so he came in at 8:00. He never seemed to be in a hurry, but he was always, always early.

Sheriff Meeks was an extreme sort of man. Extremely tall, extremely lean, and (for the most part) extremely just. Once in a while, his idea of justice varied somewhat from the letter of the law, and when that happened, he bent the law like a coat hanger.

Years ago, when Yam Ferguson had turned up in his own front yard with his head on pretty much backward, Early had been the first lawman on the scene. The body was behind the wheel of Yam's convertible, and the engine of the car was still warm, but Yam wasn't. Even if Early hadn't already been handed all the pieces of this puzzle, it wouldn't have taken much imagination to figure out that Yam didn't drive himself home that night.

Everybody knew that Yam had been messing around with the wives of at least half a dozen soldiers who were off fighting for their country. Knew it, and despised him for it. They also knew that Toy Moses was the only one of those soldiers who had come home that evening.

This they knew because, when Toy got off the bus in Magnolia, he caught a ride with Joe Bill Rader, who lived a few miles past the cut-off to Toy's place. As soon as Joe Bill got home, he told his wife, Omega, how Toy, who never had been much for conversation, talked the whole solid way about how glad he was to be home, and how he hadn't told Bernice he was coming because he didn't want her going to a lot of fuss and trouble getting things ready for him. When they got in sight of Toy's house, and saw the tail of Yam's car sticking out on the other side, Toy's whole face went slack for a second, and then he asked Joe Bill not to stop. Said he'd forgot he needed cigarettes, and thought he'd just go on down to his mama's store and get some. The last time Joe Bill saw Toy, he was standing in front of that store looking like a man who wished he'd been sent home in a pine box.

Omega wasted no time calling her sister, Almarie, who couldn't be blamed for passing the news on to a few trusted friends. One of those friends was Early's wife, Patsy, so Early already had a little background information when he got that phone call sometime after midnight. The one from a man whose voice he recognized.

"I thought you ought to know that Yam Ferguson is dead," the voice said. "I expect you'll be wanting to talk to me, but I'd appreciate it if you could give me a few hours first."

Early had given the man more than a few hours. He'd given him all these years, and still had not asked him a question. He knew all he needed to know, without even thinking about it. Toy had left the store and gone back to his house and walked in on something he couldn't handle. Yam had turned out dead, and Toy hadn't wanted the body to be found at his place. If that had happened, Bernice would have been the talk of the town. Of course, she turned out to be anyway, but since Toy moved the body, she could at least pretend to be as much in the dark as anybody else regarding what had become of Yam Ferguson.

There wasn't a mark on Yam's car when Early got there, but the front end was bashed in like a sonofabitch by the time he called in to the office and told the night man that he'd been passing by Yam Ferguson's house a little while ago and saw his car in the yard. He said he stopped to find out if Yam was sick or drunk or what, and when he got up to the car, he could tell it had been wrecked. Looked like maybe Yam had run into a tree, and the poor bastard must have broken his neck from the impact. How he managed to drive himself home was a mystery.

The Ferguson family didn't buy that story for a minute, and they raised a big stink, but it didn't do a bit of good. Judge Graves had lost a son in the war, and he'd been dying a little himself since that day. The way he saw it, Yam had gotten just what was coming to him.

The first thing Swan asked when she got out to Grandma Calla and Sheriff Meeks was "Who died?"

Grandma Calla said, "Nobody yet." Which Swan took to mean "You'd better watch your step today, Swan Lake."

Grandma Calla hadn't taken her eyes off of whatever she was looking at, so Swan turned her eyes in the same direction, and she practically did die, at what she saw. Over in the calf lot, Willadee was stroking and soothing a huge white horse while Uncle Toy swabbed turpentine onto the animal's oozing wounds. The horse quivered— maybe scared, maybe just hurting—but it stood the treatment without a sound.

Swan went queasy, and wanted to turn away, but she couldn't.

Sheriff Meeks made a contemptuous racket in his throat and spat off to one side.

"What's the matter with that horse?" Swan wanted to know. "How'd we get it?" What she really wanted to know was whether it could be hers, just hers. She could already see herself taking care of it and spoiling it and being the best friend it could ever have. If that horse belonged to her, it would never want for anything, not one solitary thing. She would brush it and pet it and feed it sugar cubes. Swan had read in books about kids feeding sugar cubes to horses, and it sounded like a sure way to make one come when you called it. Grandma Calla didn't keep sugar cubes in her kitchen, but she had some in the store, and Swan would talk her out of a box, she'd even work for it if she had to. Doing things for that horse—*her horse*— would not be work, it would be a labor of love, and she wouldn't mind, she'd put her whole heart into it. Shoot, her whole heart was already there.

"We didn't get *it*," Grandma Calla said. "That horse got *us*. And not for long. Soon as we find out who it belongs to, we'll have to give it back." Her mouth went tight and bitter when she said that last part.

"Give it back to whoever did *that* to it?" Swan crackled angrily.

Sheriff Meeks said, "A man's property is a man's property. The law don't say how a man can use what's his."

Which just flattened Swan. For a second. Then her eyes started snapping, and she threw her arms out like she was being crucified. *"Well, if you're not going to do anything about it,"* she hollered at the top of her lungs, *"what the hell are you doing here?"* She had forgotten about not cussing in front of any grown-up except Uncle Toy.

Sheriff Meeks looked at her for a second, real steady, trying to make her cringe. He just didn't know Swan.

"I'm here because your uncle called me," he answered, finally. And then he asked Calla, "You reckon there's any chance that kid'll ever grow into her mouth?"

Early didn't stay long. He'd promised to meet Bud Jenkins in town at the café at eight o'clock, and it was already going on seven. Counting that it took nearly half an hour to get there, that didn't leave him much time for being early. Before he left, though, he wrote down a description of the horse and promised to get the word out that it had been found.

Noble and Bienville had come outside by now and were petting the horse with syrupy fingers. Snowman didn't mind. Of course, the kids didn't know that his name was Snowman. They were fighting over what to call him. Grandma Calla resolved the matter by informing them that they were not going to keep the horse, but if they *did,* it was going to be *her* horse, it was her garden the thing had torn up, after all, and nobody who didn't act right and help with the chores was ever going to get to ride it. Plus, as long as it stayed on the premises, its name would be John.

"*John?*" Bienville yelped.

"Whoever heard of a horse named *John?*" Noble complained loudly.

Grandma Calla didn't feel she owed them an explanation, she could name her horse anything she pleased, but she told Willadee in private that she'd caught herself a couple of times lately saying her husband's name when nobody was around. Now if anyone caught her doing it, she could pretend she was thinking out loud about the horse.

Blade was fear-struck by what he had done and what his daddy would do when he found out. It wasn't a matter of *if.* Blade knew that, as surely as he knew that his arms and legs were getting scratched bloody by all the blackberry vines and saw briers that kept snaring his arms and legs.

About the time Toy Moses was returning from taking Bootsie Phillips home, Blade was crawling back through his own bedroom window, unaware that he was leaving smears of blood on the sill. The house was dark and quiet, not a sound anywhere except for Blue sucking his thumb in his sleep. Blade hated sleeping in the same bed with his little brother, mainly because Blue always let loose with the

waterworks sometime in the wee hours, but also because of that sucking sound.

Blade slid into bed, staying as far away as possible from his
brother and the puddle collected by the rubber sheet that protected
the mattress but not the little boys who slept on it. The pee was cold,
and smelled foul, and seeped into his sleepers, making them cling
wetly to his skin, but that wasn't why he was shivering.

At precisely 5:30 in the morning, Ras Ballenger headed out to his
barn to feed the livestock and discovered that Odell Pritchett's horse
was missing. Seeing that gate standing open sent shock waves up and
down his spine. Having a horse stolen is bad enough when it belongs
to you, and its hide is not laid open in a dozen places. But when it's
someone else's animal, and you're going to have to explain to its
owner how it came to be missing, and (once it's found) how it came
to be in that condition, that complicates matters considerably.

What Ras couldn't figure out, though, was how anybody got on
the place and took the gelding without his dogs letting him know
about it. Those dogs didn't go up to strangers with their tails wag-
ging—and nobody was allowed to come around here enough to be
anything but a stranger.

Snowman hadn't managed to let himself out of the lot, that much
was for sure. The gate had been fastened with a chain that was looped
around the gatepost, with the two ends held together by a clasp that
only fingers could open. A smart horse can lift a chain off a hook, but
it can't undo a clasp.

So someone had done this. The question was who. It couldn't have
been Odell Pritchett. Odell wasn't the type to come in the dark of
night—why should he, it was his horse, he could come for it in broad
daylight. And even if he had been the one, he'd have come in a truck,
pulling a trailer, both of which are noisy. Granted, he could have
parked out on the road, and walked in, and led his horse out. But
there again—why hadn't the dogs done their job?

Ras dragged his eyes away from that gate and the lot that didn't have a horse inside, and he turned around and stared for a moment at his house.

Geraldine always got up even earlier than Ras did. One thing he could not abide was a lazy woman. When she heard his boots scraping on the porch, her stomach clenched up a little, because he'd be wanting his breakfast on the table when he walked in the door, and she was just now starting the bacon. Since when did he get the feeding done in less than five minutes?

You could always feel him coming into a room, because the air changed to fit his mood. When he was boiling mad, you felt the heat, and even when he was just normal (at least for him), you could feel the tension popping all around. Right now, though, the air felt flat and dead. Which hardly ever happened.

Geraldine cut her eyes at Ras as he sauntered in, but he never glanced her way. He was getting himself a mug of coffee, which also hardly ever happened. A man breaks his back to provide for his family, he likes his coffee poured and handed to him. She'd heard him say that enough times to know it by heart.

Geraldine's insides started doing somersaults. She was used to her husband stomping around ranting and raving. But the way he was now, all easy and calm—that, she wasn't used to.

"You're awful quiet," she said. She didn't mean to speak first, but she couldn't stand the strain.

Ras sat down at the table and blew on his coffee, gazing at her over the rim of the mug. His eyes looked almost gentle.

"So are you," he said back. Sounding sly. "You was last night, anyways."

She stared at him, uncomprehending. Somehow she had done something wrong, and she had no idea what it was.

"I don't remember bein' quiet last night."

"Well you sure was. Like a little mouse, you was quiet." He skimmed his fingertips over the tabletop, like a little mouse, running silently in one direction. Skimmed them back the other way. Zig-zag, zig-zag. Back and forth. That was one busy little mouse.

Geraldine tried to remember being quiet the night before. Had Ras spoken to her and she hadn't answered? Had she walked past him without speaking when he expected to be spoken to?

The bacon was about to scorch, so she turned it over and pressed the pieces down flat with the spatula.

"Well," she said, "I reckon I was quiet while I was asleep."

Ras smiled. *Smiled*. Like she had just said the magic words.

"Seems to me you got that wrong. You was quiet while *I* was asleep."

She frowned. This whole thing had a bad feeling. Whatever quicksand she had fallen into, there wouldn't be any getting out of it now. You fall into quicksand and you do nothing, you go under. You try to get out, you go under faster.

"I don't know what on earth you're talkin' about," she flared. Might as well go under fast, and get it over with.

Ras said, "Maybe you was sleepwalkin'. Sometimes folks do things when they're sleepwalkin' that they regret when they wake up."

Geraldine wagged her head side to side, the picture of confusion.

"If I've ever in my life walked in my sleep, I don't know about it." She meant to sound emphatic, but the words had a tentative tone. As if she couldn't really be sure.

Ras played his tongue around the inside of his mouth, poking at his cheek, making a lump on the outside that pooched out and wiggled. Geraldine felt a crazy urge to laugh. She didn't, though. The way Ras was looking at her—like she was a mouse all right, and he was a cat, about to pounce—laughing probably wouldn't be the smartest thing she could do.

She took a paper sack out of the cabinet under the sink and laid it on a plate. That was to absorb the grease from the bacon as she transferred it from the skillet to the plate.

"All right," she said. "What'd I do?"

"You don't remember."

"I remember goin' to bed."

"You don't remember gittin' up."

She sighed. This was getting old. "I just got up twenty minutes ago. Sure I remember gittin' up." She brought the plate over and set it down on the table. "Now are you goin' to tell me what I did?"

"No—*you* are gonna tell *me*." He helped himself to a slice of bacon and munched on it thoughtfully, smiling again. "And since I don't have a horse to train, I've got all day."

Chapter 18

In Blade's dreams, he was running along the edge of the creek that led from his daddy's farm to the back side of the Moses place, and the briers along the path kept reaching for him—grabbing hold of his ankles and growing fast as lightning, right up his legs. He could feel them latching on with those fishhook thorns, and he wanted to get still, so the fishhooks would stop biting in deeper. But he couldn't stop, because there was a chicken hawk flying overhead—a great big chicken hawk, he'd never seen one so huge—and it was going to get him if he slowed down even a little, probably would get him no matter how fast he ran.

Blade had never felt so small. He must be no more than the size of a rabbit.

The chicken hawk swooped down, talons stretched out like long, curved knives. Blade didn't want to look up. Couldn't keep from looking up. And when he looked, he saw the chicken hawk's face. Saw it plain and clear, and wished he hadn't.

It was his daddy.

Blade screamed, but there was no sound, just suffocating silence. He tried harder and harder, screaming from his guts, from his toes. Helpless, hopeless, exploding inside, noiselessly; rabbits can't scream.

The chicken hawk laughed. Raw, acid laughter. Then it dove lower, and Blade screamed again, and this time there was sound. Sound all around, shredding the air.

Blade was jarred awake and sat up with a start. Heart thudding. So relieved he could cry because the dream was over—until he realized that it wasn't over after all, it was just beginning.

Blue had waked up, too, and was lying there snuffling, clutching the pee-stained covers. Blade told him to hush and crept out of bed.

The screaming, which had been coming from the kitchen, stopped abruptly. The next sound was even worse.

Ras had Geraldine by the neck and was bending her backward over the sink, with her face under the tap. She was struggling and gurgling. Swallowing water, and sucking it into her lungs, and trying to talk, and just gurgling.

Ras jerked her upright and leaned back out of the way while she hacked and heaved and spewed.

"How's your memory?" Ras asked.

She coughed explosively. Shook her head.

"The horse," Ras said patiently. "What did you do with the horse?"

Blade had come into the room by now, and his legs buckled. This was about Snowman! He'd thought that *he* was the one who would be in danger. It had never once dawned on him that anyone else might catch the blame.

Geraldine had recovered enough that she was trying to wrench away from Ras. Trying to pry his fingers off her neck. Which just made Ras squeeze tighter.

"—didn't touch—horse," Geraldine croaked.

Ras shook her, hard.

"Didn't touch him, but you opened the gate and let him out, didn't you?"

Geraldine's face was bloodred from all the coughing and wheezing she'd been doing. Her nose was running, too.

"I didn't—" she started.

Ras forced her back over the sink and held her head under the tap, like before. She whipped her head side to side, but it didn't help. She still had to breathe, and the water was still running into her mouth and nose. She started gurgling again.

"Stupid sow," Ras snarled. "I never seen such a stupid sow."

Blade couldn't let his daddy kill his mama, and it looked as if that was about to happen. So he grabbed his daddy's coffee mug off the table and slung it across the room. It hit Ras in the back, right between the shoulder blades.

Ras turned loose of Geraldine and whirled around, but Blade Ballenger was gone.

Grandma Calla made what she'd said stick. Nobody could go near her horse unless they'd been behaving right and helping with the chores. Swan and Noble and Bienville were so nice to each other and everybody else all day that Willadee started leaning over and sniffing them when they went past. She said any mama knows her own offspring by smell, even if they get to acting too strange to be recognizable any other way.

And work? Those children worked. They swept the porch, and weeded the flower beds, and picked a bushel of crowder peas, all by eleven-thirty. After that, the boys washed the grungy old gas pumps with soap and water and polished them up to a fare-thee-well, while Swan used vinegar and newspaper to clean every glass surface in Calla's store. It got so shiny around there that the customers started shading their eyes against the glare when they got out of their cars.

Every once in a while the kids would go up to Grandma Calla, and gaze at her adoringly, and tell her she was the dearest *old person* in the world and they were so glad to be her grandchildren. Grandma

Calla would shake her head and tell them that she didn't know whose grandchildren they were, but she was sure glad they'd stopped by to help out with things.

By midafternoon, Willadee decided that the kids had been good long enough. It was beginning to sap her energy, watching them zip around so fast. Calla admitted that she'd been feeling right dizzy herself, plus she'd already gotten more work out of them than she'd ever dreamed was in there.

The kids were set free, but Grandma Calla warned them again to stay away from her horse. She knew how kids can't resist the urge to climb up on anything that's taller than them, especially if it has a mane and a tail.

"Just think how you would feel if you was in the same shape as John," she said. "How would you like it if a bunch of young'uns got up on your back and set right square on your sore places?"

Bienville pointed out to her that they could never be in the same shape as John, they had two legs each, and he had four.

Grandma Calla didn't appreciate the logic. "Well, you better be thankful that's not the only difference," she said. "That horse has took a drubbing."

She didn't add (as she ordinarily would) that they could all get drubbings, too, if they didn't straighten up and fly right. They had already straightened up, they were flying like swallows, and besides, she didn't feel like making threatening noises that day. Something about looking at that horse, at those marks someone had laid on him, laid something bare inside her soul. This John was doing something the other John had stopped doing long before he took it in his head to kill himself. This John was bringing out the tenderness in Calla Moses.

It was Noble who persuaded Grandma Calla to let them take John along with them to the Badlands. Since they'd be tracking Outlaws through Unforgiving Terrain, they'd be traveling on foot anyway. When terrain is unforgiving, you have to squat down every once in a while and squench up your eyes real narrow, and study the ground to see whether the rocks have been disturbed, or if a bootheel has left an impression in the dust. You might also see where somebody has hawked a loogie, which is a sure sign of Outlaws. A lot of Outlaws have rattling coughs. Anyway, you can't do a good job of tracking if you're forever getting on and off a horse. It takes the starch out of you and slows you down.

Calla didn't see what the harm could be in letting the kids take the horse on an adventure, as long as all they did was lead him, but she said she'd better not find out they'd been on his back.

Leading him was all they planned to do, they promised. It was all they were gonna do, they *swore*.

"And we'd never break our word to a sweet little old thing like you," Swan vowed passionately.

Calla had never been called "old" so many times in one day, and she hadn't been "little" in so long she couldn't remember, but she let Swan's comment go. The sooner the kids were off in the Badlands looking for Outlaws and loogies, the sooner she could sit down and think about how quiet it was.

Ras Ballenger didn't have to wonder how that mug came to hit him between the shoulder blades. He went tearing through the house, heading straight for the boys' room.

Blue was sitting up in bed squalling, but for once, Ras didn't pay him any mind. He marched over to the open window and raked his eyes across the yard. There was no sign of Blade. It was when Ras leaned against the windowsill to think what to do next that he noticed the rusty smears of dried blood on the woodwork. He licked a finger and rubbed it across one of the stains, and the color came off on his skin.

"I should've chunked that boy to the dogs the day he was born," Ras said.

. . .

Ras wondered how Blade had gotten cut up when he was doing his dirty work last night. Maybe he took the horse out on the road to let it go and he fell on the gravel and scraped the hide off his arms and legs. Or maybe he ran into something he couldn't see in the dark.

Ras wasn't convinced that Blade could have "taken" Snowman *anywhere,* but whatever he had done with Snowman, he was going to regret it. More important right now, though, was finding Odell Pritchett's horse.

Ras took off in his truck, and he didn't have to go far. The first place he stopped was Calvin Furlough's, because Calvin had a reputation for knowing everybody's business and telling everything he knew to anybody who would listen. Ras found Calvin inside his shop, popping the dents out of the hood of a Nash Rambler with a rubber mallet, and sure enough—Calvin said he'd gone down to Miz Calla's store earlier for some Bull of the Woods and couldn't even get waited on, because the whole family was congregated out beside the barn, all circled around a big white horse. Finally, he'd just helped himself to the chewing tobacco and left his money on the counter.

"Sheriff Meeks was there, too," Calvin said. "Don't ask me why."

Early Meeks was tearing paper matches out of a matchbook and flipping them at a cottonmouth moccasin that sat coiled on the corner of his desk with its mouth wide open and its fangs exposed. Early had killed the snake in a bog behind his house a couple of years back, and had had the taxidermist fix it so that an ashtray would fit inside the coil. In case it was true what Early had heard about the fangs of poisonous snakes being just as dangerous after the snakes were dead as when they were alive, those had been painted over with a clear sealant that was turning yellow now.

The ashtray was half-full of paper matches when Ras Ballenger stormed into the office, braying indignantly that he'd had a horse stolen the night before. He said his dogs had waked him up barking, and he'd come running out of the house with his shotgun, but by that time, the thief was lighting out of there, riding the best horse he had on the place. He didn't shoot, because he didn't want to hit the horse.

Early leaned back in his chair and listened, the way a lawman is supposed to. He didn't interrupt Ras once, just let the little turd hustler tell him everything without meaning to.

"That animal was in top shape when it left my place." Ras banged his fist on Early's desk. "And it better be in the same condition when I git it back."

Early scratched his ear and frowned. "You don't think *I* took the horse," he said.

Ras coughed and spluttered explosively. "I wasn't accusin' you. I was reportin' a crime!"

"I couldn't tell. Sounded like you was saying you're holding me responsible for anything that might've happened to the animal."

"I wasn't sayin' anything of the kind."

Early looked blank. Like this was all deeper than he could fathom.

"So you're thinking—that the thief rode the horse off your place, and maybe decided he didn't like it enough to keep it—so he hurt it some way, just for spite—and left it where I'd be able to find it?" He scratched his ear again. "Usually, a man's gonna steal a horse, he'll back a trailer up to the pasture and cut the fence and load the critter on, and hightail it to the next county. I never heard of anybody going afoot onto somebody else's property, right up close to their house, walking in amongst their dogs and all—and taking a horse and riding it out, just so he could mistreat it—and then taking off on foot again. I wonder how the sonofabitch got home."

Ras tightened up like a spring. He knew he was being messed with, but now he had no choice except to gut this out.

"All I know is, it got stole. And it's your job to git it back for me."

Early smiled. It was a tolerant smile that he reserved for folks he wouldn't piss on if they were to catch fire. Then he stood up, like a ladder unfolding. Ras reacted by pulling himself up as tall as he could, which wasn't very. Early halfway expected him to jump on top of the desk so he could be the one looking down on somebody.

"I'll ask around," Early said.

He didn't let on that he knew where the horse was, and Ras didn't let on that he knew that Early knew. They both had their little secrets.

After Ras left, Early sat back down and tore another paper match out of the matchbook, and flipped it into the ashtray that was nestled into the coil of the cottonmouth. Through the window, he could see Ras strutting across to the curb, where the red Apache waited. The summer sun played over the little man's bronzy skin and midnight hair, making him gleam like a shiny water moccasin.

Watching Ras climb up into his truck and gun it out of there, Early couldn't help thinking that there was a man who was overdue for killing. When the time came, he'd be more than glad to do the honors, but there was no telling who or what was going to suffer in the meantime. He kind of wished he could do it early.

Chapter 19

Ras knew that pretty soon, unless he could figure some way around it, he was going to have to call Odell Pritchett and tell him that his horse was missing. It galled him to have to say it was missing when it wasn't missing at all, it just wasn't where it was supposed to be. There ought to be a way to get it back.

But there wasn't. He'd already overplayed his hand by blowing off his mouth to Early Meeks about how the horse had been stolen. Now Meeks knew whose place the animal had come off of, and that was the first place he would look if it was to go missing again.

When Ras got home, he did chores around the place, and ate what Geraldine put in front of him, and drew back his hand every time she opened her mouth to speak. He didn't even talk to Blue.

He didn't call Odell yet, because he hadn't finished thinking out how to handle the situation, and he still did not go looking for Blade, even though Geraldine blubbered and begged. He wasn't in a hurry. Let the little bastid see how he liked going hungry and sleeping on the ground. Then, in a day or so, he could see how he liked what else was in store for him.

All afternoon, Blade Ballenger hung out near the creek, watching the Lake children pretend to track outlaws. Actually, they didn't do all that much tracking, they were too busy making over the horse. They were leading it down to the creek for a drink, and scratching its ears and its belly, and when it lay down in the tall meadow grass, they lay down all around it and used it for a pillow.

Blade wanted to go play with them, but he didn't dare show himself. He didn't think the girl would run tell her folks about him (she had let him sleep in her bed that once, after all), but he wasn't so sure about the boys. Besides, those children were fully dressed and reasonably clean, whereas he was still wearing what he'd had on the night before—the same tattered shirt and underwear, filthy with his own blood and his brother's pee and dirt from hiding under the house after he jumped out the window this morning. He'd stayed under there, afraid to breathe, until his daddy tore out of the yard in the truck, and then he'd made a beeline for the woods.

So now, here he was. He couldn't go home, and there was nowhere else to go. All he could do was stay still and watch those kids playing with the horse he had saved, and wait for something to happen.

But staying still made it hard for him to keep his eyes open. He was dead for sleep, plus he hadn't eaten a bite all day, and he was running on empty. His eyes were dry and grainy, so he blinked them, hard, and that was all it took. Once his eyelids came together, they wouldn't pull apart for the longest time. When he finally got them open again, it was dark, and the children were gone.

Blade had been to the Moses place enough times that he knew the ebb and flow of life here. He knew how to blend into the shadows as he crept across the yard. He also knew where to step in the kitchen so as not to hit a board that creaked, and he knew where everything was kept. Leftover corn bread would be on the back of the stove, covered with a dish towel. Lately, there'd even been pieces of cake, or sometimes a slice of pie. Other leftovers would be in the icebox, sometimes stored in covered bowls, but often as not, in lidded mason jars. These he preferred, because he could grab the jars and go, instead of digging in the covered bowls and hoping no one heard. Blade suspected that women liked their bowls, and would get upset if one disappeared, but nobody worried about a missing mason jar.

He knew a lot for a boy his age, but he didn't know everything. He didn't know, for instance, that Sam Lake sometimes sat in the dining room, in the dark, after everyone else had gone to bed, thinking about his situation and wondering how to make it better. Samuel had spotted Blade a couple of times sneaking jars of string beans and chunks of corn bread, and he had started keeping up with whether the boy had been around by leaving his dessert on the stove after supper ("for later," he told Willadee, in case he got hungry during the night).

On this particular night, Samuel was in the dining room again, and when Blade stole out of the house, Samuel trailed him. Far enough behind that the kid had no idea he was being followed.

Blade holed up in the barn and ate his supper with gusto. When he was done, he hid the jars under a pile of spoiled hay with the growing accumulation of empties. Then he burrowed into the hay himself, curling up like a fox in its den.

He slept.

Sometime during the night, a crisp sheet settled over him like a cloud, and a set of clean clothes was laid out on top of the sheet. The sheet smelled fresh as sunshine, and when daybreak came sifting through the cracks in the old barn walls, it took Blade a few seconds to wake up and realize what had happened, and what it meant.

It meant he was home.

Chapter 20

At breakfast, Samuel asked the rest of the family whether they'd ever noticed a little black-headed boy hanging around looking like he didn't have anyplace to live, and everybody looked confused as the devil, especially Swan. She said she sure hadn't noticed any little black-headed boy hanging around, she hadn't ever noticed one solitary soul hanging around, if she had, she'd have told a grown-up so fast it would've made their heads spin.

Willadee took note of her daughter's emphatic denial and put the note in a mental file to be examined later.

"Well, I've seen the little shaver several times," Samuel said. "As a matter of fact, I saw him just last night, taking food from the kitchen again."

Grandma Calla squinted at Samuel and cocked her eyebrows way up nearly to her hairline.

She said, "Again," kind of like she was asking a question, and kind of like she was providing an echo.

"I reckon I should have said something sooner," Samuel admitted.

"He's been coming and going for weeks. At first I thought surely he had a family, and maybe they were just short on groceries, but last night made me wonder."

Then he told them about trailing the kid out to the barn, and how the kid had burrowed down into the hay to go to sleep, and how he'd looked so pitiful, like a little lost dog that had been dumped beside the road.

"I took one of your good sheets out there and covered him up," Samuel said to Calla. "I hope you don't mind."

Calla said that she didn't mind, sheets were made for covering people up, there wasn't any other reason to own one.

When Bienville found out that Samuel had also taken some of his clothes out there because the little boy was wearing filthy rags, he sat up so straight and proud you'd have thought he just found out he was kin to Abe Lincoln.

"Well, I sure don't grudge him the use of my clothes," he said grandly. "What's the use of having more clothes than you can wear at one time, if you're not willing to share?"

Down at the end of the table, Bernice was holding hands with Uncle Toy like the good wife she was determined to appear, and she was about to choke on all this milk of human kindness.

"Well," she observed in just the silkiest tone. "We have to find out who his parents are, and take him home. They must be beside themselves with worry."

Swan said, "Maybe his parents aren't good people. Maybe his daddy is a mean old sonofa——"

Samuel looked at her, hard, and she realized what she'd almost said, just in time to alter the outcome.

"—*biscuit eater,* and the kid is scared to go home."

Willadee made another mental note.

Toy Moses pushed back his plate and lit a cigarette.

After breakfast, the family gathered at the window and watched the barn for signs of life.

"I bet he's already come out and gone." Noble was disappointed. He'd been looking forward to meeting a little kid who slept in people's barns and stole food out of people's kitchens late at night. Now that kid must be *formidable*.

"If he's eating here and sleeping here, where would he go?" asked Willadee.

And Calla said, "I feel just like I'm waiting for a cow to calve."

Blade Ballenger had tried on Bienville's clothes and found that the shirt came down to his knees, which was good, because the pants were so big on him that they kept slipping down there, too.

He hated to put on such nice clean clothes, because he was so dirty, and he hated to go out into the open, because he knew he looked foolish. For a little while, he stayed in the barn, both hopeful and afraid that someone would come out of the house. For sure, they must be nice people; only nice people would come down and cover a kid up in the middle of the night with a sheet that smelled like sunshine. So that was the hopeful side. But he was still afraid.

After a while, he ventured out of the barn and sat down crosslegged, staring at the house. And waited.

They all saw him at once, and they all started oohing and aahing as if they really were watching a calf get born. All but Toy, who had figured out who Samuel was talking about even before the kid came out of the barn, and Bernice, who simply couldn't get excited about the same things everybody else did.

"There he is! There he is!" Noble was yammering, and Bienville said, "Well, I'll be dawg," and Calla said, "Now, ain't he something in Bienville's clothes?"

Willadee glanced at Samuel, proud of him for what he'd done, but he wouldn't look back. He was feeling far too much to look anybody in the eye, even Willadee.

Swan started for the door. "I think y'all better let me be the one to go talk to him," she said. "I'm good with little kids."

Willadee's mental notebook was filling up fast.

Blade didn't move a muscle when he saw Swan barreling out of the house and coming his way. She was across the yard in nothing flat, and was standing right in front of him before he hardly knew it.

"Don't let on like you know me!" she hissed. "My folks might get mad if they find out I let you stay in my room that time."

Blade's eyes got big and round, and he started to get up and run off. He didn't like to be around when folks got mad.

Swan laid a hand on his arm and held him back. "Don't worry," she reassured him. "When my folks get mad, nothing much happens."

Blade relaxed a little.

"How come you to sleep in our barn last night?" Swan asked.

Blade shrugged elaborately.

Swan said, "I mean, it's all right. It's all right as everything. I was just wondering."

Blade shrugged again and tugged Bienville's britches up under his armpits to keep them from falling off.

Swan slung an arm around his shoulders and gave him a conspiratorial look. "Well, anyhow," she said, "I'll bet you're hungry. So you just come on up to the house, and my mama will fix you something to eat, and I'll tell you on the way what to say and what to keep quiet about."

You never saw a small child eat as much as Blade Ballenger ate that morning, and you never saw so many folks gang around watching with such fascination. Swan was sitting right beside him, so she could poke him if he got mixed up on what not to say. Nobody asked him any uncomfortable questions, though. Mainly things like "You want some more butter on those pancakes?" and "You got room for another couple strips of bacon?" Things he naturally said yes to. He didn't volunteer any other information. Swan did, though.

"His name is Blade," she announced, as if that was something she'd just found out two minutes ago. "His folks got carried off by the tornado, and he doesn't have anybody to take care of him, so like as not, we're gonna have to adopt him."

Toy was on the other side of the room, leaning against the door-jamb, and he nearly fell over at the sheer magnitude of that whopper. He understood why Swan had told it, though. She'd seen the way Ras Ballenger treated the boy that day in front of the store, and he knew she wouldn't want him to have to go back to more of the same.

Toy wasn't the only one who saw the holes in Swan's story. Samuel knew for a fact that the kid had been coming around since before the storm. As for Willadee and Calla, they simply knew when Swan was lying. Noble and Bienville couldn't tell for sure, but Bernice (not having kids or maternal instincts or any experience with liars—herself excluded) bought the tale hook, line, and sinker.

"You can't adopt a child just because it's an orphan," she told Swan.

"He's not an it," Swan bristled.

"Well, of course, he's not. He's a little boy who's lost his family, and little boys who've lost their families have to be turned over to the Welfare, for their own good."

Blade gave her a look that said he didn't know what she was talking about, but he didn't like the sound of it.

"Nobody's turning him over to anybody yet," Grandma Calla put in. "Why, my goodness, we haven't even heard the whole story."

She nodded for Swan to continue, just as if she thought the truth might suddenly start pouring out of the girl's mouth.

Swan hadn't actually planned to continue. She had more or less expected that Blade would be invited to move in, and that would be that. In the back of her mind, she knew that Blade's folks would try to get him back, but some things you can't think about until you absolutely have to.

Grandma Calla was looking at her expectantly. She had to say something.

"Well," she started, "he's been right tore up over the loss of his loved ones—"

Samuel said, "Now, Swan, God's listening."

He'd always taught his children to tell the truth and trust God for the outcome, and now did seem like a good time for her to test the principle. But she had gone too far to turn back.

"I know," she said, solemnly. "And God knows how tore up he is."

Samuel didn't have it in him to call Swan on her fabrication. Not here and now, with that little boy looking at her like she was an angel of light. And looking at Samuel as if he held his life in his hands.

So it was Samuel who backtracked. "I reckon we can hear the whole story later on."

Swan was so glad he said that.

"Right now," Samuel went on, "I've got to get to work, and you children need to be some help around here."

"Oh, they don't have to be any help today," Grandma Calla chirruped. "They was so much help yesterday, I'm still not over it."

Once the kids had gone out to play, Bernice cleared off the table while Willadee filled the sink with hot, soapy water.

"I just cannot understand," Bernice said, "why nobody's concerned enough to notify the authorities about that poor little orphan."

"Because he's not an orphan," Toy told her. "His folks live around the bend, at the end of that lane that cuts off through the chinaberry thicket."

Bernice almost dropped the stack of dishes she was carrying. "He's *Ras Ballenger's* boy?"

"Who's Ras Ballenger?" Willadee asked. She'd been gone from these parts for a long time. The Ballenger family had moved in after Samuel spirited her off to Louisiana.

"Satan's stepson," Calla said. "At least, that's the feeling I get when I look at him."

"Well, the child can't stay here," Bernice protested. "I will not sleep in a house where a runaway child is being harbored."

Calla wanted to tell Bernice that there was a whole world out there she could sleep in, but she managed to hold her tongue.

Samuel said, "I'll take him home on my way into town."

Willadee and Calla tried not to look anguished, although they were.

Out back, Noble, Bienville, and Swan were showing Blade the Territory.

"Over yonder are the Badlands," Noble said, indicating the cow pasture. "And back over there"—he waved toward the creek—"is the Big River."

Blade nodded soberly and hitched up Bienville's britches. Noble jerked his head in the general direction of the chicken pen.

"Now, over here, is the saloon. You can't really go in there, because that big, speckled rooster has spurs that'll rip you ragged, but you can stand around outside and talk about how you'd sure like a glass of sarsaparilla."

Blade nodded again. There was a lot to remember.

Noble pointed at the calf lot, where Snowman was standing. "And over there's the Box Canyon, where we trick Outlaws into holing up so we can shoot 'em as they ride out."

Blade's eyes lit up at sight of the horse.

Swan put her arm around him, like they were old buddies. "The biggest thing you have to remember in the Territory," she instructed, "is that it's the Good Guys against the Bad Guys, and the Good Guys always win."

Blade hoped he'd get to be a Good Guy. From the sound of things, it had its advantages. Swan started over toward the Box Canyon, keeping her arm across his shoulders, taking him with her. Noble and Bienville hustled alongside.

"Now, what we're doing today is, we're looking for a no-good named Dawson," Swan explained. "He's been poisoning all the watering holes, because he wants to make all the ranchers go broke, so he can get their land and sell it to the railroad."

Noble said, "I'm the sheriff."

Swan said, "I'm the United States marshal."

Bienville's hands went to work signing, indicating his own identity, but Blade couldn't read sign language, so he just looked at Swan, since she seemed to always have the answer for everything.

"He's a deaf and dumb Indian scout," Swan said. "He can't talk, and he can't hear you when you talk, so you can say anything you want to around him."

As if to illustrate her point, Noble turned to Bienville, and grinned real big, and said, "You're ugly, and you smell like a cow pile!"

Bienville grinned back, nodding his head up and down as if to say that he couldn't agree more.

Blade laughed out loud. He'd never had so much fun.

Swan said, "Okay, let's figure out who *you* are."

Noble had already been thinking about that. He reckoned Blade ought to be a little Mexican boy that they had found out in the desert wandering around dying of thirst, and they had let him drink out of their canteens, and now he followed them everywhere they went. Bienville said that wouldn't do, what they needed was another Indian. Swan argued that one Indian was enough for anybody, but she could sure use a deputy.

While they were fussing about it, Blade let himself into the calf lot. The other kids heard the gate creak open, and they all spun around just in time to see Blade venturing toward the horse. They rushed into the lot to protect him, but he didn't need protection. He was reaching his hands up, and the horse was reaching its head down. The two were having a real reunion.

"You shouldn't go up to a horse you don't know," Noble warned him. "You lucked out this time, but what if it had been a raging stallion?"

"I know him," Blade said. He nuzzled Snowman's muzzle. "Don't I know you, Snowman?"

Swan sighed. She hated to upset the kid, but she had to set him straight. "You can't go naming other people's horses, either. His name is John, and he belongs to Grandma Calla."

"His name's not John, it's Snowman," Blade shot back. "And he belongs to Mr. Odell Pritchett."

Noble and Bienville and Swan all stared at Blade, wondering if he knew what he was talking about. Which was probably why they didn't see Uncle Toy, who had come out to tell Blade Ballenger to run back up to the house, because Samuel was going to take him home.

Chapter 21

As soon as Blade realized what was up, he lit out. Of course, he didn't get far. Being inside the calf lot worked against him. He set in climbing the rails, trying to get away, but Toy caught him from behind and stood there holding him while he kicked and scratched and howled like a banshee.

"Hey, now, son," Toy said, easy and quiet. Blade just went wilder than ever. It was no use, though. Toy had a good solid hold.

Noble and Bienville and Swan were watching in dismay. They could hardly stand to see this happening.

"You can't send him back there!" Swan hollered, and she started hitting Toy on both legs—one of which was bound to be feeling the blows. "His mean old daddy will do something terrible to him!"

Toy said, "We can't keep him, Swan. It's against the law. If we didn't know who he belonged to, maybe we could keep him till his folks was found, but we'd still have to give him back sooner or later."

"You make him sound like he's a dog!" she wailed. "Which is how his daddy treats him! He'll probably turn out tied to a tree, with a chain around his neck!"

She was still punching Toy's legs with her fists, and Blade was still kicking and scratching for all he was worth. Toy Moses was getting a good going-over. Then Noble and Bienville pulled Swan back and held on to her, so Toy could walk without stepping on her. And Swan lit in on them.

Noble dodged a blow and said, "Swan, you ain't helping."

It was a losing battle, and Swan knew it. She slid out of their grasp and sat down in the dirt, sobbing helplessly.

By then, Toy was up in the yard where Samuel was sitting in the car with the motor idling and the passenger door open. Toy set the kid in the front seat, and closed the door, and stood there holding it until the car started moving.

The last thing Samuel wanted was for Blade to feel unwanted, so while he drove, he spoke reassuringly to the boy, telling him that the whole family liked him, liked him a lot, and he was welcome to come back over and play anytime he wanted to, only it had to be with his parents' permission. Samuel also promised that he'd go in and talk to Blade's folks for a few minutes, and try to smooth things over a little.

"Sometimes all a family needs is to talk about what's bothering them," he counseled. "It could be, if your daddy knew how scared you are of him, he'd feel bad about it and put out a real effort to show how much he cares about you."

Blade had found a tiny hole in the upholstery, and he was working his finger into it, probing around in the stuffing underneath. Not that he wanted to destroy anything. You just do what you have to do.

"So how about it?" Samuel asked. "Do you think it might help for me to talk to them?"

They were coming up on the bend in the road, and after that, not far, would be the turnoff into the lane. Whatever was going to happen would have to happen fast. Blade curled his finger inside the upholstery and yanked, hard. The fabric (which was as old as the car, which was older than Blade) rrrrripped.

Samuel was so shocked that he hit the brakes—not stopping the car but sure slowing it down. Blade grabbed the door handle with both hands and yanked. The door flew open. And Blade flew out. He landed on all fours, in a thick patch of clover, and was up and running before Samuel could pull over to the side of the road and kill the engine.

Samuel got out and looked around, and crossed the ditch, and tried to get through the thicket, but the trees and the brush were grown up so close and tight that only a rabbit or Blade Ballenger could get through.

He couldn't leave an eight-year-old boy out loose in the woods, so he drove on to the little lane and followed it back to the Ballenger house. The most logical thing in the world was to tell those folks where their son had spent the night and what was going on. They must be worried sick.

There were a bunch of cur dogs in the yard fighting over some scraps, but when Samuel got out of the car, the curs lost interest in the food and headed in his direction with their heads down and their hackles up. The Protection of the Lord must have still been working for Samuel. He waded through those dogs like Moses through the Red Sea.

When he got up close to the steps, a timid-looking woman appeared in the doorway, with a baby on her hip and a toddler hanging on to her skirt tail. She didn't offer to come out, and she didn't invite Samuel in. Just stood there on the other side of the screen door looking like she'd rather he hadn't stopped by.

"Them dogs'll bite," Geraldine Ballenger warned.

"Yes, ma'am," Samuel answered respectfully, even though the dogs weren't showing any further signs of being in a biting mood. Then he introduced himself and explained why he was there, telling her all about how Blade had shown up at their house last night, and how he had tried to bring him home a while ago, but the kid had gotten away from him, and now he was worried that the little fellow might get hurt or lost, out in the woods by himself.

"I expect you'll want to get somebody out looking for him," Samuel finished up. "If you'd like for my family and me to help—"

Geraldine jerked her eyes away from his face to something off in the yard, and she backed away from the door so quick that he almost wondered if she'd ever been there. He turned to see what she'd been looking at, and there before him was Satan's stepson. Well, those were the words that came jolting into his mind. Calla's words. And they sure seemed to fit.

Ras Ballenger came swaggering across from the barnyard with a sardonic smile on his lips. There was a little boy scudding along beside him, aping his movements and attitude—looking up every few seconds to make sure he was getting it right.

Samuel had met a lot of men in his life, some good, some bad, but this was the first man he'd ever met who made his blood run cold. He stuck out his hand anyway, the way a gentleman is supposed to do. The way a preacher does.

"I'm Sam Lake," he said. "My family and I are staying over at the Moses place for a while, so I guess we're neighbors."

Ras ignored Samuel's outstretched hand and hooked his thumbs in his belt loops. "You come all the way over here to tell me that?" he asked.

Samuel dropped his hand. He was becoming more convinced by the second that helping these parents to get their son back might cause the child more harm than good. Maybe going to the authorities would have been a better idea. Still, he'd already told the woman the whole story, so there was nothing to be accomplished by holding back now.

"No, sir," Samuel said. "I came over here to tell you that your son is out in the woods yonder, and to offer to help you look for him."

Ballenger's smile widened and stiffened, all at the same time.

"Well, I appreciate the charity. I do. And when I need your help, I'll ask for it."

Which was pretty much the same as saying "Get the hell off my land."

So Samuel did.

Toy Moses didn't get any sleep that day. As soon as Samuel had left with Blade, Toy had called Sheriff Meeks, who put in a few calls of his own to lawmen in neighboring towns. Jack Woodard, the constable over in Camden, said sure he knew Odell, everybody knew Odell, Odell was a fine, upstanding member of the community.

Jack called Odell to tell him that his horse had been found, and Odell called Ras to ask when the hell the horse had gone *missing,* and why the hell he hadn't been notified. In the meantime, Early Meeks called Toy back to tell him that Odell had been located.

Ras Ballenger arrived before Odell did, and you'd have thought another tornado had hit Columbia County. He came slamming out of his truck and stomping across the yard like a whirlwind. Toy was in the side yard, untangling a trotline that he'd been intending to string across Calla's pond the next time he wasn't either working or resting up from it, so he saw him coming.

He wished to God he hadn't loaded that kid up a while ago and sent him back to a place where fear must live in the very walls. But he'd had no choice. As soon as it had become common knowledge that the boy was on the Moses place, someone would have come for him. The question was not whether Blade would have had to go back. The only question was who'd have to lie awake nights knowing they'd had a hand in it.

Toy dropped the trotline and stepped into Ras's path just in time to stop him from treading on Calla's double ruffled petunias.

"Help you, Mr. Ballenger?" Actually, the only way he wanted to help him was out of this world and into the next one, but he knew from experience that doing a thing like that could be hard to live with, later on.

"You already helped yourself to a horse that don't belong to you," Ras snarled. "Seems to me you've helped enough."

There were plenty of things that Toy could have come back with, but all he said was "The horse is out back."

With that, he turned on his heel and headed toward the barn. Ras had to break into a trot to keep up. When they got to the calf lot, Ras leaned against the fence and stared at the horse like he was seeing it for the first time. He couldn't have looked any more shocked if the fence had jumped out from under him.

"I don't reckon you'll own up to knowin' who done that." Ras spat, indicating Snowman's wounds.

Toy just shook his head in disgust. Some people were beyond belief or redemption.

Snowman had turned away at the first sight of Ras, and now he started to quiver slightly. Toy went into the lot and walked over to the horse's head.

"Don't worry," he said. "That's not who you're leaving with." The fact that he hadn't somehow saved the boy from going back was gnawing on him now worse than ever.

Ras heard what he said and would have torn into the lot and laid into Toy, except for two things. He didn't really think he could beat Toy Moses in a fair fight, and he was pretty sure the horse would stomp his brains out if he went in there without his whip—which he had left at home for obvious reasons. So he just smoldered.

Then, all of a sudden, Odell Pritchett's truck and trailer pulled up in the yard and Odell came spinning out, bearing down on Ras.

"That's how you train a horse?" Odell bellowed when he got a look at Snowman. He was a hefty fellow. Not as big as Toy, but there was a sight more to him than there was to Ballenger. He was soft, though, and he knew it. That showed in the way he kept clenching and unclenching his fists. Wanting to hit but not daring to do it.

Ras bowed up and stuck out his chin, the picture of righteous indignation. "That horse didn't have a mark on it when it was stole off my place," he claimed loudly. "And I don't much like you insinuatin' that I had anything to do with what's happened to it since."

"I'm not insinuating," Odell flared back. "I'm saying." He was talking through clenched teeth, like he had his mouth wired together.

Ras said, "I reckon next thing, you'll be sayin' you don't intend to pay me for the work I put in on the animal."

Odell's teeth unclenched real fast, because that's what happens when a man's jaw drops.

"Pay!" he exploded. His skin was kind of rosy-toned anyway, and now it turned red as a tomato. Even his ears lit up. "I'll pay, all right! I'll pay the newspaper for running a full-page picture of this horse, so folks can see for themselves the kind of work you put in!"

"You do that, and you'll pay more than you know."

Ras was talking low, so low Toy didn't hear. But Odell caught every word—and believed them, too. He backed off from Ras and shook himself involuntarily, trying to get rid of the feeling that had just settled over him.

About this time, Toy came out of the lot, leading Snowman. Ras was standing smack in his path and didn't make a move to get out of the way until Snowman snorted and reared and screamed as only a horse can scream when it is filled with sudden fury. Then Ras moved like lightning. Snowman's hooves crashed back to earth, slashing the ground that Ras had been standing on, but Ras had already shinnied over the fence and was inside the calf lot looking as if he'd just gotten a rupture.

Swan and Noble and Bienville witnessed the drama from Swan's bedroom window, which looked out over the backyard and the fields and pastures beyond. All of them enjoyed the sight of Ras almost getting his just deserts, but that little bit of vengeful pleasure couldn't make up for their heartbreak over Blade.

"Snowman almost got him," Noble whispered. They weren't calling the horse John anymore, since he didn't belong to Grandma Calla, and the name Snowman fit him better anyhow.

"There would have been a lot of blood," Bienville noted.

Swan was thinking that it was too bad Ras Ballenger was so quick on his feet. They watched silently while Toy and Odell loaded Snow-man into the stock trailer. Ras Ballenger left unnoticed, but the kids' eyes followed Odell's rig until it was out of sight.

"We're never going to see that horse again," Bienville said.

Swan bit her lip to keep from crying, but it didn't help at all. She'd been crying off and on all morning, and now it started happening again.

"At least Snowman is safe now," she said, sounding all wobbly. "But Blade could be dead before sundown."

If you watch what the birds and wild animals do, you can survive pretty much anywhere, because they know things humans have for-gotten, such as what's poisonous and what's not, and what it means when things suddenly get too quiet, and where to hide when what it means is danger. If Blade had known those things, he could have feasted all day on leaves and shoots and berries and flowers, plus a few well-chosen bugs to round things out. He could have listened to the woodland sounds, and if they'd stopped all at once—if they had gone in a heartbeat from a riotous chorus to stone-dead stillness—he could have holed up in a hollow log or deep back beneath the low-hanging canopy of some ancient tree. And he could have watched, the way animals do, in silence, until he knew the cause of alarm and could figure out whether he was the prey being stalked.

But he didn't know, so he did what most boys his age would have done when they had run away from home, and found another home, and lost it, and had run away from the person who was taking them back to the place they'd run away from in the first place. He went swimming.

The chinaberry thicket ran back to a stand of loblolly pines, which gave way to what used to be a cornfield, back when John Moses was still farming, but was just an overgrown mess nowadays. Blade cut through the brush and scrabble until he came to the creek, and he fol-lowed it to the Old Swimming Hole.

There's something about being in the water that makes life feel right, and Blade almost forgot for a while that it wasn't that way at all. He'd left Bienville's clothes on the creek bank, so he felt free as the minnows that were darting around in the shallows. He dove and he swam and he floated and he thought. Thought about those kids he'd been playing with earlier, and about how he almost got to be a deputy for a United States marshal. Now that would have been fine.

He had a notion that he might stay in the swimming hole all day, and then go back and sleep in those people's barn, just like last night, and in the morning, Swan would come for him again, only this time she wouldn't let anybody take him away. She was smart, Swan was, and Blade didn't think that anybody could put the same thing over on her twice.

That's what was going on in his mind when, all at once, every bird stopped singing, and every cricket stopped fiddling, and every frog stopped advertising for a mate. The world got too quiet too fast, and it was too late to hide before Blade Ballenger even realized he needed to.

Chapter 22

Willadee knew that Samuel was going to get a cool reception that evening from his children. As far as they were concerned, what he had done that morning was out of character for him. The Samuel they knew stood up for what was right, no matter what. The fact that he'd done what he *thought* was right escaped them. Willadee tried to explain it to them that afternoon, when she came out of the garden with a bucket of fresh tomatoes and found them sitting on the porch steps with their chins in their hands and sullen looks on their faces.

"Your daddy did what had to be done," she told them. "If we'd kept Blade here, there would have been trouble."

None of that made Samuel look any bigger in their eyes. They'd always seen their daddy as a man who persuaded people to change, not the other way around.

"Just because he's not a preacher anymore doesn't mean he should be as bad as everybody else," Swan blurted.

"He's still a preacher," Willadee said. They all hunched their shoulders and shut her out. She was on their bad list, too. "What on earth makes you think he's not a preacher anymore?"

"He doesn't have a church. Where's he going to preach?"

"We don't know yet."

"Then how can he be a preacher?"

Willadee felt like maybe she ought to say that Samuel was a preacher because God had called him to preach. But that wasn't how Willadee saw it. The way she saw it, Samuel had called himself. He'd fallen in love with God, and when you're in love you can't keep from talking about it, it's as simple as that.

That's not what she told the kids, though. To them, she said, "He just is."

Swan hugged her knees to her chest and glared off at the road. "Well, I hope he doesn't expect me to go to church anymore," she declared. "Because I don't have to do right if he doesn't."

Willadee had to smile. When a kid threatens something she can't possibly go through with, an adult feels easier about a situation. Like maybe it's not as bad as it seemed. Toy had not yet told her that the man Blade had run away from and the man who had mistreated the horse were one and the same, so she was thinking that, likely as not, everything had turned out just fine. The kid might have gotten a licking for running away like that, but his folks had to be glad to see him when he got home. And Samuel surely would have brought out the goodness in everybody concerned.

"Yes, you do," she said.

"Well, I don't see why."

"You don't have to see why. But you do have to mind your daddy and me. If you think that's changed, you've got another think coming."

Swan still wouldn't look at her, but Willadee didn't care. A child that doesn't have strong opinions is one that won't amount to much. She did care how Swan and her brothers treated Samuel, though.

"Now, I don't want you acting like this when your daddy gets home," she told them. "He's got enough on him right now without having to feel like his kids are disappointed in him."

Swan said, "Well, we are."

And Noble said, "I wish he could have figured out another way to handle it."

Bienville shook his head like an old man who's decided that the world is going to the dogs. "We may be the only kids in the world who ever lost a horse and an Indian scout in one day."

Swan said, "He wasn't an Indian scout. He was my friend."

Samuel had figured the kids would have a hard time forgiving him over Blade. He was having a hard time forgiving himself. The fact that Blade had escaped was something he felt as both a relief and a burden, and he said as much at the supper table, when he was telling what had happened.

Swan, who had avoided looking at him since he got home, met his eyes hopefully.

"You mean he got clean away?" she asked.

"Clean as a whistle."

"Then maybe his daddy didn't get him."

"Maybe he didn't."

There were smiles lighting faces all around that table, everybody except Bernice becoming suddenly animated. Even Toy looked glad, and he wasn't one to let his feelings show on his face.

"Maybe he'll sleep in our barn again tonight!" Bienville yodeled.

"Maybe he will."

They didn't talk about whether they'd have to give him up again if he did come back. Some things you take a step at a time, and how they'd get to keep Blade Ballenger was one of them.

"Well, if he comes in this house to steal food tonight," Grandma Calla announced, "he's going to get a big ole jar of Willadee's chicken and dumplings."

She went over to the stove and got the buttermilk pie that Willadee had made and brought it back to the table.

Samuel said, "Don't cut a piece for me, Calla. I'm so full, I don't believe I'm going to have any room for pie."

Noble said, "Me, neither. I reckon I'll have to pass up pie tonight." And buttermilk pie was his favorite.

It turned out that everybody was too full, so the pie never got cut and was transferred whole back to the stove, where a small child stealing leftovers couldn't possibly miss it.

"I hope he don't eat the whole thing at once," Calla worried aloud. "I'd hate for him to get sick out there all by himself."

"Oh, he won't be by himself," Swan assured her.

Willadee wasn't certain what she thought about Swan's idea of sleeping out in the barn, but Samuel said he figured she'd be all right, since her brothers were determined to stay with her. Toy offered to check on them, off and on, since he'd be up working all night anyway, and the kids made him promise that he wouldn't be too obvious. They didn't want to scare Blade off. If he showed up and things looked out of the ordinary, he might cut and run.

Willadee and Samuel loaded the kids down with blankets and pillows and flashlights and toilet paper, and went out to the barn to help them settle in. By that time, the offering on the stove had grown somewhat larger than usual. There were leftovers from the supper Willadee had cooked, plus an all-day sucker that Calla had brought in from the store and an old cat's-eye marble that Swan had found half-buried out in Calla's yard. Noble had added a stack of baseball cards, and Bienville had donated a *National Geographic* with foldout maps of South America. Samuel thought every little boy should have a Bible, so he laid a pocket-size New Testament on top of the *National Geographic*. Toy didn't contribute anything as long as anybody was watching, but sometime along the way, a hand-carved slingshot got added to the mix, and it was a safe bet that Bernice hadn't put it there.

Swan didn't intend to sleep. Did not intend to sleep at all. Not until Blade showed up. Willadee and Samuel spread several blankets over the old hay, and the kids crawled between the blankets with their heads toward the barn door. They lay on their bellies, and propped on their elbows, and watched their parents heading back to the house—Willadee and Samuel, talking and laughing, their voices high and deep, and soft and strong, all full of contrasts and harmonies. It was the finest music in the world.

There was other music, reverberating from Never Closes, but none so sweet. Swan and the boys listened until Samuel's and Willadee's voices faded, and then they watched until the two disappeared into the house. After that, they watched for Blade.

In her faded bedroom, Calla Moses was watching, too. She pulled her rocker over beside the window and drew the curtains back, so that nothing would obscure her view. When the boy showed up, she wanted to see him. Wanted to be a witness when he hauled his loot down to the barn and got the surprise of his life at finding the other kids there to welcome him. She wouldn't be able to see it all from where she sat, but she planned to see all she could, and imagine the rest.

All her life, she'd been a practical sort. Nonsense and Calla Moses didn't go together. These days, though, something was turning loose inside her. Maybe it was having the kids around that was making it happen. Them, with all their games and foolishness. Or maybe it was the horse, appearing like that, out of nowhere, looking, except for the stripes he wore, like something out of a storybook. And now that night-eyed boy had come and captured them all.

Whatever it was, Calla's imagination had waked up from a long sleep, and these days she had the feeling that magic and miracles might be hovering in the air all around, waiting to happen. She wasn't a great believer in such things, but she didn't push the thought away.

Willadee and Samuel watched for Blade from the living room. They'd have waited in their bedroom, but the windows opened onto the wrong side of the yard. If they'd looked out from there, all they'd have seen would have been the cars pulling in and out of Never Closes.

And they couldn't very well watch from the kitchen, since that was where they hoped Blade Ballenger would go first, when he arrived.

If he arrived.

In the meantime, they talked about everything else. About how school would be starting before they could hardly turn around, and the kids were outgrowing their clothes, but Willadee could sew, and could draw patterns on newspaper that worked as well as the store-bought kind. The dresses she'd made for Swan in the past had always turned out prettier than the ready-mades. She guessed she could make a shirt for a boy as easily as she could make a dress for a girl, and in less time, too, because there wouldn't be so much handwork. You want to totally ruin a boy's life, just try sending him to school in a shirt that shows off your cross-stitch and smocking.

Sometime in the night they went to sleep, there on Calla's settee, with their clothes on and their shoes off, and more on their minds than they were apt to let on to anybody besides each other.

Bernice didn't watch for Blade, but she watched herself in the mirror for the longest time. She sat at the little dressing table in her bedroom, and brushed her hair out over her bare shoulders, and studied the curve of her cheekbones and the hollow at the base of her throat. She stood up and stretched her arms and gazed at the reflection of her body, and she just wanted to bust out bawling, because she was every inch perfection, and it was all going to waste.

Toy Moses made a lot of trips outside that night, leaving the regulars to drink on the honor system. The customers would get themselves drinks and adjust their tabs in John's old ragged notebook, which Toy still kept. Nobody asked him why he kept stepping out into the night and standing around in the shadows, and Toy never offered an explanation. The two best things about Never Closes were that nobody owed anybody information about anything and everybody looked out for everybody else.

Half a dozen times, Toy skirted around the yard and stole down to the barn to see about the kids. They were always all right, but the last time he checked, which was just before daybreak, there were still only three.

...

Blade had never thought much about mice, but he thought about them now, because his daddy had told him that the room might be full of them, and that they could chew through walls, so they wouldn't have any trouble chewing through a boy.

That's where Blade was. In a room with a dirt floor, where he had been for hours. He wasn't sure how many.

The darkness in there was beyond black. Beyond endless. When Ras Ballenger built something, he built it airtight and solid. There was no way for light to get in, even if there was light outside, so Blade didn't know whether it was day or night. He thought it must be night, because he couldn't hear Blue jabbering. Or his daddy answering. Or the cur dogs barking and baying. Or anything at all.

He was naked. As naked as he had been in the swimming hole, when there was a sudden splash and he jerked his head around to see the water erupting the way it does when something or someone has hit the surface hard and gone under. When he saw that, his heart nearly jumped out of his mouth, because he knew what it meant. Thought he did. He started swimming for shore, but then something came up beneath him and grabbed his foot, and pulled him under, and kept him there forever.

He fought. For all the good it did. The depths of the swimming hole were clear, and he could see his daddy's face through the pale green water. His daddy, grinning at him, like this was a game and he was winning.

Blade had seen his daddy catch a catfish once with his bare hands. The man was that quick. And that's how Blade felt. Like that catfish. Caught without hope.

And then it was over. Blade's daddy, dragging him out of the swimming hole, and dumping him on the ground, and noosing a lead rope around his neck while he lay there sucking air and puking water. A lead rope. Like he was a horse that was about to be led into the barn to be cross-tied. Ras left the end of the lead rope lying on the ground while he got dressed (he'd shucked his clothes before he dove into the swimming hole), and Blade tried once to get the thing off his neck. But Ras lunged for the rope and jerked it, hard, and Blade's head threatened to come right off his shoulders, so he didn't try that again. Just stayed still and looked for chances.

But there weren't any chances. Ras drove him in front of him through the woods and home, leaving Bienville's clothes scattered on the creek bank.

And now here he was.

He was cold. It was the middle of summer, but he was lying curled in a ball, and he was shivering. His hands wanted to trace patterns in the dirt, because that always helped his feelings, but he was scared to move. Terrified of what he might brush up against, and of the thousand furry things that might come out of hiding. Swarming, hungry things. He wondered whether mice made noises while they ate, or whether his screams would be the only sounds, and whether his mother would hear and come to help.

She hadn't come yet, and he had screamed aplenty. Screamed and beat on the walls until his voice played out and his fists were bloody. He couldn't see the blood, but he could taste it when he sucked on his hands to stop the hurting.

There hadn't been any sound for the longest time, but now he heard a bobwhite call, so maybe it was morning. He sat up. Everything hurt. His hands, his arms, his legs, his neck. His skin, and his muscles, and his bones. He listened for that bobwhite to call again, and it did, and that gave him a peg to mark his place in the world. He could call this moment "day."

Then there were other sounds. Other birds, making much of morning. And now the curs stirred to life, complaining about something.

A door slammed. Blade was sure he heard a door slam. He hoped and feared that he was right. And he was. His daddy's voice came singing out across the yard, talking to the dogs, telling them to shut up and settle down.

Blade braced himself.

Chapter 23

What Swan intended to do was rescue Blade Ballenger. It had been three days now, and she was through fooling around.

The whole family had been under a cloud since they woke up to find their gifts still on the back of the stove. There'd been a lot of talk among the grown-ups (mostly in hushed tones, when they thought the kids weren't listening) about what might have become of the boy, and how they all wished they could help him, and how the law and Ras Ballenger would come down on them like a pestilence if they tried, but not a word about just marching in there and getting him.

Swan had mentioned the Battle of Jericho to her daddy and had pointed out that, if God had really given Joshua an edge like that, then surely He would bless their efforts at saving Blade. After all, Joshua and his crew had to bring down the walls to a fortified city. All *they* had to do was scare one slimy little snake of a man into having a heart attack. Or at least distract him long enough to snatch his kid. She said since they didn't have trumpets, she thought they ought to use cowbells. There were a bunch of old, rusty ones out in the barn, and they made a terrible racket when you shook them real hard.

Samuel explained to her that you can't go around trying to reproduce the miracles that happened in biblical times, and she told him you sure could if you had faith as a grain of mustard seed. That was something she'd heard him preach about a lot—how a tiny seed of faith could yield a mighty harvest.

"It's like you're always saying in your sermons," she told him, "if we show God our faith, He'll show us His favor."

"I'm just not sure that surrounding the Ballenger place with a bunch of cowbells is the best way to go about it," Samuel said.

But he didn't offer any better ideas, and neither did anybody else, so Swan decided to take matters into her own hands. The problem was that she had only two, and she needed more. Well, she knew where there were four.

Noble and Bienville nearly swallowed their teeth when she unfolded her plan to them.

"That man will kill us, Swan," Noble said.

"Not if he doesn't catch us," Swan said back. "What we've got to do is make sure we have the Lord on our side before we start this operation. And the way we do that is with prayer and fasting."

"How long do we have to fast?" Bienville wanted to know. He wasn't sure what else they were having for supper that evening, but he'd seen their mama making banana pudding the last time he passed through the kitchen.

Swan had been thinking that twenty-four hours might be about right. That wasn't as long as people generally prayed and fasted in the Bible, but this was an emergency. When she heard about the banana pudding, she cut the time down even more. It seemed to her that, if they skipped lunch (which was probably going to be peanut butter sandwiches) and spent the time on their knees before the Throne of Grace, that ought to do it. The way she saw it, they could rescue Blade and be back home in time for supper.

. . .

Swan knew how to get to the Ballenger place by taking the road and the lane, but she figured the best way to sneak up on somebody was to stay out of sight while you're doing it. There had to be a back way, since there can't very well be a front without a back, and it just made sense to her that, if she followed the creek, she would find what she was looking for. After all, Blade and his daddy had both shown up back there that day when she was looking for a place to baptize Lovey, and they had to have gotten there somehow.

There's a certain amount of preparation that goes into doing a rescue, and one of the most crucial parts is making sure that grown-ups don't come looking for you right when you're about to make your Big Move. (Not showing up for a meal is the surest way on earth to get big people out looking for little people.) Swan and her brothers took care of that problem by telling their mother part of the truth—that they were planning to spend some time in prayer and fasting on Blade's behalf. Willadee offered to join them, but they told her that wouldn't be necessary, they had the prayer and fasting pretty much under control.

Willadee told *her* mother what the kids were up to (at least what she thought they were up to), and Calla Moses got tears in her eyes. "Maybe we ought to pray and fast right along with them," she said. She'd never prayed and fasted a day in her life, and had always thought the fasting part was going overboard, but she was touched by what the kids were doing and wanted to show her support.

"I already offered," Willadee answered. "They seem to want this to be just between them and God."

Well, Calla could appreciate that. She'd always been a great believer in keeping your relationship with God to yourself when at all possible.

The kids had their prayer meeting out in the barn, kneeling on the blankets that they hadn't let their parents take back to the house yet.

"When Blade ever does show up," Swan had explained, "it would be so nice for him to find a soft spot waiting for him."

She couldn't bear the thought that he might never show up, and neither could the rest of the family. The blankets had stayed.

Noble, being the oldest, led the prayer meeting, and he did an impressive job of it. He'd been going to prayer meetings since before he could remember. The boy knew how to pray.

"Lord," he started out, "Swan and Bienville and I come before You asking for strength."

"Amen!" said Bienville.

"Yes, Lord!" said Swan.

"We need Your help in arresting Blade Ballenger out of the hands of evil," Noble continued.

"Wresting," corrected Bienville.

"Keep praying, Brother Noble," said Swan.

Noble kept praying. As a matter of fact, he kept on for so long that Swan finally decided God had heard enough. There's a time for praying and there's a time for putting prayers into action.

The hard part was going to be keeping the cowbells quiet while they approached the Field of Battle. Bienville wisely counseled that they could accomplish that by wrapping the clappers with rags and then unwrapping them, quickly and carefully, when they were ready to cut loose.

So they had to find some rags. Which was no trouble. Grandma Calla had a big box full of cleaning rags under the counter in the store. Getting them out of there without her noticing would be the challenge. Not that Grandma Calla was overly attached to those cleaning rags. She had plenty of old pillowcases she could tear up to make more. But the kids didn't want her to start asking questions.

It was Swan's job to get Grandma Calla's attention while the boys borrowed the rags. The word *steal* was not in their vocabulary today. You do not steal when you are on a Holy Mission.

Swan wasn't born yesterday. And she hadn't been living at Grandma Calla's since the first week of June without learning how to get her attention good and proper. She went up to the door of the store and stuck her head inside, and looked as guilty as her grandmother used to always expect her to be. Calla had stopped expecting that so much lately, or had at least stopped talking so much about it.

"I may have torn up some of your flowers by mistake," Swan said when Grandma Calla looked over and saw her there. Now lying is just as bad as stealing, and just as likely to result in God not blessing a rescue, but Swan wasn't lying. Exactly. She said "may have."

"I thought you kids were praying and fasting."

"We are. But I had to come back to the house for something—and I may not have watched where I was going."

"I've got plenty of flowers," Grandma Calla told her kindly. "I've got so many flowers, you can't hardly walk around the house without stepping on some of them. Which flowers do you think you may have torn up by mistake while you may not have been watching where you were going?"

Swan hesitated for an appropriate length of time before answering. This had to seem like she really hated to admit what she was about to own up to.

"Your poppies," she whispered remorsefully.

Calla Moses was around that counter and out the door before Swan could even blink. You've never seen a woman her age move so fast. She'd been trying to get poppies to grow on her place for a decade, and she'd never had any luck with them. Until this year. This year, they'd shown up and showed out, and the first thing Calla did every morning was go outside to look at them. She'd even had Toy pull the glider over there close to them so she could sit and have her coffee while she admired their colors. She didn't say anything to Swan as she went past. It's hard to talk when you're chewing your tongue.

Swan waited until Calla had disappeared around the corner of the house, and then she let out a discreet whistle. Her brothers whizzed out of hiding and into the store. Swan took off after her grandmother.

When she got around to the other side of the house, she found Grandma Calla sitting in the glider looking as if she'd thought she was having a stroke and realized it was only a hot flash.

"Why, there's nothing wrong with those poppies," Grandma Calla said.

"Maybe it was the tiger lilies I may have torn up," Swan hedged.

"You can't hardly tear up a tiger lily," Grandma Calla informed her. "They're tough as nails. That's why you see them still growing around old house places fifty years after the folks who lived there have moved off or died out."

And then she said, "You can't hardly confuse a tiger lily with a poppy, either."

There was a squint on her face when she said it. Kind of a suspicious squint.

"Where's that box of cleaning rags you always keep under here?" Willadee asked Calla later. They were leaning against the counter, munching peanut butter sandwiches, and Willadee was of the belief that, when you're eating standing up, you might as well be doing something useful.

Calla looked under the counter and saw that the box was gone.

"So that's what that was all about," she said. "I knew Swan Lake could tell the difference between a tiger lily and a poppy."

Willadee asked her what on earth she was talking about, and Calla said she wasn't sure, but at least they didn't have to worry about whether the kids were all right. Between praying and fasting and lying and stealing, they were probably too busy to get into any real trouble.

While Noble and Bienville wrapped the clappers with the cleaning rags, Swan took the additional precaution of borrowing three duck calls that she had come upon once when she was pilfering in the tool-shed. Cowbells were great for just making racket, but they weren't in any way kin to trumpets, and Swan thought this whole event would be more authentic if they had instruments they could blow through. They wedged the duck calls into the cowbells, in among the wadded rags.

The trip across the pasture was pretty much like any other trip across the pasture, except that the kids were considerably quieter than usual. The seriousness of what they were doing was starting to weigh on them. There was no turning back now, though. Blade Ballenger needed saving, and there was nobody else willing to do it.

When they got to the creek, they hunkered down and drank out of cupped hands, the way they imagined the Hebrew Children would have done. They were extra watchful while they drank, well aware that nothing they'd ever done before had entailed any true danger—and that this time was different.

Bienville wanted to do a little more praying before they set off again, but Swan told him he could pray while they walked.

"That's what the Bible means when it says to pray without ceasing," she said. "It means you gotta keep moving while you're doing it."

They didn't slow down again until they got to the high bank above the swimming hole, and then they came to a dead halt, all of them going dry-mouthed at the same time.

"Oh nooooooo," Swan moaned.

Noble and Bienville just stared.

What had drawn them up short was the sight of clothes strewn about on the ground. Bienville's clothes. The ones that Blade had been wearing the last time they saw him. There were the clothes, but where was the *boy*? He wasn't in the swimming hole, and there was no good reason they could think of why he'd be out running around the woods in the altogether.

"You think something *ate* him?" Bienville gasped.

Noble gave a disgusted snort. "If something ate him, it undressed him first. The clothes would be all ragged and bloody if something ate him."

Well, the clothes weren't ragged, and there wasn't any blood. So that was good.

Swan went around gathering up the clothes and holding them close to her heart. Her brothers examined the area for signs of a struggle. There were no signs.

"If anybody grabbed him, he didn't put up much of a fight," Noble reasoned.

Which didn't do much to set Swan's mind at ease. She remembered how hard Blade had fought the other day to get away from Uncle Toy, and he hadn't left any signs of struggle in the calf lot. When a kid is being held up in the air by someone several times his size, the ground can't bear witness to what happened.

Now they had an even greater sense of urgency, but they moved more cautiously—watching their step, and not talking at all anymore. They had to be getting close to Ballenger land, which meant they were getting closer to finding out just how well this miracle business really worked.

There are moments in our lives that we more or less stumble upon—moments that we could not have predicted, and were not prepared for, and would have done almost anything to avoid—and the Lake children were coming up on one of those.

According to the plan that Swan had laid out earlier, as soon as they discovered the Enemy, they were to march around the area seven times, just like the priests had done at the Battle of Jericho. They were not to speak or make any sound whatsoever until they'd made the seven rounds. Then they would silently unwrap the clappers and—on a signal from Swan—would shake the cowbells and blow on the duck calls. If seven trumpets had been all it took to make the walls of Jericho fall flat, three cowbells and three duck calls ought to be enough to knock the legs out from under Ras Ballenger. It would be up to Almighty God to keep him down long enough for them to locate Blade and carry him to safety.

Only, they never got a chance to implement the plan. They had just crawled under a barbed-wire fence that they reckoned (rightly) marked the boundary between Grandma Calla's land and the Ballenger place when they heard a voice. The boys didn't recognize it, although they could figure out who it belonged to. Swan didn't have to figure. She knew for sure.

"Whoops!" Ras Ballenger was saying. *Taunting.* "Where you think you're goin'? Nope. Not that way." And then, "Not that way, either."

Swan and her brothers got still as statues, afraid to even breathe. After a moment, they crept along toward the sound, which was coming from the other side of a bank of weeping willows.

They had to scrunch down low and pick their way through the drooping branches. Careful not to rustle the leaves on the trees, or the ones underfoot. When they were almost to the other side, they spied a clearing up ahead—a big open space where a couple of large pines had been uprooted, probably in the storm. The pines had fallen crossways, snapping off several of each other's limbs in the process. Broken branches littered the ground.

There in the middle of the mess was Blade. Not a hundred yards away. He was wearing clothes that were grime-encrusted, and he was just as dirty, his fine black hair matted to his scalp. He was gathering wood. Scurrying about, this way and that, faster and faster, as his father popped his hateful bullwhip and barked instructions.

"Missed a piece there!" Ballenger yelped, herding the boy back and forth. "What's the matter with you? Can't you do anything right?"

Swan was so stricken at the sight that she reached out and grabbed hold of Noble's arm to steady herself. Bienville was on the other side of Noble, and he grabbed hold of his big brother's shirttail. Noble let the others hold on to him, but he himself was having trouble standing up.

Then it happened. Blade couldn't move fast enough to escape the whip, and it caught him about the face. He let out a piteous bleating sound and stopped darting around. Stopped moving at all.

Swan and her brothers stared in horror at their friend's startled look. At the blood that was leaking from where his right eye *had been.*

Swan fainted.

Noble felt his sister letting go of his arm, and he managed to catch her before she hit the ground. Managed to let her down easy, so she wouldn't get hurt in the fall, or hit with a thud that would alert Ballenger to their presence. Bienville had turned loose from Noble's shirttail and was standing rigid, with his eyes squenched shut and his lips clamped together, so Noble was the only one who saw what happened next.

Ras Ballenger got a look at what he had done and he shook his head more like he was inconvenienced than like he was sorry. Still carrying the whip in his right hand, he went over and scooped Blade up and carried him under his left arm like a farmer might carry a squealing pig. Out of the clearing. Out of sight.

Gone.

Chapter 24

Willadee saw them coming when they topped a rise far out in the pasture and headed into the homestretch. They were following an old, worn cow path, the one they always took. She'd seen them make that trek dozens of times and never felt her heart seize up inside her chest, but that's the way it felt this time.

She was out in the backyard shelling purple hull peas, her thumbs and fingers stained all to glory and the dishpan in her lap half full. She set the dishpan aside and stood up to get a better look. Something was wrong. She knew it. For one thing, Swan wasn't in the lead, and that hardly ever happened. For another thing, she was holding Noble's hand.

Bienville was tagging along behind. Nothing unusual about that, he was always tagging along behind. But his shoulders were hunched, and he kept swabbing at his eyes and nose with his shirtsleeve.

"Toy!" Willadee hollered out. "Toy, come quick, something's wrong with the children!"

Toy was inside Never Closes when he heard Willadee shouting his name. It wasn't time to open yet. It wasn't even time for supper. He and Bernice had just arrived a few minutes before, and he'd gone into the bar early to clean it up a little. He went rushing out and saw Willadee running toward the pasture. By the time he caught up with her, she and the kids were already meeting in the middle, and Willadee was flinging her arms around all three of them at once.

"It was horrible," Noble was saying. Shuddering.

Bienville looked as if he might get sick all over his mother.

"His eye was gone!" he cried. "Just—*gone*."

Swan balled up her fists and started pounding them against her legs. "We let him down!" she shrieked. "We were right there, watching, and we let him down!"

"You didn't let anybody down," Grandma Calla said, emphatically.

They were all in the living room now. Calla, who had left the store without anyone to watch it as soon as she knew there was a family crisis, and Samuel, who had come home from work while the kids were spilling out their story, and Bernice, who had just known something this bad or worse was going to happen, and Toy and Willadee and the kids. Calla sat in her rocker, holding Swan. Bienville was in Willadee's lap with his face pressed hard against her shoulder. Noble sat by himself on a hassock, holding on to the sides with both hands.

"We let him down something terrible," Swan sobbed. "We never even got the clappers unwrapped."

"What clappers?" Willadee wanted to know.

"We were going to try to scare Mr. Ballenger by ringing cowbells and blowing on duck calls," Noble explained. You could tell he was embarrassed to admit it. After all, he was the oldest, and should have been the voice of reason.

At the word *cowbells,* Samuel cocked his head to one side, looking heartsick through and through.

"Like the priests with the trumpets at the Battle of Jericho," Noble continued. "Only we had to wrap the clappers with rags so they wouldn't make any noise until we were ready."

At the word *rags,* Willadee and Calla cocked their heads, too. The pieces were falling into place, and the picture that was emerging would have been beautiful—if only it hadn't all turned out so badly.

"And then, when Blade needed help the most, I just lost the use of myself," Swan grieved. "If we'd stuck to the plan, we could have saved him."

Willadee said, "You couldn't have saved him, honey. You'd just have all gotten yourselves killed."

"There's wickedness in this world," Grandma Calla told the kids, taking them all in with her glance. "And you might as well know it now. There are people who are evil to their core, and nothing they do is your fault."

Noble said, "Well, somebody needs to stop him."

It was quiet for a moment. The kids, waiting for one of the grown-ups to promise that somebody would, indeed, stop Ras Ballenger. The grown-ups, knowing that wasn't a promise they could make.

Samuel got up silently and walked outside. The rest of them could hear him when he raised his voice, calling on God.

Toy Moses didn't bother with calling on God, since he'd had so little practice at it and had never been convinced that it carried any benefit. Instead, he just picked up the phone and called the law.

Later that night, two deputies dropped by Never Closes and filled Toy in on the details of their investigation. Yes, the Ballenger boy had lost an eye that afternoon, but the father claimed the kid had fallen on a stob while he was picking up firewood, and the mother backed up his story.

"The mother wasn't even there," Toy pointed out.

"Were you?" one of the deputies asked. This particular deputy,

Bobby Spikes, was a newcomer to the area (he'd lived in the county for only eight or nine years). He was also one of the few officers around who had never once raised a glass in Never Closes.

"If my kids say she wasn't there," Toy said, "she wasn't there."

"*Your* kids?" Spikes said.

The other deputy, a fellow named Dutch Hollensworth, had known Toy Moses since God made dirt, and he didn't much care for the way Spikes was talking to a man whom he personally respected and got a lot of free drinks from.

"They're his *kin*," Dutch told Spikes. "And they're Moses to the bone."

"Right," said Spikes, kind of dry. "And a Moses will not lie."

So at least he knew the local lore, even if he didn't put much stock in it.

"Anyway," Spikes went on, "the Ballenger boy wouldn't say a word, one way or the other. But his parents got him medical attention, the way any caring parents would, and the doctors wrote it up as an accident. In a case like this, there's nothing the law can do."

"Not in Columbia County, right?" Toy Moses said. He didn't really mean for it to come out sounding like it did, but Spikes had gotten under his skin.

The deputy gave him a look and licked his tongue around the corner of his mouth for a second. "Once in a while, a crime goes unpunished."

Which was about as close as anybody had ever come to accusing Toy Moses, to his face, of having committed a murder he never had to pay for. That wasn't what Toy thought about, though, after the deputies had gone. What he puzzled over, off and on for days, was whatever had possessed him to say "my kids."

Two weeks went by.

The kids had nightmares. Noble woke up once, in the middle of the night, to find Bienville crawling into bed with him. Shaking like a leaf.

"You, too, huh?" asked Noble.

"You mean I'm not the only one?"

"Not by a long shot," Noble told him.

As for Swan, she took to sleeping in a chair. That way, when she jarred awake after seeing Ras Ballenger's face in her dreams, at least she didn't find herself trapped and tangled in her covers, unable to escape.

During the daytime, the boys stuck close to the house. Swan stayed to herself as much as possible. Willadee tried to draw them all out by offering to let them help her make tea cakes, and Calla offered the most precious gift she knew—the chance for them to help her with her flowers. Samuel offered to take them into town for ice cream. Calla kept ice cream in the store, but he figured ice cream is more of an event when you go a few miles to get it.

Nothing worked. The kids didn't know what had become of their friend, and their misery was all they had to hold on to. In their heart of hearts, it felt as though letting go of their hurt, even for a little bit, would be the same as letting go of Blade. Forever.

"You can't keep on like this," Willadee told Swan one day, when she caught her moping in her room.

Swan, who had never heard the word *can't* without arguing it to death, didn't say a word.

"I know you're worried about Blade," Willadee said. "We all are. But we mustn't draw up in a shell and shut the world out. That's no way to live."

Swan turned away.

Willadee came over and stood beside her. She didn't try to put her arm around her daughter. Didn't try to draw her close. Swan had been shrugging off every hand that reached out to her lately, and Willadee could understand. Sometimes a sense of loss can be so great that anyone who offers comfort seems to be making small of it.

"Well, here's a list of chores," she said, and she laid a slip of paper on the windowsill. (She had two more of those in her apron pocket— one for each of the boys.) "When you're done, you can come back up here and be sad until supper if you need to."

The kids hadn't had to do any work around the place since the day Snowman arrived, and Willadee had come up with the idea of putting them back to work now as a last resort. To be honest, she wished that every day of their childhood could be endless summer, filled with play-pretend and make-believe and enchantment. But this summer was turning out to seem endless in a different kind of way. Endless in that the kids were all running one horrible scene over and over in their minds. Maybe giving them some responsibility would force them to think about something else.

So the kids all did chores, and they thought about Blade Ballenger while they worked.

Samuel found Swan sitting out in Calla's glider by herself one evening, and he told her how sorry he was for not paying more attention the other day when she ran that idea past him about the cowbells. If he'd taken her seriously, he said, he might have been able to help her understand things better, and maybe she wouldn't have turned out having to be a witness to such a terrible thing.

"Me not being a witness wouldn't mean it didn't happen," Swan said. "What we needed was a miracle, and we didn't get one."

Samuel thought he knew where she was going with that, so he asked her if she felt it was God's fault, what had happened to Blade.

Swan thought about that for a minute before she answered. Obviously this was an issue she'd been wrestling with.

"No, sir," she said finally. "I'm the one who cut the fasting short so we wouldn't miss out on the banana pudding."

On Friday morning, another horse showed up at Calla's, this one brought in a trailer by Mr. Odell Pritchett and paid for in cash by Toy Moses. Odell had called Toy to say he'd like to do something to thank him for taking care of Snowman, and Toy had told him no thanks were necessary, but he'd appreciate it if Odell could tell him where he might find a good horse for the kids. One that didn't have any bad habits, and preferably not much in the way of speed.

"I've got just the animal for you," Odell had said. "Her name is

Lady." They'd wrangled awhile about the price (Odell wanting to give Toy the horse for free, and Toy refusing to take anything for nothing), and finally they had reached a compromise. Only they knew the terms. As a matter of fact, only they knew that there was a deal in place.

About the middle of the morning, the kids had finished their chores and were doing what they normally did when they finished, which was nothing much. Noble and Bienville were lying on a patch of bare dirt in the front yard, trying to get doodlebugs to come out of their holes. The way you did that was, you took a twig, and you stuck it in the hole, and you turned it round and round.

"Doodlebug, doodlebug, your house is on fire." That was what you were supposed to say, so they were saying it. They'd never really seen it work, and it wasn't working this time, but it was something to do.

Out back, Swan had climbed up on top of the chicken house, because that was the easiest way to get into the mulberry tree that grew right alongside it. From the chicken house roof, she had pulled herself into the branches. She was sitting there straddling a limb, with her back resting against the trunk of the mulberry. The way the tree was leafed out, she couldn't see what was going on in the world, and that suited her just fine. Nobody could see her, either, and that suited her even better.

Swan heard the rattle and clatter of Odell's truck and trailer driving up, but she didn't pay the slightest attention. Vehicles rattled and clattered into the Moses yard all day and most of the night. She did take notice, though, when her brothers commenced to whooping like Indians on a scalping raid.

"A horse?" Noble was hollering. "A horse for *us*?"

And Bienville was yelling, "You mean we've got a horse we won't have to give back to anybody?"

Well, you don't hear a thing like that without getting curious. Not if you're eleven years old. Having a horse was not going to heal her broken heart, or stop her from grieving over Blade. But it did get her attention.

She got down out of the tree.

Horses don't walk out of trailers headfirst, they back out, so the first part of Lady that Swan and her brothers saw was her behind. Which was as good a start as they could have asked for.

"Man, she is beautiful," Noble whispered.

"Yeah," Bienville breathed reverently.

"What? Her butt?" asked Swan, who wasn't going to allow herself to be made happy by one look at the south end of a horse.

Then came the rest of her. She was just the right size—not too little, not too big. Dappled gray, all the way. If she was a little swaybacked, they never noticed. Past her prime? Well, they couldn't see that. They did notice that her mane was a bit unfortunate. It looked as if some child had taken a scissors to it, which turned out to be the case.

"That mane will grow out," Odell was saying apologetically. "My daughter got a little carried away."

The kids all nodded understandingly. They couldn't care less about the haircut.

Odell said, "She's a good, sweet horse, Lady is. She's going on eighteen, so she doesn't have as much flash and dash as she used to. But she's giving."

Bienville had a feeling that the term *giving* meant something different than the ordinary when it was used to describe a horse, so he asked Odell to elaborate.

"It means if you ask her to do something, she will plumb outdo herself trying to please you," Odell said.

The kids all smiled. Every one of them. Even Swan. Toy Moses didn't smile, though. He looked gruff as all get-out, and told those kids if they asked that horse to do too much, he knew where he could cut a good keen switch off of a piss elm.

They rode the horse bareback. Toy had an old saddle out in the barn, but the leather was cracked, and the saddle was too big for Lady anyway. Plus, the kids figured if riding bareback was good enough for Indians, it was good enough for them. Toy bridled her for them and showed them how to "rein soft," so that the bit didn't cut into her mouth. After that, they were on their own.

They rode doubles, because Swan refused to get off, and the boys were agreeable enough to take turns. Around the yard. Then around the barn. Then out across the pasture. But not to the creek. The creek was like a meandering line that marked the end of safety and the beginning of unthinkable peril. They weren't ready to deal with the creek again just yet.

Lady got the royal treatment. It was carrots from the kitchen, and sugar cubes from the store, and watermelons straight from the patch out beside the smokehouse.

"Y'all are liable to colic that horse with kindness," Grandma Calla told them when she caught them sneaking apples that she had set aside for making fritters.

Colic sounded like something babies get, and they'd never heard of one dying from it, but Calla told them they couldn't burp a horse, so they'd best not give it a bellyache. After that, they cut back on stealing food for Lady and concentrated on her grooming.

Toy taught them how to use a brush and a currycomb, and how to clean her feet with a hoof pick.

"A horse's feet are the most important thing it's got," he told them. "A human being can get around just fine on an artificial leg, but a horse has to have the wheels God gave it."

The kids laughed at the idea of a horse having wheels, but there was something else in what Toy had said, and they didn't know what to make of it. This was the first time they'd ever heard him mention his artificial leg. The very first time. The way he had said it, kind of offhanded and casual, it was like he was saying something else. That he was taking them into his confidence, maybe. That he was opening a door and waving them in. Of course, they all knew that was a stretch. More than likely, he had just let it slip. He wasn't really the type to let anything slip without meaning to, but he wasn't the type to get too cozy with a bunch of kids that didn't belong to him, either, so they didn't want to read too much into it.

The Lake children all rested better that night. Swan even slept in her bed again, instead of in the chair. She did turn on the night-light that her daddy had bought for her the day after Blade got hurt. She was not at all sure that she'd ever be able to sleep without a night-light again, as long as she lived.

Chapter 25

Swan was dead asleep. The little scuffling sounds of someone coming in her window didn't wake her, but when that someone crawled under the covers with her, she sat up with a start. Before she could open her mouth to scream, she saw who it was, and that was the best minute of her life so far.

"How'd you *get* here?" she gasped.

Blade Ballenger pointed at the window. He had shown up wearing his sleepers again, and the bandage that covered his eye socket bore a suspicious yellow tinge. Swan threw her arms around him and held on. Blade relaxed, letting his head rest on her shoulder, so that his face was against her neck.

"I saw what happened," Swan told him, hating herself all over again because she hadn't done anything to help.

Blade pulled out of her arms and stared at her. So much had happened to him lately that he didn't know which thing she was talking about.

Swan explained, "Out there in the woods that day. My brothers and I had come to save you, but we were too late."

Blade's one beautiful dark eye widened in amazement, and his mouth dropped open. Someone coming to save him had never happened before.

Swan said, "We were gonna scare your daddy slap to death, but I fainted and ruined the miracle."

Blade squinted at her. He for sure didn't know what she was talking about now.

She said, "A miracle is something that can't be done, but you ask for it, and it's given. Only—there's generally a whole bunch of requirements that don't make a lick of sense, and you have to do everything to the letter. If you mess up, no miracle."

He still didn't understand, and it showed on his face. Swan patted the pillow, and he settled onto it. Then she stretched out beside him, propping her head on one hand and laying the other arm across his stomach, gathering him close to her.

"So what happened with your eye? Did the doctor sew it back in?"

Blade looked away, like he had a guilty secret and she'd discovered it. That was answer enough.

She said, "How'd you get away?"

"Waited till a cat came."

It was her turn to squint.

"My daddy kills cats," Blade said. He didn't explain that when his daddy was killing cats he was too engrossed to pay attention to anything else, but Swan got the message. Blade glanced at the window, as if afraid he might see his daddy coming through it any minute.

"I'm not letting anybody take you away again," Swan promised. "I don't know for sure yet how I'm going to keep them from it, but I'm not letting it happen."

Toy Moses had just locked the bar and was helping his mama open the store when Ras drove into the yard and jumped out of his truck like his pants were on fire. Calla looked up from sweeping the steps, and Toy looked over from propping the wood door open with a couple of Nehi cases, and both of them looked as exasperated as they felt at the moment. Which was plenty.

"Lord help my time," Calla said.

Ras Ballenger stomped over to within about three feet of them and glared at Toy malevolently.

"I've come for my boy," he said. Not snapping and yelling, like usual. His voice was kind of deadly calm.

Since Toy was unaware that Blade was on the place, he was surprised, but he didn't show it. He shook his head and also didn't show how glad he was that Ballenger's boy had gotten away from him again.

"Looks like you've come to a goat's house after wool, Mr. Ballenger. We ain't seen your boy in over two weeks."

Well, Ballenger didn't believe that, and he said so. Toy just shook his head again and told him that he sure hoped the boy was all right.

"You never know what can happen these days," he went on. "It's hard to believe, but there are people in this world who are low enough"—he paused for emphasis—"sorry enough"—he paused again—"pure pig shit worthless enough to maliciously harm a child."

Toy lit a cigarette and took a couple of deep drags before continuing. Then he said, "Me, I think those people ought to have the same things done to them that they've done to the child. An eye for an eye, you might say."

There was no way that Ras could miss Toy's meaning, and he had to wonder how the man knew so much. Like as not, the deputies who had come out to question him had driven straight over here and had sat around in Never Closes, drinking and jawing about things they should have kept to themselves. Which just about made Ras Ballenger foam at the mouth. A man was innocent until proven guilty, after all, and he was getting tired of having to pretend to be innocent of things that were nobody's damn business.

He said, "I didn't come here to hear what you think, I came for my boy. Now, are you gonna bring him out, or am I gonna have to go in and git him?"

Toy flicked his eyes real quick at Ballenger, giving him the kind of look that says, "You just try."

Out loud, he said, "What you're gonna do, Mr. Ballenger, is get back in your truck and leave. You've got five seconds."

Ballenger came undone. "I'll have the law on you, you see if I don't! You may think you've got the sheriff in your pocket, but a man has rights, and I reckon I know mine."

Toy said, "Make that three."

The first place Toy checked after Ballenger left was the barn, but nobody had been in there lately. The blankets were spread out nice and neat, with Blade's presents right in the center, the way they'd been since shortly after that Battle of Jericho thing. Nobody knew for sure when the kids had put them there, but they'd made a lot of pilgrimages to the barn, so it could have been any time.

Toy looked next where he had figured all along that he would find the boy.

Swan and Blade were sleeping like puppies, both curled up every which way, their bodies touching here and there. Nothing could have been more innocent, but it bothered Toy when he eased in the door and saw them like that. He might not be a father himself, but he had the kind of feeling fathers get about their daughters, which is that kids grow up and things change awfully fast, so sometimes adjustments need to be made ahead of time by the grown-ups who are in charge.

Not that he thought he was in charge of Swan. But he was about to take charge of this situation.

He stood at the foot of the bed and cleared his throat. Swan and Blade both jumped just about out of their skins, and all the way out of bed. Since the bed was so high, they made a pretty good commotion when they landed on the floor.

Blade started to dive for the window, but Toy stepped over and blocked his path.

"Let's not go through that again," he said. "I'm not sending you home this time."

Blade swallowed hard and looked at Swan, who was looking at Uncle Toy with sudden worship in her eyes.

"You're not?" she asked.

"No, ma'am, I am not," Uncle Toy said ceremoniously. And Toy Moses had been known to go for years without saying anything ceremoniously.

Swan blew out a huge breath and sat smack down on the floor. Blade was still watching her for a sign, and this seemed to be one, so he sat down beside her. Toy stood there looking them both dead in the eye.

To Blade, he said, "I can't promise you that the law won't intervene, because they probably will. But I can promise that, as long as I have anything to say about it, you're welcome here, and you'll be safe."

He bent down and reached out his hand, and the boy, who had probably never gone through this ritual in his life, took it and gave him a manly handshake.

Then Toy said to Swan, "Now, we've got to figure out where your friend here is going to sleep. Because it's not going to be with you anymore."

So that was it. Blade Ballenger could stay until the law intervened. That sounded fine to Swan, since the only way she'd ever heard of the law intervening around here was by making sure that no liquor went to waste.

As for where Blade would sleep, that was decided democratically in a family meeting, which took place in Willadee and Samuel's bedroom. Toy led Swan and Blade from Swan's room to her parents' room, and Noble and Bienville must have been roused from sleep by the excitement in the air, because they both slid in the door before Toy got through explaining that Blade was back and needed accommodations. Pronto.

"You'll bunk in with Bienville," Samuel told Blade. "If you can find a spot among all his books."

That was democratic enough to suit all concerned.

. . .

Since Toy figured that Ras might come back, and there could be trouble, he didn't go home to sleep. He just went into his old bedroom and sacked out beside Bernice. Which was one way of getting her out of bed early.

Bernice popped into the kitchen before Willadee could even get the biscuits in the oven and said she understood the little Ballenger boy was back. Willadee said he sure was, and wasn't it wonderful. If there was anything at all wonderful about it, Bernice couldn't see it.

As soon as breakfast was over, Bernice was in the car and gone. Toy wasn't going to wake up for hours unless Ras Ballenger showed up again, and in either case, she'd rather be somewhere else. It was a Saturday, so Samuel would be around, but he was taking even less notice of her than usual, what with that little mongrel boy hanging around again, and she plain couldn't stand being around the rest of them, they'd all gone crazy.

She was the only one who wasn't happy about Blade being there. The rest of the family was elated.

Underneath all the euphoria, there was the feeling that there was no telling what might happen next, so Samuel and Willadee told the kids to stay where the grown-ups could see them.

"You don't have to worry about us getting out of pocket," Swan vowed fervently. "This is one time that you can believe us when we promise to be good and act right."

And they were good. All of them. Blade let Calla change his bandage and give him the scrubbing of his life, and he kept trying on the clothes of Bienville's that Willadee kept altering to fit him, and the other kids didn't get into the least bit of mischief while they waited.

Later on, when Samuel headed out to the pasture to bring Lady up, so they could ride her around the yard, Swan and Blade sat in the glider, Blade with his legs drawn up and a pad of paper propped on his knees. Calla had given him the paper and some pencil nubs when she noticed him drawing in the dirt. It turned out the kid didn't draw like a kid. He drew things so that you could tell what they were. The house, the fields, Calla's endless sea of flowers. Swan took turns watching his flashing hands and watching Noble and Bienville arm wrestling over at the picnic table. Noble was winning, because he was stronger, but Bienville kept messing up his concentration by asking him what he was thinking about.

"There's something preying on your mind," he would whisper mysteriously, like somebody at a séance. "I can sense it."

And every time, Noble would falter for just a fraction of a second. Just long enough for Bienville to strengthen his grip or brace his elbow a little better. There was no way he was going to win, but he was pretty good at making Noble work harder.

Bienville's teasing would ordinarily irritate Noble no end, but today he just laughed about it. Blade stopped drawing and laughed, too. All these people being so easygoing was enough to make a person downright giddy. At least a person who'd been living with Ras Ballenger all his life.

"I'm gonna stay here forever," he whispered to Swan. Not whispered mysteriously, as Bienville had done. He whispered the way you do when you want something so much you don't dare say it out loud.

"Well, you'll have to leave someday," Swan said. "We all will. This isn't really where we live. It's just where we are right now."

Blade couldn't make heads nor tails of that, so she gave him a little background.

"See, when your daddy's a preacher, you move around a lot, only we didn't have anyplace to move to this year, and Grandma Calla was lonesome because our grandpa"—how should she put this?—"*died unexpectedly*, so we moved in with her. But before long, we'll get another church, and then we'll be moving, and if everything works out, you can go with us."

Blade was floored by that one. "We're gonna live in a church?"

"No, we won't live *in* it. We'll live in a parsonage. Generally, those are right beside the church, or right across the street, so the church members can see what you're doing all the time."

Blade said, "Ohhh," like *now* he understood.

"Church members are funny," Swan went on. This was a subject she knew well. "You can't hardly please 'em, and there's always a faction—that's a bunch of people that get together and drink coffee at somebody's house after church, when the message was too strong and they got their toes stepped on—anyway there's always a *faction* that's trying to get rid of the preacher for one reason or another. That's why you move so much. Because sooner or later the faction wins out. But mostly, church members are pretty nice. Even the faction people are nice, to your face."

"Swan, what are you telling that boy?" That was Samuel talking. He'd just gotten back with Lady.

Swan looked up and smiled proudly. "I'm just telling him what to expect when we get a church and a parsonage."

Samuel handed Lady's reins to Noble and came over to sit in the glider.

"Well, now, we don't know for sure how this will all turn out," he told them. "We don't want to start making promises we may not be able to keep."

Blade had been looking up at Samuel, but now he started drawing again, moving his hand slowly and mechanically. Like that was one thing he could control. He might not know what Swan was talking about half the time, but he for sure knew what her daddy was saying. Samuel saw the hurt in his face—saw the way he was already so good at hiding hurt—and he hated like everything not to be able to say exactly what that little boy wanted to hear. But he couldn't.

"I think what we have to do," Samuel said, "is just enjoy this time together, and trust God for the outcome. He has ways of doing things that are better than anything we could even imagine on our own."

Blade looked to Swan for translation. As always.

"Who's God?" he asked. He was whispering again.

"God's kinda hard to explain," Swan told him. "But don't worry. You stay around my daddy long enough, you'll find out everything there is to know about Him."

Chapter 26

Toy woke up around four o'clock that afternoon, not because he'd gotten enough sleep but because Swan wasn't stealthy enough when she stole his shoes from beside the bed. He opened his eyes to see her creeping out of the room on tiptoe. He would have asked her what she was up to, but he figured he'd be more likely to find out the truth if he waited to see what developed.

What Swan was up to was shining Uncle Toy's shoes. She'd never shined a man's shoes before, she'd never even shined her own. Her daddy was the shoeshine expert in the Lake family, so that's who she went to for help. Samuel got out his shoeshine kit, explained the fine art, and then let Swan take over. A gift's not a gift if someone besides the giver does all the work.

"These shoes," Swan said to Blade, who was helping her by handing her whatever she needed, "are going to shine like new money. Hand me that brush."

He handed her the brush. She brushed industriously, loosening up dirt, then puffed out her cheeks and blew the dirt off the leather.

"Uncle Toy is going to be so glad he stood in the way of you going out that window," she told him. "What we've got to do is find plenty of ways to make him know that was the best move he ever made."

Blade listened and nodded.

"For instance, flowers," Swan mused aloud. "I think we should pick him some. You pick a flower for a person, it makes 'em feel special as the day is long."

Blade nodded again, looking thoughtful.

Swan said, "And we can do him favors. You know. Get stuff for him, so he doesn't have to get up. Things like that. Hand me that rag."

She held out the brush, expecting Blade to take it out of her hand and slap the shoeshine rag in its place, but her assistant was no longer where he'd been the last time she looked.

Calla's garden didn't stand a chance. Blade had cut quite a swath through the dahlias and daylilies, and was halfway through the hydrangeas when a large and somewhat lumpy shadow fell across him. He looked up into the face of Calla Moses and then looked around for an avenue of escape. There didn't seem to be one, not unless he wanted to go through the rugosa roses, which even he couldn't do. He'd never heard the term *impenetrable hedge,* but he knew one when he saw it.

Calla was holding a bucket, and he halfway expected her to swing it at his head, but instead, she handed it to him. He took it automatically. It was heavier than he expected, because it was half full of water.

"If you're looking for something to put those flowers in," she said, "you can use this." She gestured at the armful of flowers he was holding, and the other flowers that were strewn about on the ground. "I've been thinking about picking some to put on the side table in the living room. You must have read my mind."

Actually, that was about as far away from the truth as a person could get and still be a Moses. The reason she was out here was because she'd seen what he was doing from the door of the store, and she'd almost had a heart attack. You wouldn't know it by looking at her, though. She had calmed down considerably while she was deciding not to dismember him, and by now, she looked pleasant as you please. Even the veins in her neck had stopped standing out.

Blade couldn't say a word. Just two seconds ago, he'd thought it was doomsday, but here she was telling him he'd done something right. The world was getting stranger all the time.

"I was picking them for that man," he said softly, nodding toward the house. "That *uncle*."

Calla tipped back her head and sucked air in through her nose, the way a person does when a feeling gets to be too much to handle. *When was the last time anyone did anything special for Toy?* That's the thought that took her breath away. *When was the last time anyone did something desperate and beautiful to please him?* She had no idea that Swan was also doing something special for Toy, or that Toy's life was changing in ways he could never have anticipated. All she knew was that this little boy was doing a kindness for her own little boy—the man who had been her little boy—and her gratitude knew no bounds. She smiled at Blade Ballenger, and her mouth quivered a little when she did it.

After a second, she said, "Did you know flowers bloom better if you pick them?"

He shook his head solemnly.

"Well, they do. It's like you gave them a compliment, and all of a sudden they start doing everything they can to get another one."

"Do you know everything about flowers?" he asked. Which was precisely the right question to ask that particular woman at that particular moment.

"No, sir, I do not," she told him briskly. "But I'll lay odds you're going to grow up knowing everything about how to get on a woman's good side."

When Toy came out of his bedroom, dressed for work, his shoes were outside the door, and (as Swan had predicted) they shone like new money. Lined up along the wall, there were awesome bouquets in a variety of containers—everything from Calla's best vase to quart mason jars and several small jelly glasses. All dripping flowers. Toy cocked his head, and blinked his eyes, and wondered whether the person responsible was still alive, and whether his mama had hidden the body or called the sheriff and given herself up.

Bernice hadn't made it back yet, so she wasn't on hand for supper. Throughout the meal, Swan kept Toy's iced tea glass full, and Blade passed him the butter every time Toy helped himself to another piece of corn bread. Everybody in the family kept looking at Toy and grinning, like they all knew a secret and were about to pop from trying to keep it.

Finally, Toy said, "I'd like to thank whoever took my clodhoppers this afternoon and brought me back a brand-new pair."

"Those aren't new clodhoppers!" Swan chortled. "They just look new because I shined 'em!"

He gave her an unbelieving look. "You don't say. I could have sworn these shoes were spanking new. They even feel different."

Swan laughed from her toes. Beside her, Blade was about to come out of his skin, wondering whether his gift would also be acknowledged.

Toy said, "And whoever brought me flowers had better come get a hug."

He was looking at Swan expectantly when he said it, so he was surprised when Blade got down out of his chair and stole over beside him. The boy stood there, wordless and waiting, with the family looking on.

Toy stared at him. "You did that for me?"

Blade nodded shyly. Still waiting. Toy scooted his chair back a little, and took Blade into his lap, and hugged him good. Blade didn't have the nerve to hug him back, but he was sure eating this up.

"I always wondered what it felt like to be a king," Toy said, "and I reckon now I know."

Calla Moses beamed. Just beamed.

. . .

Nothing lasts forever. A couple of hours later, the law descended on Never Closes in the form of Deputy Dutch Hollensworth, who had been sent by Sheriff Early Meeks, who had been visited (again) by Ras Ballenger, who was the picture of righteous indignation. By that time, Blade had done something none of the Lake children had ever even tried, much less accomplished. He had followed Toy into the bar after supper.

At first, Toy had ordered him out, telling him that kids weren't allowed in there, but Blade had responded by darting around gathering up last night's ashtrays and emptying them into the trash can behind the bar. The ashtrays did need emptying, so Toy let him finish that job, and before he could remember to remind him to leave, the kid had grabbed a broom and was sweeping up the floor. That was what he was doing when the regulars started arriving, and they thought it was the cutest thing ever, that little rascal with the bandage over one eye, working like a bee.

"That boy looks like a pirate," Bootsie Phillips told Toy. "Only, he's got the wrong color eye patch. A really good pirate needs a black eye patch."

Toy didn't say anything, but the other men said enough to make up for his silence. One of them told Blade he sure hoped he wouldn't make them all walk the plank, and an old codger named Hoot Dyson asked him where he kept his parrot, and then Bootsie Phillips said, parrot, hell, he wanted to know where all the gold was buried. Blade was getting more attention than he'd ever gotten in his life, and it was the best feeling he'd ever had, so he swept faster and faster, and even added a little dance step of sorts to his routine. Before long, the men were dropping nickels on the floor and telling him that anything he swept up, he could keep. He had a pretty good jingle going in his pockets when Dutch Hollensworth arrived.

Toy's heart sank. Maybe this had to happen, but he wished it didn't have to happen so fast. And all at once, he wasn't one bit sure he was going to let it happen at all. He motioned to Blade, trying to signal him to scoot out the back door, but Blade was too busy entertaining the regulars to see.

Dutch saw, though. He saw Toy, and he saw the boy, and he kept his eyes on that youngster as he made his way across the room. When he reached the bar, he leaned his big frame sideways against it, so that if Blade cut and ran, he could go after him. Toy pulled a beer from a tub of ice at his feet, uncapped it, and put it into Dutch's hand. Dutch held the icy cold bottle up against the side of his face.

"I believe I'd like to take a bath in that tub of ice," he said. And then: "Sheriff told me if I saw that boy yonder, I had to pick him up and take him home, much as we all hate it."

Toy blinked at Dutch as if he didn't know what in the world he was talking about. "What boy?"

"Ras Ballenger's boy," Dutch said, pointing at Blade. "That boy right there."

Toy cut his eyes in the general direction of where Dutch was pointing and scratched his head, like he was trying to unravel a great mystery.

"Hey, fellas," he called out to the room, "anybody here see a little boy?"

At that, Blade glanced over, and sized the situation up, and stood still as a stone.

The regulars understood immediately what Toy Moses wanted them to say. The idea fell over them like a revelation. They might not carry much clout in the world, but by damn, this was one time they could make a difference. One by one, they looked first at Blade, then at the deputy—and shook their heads regretfully.

"Maybe your eyes is goin' bad, Dutch," Bootsie Phillips said.

And Nate Ramsey put in, "You haven't been doin' any of them things my mama used to tell me I better not do 'cause they'd make me go blind, have you, Dutch?"

Somebody let out a snicker, and then everybody in the room cracked up at the same time. Dutch stood there watching them all carry on, and he knew there was no way he was going to walk out of there with the kid. In a situation like this, his badge wouldn't mean a thing unless he used his gun, and he did not intend to draw his gun on his friends. Not over a thing like a little boy hiding from a man who had more than likely put his eye out with a bullwhip.

"Y'all *sure* you don't see him?" Dutch asked the crowd. The question had a going-once-going-twice sound to it, kind of like, if there were no more bids, this auction was over.

They all shook their heads again.

Dutch drank down his beer, and belched, and wiped his mouth with the back of his hand. "Well, then," he said, "I reckon I must've been seeing things."

And that was the end of that. For the time being, anyway. The regulars cheered, and somebody went over and slapped Dutch on the back and told him he was a good man, and several people bought him beers, even though he protested. Blade Ballenger's heart quit trying to jump through his throat, and the next time Toy motioned for him to get out of there, he slipped out the back door into the kitchen, quick as a lizard.

The other kids were sitting around the table, waiting for him, their eyes glued to the door.

"What was it like in there?" Bienville wanted to know as soon as Blade made it into the room. "Was it *tawdry*?"

Blade wasn't sure what he was confirming, but he said, yeah, he guessed it was tawdry enough.

Noble said, "There's a law car outside. Did that deputy see you?"

Blade plopped down into a chair beside Swan, and took the nickels out of his pocket, and stacked them on the table in front of him. There were eleven in all.

"He thought he did," Blade answered, "but he changed his mind. Do y'all think I look like a pirate?"

When Ras Ballenger found out that his son was being harbored at the Moses place, and that the law and a good portion of the community were conspiring to keep him there, he was fit to be tied. He'd kill Toy Moses, that's what he'd do. He'd walk in and shoot the S.O.B. right between the eyes.

"You'd get the chair," his wife told him, after about the tenth time she heard him make the threat. She didn't even duck when she said it.

"Don't get your hopes up," he snarled.

She did have a point, though. You kill somebody in cold blood, especially in public, there's generally a price to pay. When it comes to justifiable homicide, the law doesn't necessarily see things from the point of view of the person who felt justified.

Ras spent every waking minute thinking about how to get back at Toy and the whole Moses clan. With everybody in creation knowing about the hard feelings between the two families, Ras would get the blame for anything that happened over there. If that house burned down, he'd be arrested for arson. If somebody fell off a ladder, he'd be accused of sawing through the rungs.

Finally, one morning, he hit upon a plan that was so beautiful, and so simple, that he didn't know why he hadn't thought of it sooner. He was sitting in the backyard, in a straight chair, when the thought came to him. Sitting there looking over his yard and his outbuildings and his maze of pens and feedlots, while Geraldine gave him a haircut. Up until that moment, he'd been a ball of nerves, all mad and twisted up inside, but once he knew what to do, he relaxed all over. It was the best feeling he'd had in a *while*.

This plan wasn't the kind of thing that could be carried out overnight, not if it was done right, and he'd be damned if he'd do it any other way. He'd have to be patient, and in the meantime, his high-and-mighty neighbors could stew in their own juices. Let 'em lie awake nights wondering why he hadn't made another move to get his boy back, and what kind of hell would rain down when he did. Come to think of it, that helped make the waiting worthwhile—just knowing that there was no way those folks could be sleeping easy.

Geraldine finished the haircut and blew the snippets of hair off the back of his neck. Ras got up out of that chair feeling like a new man. By the time dark started coming on, he had cleaned up his tack room, trimmed all his horses' hooves, and set the posts for a new feedlot.

Chapter 27

Time rocked on.

The Moses family and the Lake family knew in the back of their minds that Something Terrible Could Happen, but the more days that passed, the less that idea seemed real, at least to the kids. Swan and Blade and Noble and Bienville spent the rest of that summer riding Lady and playing pirates and digging for buried treasure. Sometimes they all crawled under the house, and lay on their bellies, and drew pictures in the soft dirt with their bare fingers—something they'd learned from Blade. There were days when they'd start drawing under the porch and not stop until they'd covered every inch of ground from there to the other side of the house.

The grown-ups watched the kids playing, and smiled at how happy they all were, and marveled over how fast they were all growing—especially Blade. That boy was filling out like a young calf on new grass, his skin gleamed like burnished copper, and anytime he wasn't smiling, he was about to.

Samuel, meanwhile, spent his days doing work that was not what he was called to do. His nights were even worse. He tried not to let anyone see the desperation that was building inside him, but the music and laughter from Never Closes often drove him upstairs to his room, where he sat listening to *Radio Bible Hour* and calling on God for answers. Sometimes he'd go off in search of a church service somewhere. He went to prayer meetings. To revivals. If none of the white churches in the area had anything going on, he went to black churches, where the spirited music lifted him up and soothed his soul.

As he came and went, Bernice was constantly putting herself in his path. She felt the need to go to services tonight. Would he mind if she rode with him? He couldn't very well say no, but he always asked Willadee to come along. Willadee had enough to do already, what with taking care of the kids and canning food out of the garden, but she made the time. It was more church than she was used to, though, and after a while it started to wear on her.

"Maybe we could just all stay home and be together as a family," she told Samuel one night. He was getting ready to go to a prayer service over at Emerson, a little spot-beside-the-road community a few miles away. Willadee was supposed to be getting ready to go, too, but she had put up twelve quarts of string beans and that many quarts of pear preserves that day, plus, she'd done the wash and cleaned the house and made the meals, and she was tired. "I think sitting in the backyard watching the kids catch lightning bugs is a pretty good way of worshiping God every once in a while."

Samuel told her she didn't have to go if she didn't feel up to it, but he was determined not to let up on seeking answers from the Lord until he got them.

"Maybe the answer is that we're supposed to cut a watermelon and let the juice run down our chins," she said. Which only made Samuel feel that she was making light of the whole thing, although she wasn't. As far as she could see, God made watermelons for people to eat in hot weather, and He made people to love each other and enjoy life. It seemed to her that, when you're constantly seeking God's will, you may just be ignoring the obvious.

But she got ready, and she went. And so did Bernice.

August ground along, hot as a pistol, and dry as a bone. Samuel's residual income had been petering out as farmers' crops baked in the fields, and now the few folks who had actually been making their Not So E-Z payments no longer saw fit to do so. Some of them no longer saw fit to answer the door when Samuel came around to collect, either.

Samuel hated collecting from people who couldn't afford it, and he didn't have the heart to employ any of the hateful intimidation tactics that Mr. Lindale Stroud endeavored to teach him. Robbery was robbery, whether you used a gun or an insult to get the goods. He kept expecting God to open up some new source of income, but God's plan was turning out to be more complex than that. No matter how many applications he put in around town, there was no work available. He'd kept on contacting his preacher brethren, but the response was always the same: if they needed someone to fill their pulpits, he'd be the first person they would call. Now summer was almost over.

With school starting back, Samuel and Willadee took the four children into Magnolia and bought them all new shoes. Swan wanted black-and-white saddle oxfords, but her mother told her she'd get awfully tired of all that black and white before she wore the shoes out or outgrew them—which was how long she'd be wearing them. They settled on penny loafers, and Blade (who had all kinds of coins these days, from his friends in the bar) supplied the pennies.

The boys each got high-top tennis shoes and two pairs of jeans. Ordinarily, what would have happened next was that Samuel would have taken the boys to buy shirts while Willadee and Swan browsed the fabric counter. Actually, Swan looked forward to that. Imagining what could be created from this bit of fabric and that bit of trim was ever so much nicer than plowing through the racks of look-alike dresses in endless stripes and plaids, with their cheap buttons and tacky bows.

This year, Samuel didn't say a word about taking the boys to buy shirts, and they passed the fabric counter without even slowing down.

"What do you mean, pick out the ones I like?" Swan asked. Her mother had just summoned her to the living room, where a couple of dozen pieces of fabric were draped over the settee, the chairs, the various side tables.

"I mean, which ones do you think are prettiest," Willadee said. "I kind of favor the ones with the smaller prints."

Swan squenched one eye shut and peered at the fabric with the other one. There were bright colors and subdued colors and bold designs and delicate designs, with one common thread running through the mix: they were all feed sacks.

"Are you and Grandma Calla going to piece a quilt?" she asked. Although she knew the answer. You don't grow up the child of someone who lived on a farm during the depression without hearing about feed sacks and their many uses.

"Your grandma's got more quilts than she's got people to sleep under them," Willadee said. "We're going to make some darling dresses."

Swan didn't think she'd ever heard her mother use the word *darling* before. She opened the eye that was shut and closed the other one. For a long second, she stood there with her mouth hanging slack and her breathing on pause.

"I thought people had pretty much stopped making dresses out of feed sacks," she said finally.

"People have pretty much stopped needing to." Willadee sounded as cheerful as what she was being at the moment—a saleslady trying to sell somebody something she didn't want. "But you need dresses, and the boys need shirts. You get first choice."

Swan wanted to say that her choice was to go back to town and look at some polished cotton and maybe some pretty eyelet, but there was something in her mother's determined smile that kept her from it.

She drew a deep breath and eyeballed those fabrics again. After due consideration, she announced her decision. "You'll never get the boys to wear pink or lavender, so I'll take those. They can have the blues and greens."

Willadee breathed a sigh of relief. She'd gambled on Swan, and it had paid off.

Swan said, "This means we're really poor, right?"

"Not really poor. Really poor people don't have enough to eat, and can't afford to go to the doctor when they get sick. There's a difference between being poor and being prudent."

Swan sighed. "I don't suppose there's any way to know how long we'll be prudent, is there? Because I'd sure hate to still be prudent at Christmas."

"If we're still prudent at Christmas," Willadee promised, "we'll find ways to make up for it."

September showed up right on schedule, and lasted a whole month. The first day of a new school year had always been a big event for Swan. This year, she had mixed feelings about it. On the plus side, there was Blade, riding beside her on the school bus, looking up at her, so excited he couldn't sit still. Uncle Toy had bought him a black eye patch from some mail-order company, and he really did look like a pirate now—a small, full-of-mischief one. Living in a place where he didn't have to be afraid was bringing out his true nature. He was buoyant. Exuberant. Carefree. You couldn't have found the frightened, silent little boy that he had been if you'd followed him around with a divining rod.

Willadee had made his shirts out of the scraps she had left over from the other kids' clothes (*all* the other kids' clothes), and he'd insisted that morning on wearing the shirt that matched Swan's dress—which was pink, with tiny yellow flowers. Bienville had groaned, and Noble had told him the other boys would call him a sissy. Blade wasn't bothered in the least.

On the minus side, for Swan, was the bus itself. She'd always walked to school and had never even thought about what it might be like to lurch along, packed in tight with a bunch of rawboned farm kids who looked as though they might have wrestled steers before breakfast. Blade was going into the third grade this year, so he was an old hand at riding the bus, and he told her there was nothing to it. All she had to do was scoot over real fast if a big kid tried to sit on her.

The schoolhouse was in Emerson, with grades one through twelve all scrunched together in one building. Swan had plenty of experience enrolling in new schools where she didn't know anybody, so that didn't bother her. What bothered her was that she didn't know who *she* was anymore. She didn't even know what to write on the school admission form next to "Father's occupation," so she just left the space blank. Her father had lost his identity. And she'd lost hers. Being a preacher's kid may have had its drawbacks, but it was something. Now she was nobody. At least she didn't have to worry about anybody making fun of her feed sack dress. There wasn't a dress in sight that could match Willadee's handiwork.

Bienville fared better than Swan. He was there for the books. If nobody paid any attention to him, so much the better. That just left more time for reading. And if anybody gave him a hard time? He'd ask them questions they couldn't answer about some topic they'd never heard of, until they either left him alone or got curious enough to ask *him* questions that he *could* answer, in which case, he'd hold forth. At length.

Noble fared worst of all. Maybe it was the thick glasses that gave the school bullies the idea he'd be an easy mark. Or the way his voice squeaked when he had to stand up and introduce himself to the class on that first day. Anyway, he was no match for the backwoods boys—and Becoming a Tree proved to be an unworkable tactic. By the time noon recess was over, a couple of bruisers had knocked him down and dragged him around the school yard by his heels. He arrived back at Calla's that afternoon with a black eye and patches of hide scraped off both arms.

. . .

"The most manly thing to do," Samuel counseled him at supper, "is to walk away from a fight."

Noble stared at his plate. He had spent the afternoon in his room, too humiliated to show his face.

"You can't walk away when somebody's dragging you by your heels," Swan pointed out. She was hot under the collar about the whole thing.

"The idea is to prevent it from happening," Samuel said. "There's always somebody spoiling for a fight. If we sink to their level, we'll get to be just like them. You don't want that, do you, Noble?"

Grandma Calla heaped some extra roast beef and mashed potatoes onto Noble's plate and smothered it all in gravy. "You eat," she said. "Put some meat on your bones. Bullies don't pick on anybody they think might mop the floor with them."

Samuel shook his head gravely. "Now, Calla, that's not the answer. No matter how big he gets, there'll always be somebody bigger." And to Noble he said, "What I'm telling you, Son, is that the place you need to be strong is on the inside."

Noble gripped his fork tightly and stabbed at his roast beef.

"I don't think me being strong on the inside is going to keep those boys from stomping my guts out," he said. "They've decided to get me, and they're going to do it."

Samuel was not to be swayed. He had a way of looking at the world that worked for him, and he was convinced that it would work for all mankind.

"I imagine they got that out of their systems today. The thing you've got to do is find some good in those boys. That may not seem possible, but if you look for it, you'll find it. And once you do, I guarantee you their attitudes will change."

Toy got up from the table. So it wouldn't look like he was leaving because he disagreed with Samuel (although he was, and he did), he rubbed his belly and told Willadee that was a mighty good supper, he just hoped he hadn't hurt himself eating so much. As he walked behind Noble's chair, he gave the boy's shoulder a good, hard squeeze.

"You have any time one afternoon this week, I need to pull the motor on your granddaddy's truck, and I could use some help." He wouldn't presume to tell Samuel how to raise his son, but he could damn well treat the boy like a man.

Noble actually lifted his eyes. "Yessir," he said. "I'll make time."

Chapter 28

The first thing Toy did after he got to his mama's house the next afternoon was start taking the hood off Papa John's old pickup. He had the first bolt out and was about to go after the second when the school bus pulled to a stop out front. Toy glanced up, expecting to see Noble hotfooting it over to join him, but the boy was walking with his head down and his shoulders hunched. He wasn't even watching where he was going. Swan, Bienville, and Blade trailed silently along behind him, all of them obviously unnerved. Another good look told Toy why.

Noble's entire face was swollen, his nose was blue and misshapen, and the front of his shirt was caked with patches of dried blood. Toy felt sick at heart first, mad as hell second, and determined to fix this situation third and last. He went striding across the yard to meet the kids, barking instructions every step of the way.

"Swan! You take Noble's books into the house and tell your mama that we'll be in directly. Bienville, Blade, you boys go do your homework, and if you don't have any, make some up. Noble—you come with me."

No one argued. They didn't ask questions, either, although they had plenty. Toy headed for the barn, walking stiffer than usual, because he was moving faster than usual, and Noble hurried to keep up. When they got to the barn, they disappeared inside, and Toy pulled the big, faded wood doors shut behind them.

Swan and Bienville and Blade just stood there, staring.

"You think Uncle Toy is going to give him a whipping for letting himself get beat up again?" Bienville asked his sister.

"I don't know. He sure looked mad."

Blade said, "I'll bet he's finding out who did it, so he can go do the same thing to them." And he added, "I think he's always on our side."

Swan and Bienville were pretty sure that their uncle was on their side, too, but they didn't know what to make of all this.

Grandma Calla came out of the store, and Willadee came out of the house, and both of them asked the same question at the same time.

"Where's Noble?"

"In the barn," Swan answered.

"With Uncle Toy," Bienville said.

"Noble got his nose busted," said Blade.

Calla and Willadee exchanged a worried look, wondering what would become of Noble if things kept on like this. Willadee wanted to go right down to the barn and see about her son, but Calla wouldn't hear of it.

"You let those two alone, Willadee, and I mean it. Some things, a man has to handle."

Calla didn't point out that the reason Toy was handling this was because the man who should have been, wasn't. She didn't have to.

Out in the barn, Noble was perched on the metal seat of an old tractor. Uncle Toy was leaning against the tractor fender, looking up at him.

"All right," he said. "Those boys have whupped your ass twice now. And I wasn't there, but I can tell you this much. Both times, it was because you asked them to do it."

"Oh, hell, no, I didn't," Noble protested. Swan wasn't the only one who felt free to cuss around Toy. "All I did was mind my own business."

Toy wouldn't let him off that easy. "We always ask for what we get, boy. One way or another, we ask for it. And one way or another, we get it."

Noble flared. Furious. "I guess that means you asked to get your leg blown off!"

He felt hateful and small for saying that, but life and Toy Moses had pushed him past his limit.

"You bet I did," Toy shot back. "And I'd do it again. There's a lot in my life that's not the way I'd like, but every bit of it is just what I've signed up for. You decide what you want, you get what goes with it."

Toy lit a cigarette and smoked silently for a moment, looking off at nothing. Like he was still sifting through all those words he'd just said. After a little bit, he looked at Noble again.

"What are *you* gonna sign up for? You might as well decide right now. What do you want, Noble Lake?"

At first, Noble said that what he wanted was not to get beat up anymore. Toy gave a little grunt of a laugh and shook his head. "You sure don't ask for much."

So then Noble said he wanted to be able to beat shit out of anybody who tried to beat shit out of him.

"Measly," said Toy.

Noble jumped down off the tractor seat and stood there facing his uncle, with his fists clenched and his eyes blazing.

"Well, what the hell am I supposed to ask for?" he bellowed.

Toy gave him an easy grin. "Well, damn, boy. Ask for something big."

Which brought Noble up short. And made him think. Finally, he set his jaw, and looked Toy Moses in the eye, and asked for what he'd wanted all his life.

"I want—to be formidable."

And Toy Moses said, "Now we're gettin' someplace."

When Toy and Noble came out of the barn an hour later, the two were walking easy and relaxed, and laughing about something. Nobody asked them what had gone on in there, and they didn't volunteer any information.

At supper that night, Noble ate like he'd been hauling hay all day, and he held his head up like a champ. His daddy, dismayed at the shape his face was in, asked him what had happened.

"Ran into something," Noble said, cracking a grin that had to hurt.

"The same boys?"

"Yes, sir."

Samuel blew out a frustrated breath. "I may have to go to that school and talk to the principal."

"No, sir. You won't need to do that."

Samuel studied Noble's face for a moment. You could tell he felt partly responsible. "You sure? Looks like they worked you over pretty good this time."

"They did, for a fact," Noble agreed. "I reckon I wasn't looking hard enough for the good in those boys."

After that, Toy made it a point to be on hand when the kids got off the bus every afternoon, and he and Noble always disappeared into the barn immediately. An hour or so later, they'd emerge, sweaty and limping. Both of them. A couple of times, Samuel arrived home from work while their sessions were going on, and both times, the "little kids" (as Noble now referred to Blade, Bienville, and Swan) started playing Cowboys and Indians in a heartbeat. Blade would let out a bloodcurdling war whoop, and the others would set in yelling the magic words.

"There he is! There's the chief! Riding into camp!" Then they'd yell a lot of other stuff to throw Samuel off, just in case the warning had been too direct. *"How!"* and *"Me Friendly!"* and *"Gottem Wampum?"*

There was an unspoken conspiracy, and Samuel never suspected. When he'd see Toy and Noble coming out of the barn minutes later, with their hair plastered to their scalps, and their clothes plastered to their bodies, he just figured the man had been getting some work out of the boy.

Around the place, Noble had now started pitching in with the work, especially the heavy lifting. Anything that would build a muscle. The best part, though, was the way he handled himself these days. The way he stood up straight and looked relaxed at the same time. And never seemed to be moving fast but always looked as if he might—without warning. He was going from awkward and gawky to graceful and sure, right before the family's eyes. And it was more than a physical thing. He was doing what Samuel had advised—getting strong on the inside. Just not quite the way that Samuel had intended.

"What's got into Noble?" Samuel asked Willadee one night, when they were getting undressed for bed.

"Maybe he's coming into his own," she replied.

She didn't bother to tell him the rest—that Toy was taking their son in hand and showing him how to survive. Or that she was so blessed glad. She was well aware that whatever lessons Noble was learning could someday get him hurt. Or worse. But so could walking away from a fight, she thought. So could walking across a street. The main thing was, if he learned the right lessons, and learned them well, he'd be facing whatever came at him head-on for the rest of his life. He'd never have to hang his head ever again.

Noble's test came six weeks later, which was sooner than he'd hoped, but it turned out he was ready. The way Swan told it that night at supper, a trio of husky farm boys had cornered Noble behind the schoolhouse, and informed him that he could lick their boots or eat them. His choice.

"That's what they said," she babbled excitedly. " 'You can lick 'em, or eat 'em. Your choice.' And Noble said, 'Got any salt?' "

She let out a hoot of laughter and pounded the table so hard the dishes rattled.

"Cross my heart," she howled. "Those were his exact words." She made her voice low and, well, formidable—like Noble's must have been. "He said, *Got any salt?* Like that."

Everybody except Samuel had been hearing this all afternoon, and they were laughing, too. Noble wasn't, of course. He was sitting across the table, very nearly as bunged up as he had been the last time this happened, only this time, he was soaking up praise.

Samuel looked at the happy lot and listened without a word.

"And then they lit into him," Bienville announced. This was too good a story to let Swan do all the telling.

Blade jumped up from the table and made as if to be Noble, dodging farm boys.

"Only he wasn't there!" he exulted. Dancing. Darting. "All they were doing was running into each other."

Bienville said, "Hard."

"When it was over," Swan bragged, "Noble was the only one standing."

Blade pretended to be a farm boy, falling down. In pain.

Samuel said, "Blade. Get back to the table."

Blade climbed back into his chair but fast.

Samuel focused on Noble. Only on Noble. "I guess you're feeling pretty good right now."

Swan said, "Well, it's not like he started it. When there's three against one—"

Samuel lifted a finger in her direction, never taking his eyes off his eldest.

"You'd rather I'd licked their boots?" Noble asked. He'd never used that tone with his father before.

"I don't think you should have egged them on."

"They were *coming* on, Daddy. Me saying that just threw them off a little. Gave me an edge. Right, Uncle Toy?"

Samuel's face froze for a split second, not even his eyes moving. Then he looked over at Toy, who was looking back. Unapologetic.

"I've been giving the boy some pointers," Toy said.

Everybody watched Samuel, holding their breath. And now he understood. The way he'd been shut out and overruled. Even by Willadee. He felt all at once that he was in a room full of strangers, and it was all he could do to keep sitting there. Sitting there feeling useless and impotent and betrayed.

He wanted to tell them, bitterly, that it was good to know how much his opinion mattered. He wanted to let loose with the fiery temper he used to have but had been dampening for years. Wanted to just leave. But he couldn't say or do any of that, because whatever he said or did would prove whether everything he'd already said to Noble had been empty words or words a man could live by.

When he finally spoke, it was to Noble—his voice sounding loud, because the room had been quiet for so long.

"I'm glad you're all right," he said.

Later on, when Willadee and Samuel were in bed, she apologized for helping to keep him in the dark about Noble and Toy.

"I imagine you did what you thought was right," he said.

"No, I didn't. I thought it was right for Noble to learn to look out for himself. But it was wrong to hide it from you like that. I should have just argued with you. There's nothing wrong with a good healthy argument."

When he didn't answer, she said, "I didn't mean for you to be hurt."

"I know you didn't." Those were his words. What he was thinking was, You didn't mean for me to find out.

Willadee put her arms around him and held him close. "I won't do anything like that again. I promise."

They lay there silent for a moment, then he gently shrugged out of her arms and turned over on his side, facing away from her. She kissed his back. Spooned him.

"Are we okay?" she asked. "You and me?"

He said, "You know how much I love you, Willadee."

For Sam Lake, every day just got harder. He didn't say a word to anybody about his sense of defeat. Didn't let on that it bothered him to witness the deepening bonds between Toy and the kids. Truth be told, he was glad for Toy. That childless man, who had suddenly become a hero to all of Samuel's children. And one of Ras Ballenger's.

Some mornings, Samuel woke to find that Toy had already gotten the kids up and had taken them down to the pond for a little fishing. Sometimes he came home in the afternoon to find the kids raking the yard with Toy. Burning leaves with Toy. Having a weenie roast with Toy. Or coming out of the woods from some trek they'd all been on. He saw Toy growling at them and bossing them and loving them, and he sensed that an emptiness inside the man was being filled. Knew that Toy was sharing with those children things he hadn't been able to share with anyone since his younger brother's death. The woods. The water. His world. He was glad for Toy, all right. It was himself he wasn't glad for. Himself he was feeling bad toward, for letting everybody down. Himself he stared at in the mirror and didn't know anymore.

Samuel had no solace. He took his fiddle down to the swimming hole and sat on the bank listening to the wind in the cottonwoods, and when he pulled his bow across the strings, the music skimmed over the water and swooped through the woods and always came back to him sobbing. Samuel never shed a tear. His fiddle did it for him.

Chapter 29

Ras Ballenger didn't think much of people in general, and he loathed the Moses family in particular. Over the months since that thing with Odell Pritchett, business had fallen off considerably, not to mention Ras had noticed folks talking behind their hands when he'd go into town to buy feed for his livestock. The hatred he felt for his neighbors had grown into a poisonous, festering abscess that plagued him day and night. Lately, he'd been powerfully drawn to the Moses place, and he had taken to driving past there at odd times, just to see what was going on.

Across the road from Calla's was sixty acres of land that belonged to a family named Ledbetter, who had raised cotton there until a few years back, when Carl Ledbetter died and his wife, Irma, moved into town. Nothing was there now except empty fields that had been taken over by scrub brush, a weighing shed that had been taken over by poison ivy, and a For Sale, Reasonable sign that some drunk had run over and nobody had ever bothered to set back upright. Sometimes, late at night, Ras would turn his truck in to the field, and pull over behind the weighing shed, and watch the Moses place for hours.

Toward the end of October, it rained unexpectedly and turned cold. Toy woke late that afternoon to find the rain gone and the air crisp as apples. It took all he had to force himself to open the bar. No man should be shut up all night in a place like that.

Bootsie Phillips, who wouldn't have minded being shut up in a place like that for the rest of his life, got so drunk that night that he fell off his barstool and rolled under a table. Toy and the regulars just left him there. It wasn't the first time this had happened. Sometime around 4:00 A.M., when the crowd had cleared out, and Bootsie was the only one left, it dawned on Toy that tradition was one thing and being a damned fool was another. It was just plain ridiculous for him to stay there with nothing to do but watch Bootsie Phillips sleep, when that wasn't making any money and he wasn't getting to do what he loved most, which was welcome the pearly grays. Keeping Never Closes open all night every night meant that by the time he made it into the woods these days, dawn had usually cracked and broken, spilling sunlight through the trees and painting splotches on the ground.

He didn't want to wake Bootsie up and make him drive home drunk, so he grabbed an old overcoat of his daddy's that had been hanging on the coatrack by the door since whenever John had put it there, and he covered Bootsie up. Then he cut the lights and left the bar, locking the door behind him.

For a second, he stood out in the yard, sucking in air that smelled of damp earth and autumn, and he wondered why people even had houses. He, for one, could do without the walls, and not having any around him at the moment made him so glad he trembled inside.

Ras Ballenger sat in his truck, imagining what it was going to feel like when he finally settled his debts with that bunch. They had ruined his business and stolen his son and made him look like a half-wit. For all of that, they would pay, and pay dearly. The pieces of his plan were in place. Now it was just a matter of picking the right time.

He couldn't see the bar, since it was on the back side of the house, but he could see the glow from the lights—the muted way they lit the yard. He watched the customers coming and going until they were going, going, gone. When the lights went out, in the wee hours, he came to attention, wondering what that meant. He'd never seen the Moses yard dark before. Not once.

With daylight not due to come calling for at least another hour, he considered going over there and prowling around. Maybe snatching his son and making off with him. See how safe those bastids felt when they woke up in the morning to find that the child who didn't belong to them was gone.

While he was thinking those thoughts, a light winked on in the side yard. The dome light in Toy's truck. The truck and Toy Moses, materializing in the darkness. Ras saw the big man reach inside and take his rifle from the gun rack. Saw Toy Moses reaching behind the seat, and bringing out a vest, and pulling it on. A hunting vest, Ras knew. The truck door closed, and the yard went dark again for a moment. Then the bobbing beam of a flashlight came to life, moving away from the house, and Ras's mind filled in the blanks of all he couldn't see. Toy Moses, leaving the yard and heading for the woods, his gun across his shoulder. *Hisgunhisgunhisgun.* Those words went buzzing through Ras Ballenger's brain, buzzing and humming and buzzing, it was the damnedest thing, the damnedest damn thing, the way he knew all at once that he could take his revenge right now, and still carry out his original plan later on, easy as pie and twice as sweet.

The slender little creek curved and twisted through the Moses pasture, slithering on and off the Ballenger place on the east side and the Hempstead farm, to the north.

Toy moved along, not following the creek exactly but keeping it in sight. Before sunup like this, a man could get turned around in deep woods, even woods he knew, if he didn't notice things like which side of a creek he was on, and which way the water was flowing. He'd have found his way out, of course, but that wasn't the point. The point was that this was stolen time, time treasured, and Toy didn't want it marred by the rough edge of frustration. He wanted to feel as free as the water in that creek. And when the dawn washed across the sky, as it would before long, he wanted to drink it in, drink it up, drink it down. He wasn't here to hunt for game (he wasn't sure why he'd even brought the gun), he was here for a baptism—the only kind he knew and believed in. Immersion in silence and anointing by the pearly grays.

About the time Toy got to the first big curve in the creek, Ras Ballenger got back home. He took his own rifle from his own gun rack, then crossed his yard and faded into the woods. He had no way to know where Toy Moses was headed, but hunting was hunting. You looked for tracks and traces, and you tried to reason like the creature you were hunting, and you didn't make a sound.

Sometimes you don't think. You don't dream. You don't ask for anything or wish for anything or need anything, you just let yourself *be*. That's what Toy was doing when the pearly grays arrived. *Just being.* He was squatting on the bank of the creek, looking down into the water—watching as it turned from dark to light, matching the sky tone for tone. There was an orange leaf skimming along on the surface. One bright orange, gently curling leaf, stark against the singing, silver water, and he couldn't take his eyes off it. It was that perfect.

When Toy fell forward, he had the giddy impression that the leaf was flying toward him, flying hard, and bringing the water with it. He was thinking that it was crazy as the devil for a leaf to behave like that when he heard the sharp *crack* that told him he'd been shot.

Chapter 30

Millard Hempstead and his buddy, Scotty Dumas (who lived in town and liked to come out to Millard's a couple of times a year to hunt), had hit the woods early that morning. They were out there after squirrels, but then Scotty saw a wild hog and just had to take a shot at it—shooting wild, because he was too excited to think straight. Town types didn't see many razorbacks, much less get trophies to put over their mantels, so he didn't want to miss his chance.

He didn't miss his chance, but he missed the hog, although he didn't have sense enough to know that. The hog whirled and crashed back into the brush, and Scotty crashed along after it.

"Got 'im!" he hollered over his shoulder to Millard.

"Boy, you ain't got nothin' but shit for brains!" Millard hollered back. "If you'd hit that hawg, you'd have just made him mad. You can't kill a razorback with a squirrel rifle!"

Scotty wasn't listening. He was going after the hog. Millard hollered at him again, telling him to get his ass back out of that brush if he didn't want to go home in more pieces than he came in, but Scotty was determined to get that trophy head. What he thought was, if the hog had been hit, it would start to weaken sometime. All he'd have to do would be to shoot it again when he found it and finish it off.

Scotty went lumbering along in the general direction the hog had gone, and it was hardly any time until he came upon the creek bank where Toy Moses had been just a moment ago. There was no sign of the hog. Scotty went on up to the edge of the bank, and looked down into the water, and then his knees went clean out from under him.

"Millard?" he yelled. "Millard, you better get on over here. I just shot Toy Moses!"

Ras Ballenger had picked up Toy's tracks and was having no trouble following them. Yesterday's rain had left the dirt soft and the leaves on the ground slicked over. Toy might as well have been carrying a sack of corn with a hole in it, the trail was that easy to see. When Ras heard the shot, he knew he was getting close and figured Toy must have just gotten himself a squirrel. His last, unless he managed to get another one before Ras got to him. That big bastid had gotten his last of everything.

Of course, what he heard next was all that racket that Scotty Dumas made going after that hog, and then the man's voice, blubbering about how he'd shot Toy Moses. Ras's first impulse was to scram out of there, so nobody would ever know he'd been in these woods today. But what difference did it make? He hadn't been the one to pull the trigger.

He scuttled toward the voices (there were two voices now), and when he got to the creek, he could see two men going over the side of the bank. One of them was Millard Hempstead, and he was white as a sheet.

"God a'mighty, Scotty," he was saying. "I think you killed him!"

Then Scotty said he didn't believe Toy was dead, and Millard said as much blood as there was in the water, he ought to be, and Ras Ballenger came forward and did what any good neighbor would do in a case like that. He offered to help them get that poor man to a doctor.

Toy didn't exactly hear angels singing, but there was once that he thought he heard one calling his name. The way he was hurting, if she had told him to come on home, he wouldn't have argued.

Mostly, the trip into town was a bloody haze. Blood all over his soaking wet clothes, and blood in his mouth, with every breath he tried to draw and couldn't. That bullet got a lung. He knew. And he was losing blood fast. He knew that, too.

He was dimly aware of the men who hauled him out of the creek and carried him, running, jostling, shouting to each other—"my truck's up there on the ridge"—"lay him in the back, and somebody sit back there to hold him"—"if we can get him into town before he bleeds to death, it's gonna be a wonder"—"dammit won't this truck go any faster"—

Those men. The men who saved him. Millard and Scotty and, of all people, Ras Ballenger. Toy kept thinking that maybe Ras had been the one who shot him, but Scotty was the one who kept apologizing over and over, at least he thought it was Scotty. Every sound seemed to be coming from far away, voices mingling three into one, and some soft, gurgling sound he didn't recognize until it struck him that he was the one making it. After that, it seemed to him that he was way up above the men, looking down, thinking that he ought to tell them to let off the gas and take it easy. Life was too precious to live in a hurry.

All the adults in the Moses family spent the day in Magnolia at the hospital, all except Aunt Nicey, who volunteered to keep the children at her house. Swan and Noble and Bienville and Blade were beside themselves with grief and begged to go to the hospital, so they could be there when Uncle Toy came out of surgery, but Samuel wouldn't hear of it.

"You can go later in the week," he promised, "after Toy's condition has stabilized." He didn't say *if*, he said *after*.

"But he needs to know we're there!" Swan wailed. "We're the best love he has!"

Calla couldn't imagine where the child got that kind of wisdom, but the words made her cry. She gathered Swan and the three boys all into her arms at once.

"You're mighty right you are," she said. Bernice was standing right beside her, looking all beautiful and insulted. Calla didn't care. She wasn't even done yet.

"Everybody on earth needs to know they're loved, and I guess you four kids have given your uncle Toy something he's had way too little of." So there. "Now y'all go on to Aunt Nicey's, and be good children, and I'll tell Toy you're doing him proud."

So they went.

When Bootsie Phillips came to, around noon, there wasn't a sound to be heard anywhere, and he couldn't figure what the hell had happened. There he was on the floor, covered up with a musty old overcoat, and nobody on hand to serve him a drink.

So he served himself one. And then another. And another. It was on the third drink that he got to wondering what was keeping Toy, who was well known for stepping out into the night air and staying a few minutes when the bar wasn't too busy. But this had been more than a few minutes.

Bootsie wandered over to the window and pulled back the curtain. All that daylight, when he'd been expecting darkness, just about put his eyes out. He dropped the curtain, then lifted it again and looked back out. Nothing was stirring on the whole place.

This had to be investigated. He went over to the door and tried to fling it open, but it refused to be flung. He was locked in. Which could be one of the best or worst things that ever happened to him. He wasn't sure which.

Suddenly, he had to take a leak, and the bathroom that belonged to the bar was on the outside of the building. Some men would have just marched over and peed in the sink behind the bar, and Bootsie might have done that himself if it had been anybody else's sink, but it belonged to his friends. He couldn't just go peeing in the Moseses' sink when these folks had been so good to him over the years. Not to mention he was hungry. So he tried the other door, the one that led into the house, and discovered that he wasn't locked in after all.

He proceeded into the house.

The bathroom was easy to find, and so was the food. There was a plate of ham and biscuits on the table, covered up with an extra table-cloth, and Bootsie couldn't imagine that Calla would mind if he helped himself. While he was eating, several cars pulled up out front and then drove off, and that set him wondering again what was going on here. His mind hadn't come out of the fog enough to be working with any real efficiency, but it was working well enough now for him to realize that something was wrong. Maybe bad wrong.

He went in search of answers and found the rest of the house as empty and lifeless as the bar and the kitchen. He also found that the door between the living room and the store was as unlocked as the one between the kitchen and the bar.

He proceeded into the store.

And wouldn't you know. No sooner had he gotten in there than another car arrived. Mindful of how the Moses family was about never closing regardless of circumstances, Bootsie went over and un-locked the door, and opened up for business.

The new arrival was Joy Beekman, who was known for coming in and taking over when anyone in the community had a tragedy. She was bringing a casserole, saying she was just so glad there was some-body there, she didn't want to leave chicken delight out on the front steps, it might spoil, but she had wanted to bring something over to show the family she was thinking about them.

"I want them to know they're in our hearts and prayers," she said. "It's so hard on a family when something like this happens, and no-body feels like lighting a match to a stove burner."

Bootsie could see that he'd been right about there being something wrong, but he still didn't know what it was, and he hated to admit it. So he asked the obvious question.

"Have you heard anything?"

Joy shook her head sorrowfully. "Not anything that you wouldn't already know. Just that Toy had that horrible hunting accident this morning, and they don't know whether he's going to make it or not."

Bootsie went numb all over.

Joy said, "And, if he dies, I hope to goodness they try Scotty Dumas for manslaughter and take away his hunting license."

After she left, other people kept coming, some of them to buy, some of them to express their concern, and almost everybody bringing food—cakes and pies and what have you, every woman having prepared her specialty. Bootsie didn't know what to do with all of it, so he let it collect on the counter until the ladies started bypassing him and carrying it into the house.

Bootsie took care of customers, and thanked everybody for being such good neighbors, and told them all he'd let Miz Calla know they'd stopped by. After a while, Millard Hempstead's wife, Phyllis, came over and offered to tend to the house, since folks would like as not be coming and going all night, and you know how dishes can stack up when you have that many people at the same time. She said nobody could get into the hospital waiting room to even ask how Toy was doing. There were so many people in there, you couldn't stir them with a stick.

After a while, Bootsie decided that Moses tradition could probably be honored just as well by keeping one of the businesses open as the other, so he locked the store and went back through the house, nodding and speaking to people along the way. For a man who hadn't had a bath in two days, and had slept on the floor of a bar the night before, he was a gracious host. Phyllis handed him a plate loaded with food and told him he was a good man to help the Moses family out like this. Bootsie told her it was the least he could do.

Nobody knew where to find a key to the outside door of Never Closes, so Bootsie opened that establishment by propping the kitchen door open with a straight chair and telling the folks they were welcome to drink on the honor system. Women who had never laid eyes on the inside of a bar took guarded peeks as they walked past, and quite a few of the men took Bootsie up on his offer.

Nobody played the jukebox, though. There was no dancing or loud laughter, either. Everybody kept their voices low and their footsteps light, as they waited for word about Toy Moses.

Chapter 31

The surgery was tricky and took hours. According to Doc Bismark, who came out into the waiting room to tell the family, Toy would spend at least a month in the hospital, and another month or two re- cuperating at home. Bernice Moses wept. Apparently, for joy.

Calla all but shouted. Her boy would live! Her other boys hugged her and said they had known that old scudder was too tough to get done in by a .22. Then the rest of the family was hugging her, too, and telling her that God was good, and this was an answered prayer, and Calla agreed with every one of them.

After Doc Bismark left, the family went over and converged around the men who had brought Toy in. Everybody thanking them. Everybody blessing them.

"Doc says you boys got him here just in time," Sid Moses told them. "Another few minutes, he'd have been too far gone to save."

Scotty set in to apologizing again for shooting Toy, but the Moses crew didn't want to hear it. They told Scotty to stop blaming himself and advised all three of them to go home and get some rest, and topped it off by inviting them to drop by sometime for supper. They didn't even draw the line at Ras Ballenger. If anybody thought about how awkward it might be for that man to come sit at their table right across from his estranged son, or of the possibility that he might refuse to leave without the boy, they dismissed those thoughts as unworthy. Maybe losing his son had made him take a hard look at himself and his ways. Maybe he had changed.

Aunt Nicey was a dimpled little dumpling of a woman, but her house was the worst place in the world for a child. There were starched doilies everywhere, and crafty things that she had made, and pressed glass lamps, and the sweetest little porcelain candy dishes sitting around with no candy in them.

Swan, Noble, Bienville, and Blade huddled on the couch, afraid to stop thinking about Toy, because then he might die, and afraid to move, because they might break something. Lovey, who still was not their favorite person, instructed them what not to touch.

They didn't want to touch anything anyway. Every few minutes, they asked Aunt Nicey if she would please call the hospital again to see how Uncle Toy was doing, but she said if she drove those folks crazy, that wouldn't do Toy one speck of good, plus Sid would call as soon as he knew anything.

Then she made them sit around the dining room table while she set up this contraption that looked like a big blackboard covered in felt. (She had another such board at church, but she kept this one at home, for when her Sunbeams came over.) Maybe hearing a nice Felt Board Story would help take their minds off things, she cooed. Swan and her brothers had seen so many felt boards during their Sunday School careers that they didn't care whether they ever saw another one, but Blade had had no such experiences, so he was game.

Aunt Nicey brought out a host of paper cutouts of biblical characters and biblical props (a palm tree, a tent, a stretch of desert sand, some sheep and camels) that all had felt glued to the back of them. These, she let Lovey place on the felt board at strategic times (they stuck, like magic) as she (Aunt Nicey) launched into the story of David and Goliath. When she got to the part where the giant was stepping on little people and squashing them to mush, Blade narrowed his eyes and clenched his fists.

"That mean old sonofabitch," he sputtered indignantly.

Aunt Nicey said, yes, well, there was a price to pay for sin, and Goliath had turned out paying it.

By midafternoon, Aunt Nicey (worn out from being so nice) suggested that a nap might be simply delicious. That plan met with considerable resistance, so she set a stack of storybooks on the coffee table and disappeared into her bedroom with Lovey in tow.

When Sid called, a little later, to announce that Toy would live, Swan answered the phone and delivered the news to the boys. They opened their mouths wide and squealed silently, careful not to wake anybody who was less bother when they were asleep. After that, it got harder and harder to be good, so they gave it up. Bienville and Noble got into a wrestling match, right on Aunt Nicey's nice hardwood floor, and Blade kept poking Swan in the ribs and running off. After the fourth or fifth time, Swan took out after him and cornered him over beside a table loaded with carnival glass.

"What has gotten *into* you?" she demanded.

"Nothing," he shrieked, through peals of laughter.

Then he kissed her smack on the mouth.

Toy was allowed to have one visitor. Being the wife, Bernice got the honor. Toy was hooked up to several machines, and he didn't really have the strength for talking, but he tried.

"Looks like you'll still have me to put up with," he rasped, painfully.

Bernice stroked his arm, and kissed his forehead, and gave him the tenderest smile in the world. "Thank God you're alive," she lied.

Chapter 32

It wasn't so much *decided* that Willadee would take over running Never Closes as it was *assumed*. There was no one else to do it, and the family had to have the money. When Samuel realized what was about to happen, he began to feel that God was grinding him to dust.

"You don't have to do this, Willadee," he told her the morning after Toy got shot. "God has always provided for all our needs."

Willadee was rushing around straightening the house and doing laundry, hoping to get everything done in time to get some rest before the kids got home from school. There'd been precious little sleep the night before, and tonight would be even worse.

"Well, let me know when He starts back," she said. She was feeling ground under, too.

Samuel didn't argue. When he and Willadee had gotten married, and the preacher had asked her whether she would love, honor, and obey, she had answered like a Moses. "Yes, yes, and that all depends," she had said with a grin.

The Moses family had laughed, and the Lake family had winced, and Sam Lake had taken his bride with the conditions laid out. Up until now, those conditions had never caused any real problems.

On the way to work that day, Samuel asked God to give him a sign, to show him what to do.

He was on the outskirts of Magnolia when he uttered that prayer, and he hadn't driven a city block before he saw a line of vehicles passing through town. Big, mud-crusted, grease-streaked trucks of all sizes, with rough-looking drivers, and gears that creaked, and fantastic pictures painted on the sides. Pictures of lion tamers and trapeze artists and big tops. The circus, on its way somewhere.

Well, Samuel had his sign. He didn't think for one minute that God was telling him to go off and join the circus, but *"Come one, come all!"* was suddenly ringing in his ears. When he got to the Eternal Rock Monument Company, he turned in his three-ring binder to Mr. Lindale Stroud and made the man a deal.

"If you'll let me make some long-distance calls on the office phone, you can take the charges out of whatever commissions I've got coming."

In less than fifteen minutes, Samuel had located a company down in Shreveport that would rent him a tent and some folding chairs and a loudspeaker system, and let him pay for it when he started taking in offerings.

There were plenty of places Samuel could have set up his tent, but the Ledbetter place seemed to have the most advantages. For one thing, the use of it was free. Irma Ledbetter might live in town now, but she knew the strain her old neighbors were under. She'd have died before she let Samuel pay money to use that land. Especially since he was going to clean it up for her, and once he got it looking good, somebody might buy it.

Another advantage to this location was that, being there (right, precisely there) made a statement. There was a steady stream of lost souls flowing in and out of Never Closes every night, and they could neither come nor go without seeing Samuel's banner, which would read, CHOOSE YE THIS DAY WHOM YE WILL SERVE.

"A revival," Willadee said, when Samuel told her the news.

"A tent revival," said Samuel.

"Right across the road."

"Right square across the road."

"Well, I think that's real good," she told him. And she meant it, too. Samuel hadn't looked this happy in a long time.

She'd been surprised when he had come home from work early, and surprised wasn't the word for how she'd felt when he told her that he'd quit his job. This revival thing made three surprises in less than five minutes, and she was glad for every one of them. At least now Samuel would be doing something he believed in, so maybe his spirits could heal.

"How big a revival?" Willadee asked. She was sitting at the kitchen table folding laundry, and Samuel was getting himself a glass of iced tea.

"Big as I can make it."

"Maybe I can put the regulars on the honor system long enough to come over and hear you preach."

"Maybe you can bring the regulars with you."

She got up and went over behind him, and laid her head against his back, and kissed him through the fabric of his shirt.

She said, "I hope you know I believe in you."

"That goes both ways," he said.

"Even though I'm working for the devil these days?"

He set his tea glass down, and turned around, and gave her a pained smile. "Willadee, you're just drawing the devil's troops in close enough so I can get a crack at 'em."

After supper, Calla put the kids to bed and Willadee went to work for the first time in Never Closes. Samuel drove over to the hospital to take his turn sitting up with Toy, so Bernice could come back to Calla's and catch up on her sleep.

When Willadee closed the bar the next morning and trudged into the kitchen, Bernice was just getting home, looking no worse for wear. She and Samuel had sat up all night talking, and she was just amazed that she barely felt tired at all.

Willadee, who wanted nothing so much as to go wash off the stale smell of the bar and get into bed but couldn't yet, was more than slightly rankled. "I thought the idea behind Samuel going to stay at the hospital all night was so you could come home and get some sleep."

"It was," Bernice explained happily. "But then he told me about the revival, and we started making plans, and we just couldn't find a stopping place."

"Plans?"

"I'm going to help him with the music. You know we used to sing together a lot, back when we were—back a long time ago."

Willadee nodded, dully. She knew, all right.

In one of the lower cabinets, there was a fifty-pound sack of flour, and in that sack, on top of the flour, was an old blue speckled enamel pan. Willadee got the pan out, and filled it with flour, and set it on the cook table. Then she took milk from the refrigerator, and baking powder and salt and lard from an upper cabinet, and she set those things out, too. All that time, she was thinking that this situation had the potential for disaster.

"Don't you ruin this for Samuel," she said.

Bernice had been about to leave the room, but she stopped now and stood there in the doorway, staring back at Willadee like she couldn't believe her ears. "Willadee Moses, whatever are you talking about?"

Willadee poked her fist into the flour and dumped the other ingredients into the crater she'd made, not bothering to measure. She'd been making biscuits every day for fifteen years, which came to more than five thousand batches of biscuits. With one hand, she squished and mixed. With the other, she turned the pan, little bit by little bit, working in more flour from the wall of the crater as she went along.

"I'm a *Lake*," she corrected. "*You're* a Moses. And you know very well what I'm talking about." She had never let loose on her sister-in-law before, but her instincts were screaming that there was danger ahead, danger for Samuel, who needed, desperately needed, for something to finally go right. "This is the first chance at happiness Samuel has had for a while, and he's got his work cut out for him. People are going to be watching him, and you can bet your boots, they'll be watching you."

Which was true as a blue sky, but Bernice wasn't about to admit it.

"Well, I cannot begin to imagine—" she started.

"Oh, yes, you can," Willadee said. And all of a sudden, she was loaded for bear. "You're real good at imagining. I figure you began to imagine that you were somehow going to get Samuel back the day you found out we were moving back here. You even got religion because you imagined that would throw the two of you together more. And you probably imagine that this revival is the answer to your prayers—what with me working nights now and you with nothing to do but look pretty and act holy. But don't go after Samuel, because you won't win."

Bernice glared at Willadee. She wasn't pretending to be innocent anymore. For a fraction of a second, her eyes fairly glittered.

"You won't win," Willadee went on, "not because I'm a better woman than you, but because Sam is too good a man to be corrupted. You can't get him away from me, but you could mess this up for him, and if you do—I swear to God, I'll pull you bald-headed."

Bernice said, "My, my, my, Willadee. One night in the bar, and you're already talking like the regulars."

Then she took off her shoes, and started languorously unbuttoning her blouse, and informed Willadee that she was going up to bed.

"You might want to get some sleep yourself," she said helpfully, as she was leaving. "You're looking downright haggard."

When Bernice drove back to the hospital that afternoon, Willadee went along with her. She was thinking it might be nice to visit for a while with Toy. She also figured Bernice would tattle to Samuel about the dressing-down she had given her, and she wanted to be on hand to defend herself. It was almost time for the kids to get home from school, so Willadee left a pan of baked sweet potatoes on the stove for a snack, along with a note telling them to do their homework and not leave the yard. Calla would be busy in the store but had promised to check on them from time to time.

The two women didn't talk along the way, Willadee having said what was on her mind that morning, and Bernice having her own thoughts that she didn't care to share. The silence was like the still before a storm.

Samuel was standing around talking to a cluster of elderly women who were soaking him up like sunshine. When he saw the car pull into the parking lot, he shook hands with each of the ladies and walked over to open the door for Willadee. Bernice slid out from behind the wheel and waited patiently while Samuel kissed his wife. Then she told them both, in a strained little voice, that she'd like to talk to them, if they could spare a few minutes. Willadee was not surprised. Yet.

"Well, of course we can," Samuel assured. "Toy won't even miss us. The nurses are giving him a sponge bath."

As if Bernice wanted to even think about Toy getting a sponge bath.

The three walked over onto a patch of grass where they'd have some privacy. When they got to a spot that looked private enough, Bernice turned and faced them with her heart in her eyes.

"You don't need to feel obligated to let me work in the revival," she said to Samuel. "The last thing I want is to be a stumbling block to some poor sinner who needs to find the Lord."

Willadee blinked at her incredulously.

Samuel said, "Well, of course you're going to work in the revival. Where'd you get the idea that you shouldn't?"

Bernice looked from one to the other, as though afraid she might have spoken out of turn.

"Well, from what Willadee said this morning—"

Willadee blinked at her again. Samuel frowned.

"That's not what I said," Willadee protested. "That's not even kin to what I said."

"You said people would be watching us," Bernice faltered. Her lips were trembling. "You said everybody knew I didn't really get religion, and if I sang with Samuel at the revival, folks would think I was out to get him, and I mustn't ruin this for him, because it's his only chance to make something of himself after the way he failed as a pastor."

Willadee didn't blink this time. Her eyes and her mouth were locked wide open.

"Dear God in Heaven," she finally managed.

Willadee turned her gaze toward Samuel, hoping to see in his eyes that he knew how preposterous this all was, but his eyes were leaden.

"I didn't say those things," she argued. And then, because she was Moses Honest, she amended. "Well, not exactly."

Samuel stood there for a minute like a punch-drunk boxer taking body blows. Then he said, "Bernice, I imagine Toy is finished with that sponge bath by now."

Bernice looked sick with regret. "Don't be upset with Willadee," she told Samuel. And to Willadee, she said, "I know you didn't really mean it when you said you were going to drag me off the stage and pull me bald-headed."

"You go see to your husband," Samuel told her. "And call the house if you need anything."

Bernice nodded obediently and started walking toward the hospital entrance. Samuel went over to the car and opened the door for Willadee.

"I didn't say those things," she told him again, as she slid into the seat.

Samuel said, "Willadee—don't."

On the drive back to Calla's, Willadee tried to make her husband understand what had happened. Yes, she had had a talk with Bernice. Yes, she had warned her to leave Samuel alone. Yes, she had said that people would be looking at them. She had mentioned the music, she had pointed out that this revival was important to Samuel's happiness. But most of what Bernice had said was all a bunch of hooey.

"What 'most'?" Samuel asked. "You just admitted to everything she said."

"No, I *didn't*!" She ticked the items off on her fingers. "I didn't say you failed as a pastor. I didn't accuse her of being a stumbling block to sinners. I didn't say that anybody besides me doubted her religion! She's taking one or two words out of every sentence I said, and weaving lies around them, and coming out with something totally different."

"It doesn't sound all that different to me, Willadee. And as for Bernice's conversion—"

"She hasn't had a conversion."

"You have no right to say that."

Willadee rolled her eyes and blew out a mad breath. "That's right, I forgot. Nobody knows her heart but you and God."

Samuel gave her a reproving look and shook his head. "This isn't like you, Willadee. I'm starting to feel as if I don't even know you anymore."

Willadee stared at him. Unbelieving.

"Then she's finally done it," she said.

"Done what?"

"What she set out to do years ago, the day you told her you were in love with me. She's finally managed to come between us."

Samuel kept his voice even, but his words were jagged as shale.

"What's come between us didn't start a few minutes ago, Willadee. And I can't see that Bernice had all that much to do with it. What's come between us is that I used to know—I mean, I knew, without a doubt—that you were always on my side, and I don't feel that way anymore. I try to, but I can't."

Willadee's mouth went dry. Somewhere inside herself, she had known this conversation was coming. Sometime. Had known that it would come, and where it might go.

"I *am* always on your side," she insisted.

"Sure didn't feel like it," he said bitterly, "that night at the supper table when all that business came out about Noble and Toy. As far as I could see, there wasn't a soul in the world on my side that night."

"I've apologized for that. I was wrong. I'm sorry." She wanted to scream the words.

Samuel went on, as though she hadn't spoken. Everything he'd been holding back was coming out all at once.

"There I'd been, going along, like a big, dumb ox, with everybody in the family knowing what was happening and working together to hide it from me. Do you have any idea how foolish that made me feel?"

"I said I'm sorry." She wasn't just sorry. She was beginning to feel afraid.

"And what do you think you were teaching the kids during all that? *If the old man won't like it, just don't let him know?*" (He had never referred to himself as the "old man" before.) "*If the truth hurts, who needs it?*"

"I'm sorry, I'm sorry," she said, crying now.

They'd reached Calla's, and Samuel turned in to the drive. They could see the kids back by the barnyard, feeding something to Lady through the fence. Samuel sat there for a minute, staring first at the children and then at Calla's sign. MOSES.

"I used to love that saying about how a Moses will never lie," he said. "But I tell you the truth, Willadee, it almost makes me sick to hear it now. And do you know why? Because what it really says is that a Moses will not lie, but they don't necessarily tell the truth."

Chapter 33

They'd never had a fight before. They'd never even had a real argument. Ever since the day they met, they'd been reveling in each other—rolling along without rules or restrictions, expecting only the best of each other, and believing nothing less. Willadee had looked at other marriages, the bad ones and even the good ones, and felt sorry for all those people, because they just didn't know— they just had no idea—what love could be like when it was this right.

Now it wasn't right at all anymore, and she didn't see how it ever could be again.

Samuel didn't even go into the house. He just went out to the barn and started fooling around with John's old tractor, trying to get it running. Willadee went in and threw some supper together and hollered for everybody to come eat, then hustled into Never Closes and shut the door, so nobody would see the shape she was in.

. . .

Calla didn't have to see her daughter's face to know something was wrong. She could sense it, and she lay in bed that night worrying and wondering. When she couldn't stand the uneasiness anymore, she got up and went into the bar for the second time in her life. Willadee was washing glasses at the sink, and there wasn't a soul in the place.

"I don't know why we make such a religion of keeping this place open all night," Calla said. "It's crazy to stay open after all the customers are gone."

Willadee said, "Yes, well, Toy tried closing early that once, and look what happened to him."

Calla laughed. That wasn't funny, but it was.

"Are you going to tell me what's going on?" she said.

"Trickery and deception, Mama," Willadee said wearily. "Trickery and deception."

"Bernice," Calla guessed immediately. "What's she up to now?"

"Oh, she's up to plenty," Willadee told her. "But it's not her trickery and deception I was talking about."

Later on, after Willadee had filled her in on the situation, Calla said, "Well, if you think you've done something wrong, make it right and be done with it."

"What if Samuel won't let me?"

"Good Lord, Willadee. Samuel can't keep you from making something right. Just don't make the mistake I made with John, by waiting too long. And as for Bernice—you're smarter than she is. Outthink her."

Willadee put the last glass in the rack and drained the soapy water out of the sink.

"I may be smarter than she is, Mama, but she gets more sleep. She's thinking circles around me."

Calla took the wet dishrag and wiped down the bar. She was feeling suddenly energized.

"Let me tell you something," she said. "No matter how much

damage you think Bernice has done, you've got her beat, hands down. But if you ask me, it's high time you fix that heifer's wagon."

"I don't know *how* to fix that heifer's wagon," Willadee wailed.

And Calla said, "Well, I do."

Willadee closed the bar right on schedule, and made breakfast, and got the kids off to school. Then she took a bath and went in search of her husband. She found him out behind the barn, chopping down the elderberry thicket that had grown up through the brush hog equipment.

"I want to thank you for everything you said to me yesterday," she told him right off. Anything else would have just been words wasted.

Samuel quit chopping, sank the ax head into the earth, and leaned against the handle. He didn't smile, but at least he was listening.

"You were right," Willadee continued. "Not for believing Bernice, but this isn't about Bernice. This is about how wrong I've been. The sad part is that I would have never realized any of it, if you hadn't pointed it out to me."

She was standing a little apart from him, not daring to take anything for granted. Not about to move in close or reach out to him, for fear he might pull away and a dark wall would spring up between them.

"Is this Moses Honesty," he asked her, after what seemed like forever. "Or Just Plain Honesty? Because I don't want to stand here swallowing something that might have to come back up later."

"Plain honesty," she said. "The only kind you'll get from me from now on." Then she added, "You may not always like it, but you'll get it."

Samuel nodded once, accepting that.

"And know this, Samuel Lake," she said, fiercely. "I am always on your side. Maybe you don't believe me right now, and maybe there have been ways I didn't show it. Like setting a bad example for the kids. Teaching them it was all right to put things by you. But I wasn't looking at it as right or wrong. I was looking at it as necessary. I'll talk to them, and explain how dishonest I was. How unkind we all were. And I'll tell them we're going to do things differently from now on."

Samuel nodded again.

Then he said, "I still intend for Bernice to sing at the revival. Will you be all right with that? With her singing?"

"I reckon I'll be as all right with that as you are about me working in Never Closes."

Samuel grinned, reluctantly. "Did you really tell her you'd drag her off the stage and pull her bald-headed?"

Willadee threw her head back and laughed out loud. "I told her I'd do it. But it wasn't the stage I was figuring I'd have to drag her off of."

The dinner for Samuel was a surprise, and the kids helped to make it. Not a one of them had ever cooked anything before, not so much as a piece of toast, but Willadee taught them the fine art of making meat loaf and mashed potatoes. While she was at it, she kept her promise to Samuel.

When she was done explaining the difference between Moses Honesty and Just Plain Honesty, and how the best thing was to keep the truth out in the open and let the chips fall where they may, the younger kids had turned into penitents.

"We broke his heart," Bienville said, contritely.

"We did," Willadee told him. "But there's a way to mend it." Then she told them about how she had apologized to their daddy and how much better she'd felt ever since. There were some other things that had happened upstairs, after they'd made up, that had also made her feel better, and they had done Samuel a world of good, too, but that wasn't news they could use.

Swan said, "Maybe we should make him a poster that says we're sorry and we'll do better." She had learned in Bible School one summer how to make finger paints out of cornstarch and water and food coloring, and she figured Grandma Calla would let them have a big piece of the white paper she used to wrap meat for her customers.

Blade said he'd help with the poster, but first he was going to pick the daddy some flowers. The only flowers left outside at this time of year were mums, but blooms were blooms. That child remembered full well how much those other flowers had lifted the uncle's spirits a while back, and anything that worked on an uncle ought to work on a daddy.

Noble couldn't see that he needed to make any amends. "I don't feel all that good about the sneaking around," he said. "But what choice did I have?"

Willadee didn't have an answer for that. She was awfully glad that all this being Just Plain Honest was starting after Noble had been taught to defend himself.

"Maybe you could at least tell him how you feel," she suggested.

"Then he'd just preach to me."

"So what?" Willadee said. "You were brave enough to face those Emerson boys. You can stand up to a little preaching. This is not about you and your daddy seeing eye to eye, it's about you letting him know that you care about him."

Calla took her supper to her room that night. Said she'd been needing some time to herself. Sid was staying at the hospital with Toy, so Bernice was spending the night with Nicey. It was the first time Samuel and Willadee had had a meal alone with the children in months.

Samuel marveled over the kids' cooking, and he absolutely loved his flowers, and the poster was just to his liking. The things the kids said meant the most, though. Noble went last, and his apology wasn't an apology at all, but it brought tears to Samuel's eyes.

"I love you" was what the boy said.

The kids hadn't seen Uncle Toy since the shooting, and it was wearing on them. It was Samuel who decided on Saturday morning that the sight of a few tubes wouldn't be nearly so hard on them as whatever they were seeing in their heads.

"Now, he's still looking pretty weak," he explained to them as he and Willadee shepherded them along the corridor of the hospital. "But don't let that scare you. He'll be good as new after a while, but it'll take some time for him to get his strength back."

"Are you sure he'll know who we are?" Bienville asked. He'd heard about people who had almost died not recognizing their families when they saw them.

"Sure, he'll know who you are," Samuel told him. "And there's no one on earth he'd rather see than the four of you."

Samuel might have been ground down by life of late, but there was nothing small about the man. He was proud to be sharing the gift of his children.

Bernice had been told that they were coming, so she was somewhere else when they got there, and they had Toy all to themselves.

"Now, this is the best medicine I've had yet," Toy said. His voice was raspy and uneven.

Though they were thrilled to be with their uncle, the children were stricken by how weak he seemed. He was the strongest man they knew—or he had been. Now his usually ruddy complexion had a grayish tinge, and he no longer looked larger than life, especially since he wasn't wearing his artificial leg. They could see the outline of the stump though his covers, could see where that part of Toy Moses ended well before it was supposed to.

"Where's your leg?" Blade asked.

Noble and Bienville winced. Swan poked Blade in the ribs.

Toy didn't bat an eye. "I think they stuck it over there in the closet. I get to put it on later today and run a footrace."

Blade made a surprised face and then laughed gleefully. If Toy was kidding around with them, everything must be okay.

Toy said, "Did you know your daddy helped save my life?"

Blade knew it, all right, he'd heard enough about it from everybody, but he didn't trust it. Didn't trust his daddy in any way. He dropped his eyes and stepped back from Toy, as if retreating from the question would keep some distance between him and his father. Toy got the message.

"I've been talking to the doctors," he said, "and they told me about a place up in Little Rock where we can get you an eye made that'll look just as real as your other one. We'll have to talk about that when I get home."

Blade was awestruck. "Will I see out of it?" he asked.

Toy shook his head. "No. But it'll look so pretty all the girls will be chasing you."

Blade went up on tiptoe and whispered to Toy, "I don't want girls chasing me. I'm going to marry *Swan*."

Samuel and Willadee exchanged an amused glance. Noble and Bienville made gagging sounds.

"Stop saying that, pip-squeak," Swan hissed.

"I can say it if I want to."

Toy said, "Well, y'all can argue about the engagement later. Right now, I want to be the center of attention."

He asked each of the kids how things were going at school, and he asked Willadee how Calla was holding up. Then he asked Samuel how the plans were progressing for the tent revival.

"Things seem to be moving in the right direction," Samuel told him.

"Well, I reckon Columbia County is in for a rumble," Toy said with a grin. "Sounds to me like God and the devil are about to duke it out."

Chapter 34

"How long are you intending for this revival to run?" Calla asked Samuel late one afternoon. In the past week, he'd gotten John's old tractor and the brush hog equipment working and had mowed the Ledbetter cotton field. And just today, some men from the rental company had come out to set up the tent. Calla had been watching from the store window all afternoon and had come across the road as soon as the men were gone, to check out the competition.

"Until God leads me to close it down," Samuel answered.

Calla pulled her sweater around herself, and crossed her arms in front of her bosom, and stood there looking at the newly mown field, the newly erected tent, the newly painted banner that read just like Samuel had envisioned. CHOOSE YE THIS DAY WHOM YE WILL SERVE. She couldn't help thinking that if Willadee got to choose whom she was going to serve, some of the regulars in Never Closes would have to find a new place to drink.

Samuel said, "I don't know how this all sets with you, Calla, but it's something I've got to do."

Calla said, "Sakes alive, Samuel, I don't care if you have a revival out here till the saints go marching in. Like as not, we'll bring each other business."

The way the revival was going to work without upsetting any of the local pastors was that Samuel would hold services when they didn't. Monday night, Tuesday night, skip Wednesday night for everybody else's prayer meeting, Thursday night, Friday night, Saturday night. On Sundays, Samuel and Bernice would visit one of the churches in the community and maybe sing a song or two. The preachers, in turn, would tell their congregations about the revival meeting and urge them all to attend.

Samuel had some flyers printed up with the words SPIRIT-FILLED REVIVAL! emblazoned across the top. Under the words, there were pictures. One of Samuel holding an open Bible, one of Bernice holding a microphone, and another of the two of them singing, with their heads close but not too close together.

Samuel and Bernice drove all over the country, mounting flyers on fence posts and in store windows, and handing out more flyers to people he met on the street. Just about everybody he talked to promised they'd come or break a leg trying. A tent revival was a big event, especially with Sam Lake singing and playing five different instruments, and that pretty sister-in-law of his singing harmony. People hadn't forgotten Samuel and his music.

The revival opened on a Monday night, and the local folk came out in droves. Carloads of people. Truckloads of people. Busloads of people from churches all over the county, and from neighboring counties as well.

Samuel stood in the open welcoming the crowd. "Good to see you." "Thanks for coming out." "Are you ready for a blessing?" And the people said, "How do, Preacher." "Evenin', Samuel." "Sure hope you brought your banjer." Bernice stood right beside him (she had never looked lovelier or more virtuous), and the realization settled over both of them at once that this was really happening. A swell of emotion was building inside Samuel—building so he could hardly contain it. Gratitude. Joy. And a feeling that he hadn't had in a while. The feeling that he was of value to the world in general. These folks— all these good folks—were coming out because they were hungry for something. Maybe for spiritual renewal, maybe for music, maybe just for a break from their routines. Whatever they had come after, they were going to get a double portion.

The weather was chilly but not downright cold, and the people came only slightly bundled up, with blankets to make pallets for their smaller children. When it was almost time to start the service, Samuel and Bernice went up onto the platform and he checked to make sure the instruments were all tuned just right. The crowd was settling into their seats, most of them talking back and forth, and the sum of the voices was a sort of subdued roar. Samuel spotted the four kids in the front row, sitting two on either side of Calla Moses, who had dressed up for the occasion. He gave them a wink, and they gave him back grins. They looked to be almost as excited as he was.

Bernice sidled up to Samuel and asked, "Do you believe this?"

"I'm beginning to," he said.

Samuel clicked on the microphone and said "Testing, testing," and when they heard his voice go booming over the loudspeakers, the tent went quiet in anticipation. He didn't bother to introduce himself. They all knew who he and Bernice were.

He struck a chord on the guitar, and gave Bernice a nod, and they launched into "I Saw the Light." Samuel and Bernice, singing into that microphone, voices melding like Heaven come down. Pretty soon feet started tapping, and hands started clapping, and somebody in the congregation hollered, *"Glory!"* Samuel responded by upping the tempo.

Once, when his eyes rambled over the crowd, he could have sworn he saw Ras Ballenger at the back of the tent (*Ras Ballenger, smiling benignly*), but when he looked back, there was no sign of the man. So maybe he'd been wrong.

It was the first time in his life that Samuel had ever been glad to think someone hadn't shown up for church.

Calla had been right in her prediction that the revival and Never Closes would bring each other business. Not everybody at the service was there because they wanted to be. Some were there because they'd been dragged by dominant spouses. And some of them didn't stay where those spouses parked them. Henpecked husbands sneaked across to the bar for a few drinks while their wives were caught up in the Spirit. Of course, the tide flowed both ways. Sinners in the bar, who couldn't help but hear the gospel music, would get to thinking about how they ought to change their miserable ways and would venture across to the tent revival in search of salvation. It was a tug-of-war between God and the devil, with both sides winning a few and losing a few.

The revival was such a success that there was no telling how long it would go on. People talked a little about how it was a shame that Samuel's wife was working in a honky-tonk while he was over there preaching his heart out, and other people talked about how Samuel wouldn't be having to put on a tent revival if he hadn't gotten himself kicked out of the Methodist conference, but they didn't let Samuel hear them, and he wouldn't have let it get the best of him if they had. There were souls coming to salvation every night, so this had to be God's plan in action.

Samuel was a happy man.

Bernice was in her element.

Toy was mending, no thanks to his wife, who couldn't just hold his hand all the time. How could she hold his hand all the time, when she had so much to do? There was helping Samuel with the services every night, and talking to Samuel after the services about every spiritual thing she could think of, not to mention running all over the country with Samuel during the daytime, printing up more flyers and inviting folks to come out and worship. And then, she had to take care of her own needs sometime, looking perfect every minute can just take hours. Anyway, it wasn't as if Toy was still in any real danger of dying. Dammit.

Willadee was so tired from being on her feet twelve hours a night, and still trying to keep up with the kids and the house in the daytime, that she was already wondering how long she'd be able to keep up this pace. By the time she made it into bed every morning, Samuel was just getting up to start his day. It was John and Calla, all over again.

Calla Moses helped with the kids and stayed ruffled out like a wet hen, because Bernice didn't help with diddly.

The kids were kids.

Thanksgiving came and went. All the children were in school programs, and Willadee somehow made it to every one of them except Noble's, which took place at night. (Calla went in her stead.) Samuel made it to Bienville's and Blade's, which were both in the daytime, on the same afternoon, but the rest of the time, he was tending to the Lord's business. Swan hardly noticed that her daddy wasn't at her program. He'd been tending to the Lord's business since before she was born, so she was used to it.

Ras Ballenger showed up at the revival again (Samuel was sure he saw him this time), but he still didn't cause a speck of trouble. Blade felt his presence, and looked around and saw him, and had nightmares for a week. After that, he started creeping into bed with Samuel every night, and the bad dreams stopped as abruptly as they had begun.

Toy came home from the hospital. Home to Calla's, not home to his own house. Life would have been lonesome stuck over there by himself while Bernice was out helping Samuel promote the revival. Plus, Willadee and Calla wanted Toy where they could see to him.

Bernice thought the hospital had let him go a little early.

Christmas arrived, and Swan was relieved to discover that the Lake family was no longer prudent. Attendance had fallen off at the revival when it got too cold for most people to stand it, but the offerings had been good up to that point, and Samuel had saved money back. There were presents for everybody.

All the aunts and uncles and cousins came over for Christmas dinner. You could hardly find room to walk through the house, there were so many people, which suited Calla fine. This was her first Christmas without John, and she didn't want to spend the day missing him. Still, after everybody who didn't live there had gone home, she went out to the cemetery and stood in the cold beside his grave for the longest time, wishing she could turn back time.

Ras Ballenger showed up, late in the day, bringing presents for Blade. Calla thanked the man again for helping to save Toy, but Blade hid in Bienville's room until after his daddy was gone and then refused to open the packages.

His nightmares returned.

It got to be January. The crowds were slimmer over at the tent revival, but not slim enough for Samuel to even begin to think about closing it down. With the smaller crowds, the services grew more intimate. Folks gave their testimonies (Bernice gave hers every night, and it touched folks' hearts, every time), sinners still came forward at the end of every service, and the music just kept getting better and better.

Swan turned twelve, and Noble turned thirteen, both in the same week. Swan asked her mother for a bra and got a camisole instead. Mail order, from the Wish Book. Toy gave Noble the keys to Papa John's truck, which still wouldn't run right, since it still needed the motor pulled. Calla made pineapple upside-down cake, which is not the kind of cake you put candles on, so there was nothing to blow out and make wishes on. Nobody missed the candles, because when you're eating pineapple upside-down cake, there's nothing much left to wish for.

Toward the end of January, Toy announced at breakfast that, in another couple of days, he'd be ready to go back to work at Never

Closes. Willadee was so happy she could have danced on the table. Bernice wasn't at all sure it was the right thing for him to do; after all, he'd been close enough to death's door to look inside, and he still didn't have all his strength back.

What was really bothering her was that, once Toy took over his duties, Willadee would be free to take over hers, which wasn't the least bit fair. Here Bernice had earned Samuel's trust and gotten him believing in her, and sometimes when they were singing, their voices melded so sweetly that it was as though the two had become one, and now Willadee was going to ruin everything. Bernice was well aware that a woman who's in a man's bed at the same time he is has a diabolical advantage over a woman who's never managed to get into bed with that man at all, and she could see her chance (or what she believed was her chance) slipping away.

Her plan had always been to finesse the situation so that Samuel thought the whole thing was his idea, but she didn't have forever, and that's how long it was taking him. He wasn't leaving her any choice except to seduce him. If he'd wanted to make the first move, he'd had plenty of chances.

If everything worked out in her favor, she and Samuel would come together in a rapturous fusion that would be the start of a lifetime of happiness. If it all fell apart, life wouldn't be worth living anymore, so she guessed she'd just have to kill herself.

That night, the service was a particularly emotional one. Bernice was so glad of that, since emotions of the spiritual kind can lead to emotions of another kind like a stream feeding into a river. She and Samuel were both still feeling the glow after the crowd had dispersed.

"I can't tell you how thankful I am to God for this whole experience," she told him after they'd finished straightening the chairs and putting things in order. They were at the back of the tent, and Samuel was about to turn off the lights. It seemed like a perfect moment for this conversation, and Bernice thought that tucking in a reference to

God had lent just the right touch. "I've had more happiness in the last several weeks than I've had in the rest of my life put together."

Samuel smiled and said, "You've done more than your share to make this whole thing work, Bernice. I don't know what I'd have done without you all these weeks."

She reached over and turned off the lights.

"I don't know how we've done without each other for so long," she whispered, moving in so close that strategic parts of her body brushed against him. Samuel recoiled instantly and switched the lights back on. He was so horrified, his hands were shaking.

"What on earth are you doing?" he demanded, his voice hoarse.

That set her back a little, but she figured his voice just sounded that way because he was so excited he could barely talk.

"Samuel . . . ," she sighed.

"Bernice, we need to get back across the road, where we belong. You've got a husband waiting, and I've got a wife."

"You feel the same way I do," she insisted, taking his hands so that she could guide them where she was positive he really wanted them to be. "You know you do."

Samuel jerked his hands away and just stared at her. "No," he said. "I do not. And, if you're feeling anything out of the way, you need to ask the Lord to help you overcome it."

"Anything out of the way?" Oh, she was indignant now. "*Anything out of the way?*" Her voice was rising, getting shrill around the edges.

Samuel said, "Bernice, I'm taking you to the house."

He took her arm.

She jerked it away. "Like hell you are," she seethed. "You think you're just going to take me back over there and drop me in Toy's lap, and say, 'Here she is, I'm finished with her'?"

Samuel backed away in disbelief.

"Well, we're not finished, Samuel. We won't ever be finished. I'm the one who stood beside you when everybody knew you were floundering. Why, I've been more of a helpmate to you than your own wife, who's over there tending bar and probably being rubbed up against by the regulars right this very minute."

Samuel shook his head and looked away. Bernice knew she'd just touched on a sore spot, so she pressed her advantage.

"I've heard stories about Calvin Furlough spending an awful lot of time in Never Closes since Willadee started working in there," she informed him. "And you know, Calvin's got a way with the ladies. He could wake a woman up sauntering through her dreams at night."

Samuel rubbed his eyes and laughed. It was a sort of hollow laugh, but it was still a laugh, and nobody laughed at Bernice Moses.

"Don't you laugh at me, Sam Lake," she warned him.

"I'm sorry," he said. "I'm sorry for laughing. It's not funny anyway, it's pathetic."

He'd said it was pathetic. Which meant she was pathetic. Bernice glared at him. Hating him suddenly. Despising him.

"It's pathetic," Samuel went on, "because you can't let a good thing be a good thing. You can't even stand for a good thing to live. You poison everything you touch."

"Poison," she said. "Now, there's a thought."

And with that, she walked away.

Samuel lay awake that night wondering whether Bernice had been trying to make him believe that she was going to kill herself or somebody else. Whichever one it was, he was sure it was an empty threat. Bernice could be spiteful and devious, but she'd never do anything to jeopardize her own comfort or safety, much less her freedom. She had driven off in the direction of her own house, and he assumed that was where she'd ended up. Probably, she would show up at the revival tomorrow night trying to convince him that he'd imagined the whole thing ever happened.

He considered waking Toy and telling him about the incident. But what would that accomplish? There'd be a lot of hard feelings, and Toy would have one more piece of unpleasantness to have to live with, and Bernice would just turn everything around to make it sound as if Samuel had been the one making the advances.

So maybe he shouldn't say a word. Maybe sometimes the best thing a man can do is let folks believe whatever makes them happy. It didn't occur to Samuel that this kind of reasoning was the very thing he'd hated most about Moses Honesty. All he was thinking as he drifted off to sleep was that he could hardly wait for morning and for Willadee.

Chapter 35

At dawn, when Willadee dragged herself up the stairs and into their room, Samuel grabbed her and hung on like a drowning man. Kissing her hair, which reeked of smoke. Kissing her eyes, which were red with fatigue. Kissing her mouth and her neck and her shoulders and all the other familiar territories, which he'd been neglecting of late.

She tried to pull away. He wouldn't let her.

"I love you," he said. "Willadee, I love you like a bird loves the sky."

"I smell like the bar," she protested.

"I don't care, I don't care, I don't care."

"What's happened to you, Samuel?"

He was laughing now. Loud enough to be heard through the walls, if anybody was listening. And if anybody was listening, he didn't care about that, either.

"I had a vision last night," he said. "God gave me a vision. He showed me clear as day what my life would have been without you."

...

It was all Bernice could do to stay inside her own skin. She paced the floor of her house like a caged cat, weeping and yowling. All this time, she'd been planning what her life would be like with Samuel, and now that her plans had been shattered, she couldn't think of one thing in the world that she wanted or cared about.

She didn't really want to die, but she didn't really want to live, either, plus she'd made that comment to Samuel about the poison, so she had more or less painted herself into a corner. It seemed to her that committing suicide or attempting suicide or at least *appearing* to attempt suicide would be the only way she could save face and punish Samuel at the same time. He would surely blame himself for driving her to that, and once word got around, everybody else would blame him, too. His reputation would be sullied, if not destroyed.

As for her own reputation, she really didn't care what happened to it. She knew full well what folks around here had thought of her, ever since Yam Ferguson died. The only reason they looked at her with any kind of respect nowadays was that she'd been making such a show of having religion, and she was not about to keep that up. Acting the part had been kind of a lark, as long as she'd thought it might win Samuel over, but she'd be damned if she would spend the rest of her life acting all holy. If Samuel had really cared about her salvation, he'd had his chance to help her stay on the straight and narrow.

Besides, she wasn't going to stay in Columbia County. She wasn't even going to stay in Arkansas. Why should she? There had to be someplace better, and in another day or so, she was going to go looking for it.

But first things first.

Knowing Samuel, he must be torturing himself, wondering what she'd meant by what she said, and whether she was going to do something desperate. She figured that, after last night, he'd be way too gun-shy to come to check on her himself, but she was confident that he'd send somebody.

By late afternoon, Bernice had gathered everything in the house that she thought might be poisonous and had the items lined up on the kitchen table. Bleach, ammonia, Drāno, furniture polish, floor polish, rat poison, a small bottle of Miltown "happy pills" that the doctor had prescribed for her back when Toy was in the hospital and she was acting distraught, and a large bottle of Cardui that Calla had given her once when she made the mistake of claiming to be having trouble with her monthlies.

Deciding what to take was easy. Besides not wanting to die, she didn't want to suffer while she was waiting to be saved, so she ruled out all the household products right off the bat. She left them on the table, though, for the impact they would have. Whoever came to check on her would be talking for the rest of their life about how it was a good thing she didn't drink that bleach or eat that rat poison because then there would have been no saving her. Just for fun, she uncapped the can of rat poison and laid it over on its side so that some of it spilled out onto the tabletop.

All she intended to take was a couple of Miltowns, and she wouldn't down those until her rescuer arrived and was coming in the front door. No sense tempting Fate. She'd never been much of a drinker (liquor hit her too hard and too fast), but she needed something to ease the knotted-up feeling in the pit of her stomach, so she helped herself to a fifth of spirits from the liquor supply that Toy had stockpiled in the spare bedroom back when he was still bootlegging. Then she took a hot bath that lasted for over half the bottle.

When Bernice didn't show up at the tent revival that night, Samuel didn't know whether to be troubled or relieved. The temperature had dropped down below freezing, so the congregation was a bit sparse, but the folks who had bundled up and come out kept asking him while he was tuning the instruments where Bernice was and why she was late. The only thing he could tell them was that he hadn't talked to her all day, and he sure hoped she hadn't come down with a cold or the flu. He was getting more Moses Honest all the time.

He couldn't escape the thought that somebody ought to go over and look in on her, to make sure she was all right. He would have bet his life she was, but he'd never stop feeling guilty if it turned out she wasn't and he hadn't tried to help.

He couldn't send Toy, because Toy had already been through so much and didn't need to be worrying about problems that more than likely didn't exist. Willadee was working, besides which no good could come of throwing Bernice and Willadee together right now. Calla didn't drive, so she was out. That pretty much left the law and members of the congregation, and Samuel didn't relish the idea of getting any of those people involved. They might all be the finest folks in the world, but they weren't family.

Neither was Bootsie Phillips, but he suddenly came to mind. At first, Samuel thought that was the craziest idea he'd ever had, but then he remembered what Willadee had told him recently—that ever since the day Toy was shot, Bootsie had developed a whole new image of himself. He'd stopped drinking quite so heavily, frequently said things that made sense, and had appointed himself Willadee's protector when she started working in Never Closes.

Samuel looked around until he spotted Noble and waved him over. Noble bounded up onto the stage with his daddy, glad to be of service. Samuel put his arm around the boy, leaning down close to his ear. "Run across the road and dig Bootsie Phillips out of Never Closes, and bring him over here." He kept his voice down to a murmur.

Noble did a double take, thoroughly confused. "*Bootsie?* What on earth do you want with—?" But the look on Samuel's face reminded him who was the kid and who was the grown-up here. "What if he's not in there?"

"The place is open, Noble. He's in there."

"I thought it was against the law for me to—"

"You don't have to go all the way inside. Go through the house and stick your head in the door and ask your mama to tell Bootsie I need him to do something for me."

"What if he's drunk?"

Samuel was trying to be patient, but the more Noble balked, the more tense he felt. On top of that, his little crowd was getting restless. He was about to have to either start the music or tell those folks to go on home.

"Just do it," he said. "Do it now."

Noble took off for the house. Samuel blew out a sigh, slipped his guitar strap over his head, and walked over to the microphone. The congregation settled down, waiting expectantly. Samuel plucked at the strings, running songs through his mind, trying to choose the right one for this moment. He and Bernice always had a music list planned out, but most of those songs begged for harmony, and that was one thing he couldn't manage on his own. After a moment, he opened his mouth, and his sweet tenor rang through the night.

"I am weak but thou art strong," he sang, and it was like he was casting a spell. Every man, woman, and child in the place got easy at the same time, smiling gently and swaying like grass in the wind.

Willadee didn't know what to think when Noble stuck his head in the door and told her his daddy needed to see Bootsie Phillips.

"What on earth does he want with Bootsie?"

"I asked him that," Noble told her. "But he didn't tell me."

Willadee shrugged and turned to Bootsie, who was seated at the bar in a semi-sober state, keeping an eye on the regulars.

"Need anything, Willadee?" he asked eagerly as soon as he saw her looking his way.

"Samuel wants you, across the road."

"What on earth does Samuel want with—?"

"Nobody knows. But it must be big for him to send Noble over here to get you." She didn't really figure it was all *that* big. The last time there'd been a crisis at the revival, Samuel had found a rat snake in his amplifier and couldn't get it out. But it was good for Bootsie to feel needed.

Bootsie was off his stool before Willadee finished talking. He stood up straight as a master sergeant, motioned for Noble to lead the way, and off they went.

"Now, y'all behave yourselves while I'm gone," he called over his shoulder to the customers, "or you'll answer to me when I get back." To Willadee he said, "I won't be gone any longer than I have to."

Willadee smiled, the way she always smiled when Bootsie delivered some solemn pronouncement or made a show of looking out for her. Actually, she'd never felt she needed any protection in Never Closes. All the regulars seemed to consider themselves responsible for her safety. They even watched their language when she was nearby, and Bootsie wasn't the only one who had cut down on his drinking.

"Crazy Arms" was just winding down on the jukebox, and all of a sudden, Willadee could hear the music from across the road. Samuel singing, high and clear. Just Samuel. Willadee listened for a second, wondering why Bernice wasn't singing, too. Then Samuel's song ended just as a rompin', stompin' hillbilly number started playing on the jukebox, and Willadee couldn't hear herself think.

Samuel had all the little kids in the congregation lined up at the edge of the stage singing "This Little Light of Mine." When Noble and Bootsie stepped inside the tent, Samuel saw them and nodded for Noble to go take a seat. Then he and Bootsie ducked back through the tent flaps into the frigid night air.

Bootsie stood there, fairly steady on his feet, looking Samuel in the eye. "What's up, Preacher?"

Samuel explained that his sister-in-law hadn't made it to services, and hadn't called anybody to say she wasn't coming, so he was concerned and he needed somebody dependable to go check on her.

"More than likely she's fine," he said. "But you never know. It's possible she had a flat tire or some kind of car trouble." He didn't add that she might have poisoned herself or that she might be sitting at home planning a murder.

Bootsie swelled with pride at being trusted with such an important responsibility and assured Samuel that he'd be glad to go, there wasn't much he wouldn't do for the Moses family or the Lake family, either.

"Well, I'm grateful for the way you've been looking out for Willadee. You're a good man, Bootsie."

Samuel gave Bootsie a hearty pat on the back. Bootsie rocked back and forth like a sailor on a ship deck, managing somehow not to lose his balance and fall slap over.

"I'm sure tryin' to be," he said gravely. "It ain't as easy as it looks."

All the way to Toy and Bernice's house, Bootsie kept thinking how nice it felt to have people depending on him and calling on him when they had a problem. Not too long ago, there wasn't a soul in the county who would have trusted him to check on their family dog, much less a beautiful, delicate woman like Bernice Moses.

Bootsie's log truck was a worn-out old piece of embarrassment that rattled and clanked and shuddered and wheezed and listed to the left. He always had to grip the wheel with both hands and wrestle mightily to keep from flattening oncoming traffic. Ordinarily, he drove hard and fast, as though he couldn't wait to see what would happen when the wheels came off. Tonight was different. He poked along, scanning the roadside for a broken-down car and a frantic woman, but the only frantic thing he saw was a squirrel that was spinning around and around trying to decide whether it wanted to run under his wheels or head for the woods.

When he got to Toy's place, there were no lights on anywhere, not even on the porch. Bootsie felt his way through the darkness, going across the yard and up the steps.

"Anybody home?" he called out. The only sound was a tree limb scraping against the side of the house.

He knocked several times, but no one answered, so he opened the door, eased inside, and switched on the lights. The living room was so neat it looked as if nobody lived there.

He moved on, through the house.

The tiny little dining room was as fastidiously kept as the living room, and so was the kitchen, except for the table. Bootsie saw the jumble of cans and bottles—the cleaning supplies and the medicines—and he figured he knew why she hadn't shown up at the revival. She had obviously worked herself to exhaustion cleaning house, plus she must have cramps, which he knew from his wife could be more painful than anything a man could ever imagine, so she'd taken some Cardui and a nerve pill and had gone to bed early. Probably she was sound asleep by now, conked out by the Miltown. He didn't have any explanation for the spilled rat poison, but he'd already done more thinking in one night than he usually did in a week, so that one little detail didn't bother him.

He thought about heading down the hallway and finding the bedroom and looking in, just to make sure that his theory was correct, but he had certain qualms about that. What if Bernice waked up and thought he had broken in and was intending to do her harm? What if Toy came home and misinterpreted the whole situation and Bootsie wound up like Yam Ferguson, with his head facing in the wrong direction?

As far as Bootsie was concerned, he had done what he was sent to do. He tiptoed toward the front door.

And then he heard something. A low, guttural moan.

He turned and followed the sound. The first room he looked into was the one where Toy kept all that liquor, and Bootsie almost didn't make it to the next room. There were cases of bourbon and sour mash and scotch and vodka and gin and rum and God knew what else—everything a truly dedicated drunk could dream of, and all of a sudden Bootsie thought maybe he'd had enough of being semi-sober.

He took a guilty step toward a case of Wild Turkey. This was going to change everything, he knew that. Nobody would ever trust him again, but dammit, he wanted a good chug of Bombed Tom, and he wanted it now. He reached into the case, took out a bottle, and opened it, forgetting why he was here.

He was just about to take a drink when he heard another, louder moan. The sound jarred him back to reality with such a start that he spilled a couple of precious ounces all over himself.

"Well, hell," he said plaintively, as he set down the bottle and backed out of the room.

He found Bernice sprawled facedown on the bathroom floor, wearing nothing but the clothes God gave her. She was every bit as flawless as he and every other man who'd ever laid eyes on her had imagined, but Bootsie didn't even notice that, because of all the blood. There were thick red stains on the side of the tub and matted in Bernice's hair and more streaks here and there on her skin.

Bootsie felt like he'd been hit with a two-by-four. He couldn't even breathe. He hung there for a couple of seconds, unable to make his legs work at all. Then he bolted into the kitchen and grabbed up the phone. What with barking at elderly ladies to please get off the party line so he could make an urgent call, it took forever to get hold of Early Meeks. He was so torn up he didn't even hear the telltale clicks when those old biddies picked up their phones again to find out what all the excitement was about.

Early listened to Bootsie's babbling long enough to make out that Bernice was badly hurt, maybe dying, and there was blood all over the place.

"Is she responsive?" Early asked.

"Is she what?"

"Can she talk? Can she open her eyes and look at you?"

"I don't know. I don't know!" Bootsie was crying now, scared to death and sick inside. "She's facedown, and I'm afraid to touch her."

"Well, how do you know she's still alive?"

"Dead people don't moan," Bootsie said. "She keeps moaning."

"I'll call for an ambulance and be there directly," Early told him. "Don't you go anywhere, do you hear me, Bootsie?"

Bootsie heard him all right, and he knew what Early was really saying. He was saying that, whatever had happened to Bernice Moses, Bootsie Phillips stood a really good chance of getting the blame.

. . .

When Early got out to Toy's house, he found Bootsie dry-heaving on the front porch.

"Where is she?" Early asked as he came up the steps.

"Bathroom," Bootsie managed between spasms.

Early strode past, into the house. Bootsie listened to his footsteps, and when they stopped, he braced himself for whatever would come next. There was a full minute of awful silence, and then Early's voice boomed like a cannon.

"Bootsie! Get in here!"

So this was it. Bernice must have died, Bootsie was the prime suspect, and if he ran, there'd be no place to hide. This, he told himself grimly, was what came of going around semi-sober. If he hadn't adjusted his drinking habits, he'd be holed up in Never Closes right now, safe as a baby in its mother's arms. He'd be gloriously drunk, and quite possibly asleep under the pool table. But no. He'd let himself care what other people thought of him, and had mended his ways to impress them, and that had been the start of his troubles. Now there was nothing he could do except face the music.

Reluctantly, he went inside the house. Sirens sounded in the distance, getting more and more shrill as they screamed closer. Bootsie felt his legs buckle but managed to keep putting one foot in front of the other. At the door to the bathroom he stopped, unable to make himself take another step.

Early was standing beside Bernice (*beside Bernice's body*), holding an empty liquor bottle.

"You know what this is?"

"I didn't drink a drop of liquor," Bootsie protested. "I started to, but I didn't."

"Maybe you didn't," Early grunted. "But she sure did."

He turned the bottle upside down, and blood dripped out onto the floor. Well, it looked like blood.

"Sloe gin," Early said. "Looks like she got drunk as a skunk and tripped getting out of the bathtub, and passed out lying on top of the bottle. If you didn't reek of whiskey yourself, you'd have smelled it."

Bootsie backed up to the wall and leaned against it, going weak with relief.

"So she's not gonna die?"

"Not unless the hangover kills her. What were you doing over here, anyway? Another man's house—another man's wife—"

"The preacher sent me," Bootsie said. "He was worried about her because she didn't make it to church."

"He better not send anybody to check on my wife when she doesn't make it to church," somebody said from behind them.

Bootsie and Early both looked over at the same time to see two medics standing in the doorway. The one who had spoken was a short, muscular loudmouth named Lawrence something or other who'd been in the bar a few times lately while his wife was over at the revival. The other one was Joe Bill Rader's brother Ronnie. They'd heard enough to understand that there wasn't any real crisis here, and they were feeling chafed about it.

"Sorry to get you boys out here on a wild-goose chase," Early said. "Y'all can head on back to town. And I imagine the family will appreciate it if you two don't go tellin' everything you know."

"Don't worry," Ronnie assured him. "The first thing you learn on this job is how to keep your mouth shut."

Of course, they didn't keep their mouths shut, and neither did the women who had eavesdropped on Bootsie's phone call. Between the four of them, phone lines were buzzing all over the county with the juiciest tidbit to hit the area in quite some time. There wasn't enough information available for anyone to piece the whole story together, so everybody formed their own conclusions, the most common one being that Bernice was a secret alcoholic and Samuel must have known about it. Why else would he have sent a disreputable character like Bootsie Phillips out to see about her, when there were plenty of good, God-fearing people who would have been more than glad to go?

Naturally, there were also those who assumed there must be something illicit going on between Samuel and Bernice. After all, those two had been spending an awful lot of time together for months now, not to mention they used to be sweethearts, and neither one of them was the kind that anybody could ever really get over being in love with.

The one thing nobody anywhere ever thought of even once was that perhaps Bernice Moses had for a single moment considered suicide.

By the end of the service, several cars had pulled in at the revival grounds bringing individuals who weren't there for the music or the spiritual awakening. Some of the drivers sat in their cars, keeping the motors running and the heaters on, waiting for the moment when the last prayer was said and the worshipers came out of the tent. Others got out and stood around smoking near the entrance, determined to be the first to enlighten the congregation.

Across the road, another car was parking out beside Never Closes, and this driver didn't wait for anything.

Willadee wondered what was taking Bootsie so long, and shortly after Hobart Snell arrived, she found out. Hobart was an old-timer who was bent at the waist from arthritis and crooked from head to toe in his business dealings. He didn't often come to Never Closes to drink or for anything else, but tonight he hobbled in and headed straight for the bar.

"Gimme some sour mash," he told Willadee. "I don't care what kind."

Willadee thought if he didn't care what kind, she shouldn't care, either, but she poured him a glass of Jack Daniel's just to be nice.

Hobart took the drink and held it under his nose, sniffing it, while he looked around the room, sizing things up. "I see your permanent fixture's not back yet," he said.

"What permanent fixture?"

"The logger. The drunk. Bootsie Phillips."

Hobart's voice had a snide overtone that Willadee didn't much care for and didn't feel obliged to tolerate.

"For one thing," she said, "Bootsie is a friend of mine. For another thing, since you just got here, how'd you know he'd been gone?"

Hobart snickered and took a sip of Jack.

"I reckon near 'bout everybody in these parts knows where Bootsie's been tonight," he said. "How come your husband picked a fool like him to send to check on his girlfriend?"

"Looks like my tent revival days are over," Samuel told Willadee later, when they were lying in bed side by side.

The rumormongers had had themselves a time spreading the word after church that the reason Bernice Moses hadn't been there to sing was because she was passed out drunk on her bathroom floor, naked as a jaybird and so covered in sloe gin that Bootsie Phillips, who had found her, thought she was bleeding to death.

"You don't have to close down the revival just because of Bernice," Willadee told him. "There are plenty of people around here who can help you with the music."

"Not every night," he said. "And anyway, revivals aren't supposed to go on forever. The way attendance has been falling off, pretty soon I could be in debt to the rental company, and then I'd be in worse shape than I was to start with."

They were quiet for a moment, and then he said, heavily, "I swear, I can't figure out what God wants from me anymore."

Willadee didn't know what to tell him, but she knew he needed comfort, so she wrapped herself around that man and rocked him like a baby.

. . .

In the coming days, Samuel returned the tent and folding chairs and the sound equipment to the rental company, and threw himself into cleaning up Calla's neglected land. Cutting brush and burning it. Sawing up fallen trees for firewood. There was a certain pleasure in the hard physical work, and it gave him plenty of time to talk to God, but honestly, it seemed to him that it was God's turn to do the talking.

Nobody in the family talked much about Bernice. Instead of leaving town, she went on a kind of rampage, throwing herself at males of all ages, and making sure the whole world knew about it.

Toy was flattened. With the truth too obvious to be ignored, everything that had mattered most to him was over. Except for the kids. He loved those kids so much it hurt, but he couldn't stand to be around them or anybody else right now. He still had to go into Never Closes every night and stay until daylight, but he didn't talk to the customers much, and they understood. Every one of them realized that what Toy felt like doing was going on a rampage of his own—just lashing out every which way—and that he was afraid if he got to feeling crowded, he might do it.

So Toy stayed to himself. Every minute he wasn't either working or sleeping, he took to the woods and the water, but that made it all worse, somehow. Every beautiful thing that he saw reminded him of beauty lost and gone.

He couldn't even stand to be comfortable, so after a while, he stopped sleeping in his room upstairs and took to sacking out on an old Army cot in the back of the shed. There was hardly enough room in there to turn around, but the only turning around he ever did was to come back out every evening, the same way he'd gone in. He had all the space he needed.

Willadee brought his meals, and she left his food outside the door of the shed. If they happened to see each other, they'd talk for a few minutes, not about much of anything. There wasn't anything much Toy cared to talk about these days, and Willadee respected that.

The kids were desolate. Sometimes Blade would "draw the uncle a letter," using pictures instead of words to communicate. These he would leave outside the door of the shed. The next day the drawings would be gone, but Toy stayed as remote as before.

Swan haunted the shed and tried a couple of times to talk to Toy through the walls, but Willadee told her to leave him alone. He worked all night and didn't need his sleep interrupted.

"It'll take him some time," she explained to the kids when they pestered her about the change in the man they adored.

"But he doesn't even like us anymore!" wailed Swan.

Willadee said, "Oh, yes, he does. He loves you more than anything. One day he's going to come out of that shed, and you better just be ready for all the love that man will show you."

Chapter 36

February rolled around, and God still hadn't shown Samuel what to do, so he asked Calla what she thought about him planting some potatoes.

"Why, I think that any man who has land available is falling down on the job if he doesn't get some potatoes in the ground by Valentine's Day," she told him. "How many potatoes are you thinking of planting?"

"A couple of acres," Samuel said.

Calla pulled a surprised face. "That sounds like a kind of in-between amount of potatoes to plant. Too many for a family to eat but not enough to call a real crop."

Samuel said, "Actually, I wanted to use about five or ten acres to do it."

Well, Calla looked as confused as she was beginning to feel, so he explained that he'd noticed the way she gardened over the years, and it seemed to him she had a system that could be duplicated on a larger scale.

"You don't just plant one big stretch of any one thing," he said. "You mix everything up, and throw in some flowers where they're least expected, and you get more food from less space, without any insects or plant diseases. It's like the bugs get so bumfuzzled they don't know where to go to dinner."

Calla said, "Why, that's just the reason I do it, but you're the first person who ever noticed."

Samuel knew that real farming cost real money. Money for seeds— but Calla saved more seeds every year than she could plant in ten, so he figured he could get those from her for free. Money for fertilizer— but Calla's chickens provided more droppings than she could ever use, plus the calf lot was rich with old, rotted manure and Lady was doing her part every day, so all that would be free, too. Money for equipment—but Samuel didn't need the kind of fancy equipment that mauled the land into submission, not for what he had in mind. John's old tractor and a few hand tools would do just fine. Samuel had seen enough of his own daddy living on farm loans to know he didn't want to go that route. By the time a man got in his crops and sold them and paid everything off, he'd have to start living on the next year's loan. What Samuel wanted to do—what he thought might work—was make the soil happy with dried manure and fish scraps and wood ashes, and see if it didn't give something extra back in return.

Calla said, "You don't have to stop at fish scraps. I bury table scraps out there all winter long. By spring, the earthworms have got the ground worked up so good, all I have to do is punch holes in it with my finger and drop in the seeds. Why are you stopping at five or ten acres?"

"Because I'm still expecting God to give me a church."

Calla just nodded. She hated to think about God giving Samuel a church, as much as she knew he still wanted one. Once he got a new church, he'd be gone. And Willadee and the kids would be gone along with him.

"I'd hate to leave you with the whole place planted in all manner of crops that somebody would just have to plow under," he went on. "And I don't reckon there's a farmer in the county who'd take over tending to a bunch of marigolds."

"You don't have to tend to marigolds, Samuel. Marigolds take care of themselves."

"That makes it even better," he said.

So he planted potatoes. Half a row here, half a row there, with cabbages and pole beans in between. The more the weather warmed, the more different vegetables Samuel planted. Greens and squash and corn and tomatoes and onions and okra. And flowers, everywhere, flowers. He planted in blocks and patches that didn't run in straight lines, like crops were supposed to. There were odd-shaped plots, blending and running together, connected by winding paths, with short stretches of fence here and there for climbing plants to latch on to. Some of the land, he didn't even plow. He just covered it with old hay, or with oak leaves or pine needles. Other farmers would drive by and see Samuel out there covering up perfectly good field dirt with all manner of dead plant matter, and they'd just figure he'd finally lost it. His field didn't look like anything those men had ever seen, but to Samuel, it looked promising.

The second week of March, Calvin Furlough (who wasn't a farmer but had opinions about everything) stopped by the store on Monday morning and told Calla he was worried about Samuel.

Calla said, "You're not worried about Samuel, you're worried about Willadee. Why don't you go home and worry about Donna?"

Donna was Calvin's wife. To tell the truth, he didn't pay her anywhere near enough attention, and everybody knew it.

"Donna's all right," he said. "I just bought her a new Chevy." By "new" he meant one she hadn't had before. He was good about buying wrecked cars and fixing them up. Donna got a new one every time she turned around, but they always had For Sale signs in the window.

"Samuel's all right, too," Calla told him. She never had had much use for Calvin Furlough.

"Well, he's sure acting like a crazy man. What is it exactly that he's doing out there?"

"You'll see when everybody else does," Calla said.

Calvin wasn't the only one who stopped by the store asking questions. Ras Ballenger stopped by the same day and asked about Blade.

"It's been right hard on his mama and me," he said, sounding anguished, "having him over here instead of at home with us. But if this is where he wants to stay, so be it. At least we know he's taken care of."

Calla said that taking care of Blade was no trouble. They all enjoyed having the boy around. Ras went on about how that was a relief, and how he hated for any of his blood kin to be a burden to anybody, and how he knew what a handful Blade could be.

"It was gittin' to where we couldn't hardly keep him at home anymore," he said. "He hasn't tried runnin' off from here, has he?"

"No," Calla said. "He seems to be pretty happy."

Ras nodded humbly, as if to indicate that this all made him feel bad, but he guessed it was his lot in life. As he left, he said, "You don't have to tell him I came by or nothin'."

Don't worry, I won't, thought Calla.

For the life of her, she couldn't figure out what Ras Ballenger was doing in her store after all these months, acting like he was concerned about his son. The mother she would have expected to show up, bawling and begging the boy to go home with her. Or just grabbing him up and taking him. Back when Calla's children were little, she for sure wouldn't have let one of them be gone so much as overnight without permission. But then, she wouldn't have stood by a man who harmed one of them, either. If John Moses had put out one of her kids' eyes with a bullwhip, he'd have gone to sleep that night in one world and woke up the next morning in another.

After Ras was gone, she pondered over what it could all mean. Maybe he was just trying to improve his image in the community. Probably that was what he'd been doing that day when he helped

Millard and Scotty get Toy out of the woods and into town to the emergency room. She'd been cordial to him ever since. They all had. As grateful as they'd been to still have Toy alive and among them, they hadn't questioned his motives.

She was questioning them now, though.

"I don't know what it could mean," Willadee said that evening, after Calla told her about it. "I don't trust him, though. Seems like every time we start forgetting he's around, he rears up his head to remind us."

They had just put the kids to bed and were sitting in the living room. Willadee was turning the collar on one of Samuel's shirts, so the worn part wouldn't show. She'd just gotten all the stitches out and was pulling off loose bits of thread.

"Well, I think we need to start watching Blade closer again," Calla told her. "We've gotten lax."

Here of late, the kids had been playing all over the place. Not as far back as the creek, but they stayed out of sight a lot, especially when they were riding Lady. Which was generally from the time they got off the school bus until it was too dark to see.

Willadee eased the collar back between the yoke and the facing, with the good side up, and started pinning it in place.

"I hate to wish harm to anybody, Mama, but I don't know why people like that man get to live on this earth."

"If he bothers that boy again, he won't, for long."

Willadee gave her a look. That was strong talk, coming from Calla Moses.

Calla said, "And don't think I don't mean it."

Ras Ballenger sat on his front steps that night with a fresh chew of Bull Durham in his jaw and a peaceful smile on his face.

He hadn't been asking questions at Calla Moses's store because he needed answers. No sirree. His appearances at the revival, and that little charade about taking Blade presents at Christmas, and now this visit to the store today, had all been done for the same reason he did half the things he did to Geraldine. He just liked to make people squirm.

All the answers he needed, he'd picked up by observation—when no one had been observing *him*.

The door creaked behind him now. Geraldine stepped out of the house and sat down beside him. She didn't sit close enough to touch him, and he knew that the only reason she had come out at all was because she had no one else to talk to who was over five years old. Just to get her goat, he reached over and began feeling the little fat rolls around her middle. She went stiff as a board, immediately.

"What's the matter, you don't like me feeling your fat?"

She edged away from his hand. "Don't do that."

"Well, all right, if you don't want my lovin'. You really oughta take it where you can find it, though, a lump like you." He goosed those fat rolls again. "You wasn't hardly lumpy at all when I married you."

She pursed her mouth and sighed resignedly. Ras patted her on the back as if she were a good old dog and gave her a cheerful smile.

"I went by and asked about your boy today." That was what he called Blade these days, when he was talking to her. "Your boy." Little one-eyed bastid.

Geraldine looked away, like she always looked away when he talked about Blade. Ras couldn't tell whether she missed the boy or whether she was simply glad the kid was over there instead of over here, and she didn't want him to see it in her eyes. Maybe she thought a child would be safer at the Moses place. He almost laughed out loud, thinking about that.

He reached up and took a clump of her limp hair in his hand. Not pulling on it, the way he sometimes did. Just holding on hard enough so she couldn't jerk her head away.

"Looks like you'd do something with this hair," he told her. "You look like a plow horse with this hair."

. . .

On Tuesday afternoons after school, Blade took art lessons from Isadora Priest, who had a major in art and a minor in education, and knew artistic ability when she saw it. Isadora was sixty-three years old and did a little substitute teaching in Emerson when any of the salaried teachers were sick. The first time she'd laid eyes on Blade and his artwork, Isadora knew she'd found a diamond in a turnip patch. The way she discovered the artwork was that she was patrolling the room to make sure all the kids were writing their spelling words twenty times each, and she found that Blade was not. He was drawing. She confiscated his notebook and instantly decided that it was no wonder the boy's spelling was faulty. As many sketches as there were in that book, he couldn't possibly have had time to work on his spelling.

Isadora didn't work *all* the time, and she didn't like talking on the phone, so she had shown up at Calla's the next day and had told Willadee proudly that the boy had "an eye." After she said it, she realized how it sounded and altered her statement to indicate that he had genuine talent, the kind you don't see every day.

"It's like whatever he sees goes in through his eye and comes out through his hand," she said. She also said she thought she should work with him. She thought Tuesday afternoons would be good. She thought that she could walk over to the school on those afternoons to get Blade and walk him back to her house. She thought the lessons should last about an hour. And she thought that Willadee could drive over and pick him up afterward.

Willadee asked her whether she'd thought about how much she would charge, and she said that she had indeed. The lessons would be free. Willadee argued with her about that, and Isadora finally admitted that a pint of whiskey from Never Closes once a month would be nice. She never had the nerve to go out and buy it for herself, and there were just so many uses for it.

So it was settled.

From then on, Blade walked with Isadora to her house every Tuesday afternoon, and Willadee drove over later and picked him up, which meant that, not too long after the other kids got off the school bus, Willadee left the house. She always visited for a bit with Isadora, but she was usually back home in less than forty-five minutes.

The day after Ras stopped by the store, Willadee went to get Blade from Isadora's, just like always. Swan watched her drive away and waved to her from the porch. Samuel waved from the field. Toy didn't wave, because he was asleep in the shed. Calla had a customer, but she looked up and saw Willadee leaving, and she said to the woman she was waiting on, "There goes Willadee. Gone to pick up Blade."

Ras Ballenger saw Willadee leave—saw her from where he was crouched, hidden, at the edge of the woods. He was holding a gunnysack.

He glanced over to Samuel's Crazy Patch, which was what the locals were now calling the farming project, and there was Samuel, carting a wheelbarrow of manure from the calf lot over to where he had plowed up some new ground. Those two boys of his were trotting out to join him—none of them aware that they were being watched.

Ras headed toward the back of the Moses yard, keeping out of sight. Going thicket to thicket. Thicket to fencerow. Fencerow to outbuildings. When he got over behind the chicken house, he opened the gunnysack and turned loose a kitten.

Chapter 37

Willadee had started supper before she left to get Blade, and she had put Swan in charge of keeping an eye on it to make sure nothing burned or boiled over. Swan turned all the fires down low and went outside to take care of her one regular chore. Tending the chickens.

Swan didn't like chickens, except for the baby ones, but there weren't any chicks right now, there was just a bunch of grumpy old hens, and that danged speckled rooster with the spurs like tenpenny nails. Swan let herself into the pen and went into the chicken house. There, she opened a lidded metal drum that sat over in a corner and filled a coffee can with chopped corn, which she took back out into the chicken yard. She was about to start throwing handfuls of corn to the chickens when she heard the most pitiful sound in the world. A kitten crying.

Grandma Calla never had kept a cat. She'd always said she had enough to worry about from chicken hawks and weasels. She didn't need a cat catching baby chicks (when she had baby chicks) and batting them around until they gave up hope and died. There'd never been a cat on the place.

But there was one here now. Swan *heard* it.

She *heard* it, but when she glanced around, she couldn't *see* it. So she went searching for it. Outside the chicken pen, leaving the gate wide open. Around behind the back of the pen, not noticing that the chickens were following her, wanting their supper.

The kitten (fluffy, gray, and needy) was under a stack of brush that Samuel hadn't gotten around to burning because the weather had been so windy lately. Swan had to get down on her belly and scrooch along, reaching back beneath the brush. She knew there could be a snake in there, but she was determined to get that kitten.

And she did. She pulled it out and marveled over it for a second—and then she heard that sound again. Another kitten crying.

Well, *of course,* there wouldn't be just one. Someone must have thrown out a whole litter, and this one got separated from the rest.

Swan followed the sound along the fencerow—and there it was. Just sitting there in some weeds looking woebegone. She captured that one, too. Then she prowled along until she came to the first thicket, where she found yet another kitten. And now she heard more kittens crying. In the woods.

Swan and her brothers knew how far they were allowed to get away from the house. They were not to get out of hollering distance. She told herself that the woods weren't *completely* out of hollering distance. If someone hollered loudly enough, from the house or the yard, she could hear them. She didn't wonder whether anyone would be able to hear her if she hollered, because she didn't intend to make any noise that might scare those other kittens away.

The thing she didn't even consider was that she might need to make some noise, she might need to scream bloody murder—and not be able to. You can't make a sound when, out of nowhere, somebody throws a gunnysack over your head and binds it around your mouth fast, so fast, with a long strip of cloth, and then you're being carried at a dead run through the woods, and you know without a doubt that you're on your way to dying.

Willadee was not happy when she and Blade came home, and she found the fires under the pots of peas and mustard greens were turned down so low that nothing was even simmering. She had to feed Toy before he opened the bar, and she liked to feed Samuel when he came in from the field, and now there'd be hungry men passing through the kitchen and her with nothing ready to put on the table.

She looked through the house, then went out into the yard, calling for Swan—and practically ran over her mother, who was huffing along behind half a dozen or so confused hens that were running every which way. Calla was shaking the tail end of her apron and shouting at them to *"Shoo! Shoo!"*

Willadee said, "Mama, what on earth?"

"My *chickens,*" Calla managed, "were on the *road.* Donna Furlough just ran over one of my Plymouth Rocks."

Donna felt just awful about what she had done. As soon as she'd realized, she whipped her new (to her) Chevy into the yard and stopped it so fast the For Sale sign fell out of the window. Now she was running toward Calla, wringing her hands.

"I didn't mean to do that," Donna kept saying over and over. "Oh, Miz Calla, I'm so sorry."

Calla didn't like to hurt anybody's feelings, especially Donna's, her being saddled with the likes of Calvin, so she got hold of herself and told her not to worry about it, it was just a chicken. Donna wrung her hands again, and got back into her car. She was still apologizing as she drove off.

"I just don't understand how they got out," Calla said.

"Samuel?" Willadee called out. "Do you know where Swan is?"

Samuel looked over and shook his head, and kept on working.

"She was feeding the chickens a while ago!" Noble yelled back.

"Just before she got interested in something else and wandered off," Calla muttered. By now, she'd herded her hens back into their pen, and she was angrier than ever that they'd been let out. "When we find that girl, I'm having a talk with her."

Blade had trotted out to the barn to look for Swan, and was now coming back, stopping at every outbuilding to peek inside. There was no trace of her. He wandered over behind the chicken pen and peered up into the mulberry tree, but she wasn't there, either. He glanced around uneasily, a slight shiver starting up his spine.

"It's not like her to take off by herself," Willadee worried aloud. Then she noticed Blade on his hands and knees, poking around in the weeds at the base of the fence row.

"Blade," she said, "stop playing around in the dirt and help me find Swan."

He pulled something out of the weeds and brought it over to her. A kitten.

"For pity's sake," Willadee said. "Where'd that come from?"

And Calla said, "We're not keeping it. I've never had a cat around here, and I do not intend to—"

"My daddy catches cats," Blade whispered. "Usually, he throws them to the dogs."

Willadee and Calla froze in place, staring at him, fear flaming up in their eyes.

"God in Heaven," Calla said.

"Samuel!" Willadee screamed. "Come here, come here, come here! *Samuel!*"

Samuel and the boys dropped their tools and raced toward the house. Toy tore out of the shed. Willadee stood there babbling like a crazy woman.

"Swan's missing. Already looked. Everywhere. Ballenger. He catches cats. We found a cat. Blade did."

"Maybe somebody dumped it—" Samuel began.

"No," Willadee said. "No. You find her. You find her, Samuel."

Toy took off like a shot, and he didn't slow down until he hit the woods. If Swan was back there, he'd find her. Samuel roared off in the car. Everybody else fanned out over the farm yelling Swan's name. Only Blade couldn't move. He just stood there holding the kitten and watching the world fall apart.

Samuel drove with his foot to the floor, careening around curves and fishtailing, spraying gravel. All the way to Ballenger's house he was praying to God and hating himself. If he hadn't failed in so many ways, he was thinking, this would not be happening. If he still had a church, he and his family could be safe in some parsonage, on some quiet street, in some small town in Louisiana, miles and miles away from here. If he hadn't lost God's favor—but he knew he had. Knew it now. Why else would this be happening?

Please God, please, let Swan be all right. Let me find her. If You never answer another prayer for me as long as I live, answer this one. In his heart, and in his gut, he was terrified that Swan would be at Ballenger's—and just as terrified that she wouldn't be. The worst thing would be if he couldn't find her at all.

Chapter 38

Swan was in a dark place. A deeply dark place, with a dirt floor. She couldn't be absolutely sure about the darkness, because the gunnysack was still over her head—and she couldn't scream for help, because that sack was still tied in place with those strips of cloth that bound it over her mouth. Her clothes were ripped and soiled but were still on her body. A man doesn't have to strip a little girl naked to do the things that he had done to her.

She knew who he was. Just knew. In her mind, she was calling him "the man," because somehow that wasn't as horrible as acknowledging who he was.

There was something lying beside her. Something she'd found back there by the willows, when Everything Was Happening. (She'd found it with one of her hands. One of her two hands that were both flailing and clutching at dirt and leaves.) She hadn't known where she was before, but she knew then, because of what it was that one of her hands had found.

Actually, it was two somethings, one inside the other. A cowbell, with its clapper wrapped in rags. And wedged in among the rags—was a duck call.

Once she'd found the cowbell, she'd held on to it, and the man must not have noticed. He was too occupied with other things. Hard, hurtful things. Finding the cowbell had carried her out of what was happening. A little bit. Gave her something to focus on besides the rough ground and the tearing, and the way the man kept calling her "little pretty" while he did those ugly things. She'd thought, wildly, of hitting him with the cowbell, but she couldn't, couldn't do anything, couldn't writhe out from under him, couldn't stand what was happening, couldn't stop trying and trying to scream, couldn't make her arm rise up to hit him.

Even then, a part of her knew that hitting him with that cowbell would be the worst thing she could do. What if she missed her mark? What if all she did was make him so mad that he went ahead and did what he was probably going to do anyway, what she was so sick with fear that he'd do anyway? *What if he killed her?*

After he'd stopped—when he'd finally stopped—he'd just laid on top of her, gasping and jerking, and she'd pulled her arm slowly to her side. Her hand holding on to that cowbell. That silent cowbell.

She didn't realize the significance of what she was holding on to even when the man pushed off her and she could hear him zipping and buckling, and he still didn't take the thing away from her. So he must not have seen it. He still must not have seen it.

It was only when they were walking—when he was hustling along and dragging her by one hand (not the hand that was holding the cowbell), and she was wobbly-legged and broken and trying to keep up and trying not to trip over roots, or fall into holes, and she didn't trip, and she didn't fall, and nothing whatsoever happened to make her lose her grip on the bell—it was only then that she understood that what she was holding in her hand was a Miracle.

By the time that they got to the place where he left her, she knew he wouldn't see it. Knew without doubt that God wouldn't let him see it. God had him blinded to it. That was the only explanation.

Still, when they'd gotten here and the man had pushed her inside this place—she had fallen. On purpose. On purpose, because Something Told Her that he'd tie her up, and that, if she were holding the bell when he reached for her hands, the Miracle would be ruined. So she'd fallen on the bell and had turned loose of it, and—when the man had started tying her, hands to feet—he hadn't found it. He had crisscrossed this space (whatever space this was), back and forth, doing more tying, anchoring her on all sides so that she couldn't move in one direction or another, couldn't do anything besides lie still and cramped and suffocating. And even then. Even then. He. Still. Did not. Find it.

Now the man was gone, and the Miracle was lying beside her. She didn't know how it could help her. She couldn't untie the knots that were holding her. She kept trying, fiddling with her fingers, desperately trying—but she couldn't.

She was afraid that even a Miracle couldn't save her. So afraid that her churning stomach wanted to come up through her throat, but she couldn't afford to let it do that. If she let that happen, that would just be another way of dying, because she'd choke, and everything would be over.

So she held it all down. And she tried to hold on. To some kind of hope. To anything. There wasn't much to hold on to. Thinking about home just made her feel more helpless, because what if she never got back there? And thinking about family just made her feel more hopeless, because what if nobody found her in time?

Probably not many men have ever built a feedlot on top of a septic tank, but not many men need to have a piece of ground that can be dug up and tamped back down without somebody wondering, if they should happen to come around and notice, why there's no grass growing in a particular spot when there's grass aplenty everywhere else. Feedlots are known for not having any grass, because the livestock that are shut up in there will eat every last sprig, right down to the roots. And ground that has been dug up doesn't look dug up for long, because thousand-pound animals can tamp it down overnight to where it looks like it hasn't been disturbed in years. That is, if you keep them agitated, so they don't just stand around in one spot for hours on end. The trick is to keep them moving, but that's what dogs and whips are for. One thing Ras Ballenger was good at was making a horse go where he wanted it to go, and he could do it all night, if that's what it took.

He had already dug down and taken the lid off the septic tank and had covered the hole with a big piece of plywood. Then he had stacked bales of hay on top of the plywood and on top of the lid, to hide them from view. All this he had done early in the day, just as soon as he got back from taking Geraldine and the kids over to her mama's house.

Now there was nothing left to do except wait. Somebody would be coming around pretty soon, he felt confident. Confident that they would come, and confident that he could handle it. They would come around asking questions, just as if he was automatically the guilty party, but they wouldn't find anything, because where the girl was now was a place they couldn't figure out, and where she was going to be later, after he was done with her, was a place they'd never suspect. Then, by the next time he cleaned out his septic tank, the lye would have done its work, and there wouldn't be anything left of her at all.

With his cur dogs for company, and his best friend the bullwhip coiled around a fence post, Ras was right now grooming a couple of horses in the holding pen, over by the barn. Not customers' horses. He didn't have a lot of customers these days. He had bought these two animals at the sale barn. A mare and her colt, both with the look of good horseflesh. He could make something out of them, with a little effort. And make money at it, too, not to mention they'd come in handy today. Them and the other four head that Ras had brought in from the pasture and was keeping in an adjoining lot.

He was feeling good, Ras was. Smug and content and well tended. A little bit ago, after he'd left the girl, he had come out into the good, sweet air and had gone over to the faucet to hose cool water over his head. Just what a man needed to feel fresh.

He was going to go back in there, where the girl was, in a little while. As soon as her people had come over and done their nosing around and satisfied themselves that she wasn't there. This was what he'd been waiting for all this time, what he'd been thinking about since that first day at the store, back on old John Moses's funeral day. He'd waited until she started sprouting. He gave himself credit for that. The way he looked at it, his behavior had been downright honorable.

When Samuel's old rattletrap car roared into view, Ras lifted a hand in greeting. Samuel leapt out of the car and ran across the yard. Ran hard. The cur dogs raised their hackles briefly, then moved out of Samuel's path. Ballenger was surprised at that, but he looked over at Samuel and smiled.

"How do, Preacher. Where's the fire?"

Samuel said, "I'm looking for my daughter."

His voice was shaking, and so was he. He was shaking all over, inside and out. Ras came out of the holding pen and latched it behind him and walked over to face Samuel. His brow was furrowed in a show of puzzlement.

"Your daughter don't play over here, Preacher. My son don't, either, for that matter. I thought you was keeping up with both of 'em."

"Have you seen her?"

Ras shook his head, and scratched his neck, and blew out a regretful breath. "I sure wish I could help you, but I'm afraid you've come to a goat's house after wool."

Samuel had no idea that Ras was parroting Toy Moses, but he sensed that the man was enjoying this.

"Could I speak to your wife?"

Ras cocked his head, just slightly, as if to say that he didn't appreciate being called a liar. His tone was civil enough though. "I reckon you could if she was here, but she's at her mama's today. They're giving each other permanents."

Samuel was looking around now. Casting his eyes in all directions.

Searching for signs and hidey-holes. It was all he could do to contain himself. All he could do not to tear this place up.

"Do you mind if I have a look?" he asked.

Ras said, "I do mind. I damn sure do." And then he said, "But I'll let you put your mind at ease." He waved an arm, indicating the whole place. "Help yourself." Then he asked, generously, "What's your girl's name?"

"Swan," said Samuel. "Her name is Swan."

Ras put his hands to his mouth, and yelled the name. *"Swan? Are you here someplace, Swan? Your folks are worried about you, Swan!"*

Samuel was shouting, too, at the top of his voice. *"Swan! Swan, can you hear me? Swannnnnnnnnnnnn!"*

Of course there was no answer.

Swan heard, though. She heard both voices, and she strained against her bonds, and she tried to scream *"Here I am! I'm in here,"* but there was no sound. No sound except for her heart, which was pounding out a joyous chorus. Her father had come for her! Her father, who always tried to do the right thing, and trusted the Lord for the outcome, and walked every day in God's favor.

But then she had a horrible thought. *Used to.* He *used to* enjoy God's favor. God hadn't been smiling on him much lately, and the outcomes he'd kept trusting God for hadn't exactly been coming out wonderful.

Ras Ballenger shrugged, and went back to grooming his horses.

The man's nonchalance broadsided Samuel, making him more sure than ever that Swan was somewhere nearby. He dashed around like a wild man, still calling her name—calling her name and looking for anything, anything. In the barn. In the feed room. In the tack room. In the feedlot. In an open shed. Under the house. He even went inside the house, and rushed from room to room. There was nothing, nothing, nothing.

His heart was exploding. He wasn't finding her.

He came back out of the house, and stood in the yard, and his eyes searched the edge of the woods, where nothing was moving. He looked back over to where Ras Ballenger was combing out the mare's mane, not paying him any attention. And then he looked the only place that was left to look. He looked up.

"*Godddddddddddddddd!*" he shouted. "*Godddddddddddddddd?*"

He shot his arms up into the air, with his hands reaching, like he was pulling Heaven down, and he let loose roaring from his deepest depths.

"*Are you listening, God? Its Samuel! Sam Lake! You know me, Lord! You—know—me!*"

Ras Ballenger whirled around and stared at him. He'd heard it around that the preacher had lost his grip, but this was proof positive. "He can't hearrrrrr you" was what he wanted to sing out to the crazy man.

Inside the shed, someone could hear. Swan heard everything. She heard when her father started calling on God, and she heard it when God answered.

God's answer started quick but quiet, with the softest little scuttling sound that multiplied by the hundreds. Pretty soon that sound was all she heard, but it was all she needed. All she needed on this earth. It was the sweetest sound imaginable. She felt as if she were wrapped in rustling velvet. Velvet brushing against her skin, soothing and caressing, maybe even healing.

You wouldn't dream that mice could make you feel such jubilation.

Chapter 39

Out in the yard, Samuel was still waving his arms at God and telling it like it was.

"*I'm Yours! Yours, Lord! But that means you're mine, too! You made a lot of big promises, and I've believed every one of them! Now I'm calling on you to keep them!*"

Ras came out of the holding pen again and hollered across to Samuel. Hollered across the considerable distance that lay between them. "Go home, Preacher! Go home and see if she hasn't turned up by now. I bet you good money she's turned up by now."

But Samuel wasn't listening.

"*I'm standing on the promises, Lord! Standing right here! Me! Sam Lake! Still standing! I'm standing here, and I'm holding on, and I'm not letting go until you answer!*"

Then he heard the cowbell. The *cowbell*! Ringing and jangling to wake the dead. And on top of that sound was the throaty *quack-quackquack* of a duck call.

Samuel froze in place. And so did Ras Ballenger. Samuel, knowing what that sound meant. Ras Ballenger, confused as the devil.

"Swan?" Samuel shouted, starting toward the sounds. Those glorious sounds.

For a fraction of a second, Ras was too much in shock to move. Then he started after Samuel, snagging his bullwhip off the fence. Samuel heard the hiss of the whip as it unfurled, and he snapped around, just as quick. Just as quick. A man can't move that fast, but Sam Lake did. He threw himself through the air—*through the air, over all that distance.* Flying. A man can't do that, either, but he flew. Later on, he remembered the flying. The whip never touched him, because Ras turned to run, and Samuel leveled him. They landed on the ground, Ras scrabbling and squirming, facedown, with Samuel on his back, pinning him.

"You best lemme up, Preacher," Ras warned him. Not so sure of himself now, but still trying to act like it.

Samuel looked around, wild-eyed, trying to get his bearings, and what he saw was a peaceful farm, where hungry animals waited, some in one holding pen, some in another—waited impatiently, stamping their feet, demanding to be turned in to the feedlot.

His glance took in the contrast of brown and green, where the barren, hard-packed dirt inside the lot butted up against the vegetation outside the fence, and then, in one heartbeat, every blade of grass became crisply visible—especially the darker, denser grass that stood out starkly from the rest, leading in a telltale line from the feedlot fence off toward the woods.

The grass that grew over the septic tank field line.

Samuel blinked, the whole picture falling into place. He heard the horses stamping their feet, the sound getting louder and louder, until it was like thunder in his ears, and suddenly he understood everything. The preparations Ras had made. The plans he had for killing Swan and making it so no one would ever find the body. Making it so there wouldn't be anything to find.

He didn't even know it when his right hand streaked down and hooked beneath Ras Ballenger's chin, and yanked the man's head sideways in one savage movement. Or when his left hand planted itself at the base of Ras Ballenger's neck.

"What are you doing?" Ras squawked, sounding quivery. He clawed at Samuel's hands.

"God's sake, Preacher," Ras whimpered. "You can't do a thing like this. You're God's man, you just said so."

Samuel jerked up with the hand that was holding Ras Ballenger's chin, and he bore down with the hand that was planted at the base of Ras Ballenger's neck, and he didn't stop until he heard the cracking, popping sounds that told him it was finished. If Ras Ballenger screamed, Sam Lake didn't hear.

It took him a while to find the room. The room that didn't seem to be there. Didn't seem to exist. It was built into the barn between the feed room and the tack room, like dead space. There didn't seem to be a way in. If you walked into the feed room and looked around, you saw sacks of feed. Stacks of sacks of feed. So you thought the wall behind the feed had nothing on the other side except that tack room.

But that was where the sounds were coming from. That cowbell ringing and that duck call bleating. And now Swan, calling out to him, answering him when he shouted her name. Samuel tore through those stacks of fifty-pound sacks, picking them up and slinging them aside until he found what he was looking for.

It wasn't a door. It was just part of the wall. A panel that was almost impossible to see, but easy to remove once he discovered it. All he needed was a crowbar, and he found one of those in the tack room, stuck back with some other tools, barely noticeable.

Samuel pried the panel off and went into that wretched space to claim his daughter. It was dark as a tomb in there, so he couldn't see the pieces of rope or the strips of cloth or the gunnysack. All those things that lay shredded on the floor. He couldn't even see Swan, but they found each other in the blackness.

She was crying. He was bawling.

"There were mice," she told him, again and again, as he gathered her up and took her out of there. "There were mice everywhere. They turned me loose."

. . .

His family met him in the yard. All except Toy, who'd gone off in the truck, and had passed him on the road, and had turned around and followed him home. The boys—all three of them—hung on the edge of the porch, afraid to look. Calla and Willadee ran to the car and cried out at what they saw, and what they understood.

Samuel carried Swan into the house, and laid her on the couch, and stepped back, giving her over to the women. He couldn't talk at all. Willadee knelt beside the couch and kissed Swan's face over and over, her tears making tracks through the dirt that was there. Calla went to the phone and called Doc Bismark. Then she went into the kitchen and brought back a basin of water and some tea towels that were old enough to be soft as down. She bathed that little girl's face and arms, and started to bathe her hands—and then she saw what Swan was holding. What she was holding on to for dear life. A cowbell and a duck call.

"What's this?" she asked, although she knew.

And Samuel found his voice.

"Swan's miracle," he said.

It wasn't until Doc Bismark came and was tending Swan that Samuel took Willadee into the kitchen and told her what had happened. By then, Calla and Toy had taken the boys upstairs to get them away from everything. Doing their best for them. Those boys needed help right now, too.

Sometime during Samuel's telling, there were footsteps in another room, but the sounds didn't register on either of them. Samuel just kept pouring out the story. Later, there were more footsteps, and a door closing, but that didn't register, either. There were cars and trucks outside—people arriving and finding out that, for the first time ever, Never Closes wasn't open. All the sounds of people coming and leaving ran together, without touching Samuel and Willadee.

"I killed him, Willadee," he told her. "After standing right there, and calling on God for help—and getting it. Knowing that He'd sent a miracle. I killed that devil man, and I don't know how to begin to be sorry."

"I'll never be sorry," Willadee said, with a voice like steel. Then she said the other part. "Unless it takes you away from us."

Samuel put his arms around her, and drew her close, and rested his head on top of hers, and for a while, all they did was breathe together.

"We'll just have to trust God for the outcome," Samuel said. "I'll have to go into town pretty soon. To turn myself in."

Willadee said, "I know. But not yet. Stay here just a little bit. For Swan."

Toy Moses had come downstairs to get the boys something to drink but had stopped outside the kitchen door when he heard what Sam Lake was saying. He'd gone outside after that and found Bootsie Phillips leaning against his logging truck, waiting expectantly for the bar to open. Toy didn't explain what was going on, but he told Bootsie that Never Closes was shutting down for a while and put him in charge of heading customers off as soon as they arrived.

Bootsie didn't have to ask if there was trouble. Anything that could keep Never Closes from opening had to be serious. He told Toy Moses not to worry about a thing.

Toy went to Ballenger's first. When he drove up, he saw the cur dogs fighting over something on the ground, and he knew what it was. Knew and thought that nothing on earth could be more appropriate. He took a flashlight from the truck and went to find the place that he'd heard Samuel telling Willadee about.

When he found the room Samuel had described, he went inside that dark, dead space. He almost could not believe what he saw there.

"Dear God," he said. And meant it.

It was getting toward ten o'clock when Samuel rolled into Magnolia. He had stayed at home longer than he'd intended, first sitting beside

Swan for a while, just sitting. The doctor had given her something to make her sleep, so she may not have known he was there. After that, he'd gone up and talked to the boys, and explained things the best he could without destroying them. They all sat in stunned silence, Blade and Bienville weeping silently. Noble wept only on the inside. Calla sat like a rock, looking on, knowing full well that, if she reached out to comfort them, they'd break in ways she couldn't mend.

There was a light on in the sheriff's office. Not just in the building itself. That was always lit. But Samuel was surprised to see Early's light on. He had figured that one of the deputies would be taking his statement.

Early took Samuel into his office and listened to every word. When Samuel got to the part about how he had flown through the air at Ras Ballenger, Early took a book of paper matches off his desk, and started tearing the matches out, and tossing them at the open-mouthed moccasin—at the ashtray that was centered in the coil.

Samuel finished his story and waited to see what Early would say. For a second or two, the man didn't say anything. Then he drew a deep breath and got to his feet.

"Well, thank you for coming, Samuel."

Samuel stood up, too, not knowing what to do next.

"What happens now?" he asked.

Early said, "Now you go home to your family."

Samuel stared at him. Going home to his family was what he wanted most in the world, but he hadn't thought it would happen this easily. He hadn't been at all confident that it would ever happen. Or at least not for a number of years.

Samuel told Early that he appreciated the show of trust, and he appreciated the time to be with his wife and children. This was all going to be hard on everybody, and he was glad he'd have more time to prepare them for what was coming, before he got locked up.

"Nobody's locking you up, Samuel," Early said. "I can't hardly charge two men for the same crime. And Toy's story sounds a lot more realistic."

Samuel reached out and took hold of the edge of Early's desk to steady himself. He was that close to falling over.

While he was still too stunned to say a word, Early added, "And you don't need to be telling it around what all happened to Swan. She's got enough to deal with without feeling like the whole world's looking at her."

A few minutes later, Samuel was standing face-to-face with his brother-in-law—Early having instructed Bobby Spikes, who was on duty that night, to take him back there for a visit. Toy was standing inside his cell, lounging with his elbows hooked through the bars, looking more relaxed than he had in quite a while. Samuel was in the hallway, tensed like a spring and sick in his soul.

"You can't do this," Samuel said.

And Toy said, "It's already done."

It was a little dark back there, not much light on in that part of the building at this time of night. Toy's face was in shadow, and the effect was a softening of all the lines and creases that he'd earned the hard way.

"But you're not guilty," Samuel argued. "I am."

Toy cut his eyes over toward Bobby Spikes, who probably wasn't supposed to be listening but was. That deputy wasn't looking at them, but he had an ear tuned in their direction.

"You're mixed up, Samuel." Toy kept his eyes on Bobby, hoping that Samuel would catch on and go along. Not expecting it to happen but hoping. "When I brought Swan home, beat up like that, it must've thrown you plumb off-kilter."

Beat up like that. Not raped. Not mauled. *Beat up.*

Samuel stared at Toy, understanding why he was doing this. Why he was taking the blame, and doing his best to hide what had really happened to Swan. It was *for* Swan. All of it. So that she'd have her daddy while she was growing up, and so that she wouldn't forever have people pointing at her and talking behind their hands. But still, to Samuel, it was all lies, and no good could come of it.

"You can't do this," he said again.

"Nothing else I can do," Toy said. "I'm a cold-blooded killer, and I have to pay the price. Ain't that right, Bobby?"

Bobby gave him a look that said he couldn't wait to see Toy fry and said, "Well, I reckon it's true what they say around here. A Moses never lies."

Chapter 40

Calla grieved.

She grieved for Swan—for all she'd lost, and for all she'd found out about life that nobody should ever have to find out about, because it shouldn't ever be. She grieved for Blade—because he was losing, too. He wouldn't be able to feel that he belonged here now. Might not ever feel that he belonged anywhere. She grieved for the other boys, because their world was in shambles. She grieved for Samuel and Willadee, because it would be their job to build it all back, and she couldn't see how anything could be simple ever again.

And she grieved for Toy.

When Samuel had come back from town—when he'd unfolded the story for her (hating it, she knew he hated it), she had sat down hard in a chair, and clasped her hands together, and started twisting her wedding ring back and forth, back and forth, on her finger.

"I'm going back again tomorrow," Samuel promised. "I'll keep going back until somebody listens to me."

And she knew that he would. And that it wouldn't matter. Nobody on God's green earth was going to believe that Samuel Lake had killed a man. Not if they had to choose between believing it was him who did it and believing it was Toy Moses. Once she'd had a chance for the shock to wear off, she wasn't surprised about Toy taking the blame. That was just what she'd have expected if her mind could have stretched out that far, to probe into possibilities. But still she grieved.

She sat that night in her room with a box of old pictures that she spread out over her bed. All those pictures of her children, when they were young and coming up. Four boys and a girl. One boy taken, years ago, and now another one going away. After a while, she put the pictures up, except for one of Toy, the day he left home to join the Army. That one she held on to, while she sat up in her chair and asked God for another miracle.

She wanted to believe that she'd get it. That she'd wake up in the morning, and Toy would be home, and Early Meeks would be in the kitchen drinking coffee and saying that they weren't bringing any charges after all, since Ras Ballenger needed killing so much it didn't even matter who did it.

She knew better, though. They'd already gotten one miracle that day. A big one. Now here she was asking for another. The way she had it figured, miracles of that magnitude were probably one per customer.

Calla was right about Blade. He didn't feel that he belonged there anymore, and he was gone when they all got up the next morning. Samuel and Willadee both worried about him, and wished they could know that he was all right, but Samuel knew it was out of the question for him to drive over to the Ballenger place to check on the boy, and he wouldn't have let Willadee go, even if she had been willing to leave Swan's side—which she wasn't. Noble and Bienville both offered to go, but neither Samuel nor Willadee would consider that.

Calla went, though. There wasn't a soul in this world who could tell that woman what she could and couldn't do. She wouldn't let anybody drive her, either. She'd called the sheriff's office and found out she couldn't see Toy until after his arraignment, which wouldn't be over until around noon, so she took off walking shortly after breakfast. Out the front door and down the road. One foot in front of the other.

When she got to the Ballengers', there were cars in the yard. Not law cars. Those and the ambulance had come and gone in the night. Calla Moses had heard all the sirens. The people who were here were Geraldine's family and Ras's family, mainly. They were a rough-looking bunch. One of them, a man who looked to be about Toy's age, stepped out in front of Calla as she walked across the yard and told her she wasn't welcome here.

"I know I'm not," she said. "And I won't stay long. Thank you for letting me pass."

What else could he do but step aside?

She caught sight of Blade before she got into the house. Saw him through the screen door. His mother was sitting in a chair, holding a baby and a box of Kleenex in her lap. Blade was standing beside the chair, the way a man would do. Two younger boys were on the floor, the bigger one of the two sucking his thumb and snuffling.

When Calla came into the room and Blade saw her, she could almost see his heart lurch. Geraldine glared at Calla with red-rimmed eyes. Apparently she was finding her husband's memory a lot sweeter to live with than the man himself had been. Or maybe it was what had happened to him after he died that undid her. What the dogs had done. Calla knew about that. Early had mentioned it when they talked on the phone a while ago. Geraldine yanked a wad of Kleenex out of the box and blew her nose loudly.

"Don't come over here asking if there's anything you can do," she said. "You can't bring him back."

No, and if somebody else did, I'd sent him off again. That was what Calla wanted to say. She didn't, though. She said, "If you and your kids ever need anything, we're still your neighbors."

Illogically, Geraldine reached out and wrapped an arm protectively around Blade. As if he needed protection from Calla Moses. "You're not taking my boy again."

"No," Calla said. "I expect Blade feels like he needs to be here with you." Then she looked at him. "You're welcome at our place, though, Blade. Welcome and loved."

He looked away. Calla turned and left. When she was almost out of the yard, she heard him coming up behind her. Running. She stopped and waited until he came around in front of her, and was facing her.

"I'm *sorry*," he whispered. So he was back to whispering now. "For what happened to Swan."

Calla said, "Blade, you had nothing to do with what happened to Swan. You can't let anything that anyone else has done change the way you think about yourself."

He didn't respond to that, so she asked him if he was all right inside. If he was sad about his daddy dying. He shook his head.

"No," he said. Barely audible. "But I'm supposed to be."

Then he turned and ran back toward the house.

Swan slept off and on, sometimes waking up crying. When she opened her eyes, there was always someone there. Her mother, her father, her brothers, her grandmother. Whoever it was, she looked away, because she thought they must be seeing what had happened when they looked at her, and what had happened was even harder for her to handle now that she was safe.

"All that's over," her mother would tell her.

"No one can hurt you again," Samuel would say.

But it wasn't the idea of being hurt again that was bothering her. She knew that Ballenger was dead, and that her father had been the one who killed him, because she'd seen the crumpled body when Samuel brought her out of the Dark Place and loaded her as gently as possible into the car. What was haunting her now was what had already happened that couldn't be undone.

Her brothers didn't know what to say, except to ask her if she was all right. She always said the same thing.

"No."

Before Grandma Calla left to see Toy, she stopped in Swan's room and sat down on the bed beside her. There was misery in the girl's eyes.

"Remember you were saved by a miracle," Grandma Calla told her, trying to help her regain that feeling of wonderment.

Swan dissolved in tears. "It didn't come in time," she said. "I was only partly saved."

"Now, that's not true," Grandma Calla said. "And I don't want to hear it. Your daddy brought you home all in one piece. We got our whole little girl back."

Swan said, "I don't feel whole."

"Well, you will. You will. You will."

After she was gone, Swan asked her mother to ring the cowbell. Willadee grabbed the bell up off the table beside the bed and rang it loud and long. Swan lay back on her pillows and closed her eyes. That clanging sound made her feel easier, somehow.

"Why do you think God waited so long to help me?" she asked her mother.

Willadee had been wondering the same thing. All she could think of to say was "You're here. You're with us. That's what matters."

Swan blew out a shuddery breath and tried to keep her thoughts away from that spot by the willows and the Dark Place at Ballenger's. There were two cowbells and two duck calls still back there in the woods, and she hoped against hope that didn't mean that anybody else was going to need a miracle. Really needing a miracle was the worst thing imaginable.

Samuel took Calla into town to visit Toy, and while she was back there in the jail, he went searching for Early Meeks. When he found him, he repeated his confession. Early listened, but not as patiently as before.

"Tell me what the inside of that room looked like," he said finally. "The room where Ballenger was keeping Swan."

"It was dark," Samuel said. "I couldn't see a thing. There was a dirt floor. I remember that."

"Toy remembers a helluva lot more than a dirt floor. He remembers every last detail."

When Samuel opened his mouth to argue, Early just shook his head and told him that everybody in Columbia County knew who did the killing in the Moses family.

"Back years ago," he said, "Toy got away with murder because he was a war hero and Yam Ferguson was a spoiled, rich punk who stayed home and chased other men's wives instead of doing his part in the war effort. But as much as Yam Ferguson and Ras Ballenger both needed killing, your brother-in-law can't just go around breaking somebody's neck every few years. It sets a bad example for everybody else."

"But he didn't do it," Samuel said. "Ask my daughter who came in there and got her."

"Your daughter," Early said, "has been through something that could break a person's mind. She told the doctor that mice set her free. Hundreds of mice. And you know what, Samuel? We found shredded ropes and a gunnysack, and all, just like she said. But we didn't find any droppings in that room. A mouse can't run here to yonder without crapping little pellets all over the place. Your daughter set herself free. I don't know how she did it, but she did. Now, you go home and be glad you've still got a daughter to raise, and stop trying to take the credit for something you didn't do."

The credit. Early was letting Samuel know that he thought somebody killing Ras Ballenger was a good thing, but he had his mind made up about who did it. Or who he was going to allow to take the blame. Suddenly Samuel wasn't sure which. Either way, he knew Early Meeks wouldn't budge.

So he went to see the D.A., a stout old bulldog named Lavern Little. This time, when Samuel told his story, he left out the part about flying. Lavern didn't even let him finish.

"Folks aren't a bit happy about this," he told Samuel. "Not that anybody misses Ras Ballenger. They don't. But they don't want Toy Moses deciding who gets to live and die around here. What you need to do is quit trying to throw cogs in amongst the wheels of justice before I decide to try Toy for two killings, instead of just one. There's no statute of limitations on murder."

Samuel got the message. Anything else he said or did was just going to make it worse for Toy.

Still, over the next couple of weeks, everybody in the family tried to talk some sense into Toy. He told them he'd never done a thing in his life that made more sense.

"If they try me," Samuel argued, "they might call it justifiable homicide. But they've got you charged with murder." They could speak more freely than usual that day. Early had long since decided there was no need to post a guard to prevent Toy Moses from escaping, seeing as how he was so determined to be locked up.

"That's right, they have," Toy told him. "And if I was out there with folks, there might be another one they'd have to charge me with." He didn't have to mention that he was talking about Bernice. When Samuel was a little slow in answering back, Toy gave him something else to think about.

"Do you know why I killed Yam Ferguson, Samuel?"

Samuel was shocked. Until now, the Ferguson murder had always seemed like a myth. One of those stories that might be true but nobody expected to ever know for sure about.

"I did it," Toy said bitterly, "to defend Bernice's honor."

He laughed then. The laugh was flat, too. And sad as the ages. "I killed a man to defend something that didn't exist. So maybe that's what I'm paying for this time, and you get what I got a long time ago. A reprieve." Then he gave Samuel a level look and said the most important thing of all. "I couldn't do any good out there the way I am now, Samuel, but you still can. And you'd better. You think life would be kind to your kids, if you was in here? I can tell you the answer, in case you don't know it."

But Samuel knew it. Inside, he knew it.

. . .

Calla tried to talk some sense into Toy, but he'd already thought things through, and all the talking in the world wasn't going to sway him.

"I understand why you're doing this," Calla told him. "But I can't stand to see it happening. You don't deserve half the bad that's happened to you in your life, and there's been plenty of it. Plenty of it, and now this."

"I've done my share of wrong," Toy said peacefully.

"Well, it's wrong to take the blame for what you didn't do," she persisted. "You're trying to do right by everybody else, but you're not doing right by yourself."

Toy said oh, yes, he was. Calla reached through the bars and he took her hand in his. For just a heartbeat, a lonesome shadow seemed to pass across his face.

"I can't say I'm looking forward to where I'm going," he told her. "But leaving is just something that happens in life. We all do it someday, one way or another. There's worse things than going away with the taste of love still fresh in our mouths."

After Calla left, Willadee went back to see her brother. Her heart felt heavy as a lead weight in her chest.

"I know you're not going to listen to me," she said. "You've never listened to anything you didn't want to hear. But this time, you need to, because we all love you and we don't want to lose you."

Toy gave her one of his easy smiles.

"Y'all won't be losing me, Willadee. I'll just be someplace else."

She shook her head hard, sending a spray of angry tears flying.

"Stop it, Toy! Stop smiling and acting like this is nothing. All these years, no matter what's happened, you've pretended it didn't hurt. When you came back from the war with a leg missing—and through all the hell Bernice has dished out to you—but this is different. Surely, if we just tell the sheriff the truth—if we're Just Plain Honest—no jury in the world would go hard on Samuel."

"Don't kid yourself," Toy told her. "People turn. They've already been asking each other what Samuel did to get put out of the pulpit. Then you add Bernice's escapades, and the fact that she's telling it all over the county that Samuel chased her until she gave in, and that he was always sneaking her into your bedroom while you was working in the bar—"

Willadee gaped.

"They won't say it in front of you," Toy said. "They never said it in front of me, either, but they said it off to the side. Just because I don't talk much, people forget I can hear."

The children came. Swan, and Noble, and Bienville. They were too heartbroken to talk much, so he just hugged them the best he could through the bars, and let them all hang on as long as they wanted.

"We'll all be grown by the time you come home again," Swan said sadly.

"You will," Toy answered. "And I'll be getting on up in years. But that won't change the way I feel about you." Then, to Bienville, he said, "You being a good boy?"

"I'm always good," Bienville told him, with an old man's sigh. "I've been good so long it's getting tedious."

Toy grinned, although the kids couldn't see that. They had their heads pressed as close as they could to their uncle's chest, all of them hating the bars that were in the way.

"You all right these days, Swan?" Toy asked next.

"Grandma Calla says I will be," she said.

"Your grandma's right," Toy told her. "You hold on to that."

And then he spoke to Noble.

"How 'bout you, bud? You makin' it okay?"

Noble pulled back a little and looked his uncle in the eye.

"I'm keeping my feet under me," he said. "You taught me to do that."

Toy nodded, pleased.

"Well, then," he said, "I reckon I can rest easy."

Chapter 41

Nobody believed Swan about the mice. They didn't believe that any more than they believed Sam Lake could fly. They couldn't explain what was in the dead space at the Ballenger farm, though. All those frayed bits of rope and those minced-up strips of cloth, or the gunnysack that had been reduced to confetti.

One evening, toward the end of April, Samuel sat in the porch swing holding Swan in his lap. She was too big for that, but she was still his little girl.

"I believe you about the mice," he told her. "I don't know whether I've told you that."

"You didn't have to tell me," she said. "I just knew, same as I knew it was true about you flying." Then she told him that she was wondering whether they needed to stop telling people about those things. They'd already been Just Plain Honest, and maybe that was enough.

"How else are folks going to find out that miracles still happen?" Samuel asked her.

Swan said, "I think maybe miracles are something everybody has to find out about for themselves. Telling them about it doesn't make them believe. It just makes them think you're crazy as a bessie bug."

At his own insistence, Toy Moses got the speediest trial since hanging days. And one of the shortest. The courtroom was full of spectators for the whole hour and eleven minutes. He insisted on representing himself, waived his right to a jury, and his plea was "Guilty as hell, Your Honor." When asked to address the court, Toy did more lying in ten minutes than he'd done in the rest of his life put together. The things he'd heard Samuel telling Willadee that night, back at the house, he wove together into a terse but thorough account, and he embellished his story with every single detail that he'd gleaned from his inspection of Ras Ballenger's hidden room. When he got to the part about wringing the little bastard's neck, that was just how he put it. He also threw in that some men just needed to be dead, and he was glad he'd helped that particular man to get that way.

Samuel Lake asked to testify for the defense. The defense (Toy Moses) declined.

The judge gave Toy twenty years. Probably ten for Yam Ferguson and ten for Ras Ballenger, although he didn't say anything along those lines.

Toy thanked him sincerely.

Bernice hadn't made it to the trial. She had, however, made it down to Shreveport, where she was living with a man named D. E. Shuler. She'd met D.E. in a bar, over at El Dorado, when he'd been passing through town on his way to Nashville to take care of some important business. At least that's what he said, and Bernice took everything D.E. said as gospel.

What had her hooked on D.E. was that he was a record producer, or would be, once he got his label established, and he was looking for a dynamite female vocalist. Bernice auditioned for him that first night, without singing a note, and they'd been together ever since.

. . .

Early Meeks drove Toy out to the house after the sentencing, so he could spend some time telling his family goodbye in a way that wouldn't be so hurtful to them when they remembered it. What he was doing wasn't strictly legal, and Bobby Spikes pointed that out to him as they were walking Toy out to Early's car. Early told Bobby that it probably wasn't legal to make a deputy's life a living hell, either, but he'd been known to do it, and might do it again, if riled.

Out at Calla's, the grown-ups sat around talking, pretty much as if this were any other visit. Sid had bought a pig from a farmer down the road and had roasted it in a pit in the backyard. What with Calla's potato salad and Nicey's baked beans and Willadee's biscuits and corn casserole, it was a meal to remember. Toy told Nicey that her five-day cake was the best thing he'd ever laid glommers on, and she just lit up like a Sunbeam.

Swan and her brothers started out the visit feeling ill at ease and sad enough to die, but before it was over, they'd gotten some peace about things. Toy wasn't going away forever, he told them. Twenty years didn't necessarily mean twenty years. It all depended on how things played out.

"In the meantime," Toy said to Noble, "you get your daddy to help you pull that motor we never got around to. Then you keep that truck running right, so you'll have something to drive when you're old enough to get a license."

Noble told him he'd do it, and that the first time he was allowed to drive it on his own, he'd have somebody take his picture and he'd send it to him.

Toy spent time with each one of them, the way a man does with his kids when he's going away for a while. Maybe they weren't his kids in all ways, but they were his in the ways that mattered.

He asked Bienville to send him books to read, and Bienville asked him what he liked. Toy said he liked anything about woods and water, but that Bienville was welcome to broaden his horizons. Bienville got a glint in his eye thinking about that.

After a while, Toy picked Swan up and set her on his shoulders, and walked off with her, leaving everybody else behind. Swan held on and smiled, remembering how she'd once daydreamed about this very thing. Not the circumstances. She never would have imagined those, or wanted them. But this was the closeness she had yearned for.

When they got over to Calla's garden, Toy set her down and knelt facing her, looking her full in the eye.

"You've got my heart," he told her. "You know that, don't you?"

Swan nodded, love in her eyes.

"Now you can't throw it away while I'm gone," he warned her.

"I wouldn't ever," she promised.

"No," he said. "I reckon you wouldn't. I sure reckon you wouldn't ever throw away a heart that loves you."

They had bonded now, Swan thought to herself. Bonded soul deep, just the way she'd dreamed of that day in the store. Only, back then she really hadn't known what soul deep meant. She knew it now, though. She knew it now, for true.

There was one kid missing. Blade. Toy asked the others to tell Blade, the next time they saw him, that he loved him like a son. And he'd like it if Blade would draw him a letter or two from time to time.

After a while, Toy hugged everyone who had come, even the men. Samuel's shoulders quaked—fairly quaked, from all the feelings he was trying not to let go of in front of everybody—when it came his turn. Toy gave him a grin and clapped him on the shoulder and said, "You take care of yourself, Preacher."

And Samuel said, "You'll be in my prayers."

Early didn't have to tell his prisoner when it was time to go. Toy Moses was not a man who needed to be hustled along. He finished passing out hugs, and kissed the kids one more time, and then hugged his mama again, hard and long.

"You come back," Calla told him.

Toy nodded and said, "You be here."

"I'll do my best," Calla answered, knowing her best might not be enough. Not necessarily twenty years might still be more than she had left. She touched his lips with her fingers and drew her hand away, letting him go.

Toy stood there for one more moment, soaking in everybody and everything he was leaving. Then he turned to Early Meeks and asked him which one of them was driving.

About the middle of May, Samuel got a letter from Bruce Hendricks, his district superintendent—or the man who had been his district superintendent. Bruce had written to tell Samuel that he thought he might have a church for him, and that Samuel should come on down to the annual conference to see what could be worked out.

Instead of a letter of acceptance, Samuel sent Bruce a batch of newspaper clippings that fully detailed the facts of the trial—including a mention that one Samuel Lake, the brother-in-law of the convicted man, tried for a while to claim responsibility for the murder of Ras Ballenger.

A letter arrived by return mail. The offer of a church had been withdrawn. Samuel read the letter, and handed it to Willadee, and went out and planted some melons.

"Are you hurting over this?" she asked him later on. It must have been sometime around sunset. They were walking in one of Samuel's fields, where the crops were up in profusion.

"Not hurting."

"What, then?"

Samuel pointed out some corn that was taller than it had a right to be, and then he showed her some squash that was making like crazy, and after that, he pointed back toward the barn, where their three kids were all grooming Lady. The last of the day's sun rays were washing over the kids, painting them in all manner of beautiful colors.

"Happy," Samuel said. "Just happy."

After a time, Blade started coming back around. There was a quietness about him, and a serious air. His daddy had left marks on people while he was alive, but when he died, he left a stain—and that kind of thing takes a lot longer to wear off.

At least Blade was there. And frequently. Partly to play, partly to see if there might be a letter from Toy (there often was)—or to bring one that he had gotten five minutes before, out of his own mailbox.

At first, Blade found it hard to be around Swan—as though he had been the one to hurt her and couldn't forgive himself. Finally, one day, she took him aside and faced him with the facts.

"Look," she said. "You can't let what happened make you afraid to be my friend. You didn't do anything wrong, and neither did I."

"I know." His voice was low and tragic. "But my daddy's who I'm *from*."

She thought about that for a minute. He was right. Up to a point.

"He may be who you're from," she said, "but he's not who you are. I love who you are, Blade."

That was a lot for the boy to take in and hold. Being told that he was loved. He'd heard it plenty here with this family, but never from Swan. *Love* wasn't a word she threw around a lot.

"I love you, too," he said, shyly. Then he cut a cockeyed grin and added, "I'm still gonna marry you someday."

Swan said, "Oh, hell, no, you're not. You're gonna be my brother."

Sometimes, when it was hot as blazes, Samuel would take the four kids down to the Old Swimming Hole. He'd been meaning to teach his children to swim for years, but he was always too busy with the

Lord's business. Watching them laugh and grow, he began to suspect that what he was doing now *was* the Lord's business. The way he saw it, God had worked out the outcome just fine.

Farming for a living didn't keep Sam Lake from driving sick folks to the doctor or spreading the Good Word, just like he'd been called to do. He didn't always use words to tell folks that God is love. Sometimes his sermon was a mess of greens and a bushel of peas that he left on some hungry family's doorstep—usually along with a handful of flowers. Sometimes it was just looking some unfortunate person in the eye without flinching when most people would look away.

In the meantime, Willadee had opened Never Closes back up and had started serving home cooking to the regulars. Pretty soon, she stopped selling liquor and took to closing the place before bedtime. That was when the men started bringing their wives and kids, and Willadee told Samuel that she needed a new sign.

Samuel took down the NEVER CLOSES sign and was ready to paint another one, but Willadee couldn't decide what she wanted the thing to say. Samuel knew exactly what *he* wanted it to say, so he just painted out the N in *Never* and painted out *Closes* altogether, and painted in another word where that one had been. Then he nailed the new sign above the back door. It said, EVER AFTER.

Willadee asked him if he thought maybe it should say HAPPY EVER AFTER, but Samuel said no, he thought happiness was like any other miracle. The more you talked about it, the less people believed it was real. It was like Swan said, some things, everybody just had to find out about for themselves.

Not that they needed a sign. Folks could smell Willadee's home cooking for a mile, and they heard about it farther away than that. Ever After was open every night except Sunday (Samuel strictly drew the line at making profit on the Lord's Day). As time went by, the supper crowd grew until it filled up Ever After and spilled out into the yard. Samuel built picnic tables and benches, and set them out under the spreading oak trees, and those tables filled up, too.

Come dusk, the Moses yard would be full of cars, and people milling around visiting with each other, and kids playing tag and catching fireflies. Sometimes, if you looked close enough, you could actually see laughter bubbling in the air. Folks would sit there at the tables and load up on barbecue and potato salad and baked beans and corn on the cob and Grandma Calla's spiced pickled peaches. They'd wash the food down with iced tea that was always served in mason jars, and if they still had room, they'd top the meal off with Willadee's banana pudding or double fudge layer cake, and if they didn't have room, they made some.

Most nights, after Samuel came in from the fields and got cleaned up, he'd pull up a chair and play his mandolin or his guitar or his fiddle, and anybody who took a notion could join in and sing.

Swan would stand there behind her daddy's chair with one arm draped across his shoulders, and she'd let 'er rip all the way from her toes. The way the music poured out of her, so clear and fresh and liquid, people would hang on the notes and ride the swells. Hearing that little girl sing was like floating the rapids of the Cossatot River.

Pretty soon it got to where pickers would come from all over the county and sit in, and the old pickers would teach new, young pickers (Noble and Bienville and Blade among them) how to play hot licks. It was enough to make your heart fill up and burst, just being there.

"Sam Lake can play anything he can pick up," folks would invariably say.

"He can make strings talk."

"He can make them speak in tongues."

Nobody ever made a move to leave until Calla would get up out of her chair and say something like "If I was someplace else right now, I believe I'd go on home."

Then folks would start gathering their young'uns and heading for their cars. All those regulars and soon to be regulars and folks who'd just been passing through, and had heard about the place, and would still be talking about it when they got back to wherever they had come from.

...

And that's the way things have gone along from that day until this. Not staying the same, but always changing. And that's okay, because once one part of a thing changes, all the other pieces begin to shift, and pretty soon it's a whole new story.

Acknowledgments

My unending thanks go to:

Kevin McCormick, for those long-ago trips to bookstores, when he'd put a copy of someone else's novel in my hands, and tell me that I should write my own.

Shari Rhodes and Elsie Julian, who loved books and loved me, and were the start of so many good things. No one ever had truer friends. Fly with the angels, Shari.

Charlie Anderson and Leon Joosen, for reading my pages every night and for keeping me encouraged. Because of you two, I wrote the book instead of talking about it.

Helen Bartlett, for being such a warm, gracious, and insightful mentor.

Lynn Hendee, whose generous spirit and love of truth make her opinions all the more valuable.

Barri Evins, for faith, friendship, and story sense, for letting me read her my stuff over the phone at all hours, and for introducing this Texan to Trader Joe's.

Beth Grossbard, for fiercely championing writers, and for bringing me together with the irrepressible—

Dorothea Benton Frank, for her deep well of laughter, for taking the time to show me the ropes, and for turning me over to the wonderful—

Larry Kirshbaum and the whole terrific team at LJK Literary Management. (Special thanks to Jenny Arch for holding my feet to the fire, and to Molly Reese for always making sure things ran smoothly.)

Susanna Einstein, my irreplaceable agent, for taking me on and taking this book out to the world. You're a miracle, Susanna. And I am blessed.

Susan Kamil, my brilliant editor, for guiding me through the process of giving up things I loved that didn't work, and creating new stuff that did. And for keeping her word invariably.

Thanks also to Lynn Buckley for the unforgettable moment when I first glimpsed your altogether lovely cover design; to Susan M. S. Brown for meticulous copyediting; to Clare Swanson for making my part of the process less scary; to Sam Nicholson for telling me what to do next (and making sure I did it); and to Noah Eaker, Courtney Moran, and Vincent La Scala for handling details I never dreamed existed.

My deepest gratitude, now and always, to my offspring, Taylor, Amy, and Lori. You three are my best friends and my reason for everything.

The Homecoming of Samuel Lake

Jenny Wingfield

A READER'S GUIDE

Letting the Story Happen

Jenny Wingfield

Stories are contrary things. They know what they want to be, and they rebel at being manipulated into shapes that don't fit them. We tend to think of storytellers as creative sorts, but in writing *The Homecoming of Samuel Lake*, I had the feeling that, rather than creating, I was discovering something that was already fully formed. It's a story about family and fun and sacrifice and tragedy—and it all takes place in what I consider to be the most exciting place in the world—on a farm.

Now, I didn't grow up on a farm. Because my father was a minister, I grew up in a succession of small-town parsonages—tidy little places that had to be kept neat at all times. Daddy occasionally brought home stray animals (which never earned him any points with church members), and at one point, we had both chickens and rabbits, but there's a limit to how many and what sort of animals you can keep when you have a modest yard and close neighbors. My only experiences with farm life were when my father would take me along with him to visit rural parishioners (who invariably had wonderful

old barns, and vegetables growing everywhere, and more animals than they could
count)—or when we made our yearly pil-
grimage from Louisiana to South Arkansas
to stay with my mother's folks while Daddy
attended the Methodist State Conference.

Those were heady days for us kids—playing in the hayloft, splash-
ing in the creek, running wild through woods and across pastures,
with very little supervision. Our mother and her family didn't believe
in smothering children with too much attention. They fed us, kept
our clothes laundered, and were glad enough to have us out from
underfoot. If we'd gotten hurt, they would have taken care of us,

and if we'd gotten our-
selves killed, they would
have mourned, but they
didn't dwell on those possibilities. They just let us be
kids, and we did a bang-up
job of it.

That was the beginning
of my love for country life.
I didn't know that it would
become my ideal or that I

would someday believe that if only people would live in harmony with nature, most of the problems on earth would be solved.

As an adult, I became a writer (well, I'd always been a writer, but I eventually started getting paid), and I finally got to live on a farm. I could look out my own window and see mist hovering above a meadow, and I could have as many animals as I could afford to feed. I reveled in all that, but I didn't often think about those childhood days, and I didn't envision ever writing about them. After all, what was there to write about? Plain people who worked hard and laughed a lot? Didn't sound like great story material to me.

Sometime in the 1990s, I decided to write a play. Robert Harling (born in my favorite town, Natchitoches, Louisiana) had written one (*Steel Magnolias*), and *he* had done all right. I naively believed that writing for the stage might be ever so much easier than writing for film. (Forgive me, Mr. Harling.) At that time, my screenwriting career had progressed to the point where I could actually say I had one, and I had a small window of opportunity (about a month) before I had to get hopping and deliver pages. Considering that I'd written the first draft of *The Man in the Moon* in fourteen coffee-drenched, twenty-hour days, I figured turning out a little ole play in thirty days would be a snap. I could probably write it, polish it, and plant a spring garden in plenty of time to meet my deadline.

Now, I had no idea what I wanted the play to be about, but I started planning a set anyway. What I came up with was a house, sandwiched between a grocery store and a bar. Honestly, I intended this to be a *town* setting. Maybe Memphis. I'd driven through there a few times, and I'd read enough about it to find it dark and mysterious. I thought the bar might be a blues club, with all sorts of fascinating characters who looked tough but had their share of soft spots, and there would probably be this young woman who came there to sing and fell in love with some dangerous character, and . . .

Then I remembered that my grandmother had run a store from the front of her house. And wouldn't you know—the minute I thought of her, she marched in and took over. She would run the store, my grandfather would run the bar, and the whole thing would take place out in the country, thank you very much.

Wait a minute. Hold the phone. That was not the kind of story I wanted to write.

While I was still trying to decide what to do about my grandmother, my parents and a couple of my brothers sneaked in (and—not to be left out—so did I). Suddenly I had a decidedly ordinary cast of characters: my family. I worried about that. I especially dreaded dealing with my father. The way I saw it, there was nothing the least bit interesting about a preacher. I'd never seen one in a book or film who wasn't corrupt, a wild-eyed fanatic, or a namby-pamby sort, and my father was none of those things. He was a red-blooded country boy, but he was also—how can I put this without offending anybody?—*truly virtuous.*

But there he was, big as life, and he didn't seem inclined to let me turn him into anything he wasn't. Grudgingly, I let him stay, telling myself that I could keep him busy off scene, so the audience wouldn't have to hear him talk about the one thing he loved most—God. Now, I love God, too. *A lot.* But I knew that if I let my father's character open his mouth, a sermon would come out, and I have a strong belief that no one should try to pass moral or spiritual lessons off as literature.

My next problem was that my story (which still had no plot) didn't want to be a play. It *refused* to be a play. It wanted to be a yarn, and I swear, it started telling itself. Bits of our family history (my grandfather's suicide, my father's exile) found their way into the mix like forgotten lengths of thread willfully weaving themselves into a tapestry. New characters (some real, some figments of my imagination) showed up, rudely demanding to be included. Finally, I gave up, threw the door open, and let them charge inside. Might as well. They weren't leaving.

From the moment Ras Ballenger drove up in front of Calla's store, things began to get sinister. It came as a great surprise to me that there might have been danger in that world I'd felt so safe in. None of us ever saw it, but what if it had been there all along, lurking in the shadows, ready to pounce without warning? How would we have handled it? What would have happened to "life as usual"?

I never planned to let Ballenger become such a strong presence, but that's the thing about storytelling. Once characters come to life, they're hard to contain. Each one, good or bad, has his or her own agenda, and they constantly pursue their goals. They live and breathe, they plot and scheme to get what they want, and all the other characters have to deal with whatever they dish out.

Maybe it was because Ras Ballenger was so thoroughly evil that I let myself get comfortable with writing about the sweetness of the Moses place, and the basic goodness of that family. I couldn't write a character without getting inside his or her head, and after spending any period of time inside Ballenger's dark, twisted brain, I was happy to bring in some light.

As much as I love structure, I didn't engineer this story. At one point, I wrote a long, detailed outline, but then I ditched it as the characters insisted that they had something better in mind.

Nothing about the creation of this book happened as planned. My wild dream of penning a play in thirty days or less stretched out endlessly, as I had to stop writing to meet that pesky deadline and didn't get back to the Moses family for several years. Religion and bucolic farm life and organic gardening and animal rescue all found their places in the story because, basically, they were all deep inside me, and it's who we are that comes out in the tales we tell.

What inspired me? Life. The life I had known. The people I loved. What kept me going? The fact that we storytellers have to be honest, but we don't have to necessarily tell things just the way they happened. We can embellish, we can leave things out, we can bend the truth the way Early Meeks bent the law—all without a single qualm. We get to be Moses honest.

Above all, we have to simply let the story happen.

Questions and Topics for Discussion

1. When Swan skips out on her grandfather's funeral and spends time in conversation with her Uncle Toy, we learn that she longs for a soul-deep bond with someone—and that she fancies Toy Moses as a perfect candidate. By the end of the story, she has achieved that goal. What other relationships have deepened for Swan, and what do you think changed inside her to make her more capable of bonding with others?

2. When Samuel Lake finds himself without a church, he believes that his challenge will be to find work, support his family, and ultimately be appointed to another pastorate. How does this struggle evolve into a "dark night of the soul" for him? And do you feel that his transformation is one of convenience, or of conviction?

3. Calla Moses is a strong, practical woman. How does her outlook change as the story progresses, and why? At one point, she begins to believe that there is magic in the world. Do you think that feeling

will carry over after Toy has gone away, and if so, how will this new belief sustain her?

4. "Moses Honesty" is mentioned throughout the book. Do you feel that the Moses family is really more honest than most? And when Toy makes a false confession, is he being honorable, or just running away from a situation he can't face?

5. How would you compare the various marital relationships in the story? (Calla and John, Willadee and Samuel, Bernice and Toy). What is different about the way each couple handles conflict?

6. Could this story have unfolded in basically the same way if the location had been different? What is there about the South Arkansas location that allowed secrets to lie undisturbed for years, while everyone knew the truth?

7. The Moses place has been described as an actual character in the novel. If you agree with that description, what is the character arc of the place? What purpose does it serve in the community, and does that purpose change? Which place would you find more exciting to visit?

8. Blade Ballenger risks his life to protect a horse. Toy Moses gives up his freedom to protect his sister's husband and family. Is one sacrifice more noble than the other? Among the other characters, who else takes unselfish risks? And who refuses to do so?

9. Throughout the book, there is a struggle between good and evil. When Samuel Lake willfully takes another man's life, which side is he on?

10. When Early Meeks neglects to charge Toy for a murder he did commit, and then later charges him for a murder he did not commit, is justice served?

PHOTO: © LORI HARWELL

JENNY WINGFIELD lives in Texas surrounded by dogs, cats, and horses that she and her family have rescued. Her screenplay credits include *The Man in the Moon* and *The Outsider. The Homecoming of Samuel Lake* is her first novel.